PASSION, BETRAYAL
AND
KILLER HIGHLIGHTS

KYRA DAVIS

PASSION, BETRAYAL

AND

KILLER HIGHLIGHTS

**RED
DRESS
I N K**
™

First edition May 2006

PASSION, BETRAYAL AND KILLER HIGHLIGHTS

A Red Dress Ink novel

ISBN 0-373-89578-X

www.RedDressInk.com

Printed in U.S.A.

For my mother, Gail Davis, who always offers me an ear
when I need to vent, a shoulder when I need to cry and a hug
when I crave the comfort of her unconditional love.

ACKNOWLEDGMENTS

This book wouldn't be in print if it weren't for the hard work
and enthusiasm of my agent, Ashley Kraas.
I also want to thank my editor, Margaret O'Neill Marbury,
for all of her guidance and support.

Kathy Vizas allowed me to pick her brain and benefit from
her years of experience as a lawyer. Her insights proved to be
indispensable for the plotting of this novel. The same could
be said of the help I received from Lieutenant John Weiss,
who patiently answered my countless questions and actively
assisted me with my research. Detective Sergeant Donna Lind
was a fountain of information, as well. I hope they will all
forgive me for occasionally taking a bit of poetic license with
the facts they so generously supplied me with.

Last but absolutely not least I need to thank my stepbrother
Chris Sullivan for watching my son while
I struggled to meet my deadlines, and my mother for
all the free child care she provided and for her
willingness to be my brutally honest and
marvelously detail-oriented volunteer proofreader.

PROLOGUE

I arranged some Pacificos in an ice bucket and slipped Sarah McLachlan into the CD player in anticipation of Leah's visit. My sister and I love Sarah. She may be the *only* thing we agree on. At first glance people always assume our differences fall into the good girl-black sheep categories, with me playing the role of the rebellious farm animal, but in reality it's much more complicated than that.

First off, although in humid weather my shoulder-length hair can resemble a ball of fluffy fleece, thanks to the genes of our now deceased African-American father and our very much alive Latvian-Jewish mother, my skin tone is much more bronze than black and Leah's is a bit on the olive side. Second, I'm not *that* rebellious and Leah's not *that* good.

The difference between us lies in our approach to life. My motto is: Always be true to yourself. It's why I became a writer. Writing's one of the few careers in which I can be paid for being a nonconformist.

Leah, on the other hand, has made it her life's ambition to be someone else, specifically Martha Stewart (without all that messy felonious stuff). She's not very good at being Martha; her ethnicity makes that whole WASPy look hard to pull off (despite all the relaxers), she's not all that creative and she'd rather die than see her name stamped across any item that would ever be carried at Kmart. Yet she keeps trying, and she's certain that once she achieves her metamorphosis she'll have found true inner peace. So it wasn't a big surprise when she announced her engagement to Bob Miller. Bob's as average as his name. He's Caucasian of the mutt variety, of medium build, moderately intelligent and, when in social settings, reasonably polite if not out-and-out friendly…or personable…or enjoyable to be with in any way. But as far as Leah's concerned Bob is *Town and Country*'s version of Prince Charming.

So unless Martha had written a book about the heightened social status of imported beer, it was probably a safe bet that Leah would not be drinking a Pacifico. But Anatoly Darinsky might be.

Lately Anatoly had been starring in a lot of my more memorable dreams. He's tall, has dark brown hair that matches his penetrating eyes, a tight physique—you know, all the good stuff. But there's more to it than that—something I can't put my finger on but that makes me want to put my fingers on all sorts of other things. Not that Anatoly's perfect. At times he can be cocky, egotistical, argumentative—and don't even get me started about the defamatory statements he's made regarding Frappuccinos. He also hates me.

I suppose he has his reasons. I did frame him for assault and battery, and I kind of inadvertently got him shot in the process, but that was all due to a big misunderstanding. I thought he was a psychotic serial killer who wanted to murder me in some violent and horrifying way, and he thought *I* was the psychotic killer. Or maybe he just thought I was psychotic. That's the problem with our relationship— not enough open communication. If we just talked more, we would spend a lot less time trying to send each other to death row.

But now I had another chance with my non-murderous love interest, for Bob had given Leah reason to believe that he had been cheating on her, and as luck would have it Anatoly is a private investigator who has loads of experience proving and disproving those kinds of suspicions. I had to offer Anatoly an obscene amount of money, but I did get him to accept the case.

I kneeled down to stroke my cat underneath his chin. "Okay, Mr. Katz, our guests should be arriving—"

The buzzer echoed through my apartment.

"—now."

CHAPTER 1

"My divorce attorney gave me a list of everything we can take from Dan," she said mildly. "I'm beginning to think it would be more humane to just kill him."
—*Words To Die By*

Anatoly pushed past me into my apartment without bothering to so much as grunt in greeting. "Where's your sister?"

"Hello to you, too. Want a beer?" I popped the lid off one of the Pacificos.

He stuck his thumbs through his belt loops. "Where's your sister?"

"You see, it's like this—nobody ever told Leah about setting the clocks forward during daylight savings time, so she spends half the year running an hour behind."

He took the beer and threw his jacket over the armrest of the love seat before lowering himself onto the leather cushions. "I'm not waiting an hour."

"Oh, please, I was kidding." I took a beer for myself and leaned against the counter that separated the living room from the kitchen. "I'm sure she'll be here in forty-five minutes, max."

"She has twenty."

"Okay, I know you're pissed at me, Anatoly, but I'm paying you a lot of money to sit on your *tuchas* and drink my beer, so the least you can do is give her thirty."

"Twenty-five. Why don't you give me the details of the case while we wait? Why does Leah suspect her husband of sleeping around?"

"You know, the usual. After years of inattention he suddenly began to shower her with gifts while at the same time scheduling a lot of late-night meetings, and if that isn't code for 'I'm screwing my secretary' I don't know what is."

Anatoly waited for me to continue and when I didn't do so immediately his countenance assumed a more pleading expression. "There's more than that, right? Tell me your sister isn't as paranoid and insane as you are."

"Oh, excuse me!" I slammed my beer on the counter. "I am nowhere near as crazy or paranoid as my sister!" Anatoly took a long swig of his beer in lieu of responding. I sighed and looked up at the ceiling. "A couple of weeks ago, the night before I accidentally got you shot…"

"Accidentally?"

"We're not getting into that now. Anyway, Bob told her he had a dinner meeting with his employer so he wouldn't be at Chalet."

"Chalet?"

"His place of work, Chalet.com. They sell home furnishings via catalogs and the Internet. Think Pottery Barn but twice as expensive. Bob's the comptroller. Anyhoo, that night James Sawyer, Bob's employer, called looking for him. When Leah told him she thought Bob was with him, this Sawyer guy claimed that they had no plans to meet. When Bob came home, she asked him how the meeting went and he said it was great. Gave her all these details that she didn't even ask for. Just totally lying. The next day he got her a pair of 1.5-carat studs. God, he's such a pig."

Anatoly jotted something down in a pocket notebook. "She have any idea who he's cheating on her with?"

The buzzer went off before I had a chance to respond. "Well I guess you'll just have to ask her yourself." I pressed the intercom button. "Leah, is that you?"

"Yes."

I hesitated. Leah is one of those people who uses five words in place of the one that was necessary. When she did opt for brevity it was never a good sign. I buzzed her in and stood by the door in wait.

When she reached the top of the stairs my level of alarm rose a notch. Her perpetually saturated hair seemed unusually devoid of products. As she moved closer I could see that the tip of her nose was a little too rosy and her waterproof mascara was barely hanging on. She nodded at me in acknowledgement before wordlessly passing into the apartment. She dropped her Louis Vuitton on the floor and paused while she impassively studied Anatoly.

He rose and offered his hand. "Hi, I'm…"

Leah walked past him to the window and stared blankly out at the street.

"Great. Just what I need, one more mentally imbalanced client."

I gave Anatoly a warning look before crossing to my sister. "Leah?" I put a cautious hand on her shoulder. "Leah, Anatoly's the PI I've told you about. He's going to…"

"I don't need him."

I glanced at Anatoly, who looked incredibly relieved. I held my hand up to indicate that he was not yet free to bolt for the door. "Leah, I know you think that Bob's cheating, but it probably wouldn't hurt to get some proof before you—"

"He already confessed…this morning before he went to work. I was standing there holding my son, *our* son, and he confessed to screwing some pathetic little home-wrecker. He says he's leaving me for her. Just throwing it all away for some twenty-one-year-old whore."

I removed my hand from her shoulder and clenched it into a fist. I was going to kill the SOB. I was going to reach down his throat, grab his tonsils and—

"All right, then—"

I started at Anatoly's chipper tone.

"Sophie, thanks for the beer. Leah, it was nice meeting you. All the luck with the divorce…"

"There's not going to be a divorce."

My head snapped from Anatoly back to Leah. Either I had just misheard her or she had lost her mind. "What do you mean there won't be a divorce? You just said…"

"I'm going to fight—for him and for my family. I can win him back, Sophie. I know I can."

She made eye contact with me for the first time, and I saw the desperation tempered with what I assumed was some kind of psychotic determination. I opened my mouth to speak before I had formulated what the next words should be.

"Even better, then," Anatoly boomed. "I hope you two have a wonderful life together. See you around."

"Anatoly!" But he was already out the door.

Pig. Men were all pigs. I turned back to Leah. "Honey, you know you can't win this one. Even if he did come back to you, why would you want him?"

"I knew you'd say something like that. I'm sorry if I actually take my vows seriously—unlike some people around here. I took a vow—"

"Yeah, you did. So did Bob. But he broke the deal, Leah. You can't honestly think of being loyal to someone who has no interest in being loyal to you."

"Lots of marriages survive adulterous affairs. Just because yours didn't…"

"And thank God it didn't! Don't you get it? Finding Scott with that Vegas showgirl was the best thing that's ever happened to me. Otherwise, I might have actually done something stupid like try to stick it out in a doomed relationship. Hell, I still send that woman holiday cards."

"Sophie, I'm not you and I don't want to be you. I want to be Mrs. Bob Miller. That's my life. Everything I have, everything I do…it's all about being Mrs. Bob Miller. I'm good at it. My life with Bob…well, it's what it's supposed to be. He's just forgotten that. He's confused. But I'm going to make him see."

"Leah, you can't—"

"The hell I can't!" I involuntarily stepped back. I had never seen her like this. She swallowed and looked away. "I found a receipt from Tiffany's. He bought her a six thousand dollar bracelet. He bought it on the same day he bought me the diamond studs."

"And what does that tell you, Leah?"

"It tells me that she's using him. He bought the earrings for me because deep down he loves me, and he bought her a bracelet because he thought he had to in order to hold on to her."

"Well that's an interesting spin, if lacking in the logic department."

But Leah wasn't listening to me anymore. She brushed past me and stared at the chilled beers without reaching for one. "I am not going to take romantic advice from a divorced woman who talks to her cat." I peeked guiltily at Mr. Katz, who was sleeping through the current fireworks. Leah snatched up the phone from the end table and started jabbing her fingers against the numbers.

"Leah, who are you calling?"

"Erika."

"Bob's secretary, Erika?"

"I spoke with her earlier. She's as outraged as I am and offered to help me win him back."

"I really don't think that's a good idea."

"Erika? Erika, are you there? It's Leah. I'm coming over so if you get this message just…just wait for me. I need to come up with a plan before this goes too far." Leah slammed the receiver onto the cradle.

"Leah this is crazy. You can't put yourself through this. Plus you have Jack to consider—wait…where's Jack?"

"He's with my friend Miranda, and for your information I'm doing this for Jack." She bent over to pick up her purse and made a beeline for the door.

"Oh come on, Leah, stay and talk to me about this. Erika's not even home."

"She will be soon and if not I'll…I'll just go home and do the laundry. Bob will need his golf clothes ready for the weekend."

"Leah!"

"Goodbye, Sophie." In an instant she was gone.

Well, that had been disorienting. It had looked like Leah, but I swear to God if I had closed my eyes I would have mistaken her for someone else. It wasn't her words so much— although she had used more profanity than I was used to hearing from her—but her tone that had really thrown me. It had fluctuated from hollow to restless then back again. She seemed on the brink of losing her mind.

My eyes wandered to my unfinished beer on the counter. I picked up the bottle, then thought better of it and went to get the vodka from the kitchen. Leah would snap out of it.

She just needed time. I poured the clear fluid over some ice cubes, then added a little cranberry juice for color. I should write something…like a book, or more specifically, the book my editor thought I had already started working on. In four months I would be touring to promote my latest finished Alicia Bright mystery, Words To Die By, and it would be helpful if I could complete the first draft of the next book in the series before hitting the road.

I silently welcomed the burning sensation the liquor provided as it worked its way down to my liver. The problem was I wasn't quite ready to write another murder mystery yet. It had only been a few weeks ago that some lunatic had tried to break my head open with a golf club. Funny how being stalked by a homicidal maniac can knock the blood lust right out of you. Although I did want to kill my brother-in-law, Bob. That was promising progress.

I eyed my drink. It looked a little too red so I diluted it with more alcohol. If only Leah had gone running off to her friend Becca. Becca would have told her to kick Bob to the curb. But Becca was currently touring Europe with her boyfriend and it was doubtful Leah knew what country they were in, let alone what hotel.

I took another sip. I needed to relax. Erika may not give the best advice in the world, but evidently she and Leah had become close. She would undoubtedly offer Leah the emotional support she needed. This was good. Leah had Erika, and I had Absolut.

My pet strolled into the kitchen and blinked at me. "That's what I like about you, Mr. Katz. You're quiet, nonconfrontational, and it was legal for me to cut off your balls."

It must have been a little after 10:00 p.m., because a *Friends* rerun was on. That meant I'd been unconscious for one…no, two and a half hours. The last thing I remember was watch-

ing a *Will and Grace* rerun. I had only consumed two cocktails (albeit, two very strong cocktails), but the combination
of the alcohol and a good dose of emotional exhaustion had
pretty much done me in for the evening.

It took a little effort but I managed to get off the couch.
Unfortunately, the ringing of the phone interrupted my
journey to the bedroom. I tapped the receiver with my index
finger and considered my options. It rang again. Hell, it was
worth picking it up just to keep it from making that shrill
sound two more times. "Hello?"

"Sophie?"

I rolled my eyes skyward. "Leah, I'm tired, I'm grouchy,
I'm intoxicated and I'm going to bed."

"Sophie, please."

There was something in Leah's voice that stopped me. It
wasn't the desperation that had colored her tone earlier, but
it was unnerving nonetheless. I sighed and leaned against the
dining table. "Okay, what is it this time?"

"It's Bob…I'm home…I'm here with Bob. Oh God,
Sophie!"

I stood up a little straighter. "What? Did he hurt you?" My
bloodlust was definitely back. I was going to kill him. Actually, I'd do better than that. In my next book I'd castrate a
philandering husband named Bobby by rigging his inflatable
sex doll with explosives.

"No, no, he didn't hurt me. He can't. Oh God, Sophie…
Oh God, he's dead! Bob is dead!"

My eyes traveled to the depleted bottle of vodka on the
counter. "I'm sorry, Leah, but I think I must have misunder-
stood you—"

"He's dead! D–E–A–D. BOB IS DEAD!"

"You mean like *dead* dead?"

"How many kinds of dead are there?"

"I'm not getting this." I shook my head in an attempt to

clear it. "Bob is only five years older than I am. Thirty-five is a little young for—"

"I think he was shot or something."

"Shot *or something?*"

"I think so. I don't know. He's just lying there and there's all this blood coming out of his head. Sophie, what do I do?"

Well, I wasn't sure about her but what I wanted to do was throw up. "Leah, how exactly did Bob get 'shot or something'? Who shot him?"

"How in God's name would I know? I just came home and found him in the middle of the living room with a hole in his head! And our pictures, the framed wedding pictures that were in the room, they're all smashed up. No one even bothered to clean up the glass! What if Jack had come home with me and cut himself?"

Excuse me? I lowered myself into a chair and tried to figure out if Leah's instincts proved her to be Mother of the Year or just stark raving mad.

"Sophie, are you still there? What am I supposed to do?"

"I'm here." Big sisters taught their younger siblings how to straighten their hair and apply their makeup. They did not instruct them on how to behave at a murder scene. "Leah, I honestly don't know. What do the police say?"

"The police? I don't know, they're not here. Do you think they're coming?"

"Didn't they *say* they were coming?"

"No, no, I haven't called them yet....I called you. Oh, Sophie, he's really dead! I mean really, really…"

I couldn't hear Leah anymore, nor was I suffering the effects of the alcohol. All I could feel was the beginning of a panic attack. I took a deep breath and tried to make my voice slow, steady and clear. "Leah, I need you to hang up the phone right now and call the police."

I could make out Leah's quiet sobs on the other end of

the line. "Leah, this is really important. I'm coming over but I need you to call them right now."

She made some kind of weak affirmative noise. I hung up and for a few moments I couldn't get myself to move. This was very bad. Hours after Bob had informed Leah that he was leaving her, he had transformed into a bloody corpse, and the phone records would show that the first number Leah dialed after discovering his body was not 911, but mine.

I looked down at Mr. Katz who had wrapped himself around my foot. "What now?"

My first stop was not Leah's but Anatoly's. I double parked in front of his building, ran up to the stoop and stood methodically tapping the buzzer until he relented and came down. He threw open the glass door and glared at me.

"Get your finger off the button, *now.*"

"Anatoly, I need help."

"I'm not a psychiatrist."

"Not that kind of help—" I took a moment to turn and acknowledge a driver yelling obscenities as he maneuvered around my illegally parked Audi "—although that should probably be my next stop. I'm here because Leah's in trouble."

"Leah's made her choice, and you're going to have to deal with that. Who knows—maybe she'll get lucky and he'll end the affair."

"The affair's pretty much a nonissue now, unless of course his mistress is into necrophilia."

Anatoly's lower jaw seemed to detach from his head. "She *killed* him? What the hell is wrong with you people? Doesn't anyone in your family understand that vigilante justice is wrong?"

"She didn't do it." As soon as I said the words I realized my voice lacked the conviction to make them believable. I cleared my throat and forced myself to look Anatoly in the eye. "My sister did not shoot her husband. She loved him. Yes, they were having problems, but she was fully confident that they would work through them."

Anatoly's forehead creased and he leaned against the door frame. "What is this? Rehearsal for when you have to talk to the police?"

"Why? Didn't I sound convincing?"

"That's it. We're done here. Goodbye, Sophie."

I put my foot in the path of the door, inadvertently bringing myself closer to Anatoly. I could feel his breath in my hair and, despite his harsh words, I could see the twinkle of interest ignite in his eyes as he noted my new proximity. His mouth curved into a little half smile. I know that people often find themselves craving sex after a funeral but it probably isn't healthy to be overcome with lust right after a family member has been shot. I distracted myself by looking at his feet. I've never been into feet no matter how big they are.

"Anatoly, I'm here to hire you. I was going to pay you six thousand dollars to find out if Bob was messing around. Now I'm offering you…ten. Ten grand to find out who messed with him."

"It's not about the money, Sophie."

"What if I raise it to twelve? *Then* can it be about the money?"

He was silent for a bit and I kept my eyes glued to his boots. My friend Marcus always says that if a man's shoes match his belt it means he's gay. Anatoly must be the straightest man alive because his shoes never match anything. They are always ugly and—

"If you hire me I might uncover information that you don't want to know."

The statement was loaded with enough reality to quiet my raging hormones. I refocused on his face. "Then I'll fire you."

Anatoly snorted and looked out to the street. "I can't believe I'm going to do this."

"Great!" I pulled my keys out of my pocket and dangled them in front of him. "Get your coat and get in the car. I'll fill you in on the details on the way."

"I didn't say I would take the case."

"But you were about to. Come on, no more banter. The police are arriving at the scene as we speak."

Anatoly shook his head in defeat. "I'm going upstairs to get some things. Wait for me in the car." He retreated into the building and I ran to my car. I snapped on my seat belt and put my hand on the gearshift, ready to press it into first the minute his cute butt hit the seat. Anatoly was obviously less anxious. He strolled out wearing a generously cut leather coat and no other visible accessories. Maybe he had all his James Bond–like spy stuff hidden in his inside pockets.

Instead of taking his place in the passenger seat he came around to the driver's side and opened my door. "Move over, I'm driving."

"It's my car."

Anatoly bent down so that he was at eye level. "After your sister left your apartment, what did you do?"

"I watched some TV."

"Right. Did you have any snacks while you were watching?"

"What would I snack on?"

"Vodka."

"Vodka's a good snack. Easy to prepare, light on calories…"
Anatoly smiled. "I'm driving."

I gripped the wheel possessively. "Anatoly, you can't possibly think I'm drunk."

"No, I think your blood alcohol level is hovering around .08 but since we're going to a place that we know will be crawling with cops it would be best if we don't test fate."

I grunted in disgust but relinquished my seat to him. "You think you know me so well."

Anatoly positioned himself behind the wheel and adjusted the rearview mirror. "I guessed correctly, didn't I?"

"Maybe. Or maybe you were playing PI in the apartment across the street, spying with a telescopic lens."

"I don't have to play PI, I *am* one." He started the ignition and turned off the radio. "And I also have a life. Which way?"

"We're going to Forest Hill. You know how to get to that neighborhood?"

Apparently he did, because he turned the car in the appropriate direction. I spent the first half of the drive giving him what little information I had. He listened, only interrupting occasionally to ask a question that I inevitably didn't have an answer to. When I finished, the conversation lulled and I focused on the cars and street lamps we sped past. I hated to admit it to myself but I was pleased that he had insisted on driving. I consider myself to be a pretty independent person but in times of extreme crisis it was nice to have someone around who wanted to take control. That didn't mean I was going to give him control, but I could take some comfort in knowing that it was an option.

As we got closer I broke the silence in order to direct him but I didn't need to give him the exact address. Once we were within a block of the house all the flashing lights and uniformed officers served as a pretty clear indicator of where we were going. Anatoly parked several houses away and pulled the keys out without making any move to get out of the car. "I'm sorry, but I have to ask you again, Sophie. Are you sure you want me to investigate this?"

I should have been flattered by the note of concern in his voice, but its implication frightened me. I shook my head violently in an attempt to shake off the dark thoughts that were creeping in. "She's innocent, and yes, I want you to investigate."

We stared at each other for a beat. Finally, in what seemed to be slow motion, our hands simultaneously reached for our respective door handles and we got out and approached the crime scene.

CHAPTER 2

"Life is like a never ending play," he said between drags on his cigarette. "We all have roles to perform and there's always some critic insisting we've been miscast."

—*Words To Die By*

We hadn't gotten very far before we were headed off by a particularly butch policewoman who used her hand as a barrier. "Sorry, no one's allowed beyond this point."

"My sister's in there," I argued. "This is her house."

The woman was completely unmoved. "You'll see her later."

"Well, if it isn't Sophie Katz and her victim—er—friend, Anatoly Darinsky."

I looked up to see the tall, lean form of Detective Lorenzo. His eyes narrowed as they met mine. He had let his black curls grow out since the last time I had seen him, which made him look younger, if not nicer. I felt the muscles in my neck tighten.

"You're the detective handling this case?" I asked.

"One of them."

"I think there's a conflict of interest here. You hate me and you've been sent to investigate my brother-in-law's murder. It doesn't seem reasonable to expect you to remain objective."

Anatoly put his hand on my shoulder in what must have appeared to others to be a supportive gesture. Only I knew that there would be permanent indentation marks where his fingers were digging into my flesh.

"What exactly do you want me to be objective about?" Lorenzo asked. "And how do you know your brother-in-law was murdered?"

Anatoly loosened his grip, but not enough to eliminate all the discomfort. I'm not sure what he thought he was accomplishing. Obviously what I needed was to be smacked upside the head.

I took a deep breath and soldiered forward. "Leah called me a little while ago, distraught. She told me she had... found him."

"Do you know if this was before or after she called us?"

"I...don't know. I didn't think to ask. She loved him so much.... I'm really very worried about her—can I see her?"

"Just a few more questions." Lorenzo pulled out a pocket notebook and pen. "Did she tell you how he was killed?"

"She wasn't sure. She said there was a lot of blood and it seemed to be coming from his head."

"She called and told you there was blood coming out of her husband's head," he said flatly.

"Mmm, I think that was it. It wasn't all that clear...you know, with all the crying and all."

"And the first thing you did was go out and hire a private detective? Any particular reason for that?"

Anatoly slid his hand down to my waist. "I was with Sophie when Leah called. We've become...close. I wanted to be here for her and her family."

He pulled me tight against his side and I could feel his body heat radiating through his jacket. I reached my arm out to return his squeeze, somehow managing to "accidentally" brush it against his butt in the process.

"Right." Lorenzo made another note.

I'm not very good at reading upside down but I think I could make out the word *dysfunctional.*

"When was the last time you saw Leah?"

"This afternoon," I said. "She was on her way to see a friend...not sure who. Anyway, she stopped by to say hi."

Lorenzo made another little note. "Did she say anything else?"

"It was just a basic conversation between sisters. She asked how I was, inquired about my next book, and then told me to stop talking to my cat and find a human companion to date and converse with."

The detective glanced up at Anatoly. "She doesn't consider Mr. Darinsky here to be human?"

"Well, Anatoly has a lot of apelike qualities, so it can be confusing."

Anatoly removed his arm.

"How was her marriage?" Lorenzo said.

"Spectacular."

"Spectacular?"

"Mmm-hmm. He brought home a paycheck and left her alone," I explained. "A woman couldn't ask for more."

Anatoly made a noise of disapproval.

"That isn't very liberated of you," Lorenzo noted.

"Don't get me wrong, she loved the time they did spend together, but Leah had a life of her own. She adored Bob because he gave her the space she needed to maintain her individuality while still supporting her. And he always made time to take her out on the occasional date or family outing with their son. I mean really, how much more liberated can you get?" It was also complete bullshit. I pretended to search my purse for a tissue so I wouldn't have to make eye contact with either of my current male companions. Hopefully the picture I had painted of Leah would make her seem like the kind of gal who wouldn't get all homicidal if she discovered her husband was messing around with some college-aged slut.

"Sophie!"

I looked up just in time to see Leah hurl herself in my direction. She flung her arms over my shoulders and tucked her tear-stained face into the crook of my neck. "Oh, how can this be happening to me?"

Lorenzo looked more irritated than sympathetic, but he did have the courtesy to put the notebook away. "It's going to take a while for us to finish searching the house and dusting it for prints. Why don't you come down to the station with us, Mrs. Miller? We can finish up the questions, and if your sister here would like to follow us she can give you a ride when we're done."

"Do you expect to be finished with the house by the time Leah's through with questioning?" Anatoly asked.

"Not likely. I'm sure you understand the necessity of being thorough," Lorenzo said, directing his comments to Leah.

Leah nodded numbly, and Anatoly took a step closer to her. "We'll take Leah to the station."

Lorenzo paused and studied Anatoly for a moment. "It might be more efficient if she rode with me or one of the other detectives. That way we could ask her some questions on the way over."

"She's been through enough without being forced to ride in a police car like some kind of criminal," Anatoly said firmly.

My eyes traveled from Anatoly to Lorenzo. It was a no-brainer that Anatoly wanted to coach Leah on what to say before she answered any more questions, and it was equally obvious that Lorenzo would do whatever he could to prevent that from happening.

Lorenzo smiled and turned his attention back to Leah. "You know, Mr. Darinsky is right. You've been through enough. The last thing you need is to be dragged to some ugly police station. Why don't we just sit in the car over there—" he instinctively held up his hand to block Anatoly's predictable protest "—the unmarked car, in the front seat. I'll have one of the guys bring us some coffee and we'll finish the questions here."

Anatoly's jaw got a little tighter but he didn't say anything. Leah looked to me questioningly for what I assumed was guidance. Ironic, since if she had ever taken my guidance before she never would have married Bob in the first place. But now I was all "guidanced out," so of course I looked to Anatoly, who managed to loosen his jaw enough to speak.

"Go ahead, Leah, we'll be waiting for you here."

Leah allowed Lorenzo to steer her gently to the proper car. He stopped to talk to one of the uniformed officers, possibly to request the promised coffee, which was just stupid because the last thing Leah needed was to be more amped.

Anatoly stood silently with his arms crossed in front of him.

"Where's the hidden camera?" I whispered.

Anatoly's brow furrowed. "What?"

"You know, the spy stuff that detectives carry around with them when they go to crime scenes."

Anatoly shook his head in disgust. "I was in the Russian Army, not the KGB. I don't have any spy stuff."

Well, that was disappointing. "Not even a mini tape recorder?"

"Not even that."

"Then what the hell did you go back up to your apartment for?"

"A jacket."

"You are so not worth twelve thousand dollars."

"You wouldn't say that if you had ever given me the opportunity to get you undressed."

I opened my mouth to make a clever comeback, but then quickly closed it in order to keep the drool in. Not healthy. I really needed to try to be more somber. I thought about Bob's early demise. Unfortunately that didn't sufficiently lower my spirits. I turned my thoughts to Leah's potential incarceration. That did it.

"Do you think she's telling him—"

"Sophie, do us all a favor and shut up."

"That wasn't very nice."

"When did you get the impression I was nice?"

"Good point. So this undressing thing…is that really part of services rendered? Because it's a good marketing tool. 'Hire Darinsky, he'll catch your spouse with his pants down, and as a consolation he'll lower yours, as well.' Really, I think there could be a high demand for that. But since I'm hiring you for more solemn purposes, I think I'll have to pass."

"I didn't actually offer."

"The hell you didn't."

Anatoly smiled slightly. "I'd forgotten what you were like when you weren't busy setting people up for murder."

"Yep, this is me. Spunky and fun."

"I was thinking argumentative and insane, but you should stick to the euphemisms that work best for you," Anatoly said.

I gave him what I hoped came across as a disdainful glare. "I'm cold. I'm going back to the car."

Anatoly hesitated, then carefully removed his jacket and held it out for me. I couldn't help grinning while I slipped my arms into the sleeves. This is what I liked about Anatoly: he was full of contradictions. Though the jacket was about eight sizes too big, I managed to find a way to get my hands into the pockets. Anatoly reached out to stop me but it was too late—I had already felt it.

"What's this?"

"Nothing, now just—"

"It's a tape recorder! And it's on, isn't it."

"Shh!"

"You *do* have spy stuff," I hissed.

"Sophie, this is not the place. We'll talk about it when we're alone."

"Oh, please, no one's listening. You just don't want to admit I was right."

"You were right. Now shut up."

I wasn't quite as offended by the command now that I knew I was right. I simply spent the rest of the time smiling smugly at him while he ignored me. Finally, Leah emerged from the car and came over to us.

"Please get me out of here."

My smugness was instantly squashed. Hopefully the fact that I kept forgetting about Leah's plight was due to shock and denial and not extensive egocentrism. I ushered Leah to my car, where Anatoly once again assumed the role of driver. Leah refused my offer of the front passenger seat and tried to open the back door for herself. Unfortunately her hand was shaking so badly that she found even this task too diffi-cult. I opened it and buckled her seat belt for her before crawling into the seat next to Anatoly.

The first five minutes of the drive were silent. It occurred to me that it would have been better if this had happened back when Leah was under the illusion that her marriage was successful. That way her final memories of Bob likely would have been positive. As it stood now, she had been robbed not only of her husband but also of the right to be angry with him. Unless of course it had been that anger that had led to his death. I shook my head vigorously and Anatoly gave me a questioning glance that I didn't bother responding to. I wasn't going to allow myself those thoughts. Leah was a lot of things—neurotic, insecure, judgmental—but she also had a good heart. She was simply not capable of murder.

"Jack! Oh my God, I forgot about Jack!"

I quickly turned toward Leah. "Forgot him? Forgot him where?" Images of Jack suffocating in the back seat of her Volvo flashed in front of my eyes.

"I dropped him off with Miranda for a playdate this afternoon. Oh Lord, what am I going to say to him?"

I doubted it was necessary to explain a father's death to an eighteen-month-old child, particularly if the victim was a man that had a stronger relationship with his laptop than his son. "Why don't you call Miranda and see if Jack can sleep over?"

"I couldn't. It's asking too much."

"She'll understand."

"Sophie…"

"Phone." I stuck my hand between the seats and Leah reluctantly pressed her cell phone into my palm. I looked up Miranda's number in the memory and pressed Call.

"Allen residence." The woman on the other end of the line spoke with a Mexican accent and sounded extremely harried.

"Hi, this is Sophie Katz, Jack's aunt…."

"Oh, thank goodness! You're coming to get Master Jack."

Master Jack? Who instructed their ethnic nanny to call their charge's playmates "Master"? "Well, actually I'm not. You know I think I should explain this to Mrs. Allen."

"But you *are* picking him up?" The desperation in the woman's voice was palpable.

"I really need to talk to Mrs. Allen."

"Of course." Was she crying? "I'll get her."

My heartbeat quickened as I waited for Miranda to pick up the line. What had Jack done now? Polluted the family's drinking water with Epsom salts? What if they didn't let him stay? I empathized with the nanny, but this felt like a her-or-me kind of situation, and I'd be damned if I was up for dealing with a Junior Moriarty.

"Hello? Sophie? It's Miranda. Is Leah all right?"

"Hi, Miranda. Leah's…" I looked behind me to see Leah methodically rotating her wedding band around her finger. "Leah's had a rough night."

"Yes, she told me about the affair…."

"It's more than that," I began. "There's been a…an unexpected death in the family."

"I am so sorry to hear that, Sophie. Was it your mother?"

"Mama? Oh, no! Nothing that bad, it was just Bob." As soon as the words came out I realized how bad they sounded and how horrible I was for saying them. Fortunately my rabbi had informed me there wasn't a hell to go to. I just had to learn to live with guilt.

"Bob? What happened to Bob?"

There was absolutely no delicate way of putting this. "He was shot." I thought I saw the corners of Anatoly's mouth twitch in amusement.

"I don't understand."

"I know it's shocking. We have no idea who did it—a burglar maybe. Leah's an absolute wreck. Would it be all right if Jack spent the night with you?"

"Of course, of course." Miranda sounded a little dazed. "Consuello will make sure he's comfortable."

Sorry, Consuello, you lose. "Great, Leah will pick him up tomorrow, before nine."

"No rush, you can pick him up as late as eleven-thirty if you like. Just…give Leah hugs and kisses from us."

"Will do. I'll have Leah call before she comes over." I hung up just as Anatoly was pulling into a parking spot five blocks away from my home.

He tossed the keys onto my lap and made eye contact with Leah through the rearview mirror. "Leah, I'm going to have to ask you a few questions."

"No more questions. I can't take it."

Anatoly sighed. We both got out of the car and Anatoly opened the door for Leah. "I know how hard it is to lose someone you care for," he said, "but if you're going to get through this, we're going to have to put the pieces together so we can figure out what happened tonight."

"The police are already doing that."

"Yeah, but unlike the police, Anatoly works for us, not the state," I said. "He'll be more sensitive in his approach to this and he'll conduct his investigation in a way that will best ensure your protection."

"*My* protection? Do you think whoever did this is planning on shooting me?"

No, I thought that the police had plans to arrest her for being the "whoever" who did this. "I think you should answer Anatoly's questions."

Leah shifted her weight from foot to foot. She is an inch taller than me, but right then she seemed much smaller.

Anatoly put a gentle guiding hand on her shoulder. "Let's walk."

Leah nodded and fell into step with him as I trailed behind.

"When was the last time you saw Bob?"

God, Anatoly's tone sounded so comforting that even I felt myself lulled into a sense of tranquility.

"This morning when he…told me."

Anatoly nodded and slowed his pace. "Sophie tells me you went to see Bob's secretary after you left her place a little after five."

"Erika wasn't home."

Anatoly's pace didn't change but his shoulders seemed to get a little more rigid. "What did you do then?"

"I parked my car in front of her house and waited for about a half hour. Then I just drove. Erika lives in Daly City, so I got back on Highway 1 and drove down the coast for a while. Then I came back up to the city and drove around the Presidio. I just drove."

"So you have no—you were alone." His voice remained steady.

"Yes, that's right. I needed some space so I could figure out how to get Bob back, and now—now he's gone forever. I'm a widow." She stopped in her tracks and turned to look at me. "I don't know how to be a widow, Sophie."

Leah didn't look so steady on her feet, and I contemplated whether it was necessary to remind her to breathe.

"Let's keep walking," Anatoly said. We all resumed our journey to my apartment. "When you came home did you see anything unusual? Any people walking around nearby or cars pulling out of parking spots?"

"No, nothing unusual or out of place. I don't think there were any pedestrians out, and the streets were quiet. I had no idea…I just had no idea."

"Was the front door locked when you came in?"

"Yes, double locked. Bob is always so careful."

I stopped myself from correcting her use of the present tense.

"Sophie said that when you got inside there were a few frames containing your wedding pictures that had been smashed on the floor."

"In the living room, next to him. The rest of the house was in order, just as I had left it. But all three of the framed photos we display in the living room had been broken, and there was a broken highball glass."

"A highball glass?"

"Shattered right next to Bob. And there was all this blood." Leah blinked a few times. "Do you think it will always be there?"

Anatoly shook his head uncomprehendingly.

"The blood. Will it stain the floor? I have a book that tells you how to get the worst stains out...but there was so much."

Leah was in shock. That was obvious. I wanted to reassure her that Pergo didn't stain, but it didn't seem appropriate at the moment. "The blood's going to go away, Leah. It's all going to get better. Why don't we go upstairs and I'll make you a little tea with brandy?"

"Yes, if all else fails, get her drunk," Anatoly muttered.

I shot him a warning glance before escorting them up to my place. Leah took a seat on my couch without bothering to take off her jacket, and I went to the kitchen to put the kettle on. Mr. Katz strolled into the living room undoubtedly hoping to cajole some food out of me, but once he saw both Leah and Anatoly he pulled a U-turn. He was too proud a cat to beg in front of company.

"After you found him you called Sophie. Did you call anyone else before you talked to the police?"

"Not before, no. After the police arrived and right before I came out and saw you I called Cheryl, Bob's sister."

Shit, I had forgotten about Cheryl. Usually that was a good thing, but in this case even Ms. Shallow deserved some consideration. "That couldn't have been a fun phone call," I said. "How did she take it?"

It was hard to tell from where I was standing, but I could have sworn that I saw a spark of annoyance in Leah's eyes.

"She reacted like she always reacts—lots of dramatics and lamentations. You'd think that this whole thing was a personal assault against her, as if I weren't suffering at all."

I did a quick double take. That was a bit judgmental. Maybe Leah was returning to her old self again. "Well, he is her only living relative," I pointed out.

"*Please.* She reacted the same way when Jason Priestley crashed at NASCAR."

Yep, she was definitely coming around.

Anatoly seemed less impressed with her sarcasm. "Did the police find the murder weapon while you were there?"

"No, I showed them where Bob kept his gun, but it was missing."

Great, just great. I could easily remember the debate Leah and Bob had over that stupid gun. She didn't want to have one with a child around but he had insisted that it was a good security measure for the family. Apparently Bob was wrong.

Anatoly leaned against the counter that divided the living room and kitchen and shot me a look that said *We're in deep doo-doo.* "Leah, I'm almost done. Do you know of anyone who might have wanted to kill Bob, or for that matter, anyone who held any kind of grudge against him at all?"

"No, everybody loved Bob."

What drug was she on? Nobody loved Bob, not even her.

"He had lots of friends," she continued. "The people who worked with him loved him. He was just offered a promotion. It was going to be announced in a few days. His employees couldn't have been more loyal. Erika thought the sun rose and set around his head. No one wanted to hurt him— to my knowledge. Unless that slut he's been sleeping with wanted to do him in. That's always possible."

I felt like screaming. The woman he had been sleeping with had no motive. Leah did. She had to see that. She had to realize how bad this all looked.

Anatoly cleared his throat. "Last two questions. Did you tell the police about Bob's affair, or that he told you he was leaving you?"

"No, I…I couldn't. The only people who know about that are the two of you, Erika and Miranda."

I could tell by the look on his face that we were thinking the same thing. That was two too many.

"Leah, what's Bob's e-mail and password?"

I handed Leah a Post-it and she scribbled down Bob's private e-mail address and handed it to Anatoly. "The password is June21." She hesitated a moment before adding in a much quieter voice, "That's our anniversary."

Anatoly waited a few seconds for her to reflect, but I sensed his chivalry was close to used up.

"Any other addresses? His work e-mail, for example?" he asked.

"It's bmiller@chalet.com. I don't know what password he used there. I tried accessing his messages when I suspected…" Leah got another faraway look in her eyes.

Anatoly motioned with his hand for her to continue. "I know what you suspected. So what passwords did you try?" he prompted.

"Well, I started with our anniversary, of course. We use that code for all of our accounts, our checking, our various online retailers…."

"What other passwords did you try?"

"My birthday, the date of our engagement, my name, and I tried one other before I gave up…what was it? Oh, of course, the day we first met. None of them worked."

Anatoly jotted it all down. "Did you try *narcissistic?*" he whispered under his breath.

I shot him a dirty look, but Leah didn't appear to have heard him.

"Last thing," he said. "Are there any questions that the police asked you that I haven't, or vice versa?"

"No, I've answered all these questions before," Leah said. "I don't think newly widowed women are supposed to answer all these questions right away. I think they're supposed to be too distraught to talk. Maybe I'm being callous."

Maybe she was being crazy.

Anatoly studied her. I got the feeling he was trying to pull information out of her—that she didn't want to voice. Finally, he shrugged and joined me in the kitchen.

"Come to help me with the tea?"

Anatoly didn't even bother acknowledging the question. "Meet me at Leah's at ten-thirty tomorrow morning."

"Is that a request or an order?"

"Ten-thirty, Sophie. And if you hear anything from the police, call me." Anatoly left as the kettle began to whistle.

Leah entered the room and crossed to the stove to turn it off. "Skip the tea. Just give me the brandy."

The next morning I awoke to the sound of grinding coffee beans, which would normally fill me with the kind of inner peace others only experience after visiting the Dalai Lama. However there was an odd pattern to the noise this morning. Normally when you grind coffee you press the top of the coffee grinder for a minute or so until the beans are as fine as grains of black sand. However the person preparing these beans was pressing the grinder for five seconds at a time, and, taking two-minute breaks in between to utter phrases like "Oh, my head!"

I pulled on a robe and went out to the kitchen to see Leah braced against the sink, the grinder currently silent beside her.

Her angry, bloodshot eyes zoomed in on me. "Look at me! Look what you've done to me!"

I didn't immediately answer. I understood that she was hungover but I missed the part that made it my fault.

"Why did you let me drink all that brandy?" She ran her fingers through her hair, inadvertently molding it into a wing formation. "How am I going to reevaluate my life if I feel like my head is going to explode?"

I pulled out a filter and began to prepare the coffeemaker for the beans that I was clearly going to have to grind myself. "Maybe you shouldn't reevaluate your life just yet."

"Of course, I have to reevaluate! Weren't you listening to

me last night? I'm not the wife of a comptroller anymore. I'm the *widow* of a comptroller. That's an entirely different situation. I have to figure out—OH MY GOD!"

I almost dropped the coffeepot. "What? What is it?"

"This nightgown I'm wearing! You lent me a pink nightgown!"

I blinked. "I thought you liked pink."

"I'm in mourning! I'm supposed to be wearing black."

"To the funeral maybe…"

"No, no, no, no." Leah shook her head hard enough to cause her hair wings to make a flapping motion, then abruptly stopped as she struggled to regain her equilibrium. "There is a period of time in which widows are supposed to wear black, I'm sure of it."

"Leah, this isn't *Gone with the Wind.* No one is going to blackball you for wearing a pink nightgown."

She started pacing the narrow kitchen. "There's a way to do this…I know, a book! There's got to be a book that explains the proper protocol for a newly widowed woman."

"Like what? *Mourning for Idiots?* Why don't you pick up Emily Post's book on how to be a socially gracious murder suspect while you're at it, because that seems to be the more pressing problem."

Leah stopped pacing. "Murder suspect? I didn't kill Bob."

"I didn't say you did, but I'm sure you've heard the saying 'perception is the greater part of reality.' And I'm pretty sure I know what the police department's perception is right now."

Leah looked bewildered, although how this could have been news to her was beyond me.

"But once the police start investigating, they'll see it wasn't me. There's no evidence that could say otherwise because I really am innocent."

"Wake up, Leah. Innocent people go to jail all the time on

bogus charges. It was barely a month ago that Anatoly was charged with assault and murder."

"But that's because *you* set him up, Sophie. You invited him up to your place, kicked a few chairs over or something and then called 911."

"Okay, forget about that. How many times in the past couple of years have forensic scientists used old DNA evidence to prove that some of the people who have served time for various crimes were actually innocent? While researching *Words To Die By,* I found out that Ray Krone was in prison for *ten years* before DNA evidence proved him innocent. What about the cases when DNA evidence isn't available? Do you think the courts get all those right? You need to look at this realistically and prepare to fight the accusations that are going to come your way."

In one fluid movement Leah picked up an empty coffee mug and threw it across the room. It exploded against my cabinet door in a burst of ceramic. *"I didn't do it!"*

I stood motionless, looking at the remnants of the cup. I had a long history of throwing things, but that's because I have no self-control. Leah, on the other hand, had always managed to be on the verge of a breakdown without ever actually having one—until now.

Her action must have surprised her, as well, because she had become completely still. Then she slumped against the counter. "I know it looks bad, but I honestly never wished him dead. I wanted the chance to make it work. Why wasn't I given that, Sophie? Why would anyone do this?" She slid down to the floor, buried her face in her hands and cried.

I reluctantly crept forward and sat down beside her, careful not to get shards of ceramic stuck in my butt. I understood where Leah was coming from. I'm not sure she valued Bob the individual all that much, but she did value their union and the life they had made together. Her choices were not ones that I would ever have made for myself, though they apparently worked for her. But Bob's extramarital affair had not been one of her choices, nor had his murder. At least I hoped it hadn't been. Now, after spending years perfecting her role as Mrs. Bob Miller, she was forced to redefine herself, and she had no clue how to do it.

I put my arm around her shoulders. "I'll ask Mary Ann about the black," I said, referring to my friend who worked at Neiman Marcus. "She'll know what you should wear."

Leah choked back a sob.

"Do you want to cover the mirrors?" I asked.

Leah lifted her tear-stained face. "Cover the mirrors? Bob would have hated that. He wasn't even Jewish."

"Look, God's got Bob covered, so now we've got to do what's necessary to get *you* through this. The rabbis wrote out some pretty clear instructions on what we Jews are supposed to do when we lose a family member, and you need guidance, soooo…"

Leah nodded and chewed on her lip. "I guess it's not such a bad idea, but do you think…perhaps just for this morning…?"

"You want to wait until you've finished with your makeup and hair."

"Am I completely shallow and horrible?"

"Maybe, but if so, it's hereditary, because there's no way that I'm going to go through the day without my under-eye concealer."

Leah rested her head against my shoulder, which required some contortionist moves on her part, but the gesture was irresistibly sweet. "If you ever try to remind me that I said this I'll deny it, but honestly—I don't know what I would do without you."

"You're never going to have to find out," I said, then reached forward and patted her knee. "And you can count on me reminding you."

★ ★ ★

If anybody else had lost her husband I would have had the courtesy to let them shower before me. But it was an undisputed fact that Leah's particular bathing rituals were the primary reason for California's water shortage, so I made it a point to sneak in first. When I had finished making myself beautiful, I searched the apartment for something appropriate to cover the mirrors with. It took about five minutes for me to figure out that I had nothing. My downstairs neighbor Nancy sewed. She'd probably have some spare fabric. But there were so many things I'd rather do than ask her for a favor—like go snorkeling in a tanker full of plutonium.

I heard Leah turn off the shower. She'd be done in forty-five minutes max. I had promised her I'd cover the mirrors and I didn't want to renege on that, especially since it was the only thing that seemed to perk her up. I opened one of my dresser drawers for the eighth time and glared at its contents. Of course there was nothing of use in there. Gym clothes, bathing suits and...

My hand reached in and pulled out the first of my many sarongs that I had collected over time to use as bathing suit covers and skirts during the years that it was fashionable. I shook it out and held it up to the full-length mirror fastened to the closet door. It was the right length. I had seven sarongs and five mirrors. Perfect. I hurried around the apartment hanging up my exotic mourning sheaths. By the time Leah was done I was waiting outside the bathroom holding the sarong I intended to hang in there. Leah opened the door and looked at it questioningly.

"Are you going on a cruise?"

"These are for the mirrors. I didn't have any black cloth."

"Are you kidding? It's going to look like we're holding a luau."

"A very somber luau."

Leah shook her head. "Sophie."

"I put the black one with the purple and turquoise fish in the living room."

"I gave that to you when you got accepted into USF! I can't believe you still have it!"

"I take it with me on every beach vacation."

"Well, I guess it's okay. After all, you're putting the red one in the bathroom and the one I gave you *is* predominantly black...."

"And if you'll recall, the fish on it are wearing very serious expressions."

"Bob loved fish." And that was it—Leah was in tears again.

I hugged her and tried to conjure up some fond memories of Bob ordering halibut. I wanted to feel more sad about this, if for no other reason than to prove to myself that I wasn't a sociopath, but my main emotion at the moment was relief. If Leah could just have another breakdown over Bob's eating habits in front of the police, that might sway their opinions in the right direction. Leah wiped her tears and tried to smooth a crease in a skirt that I had lent her. I slipped past her and covered the last mirror. I heard Leah gasp in what I took to be horror as I pushed in the last thumbtack. "Oh, come on, Leah, it's a mellow red."

"It's not the sarong—I just remembered what I forgot."

"Which is?"

"Mama."

"Shit!" I locked eyes with Leah. If Mama came for a visit and discovered a tube of Monistat 7 in the bathroom drawer you could count on her demanding to know why the offending offspring hadn't called her the minute she felt an itch. Forgetting to call to let her know her son-in-law was murdered was not going to go over well. I glanced at my watch. "She must not have watched the morning news or she would have called by now—"

The phone rang. Leah looked like she had just swallowed her tongue and I felt the threat of a migraine.

"It could be a reporter looking for a quote," I said.

"Do you have caller ID?"

"No, but I'm going to get it any day now."

"How helpful."

Leah and I walked over to the phone and stared at it as it rang for the fourth time. I decided to live dangerously and pick it up right before the answering machine did it for me. "Hel—"

"What kind of child doesn't call her mother when her sister's *schlemiel* husband has come to a *schwartzen sof*?"

The more excited Mama got, the more Yiddish she used. I wasn't exactly fluent in the language but I knew that to come to a schwartzen sof was to come to a bad end and that schlemiel was a polite way of calling Bob a prick. I cleared my throat.

"Mama, it really wasn't my place to call you—Leah should have done that." I winced as soon as I said it. It was an unfortunate force of habit to transfer my mother's wrath onto my younger sister. I mouthed the word *sorry* to Leah. She in turn gave me what I had come to know as the "I'm going to get you for that" look.

"So where's your sister and the *lobbus*? Are they all right?"

"Leah and Jack are fine. Jack slept over at a friend's house and Leah's…" Leah began to shake her head furiously at me. "Leah's here, but she's asleep."

"At ten in the morning she sleeps?"

"Well, she didn't sleep much last night. As you pointed out, her husband was killed."

"So who shot him? Was he some kind of criminal? If I find out that he got my Leah mixed up in any kind of monkey business I'll…I'll give him the Einhoreh, that's what I'll do."

"What good—or bad—is the evil eye going to do now that he's already dead?" I heard Leah choke back another sob and I mentally slapped myself.

Mama muttered some more Yiddish before coming back to English. "Enough with the sleeping—put Leah on the phone."

It was tempting to think that Mama was just being insensitive to my sister's need for rest, but it was more likely that she knew I was lying, which was impressive because I'm a pretty good liar.

I took a moment to weigh my loyalty to my sister against my desperate desire to get off the phone. Fortunately, I didn't have to make the choice because Leah, in what I assume was an unexpected attack of altruism, took the phone from me.

"I'm here, Mama. Yes, I'm okay…Jack's okay… No, I haven't eaten anything today…"

I left the room to allow Leah some privacy and to avoid being stuck with the phone again.

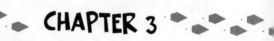

CHAPTER 3

Alicia let out an exasperated sigh. "Dead people are always so much more likable than the rest of us."
—*Words To Die By*

Leah and I were only fifteen minutes late in meeting Anatoly at her house. This was a new record for Leah, but for some reason Anatoly didn't look like he was in the mood for handing out gold stars.

"Can we go in now?" he asked.

"Hello?" I suggested. "When you greet someone you're supposed to say hello. Otherwise people accuse you of having Asperger's."

Leah looked around the front yard and then stared at the still closed front door. "Where's the police tape?"

"What's the point of having police tape if there are no police here to enforce the restriction?" Anatoly asked. "Unless the goal is to entice troublemaking teenagers to mess with the crime scene."

Leah threw him a confused look. "But in the movies…"

"Hollywood has a very different approach to crime fighting than the police." Anatoly looked at his watch impatiently. "The police may or may not come back to look for more clues, but they have to accept the fact that by that time things will have been altered."

"Okay, so let's go in and alter them." I looked expectantly at Leah, who was examining the doorknob as if it were attached to the gates of hell.

Anatoly cleared his throat. "Leah, if you want to wait out here I'll understand. Just give me the keys and I'll come get you if I have any questions."

Leah shook her head. "I've got to go in eventually." She pulled out her keys at a speed that underscored the meaning of the word *eventually,* and after several deep breaths (each one resulting in the further extension of Anatoly's chin) she opened the door. She stood in the entryway for a full two minutes before Anatoly and I gently pushed past her.

Our first stop was the living room. Things looked eerily normal. If there had been broken picture frames on the floor, they were gone now, with the exception of a few neglected slivers of glass. Anatoly sighed and looked around the room.

"I'm sure they confiscated everything that could possibly qualify as evidence. I doubt we'll find much."

"You mean they took my wedding pictures?"

We turned to see Leah standing behind us.

"Can they really do that without asking me?" she asked.

"As long as they have a warrant," I said. I walked over to the middle of the room and tapped my foot against the bloodstained floor. If I didn't know better I would have assumed it was spilled burgundy.

Anatoly was now walking slowly around the room, taking it all in. "Show me where the gun was kept."

Leah led him to the safe, which was tucked into the cabinet below her showcase of Waterford collectibles. It was such a stupid place to put a safe. Like a burglar wasn't going to search the furniture piece holding thousands of dollars' worth of crystal. Leah twisted the combination lock a few times until it released. Inside were some insurance papers, a will, a rather extravagant-looking diamond necklace and a few bond certificates that added up to an amount that was considerably less impressive than the value of the necklace. No gun.

Anatoly examined the insurance records. "No life insurance?"

"Bob thought accidental death and disability insurance was enough. After all, both of us were in perfectly good health."

"So Bob decided to wait until his health failed before approaching the insurance companies for life insurance?" I asked. "Or is it possible he just couldn't be bothered spending money on a policy that he would never be able to benefit from personally?"

Leah winced and I immediately felt guilty. I was going to have to work on holding back my reflexive insulting observations about her husband now that his previously vacant head contained a bullet.

Anatoly coughed a few times in an obvious attempt to suppress a laugh. "Let's be grateful he didn't have an insurance policy—one less reason for the police to suspect you." He stuffed the papers back in the safe. "Did you have a lot in savings?"

"Just over a hundred thousand," Leah said softly. "It's not enough. Our house payments alone are ten thousand dollars a month."

Anatoly did a quick double take.

"Well, we put down a small down payment!" Leah said defensively. "It's important to have a nice house to bring business associates to. Besides, Bob was making over four hundred thousand dollars a year and he was getting a promotion, so we knew we'd be fine...or at least we thought we would." Leah's eyes misted over. "Oh God, I'm going to have to go back to work, aren't I."

"There are worse fates," I said. "So, other than the savings account, your house and your cars, are there any other assets worth mentioning?"

Leah's face brightened. "There are the Chalet stocks! Of course, I can't cash them out yet, since they just went public and the shares are in lockdown...."

"Lockup," Anatoly corrected. "When a company goes public the employees' shares go into *lockup* for the first six months or so."

Leah dismissed Anatoly's comment with an impatient wave of her hand. "Lockdown, lockup, who cares what it's called? The important thing is that Jack and I aren't going to lose our house and I won't have to work!"

I creased my forehead. "How much are Bob's shares worth?"

"I don't know the exact figure, but it's well over a million."

I bit my lip and Anatoly let out a heavy sigh. "So much for eliminating money as a motive."

Leah took a step back from Anatoly and glared at him. "You aren't seriously suggesting that I would kill my husband for monetary gain?"

"You wouldn't be the first woman to do so," Anatoly said.

"Excuse me, but just because I'm unfamiliar with the terminology of the stock market doesn't mean I'm completely clueless about money. This is a community property state so if I had wanted to get my hands on Bob's money, any divorce attorney worth his salt could have done that for me."

"I know you wouldn't kill for money or any other reason." I inched closer to Leah and rested my hand on her shoulder. "But the police might think that you weren't really up for the whole half-sies thing."

"This is perfect," Leah said. "If Bob had been bankrupt, Jack and I would be homeless and hungry, but since he wasn't, I'm a murder suspect. No matter what the situation is I lose."

"Just because you're a suspect doesn't mean you're going to be charged with anything," Anatoly pointed out. "Let's figure out who else could have done this. Did anyone other than you and Bob know the combination to the safe?"

"No one. Just Bob and I. It was our anniversary."

"Your anniversary," Anatoly repeated. "The same combination you used for your personal Internet access, your ATM and your online retail accounts."

"You can see why neither chose careers that required a lot of creative thinking." Oh damn it, I'd done it again. I was really going to have to make more of an effort on this delicacy thing.

Anatoly did some more coughing before pulling out the necklace. He held up the pendant so that the light caught the yellow stone and the white diamonds that surrounded it. "Is this one of those yellow diamonds?"

Leah took the necklace from his hands. "Don't be ridiculous. Colored diamonds are trendy and ugly. Diamonds should be clear like these little ones. The stone in the middle is a yellow sapphire."

"I see. How much is that yellow sapphire worth?"

"I had the necklace insured for fifty-four thousand dollars."

"Are you kidding?" I squeaked. "My God, what happened to the days when a man could clear his guilty conscience for under a grand?"

"Clearly Bob had more guilt than the average philandering husband," Leah said, and shook her head in disgust. "I should have known right away. Bob was never excessively affectionate. We're both too sophisticated to be taken in by all the hearts and flowers nonsense."

I sank my teeth into my tongue to refrain from blurting

out that she had been renting *Sleepless in Seattle* on a biweekly basis for the past decade and a half.

"…but it wasn't until last year that he really became distant. He'd stay out late, make excuses for missing dinner, but he'd always make it up to me by buying me something. As the excuses became more frequent, the gifts became more elaborate." She held up the necklace to eye level. "I don't want it. I would never be able to wear it without remembering that he gave it to me just months before declaring that he was planning on trading me in for a younger model. I made such a fuss over his generosity, too. I made him gourmet dinners for a week straight. I'm so incredibly pathetic."

"You're not pathetic. Remember, Bob never actually left you. I'm sure that given the chance he would have come to his senses and stayed," I lied.

Anatoly stepped back from the safe and scanned the room. "Where do you keep the computer?"

"In the study upstairs," Leah said absently, still admiring the necklace she supposedly didn't want.

I tugged at Anatoly's sleeve. "I'll show you." We left Leah downstairs and I took him to the room that stood between Jack's and the master suite. I stepped in and did a quick visual inventory. "Wait, I know they keep it in here. Where is it?"

Anatoly walked past me and tapped a spot on the empty desk. "My guess is it was right here."

I stepped forward and examined the dust-free square on the desk where the computer used to be. "The police?"

"Looks that way." Anatoly shook his head. "Hopefully there aren't any messages on it from the mistress. It would be better if Leah could volunteer the information about that affair herself."

"You want Leah to tell the police about Bob's bimbo?"

"Assuming she didn't do it, yes, I want her to tell them

about Bob's bimbo. They're going to find out anyway, and while I recognize that in her case lying is a family trait, lying to homicide detectives will not serve her well."

I shrugged. "There was a period of time in recent history when I was lying to the police all the time. I never got arrested."

"No, *I* did. Let's not repeat the pattern, all right?"

Leah entered the room and stared at the empty spot where the computer had been. "Hold on a minute. Last night the police escorted me through the house so that I could confirm that nothing was missing and I distinctly remember the computer being right there." She looked at me and Anatoly accusingly.

"Okay, you caught us. We used Anatoly's super-microblastic shrinking machine and hid it in the drawer."

"The police took the computer." Anatoly was now looking through the papers on Bob's desk with noticeable lack of interest.

"I can't believe those people. First my wedding pictures and now this? It's just so rude! You have no idea what it was like to see the photos of Bob and me on the happiest day of our lives covered in broken glass. And now, not only am I unable to reframe them, I can't even complain about it to my online stay-at-home-moms' support group! Honestly, is it really necessary to rob me of all my comforts?"

"Not all your comforts," I offered. "I'm sure they left the ice cream."

"This is so typical of you, Sophie! My life gets turned upside down and you're making jokes."

Anatoly looked up from the papers. "Funny, I thought it was Bob's life that got screwed up."

"Shut up!" The words came from both me and Leah in unison.

She smiled at me and I exhaled a sigh of relief. At least

we still recognized that we were not each other's enemy. The real enemy was the heterosexual male.

Leah checked her watch. "Damn it, I was supposed to pick up Jack five minutes ago."

"Are you bringing him to Mama's after that?" She had already told me that she was but I just wanted to be reassured one more time that she wasn't bringing him to my house.

"Mmm-hmm. She's taking him for the afternoon."

"How about the night? Can she take him for the night, too?" Anatoly gave me a sidelong glance, which I ignored.

Leah pushed her purse strap farther up her shoulder. "Jack and I will be staying with you tonight."

"I really think you should ask Mama to take him. You have enough on your plate as it is."

"I'm the only parent he has now, and he needs me."

"You're right," I said slowly. "Jack needs stability. Maybe the two of you should stay here tonight. That way he'll be able to sleep in his own room."

Leah shot me a "you can't possibly expect me to stay here" look and then turned around to leave before I had a chance to send her a nonverbal message of my own.

Anatoly smirked. "I'm getting the sense that you have some strong feelings concerning your nephew."

"You don't know what this child is like. Rosemary's baby would be easier to deal with."

He chuckled and opened the top drawer of the desk. "I'm going to take an hour or so going through this place—there's always the off chance the police left something behind."

I pulled off my leather jacket. "I'll help. I think I'll start in the kitchen."

Anatoly nodded, although I don't think he was listening. I went downstairs and left him to his exploring.

Forty-five minutes later, I had discovered a frozen Wolf-gang Puck pizza, two Trader Joe's salads, an open bottle of Kenwood, Pinot Noir, and an entire box of chocolate-covered macadamia nuts. I flipped on the small television discreetly mounted on the wall in the corner of the dining room and turned the volume on low before getting to work on the pizza preparation. Ten minutes later the scent of freshly baked mozzarella brought Anatoly downstairs.

I gestured for him to sit at the dining table as I poured the wine. "Do you think the police found anything interesting last night?"

Anatoly glanced at the figure of Montel Williams scurrying around the TV screen, and pulled out a chair for himself. "It's impossible to know."

"So what's our next move?"

"*My* next move will be to talk to the woman Bob was sleeping with."

"Why would *we* want to do that?" I set the pizza out along with the two salads, then sat opposite him. "She has no motive—she won. Not that Bob was any great prize. Maybe that's it! Maybe she started thinking about what life would be like with Bob and freaked out."

"We don't know the details of the affair." He looked at the glass of wine offered him, then glanced at the wall clock, which read 11:55.

"My brother-in-law died yesterday," I said. "I think it would be justifiable if we started drinking early. So what were you saying about the affair?"

Anatoly sighed and reached for the prepackaged shrimp Caesar. "I was saying that it's unlikely Bob told Leah the whole story. Maybe his mistress had reason to want him dead, or maybe someone connected with her did."

"A husband! Why didn't I think of that?"

"Because you're not a PI." He tore off a piece of pizza. "You're a writer...of sorts."

"One would think that with everything we've been through together you would know better than to piss me off."

"Good point." Anatoly leaned back in his chair. "All right, who might know the name of Bob's mistress?"

"Maybe Erika, Bob's secretary," I mumbled between bites.

"I'll need you to make an introduction."

"I'll do better than that. I'll help you with the interview."

Anatoly frowned and shook his head. "I mean it, Sophie, you need to leave this to me."

"Uh-uh. Erika knows me, so she's a lot more likely to open up if I'm there. Plus, I'm good at this detective stuff. I figured out who killed Tolsky, didn't I?"

"How could I forget?" Anatoly taunted. "You're the genius who put the whole thing together just minutes after the killer confessed. Very impressive."

I narrowed my eyes. I didn't care what anyone said, writing the Alicia Bright mysteries *did* qualify me to be an amateur sleuth. In *Words To Die By* Alicia solved four murders in less than a month's time. Surely, with Anatoly's assistance, I could solve *one* murder in less than a week. "The point is, I figured it out before you. No, scratch that—the point is, I'm the one footing the bill for this little investigation, so if I say I'm sitting in on an interview, then—"

Anatoly leaned forward and grabbed my wrist. God, I had forgotten just how strong his hands were.

"This is not a game. A man was killed and the murderer may be willing to kill again in order to avoid getting caught."

I dropped the utensil I had been holding in my free hand. "You're worried about me!"

Anatoly uttered some Russian curse and attacked his salad with his fork.

"You looove me." When Anatoly didn't respond I decided to take it down a notch. "Okay, maybe you're not ready for the big *L* word, but you've got to admit you like me an awful lot."

"Careful, Sophie. I like Caesar salad and look what I'm doing to it," he said as he violently sank his fork into a piece of shrimp.

"Are you suggesting that you want to eat me?"

"Sophie…"

"*Good afternoon.*"

Anatoly and I looked up at the television to see the anchor woman who had begun speaking.

"*Thanks for joining us for Channel Two News at Noon. Today's lead story is a murder that took place last night in the Forest Hill district of San Francisco.*" Anatoly quickly stood up and adjusted the volume. "*Bob Miller, the comptroller at Chalet.com, was found last night with a gunshot wound to the head. His wife, Leah Miller, made the call to the police. This morning we had a chance to speak to Bob's sister, Cheryl Miller. This is what she had to say.*"

The camera switched to a shot of Cheryl standing in front of her place of work, Hotel Gatsby. Her overly gelled dyed-blond hair was impervious to the wind that was plaguing her interviewer. "I'm still reeling from the whole thing," she said, gently patting the corner of her eyes with a pink handkerchief. "Although, I suppose I should have seen this coming. Leah and Bob were having problems, and Leah was never the most stable of people."

"That bitch!" I screamed, standing up quickly enough to upset my chair.

"Shh!" Anatoly scolded, and turned the volume up a bit more.

"I know the police are looking at her," Cheryl continued. "Of course, she's denying it. I swear, it's just like OJ and Nicole all over again."

"How so?" the interviewer asked.

"Well, Bob and I came from a very well-respected New England family, and Leah's…well, she's black. And now she's going to try to act like the police are targeting her because of her race, which isn't the case at all. But if she's brought to trial, who knows what she'll be able to convince a jury of." Cheryl dabbed her eyes again. "Not that Leah has the money to hire the Dream Team, but she does come from *some* wealth. Her mother's side of the family is Jewish."

I wasn't so much upset as I was floored. Anatoly and I looked at each other.

"Huh," he said, "I completely forgot that your sister is black."

"I'm not sure she is anymore," I replied. "Is it possible for a person to shop in Wilkes Bashford's women's department while still maintaining an ethnic identity?"

Anatoly shook his head and cast one last glance at the television. "This is going to get messy."

Twenty-five minutes later I was clinging to Anatoly as he pulled his Harley into a parking spot right in front of Bob's office building, located in the heart of the financial district. I doubt I'll ever get over the thrill of having my breasts pressed up against his well-developed back muscles while riding on the back of that bike. There's something intrinsically sexy about a non–Hells Angels type riding a Harley. It was like Anatoly was wearing a sign that said, "I'm sexy, I'm fun and I'm secure enough with my masculinity to willingly put a large vibrating phallic symbol between my legs and enjoy it."

We walked inside and took an elevator to the eleventh floor, which was the second of the three floors that housed Chalet. I had only been there once before with Leah. Back then Bob had shared a moderate-size office with a colleague whom he had neglected to introduce me to. Since then Bob had moved up in the world. He held bragging rights to a corner office the size of my living room. Leah had told me the CFO had recently turned in her notice and Bob was to fill the vacant role. Of course, at the time she hadn't known that Bob had no intention of sharing his success with *her*...

Now the door to the office was wide open, and sitting at his desk was a petite Chinese woman. Her permed black hair hung delicately around her shoulders as she sobbed into her hands. Even without being able to see her face I recognized her as Erika. The tall man with the salt-and-pepper hair patting her shoulder was Chalet's CEO, James Sawyer, whom I had met at the occasional dinner party. As Anatoly and I stepped inside, James's hazel eyes met mine.

"Sophie." He stepped around the desk and clasped my right hand in both of his. Erika looked up and used the back of her hand to try to wipe away the tears that dampened her face.

"I can't tell you how sorry I am about Bob," James continued.

His tone was so sincere and concerned that I genuinely wished I was more upset. "I want you to know that we at Chalet have always considered the family of our employees to be part of our own extended family—no matter what their nationality, race, creed or religion."

Anatoly cleared his throat and I pressed my lips together. "I see you've been watching the news," I said.

"I...might have caught it while purchasing a coffee across the street." James adjusted his tie as if that was the reason he had suddenly gone red. He looked past me to Anatoly. "I don't believe we've met."

"Anatoly Darinsky. I'm a close friend of Sophie's."

Close—I liked that.

"I see," he said. "Well, I assume you're here for some of Bob's things?"

"Actually, we were hoping to talk to Erika for a few minutes." I tilted my head to the side so that I could see past James to Bob's grieving secretary. "Bob always spoke so highly of you, and Leah feels that your help with the arrangements would be invaluable."

"Of course, I'll help with the…arrangements. Oh, poor Bob!" She lunged for the tissues at the corner of the desk.

James regarded Erika with a mixture of sympathy and disdain. "Erika, you can go through the paperwork tomorrow," he said as he helped her to her feet and led us out of Bob's office and to her desk. "Waiting another day won't kill—won't be of any significance. Why don't you take the rest of the afternoon off?"

As Erika squeaked in agreement, James checked his watch. "I don't mean to appear insensitive, but I'm afraid I'm going to have to head out. I'm scheduled to speak to a youth group in Hunter's Point in forty-five minutes." He looked up at Anatoly and me and smiled proudly. "Chalet has built a reputation on reaching out to San Francisco's diverse community."

"Uh-huh." I eyed the navy-blue pinstripe suit once more and tried to imagine how that look played with today's troubled urban youth.

"Bob always said he wanted to get more involved in Chalet's community projects." Erika made a loud honking noise as she paused to blow her nose. "Now he'll never have the chance."

I tried not to roll my eyes. Expecting Bob to do voluntary community service was kind of like waiting for the Pope to go devil worshiping.

James's eyes were now darting between the sniffling Erika

and his ticking watch. "Yes, it's all very unfair. Sophie, please express my sympathy to your family." He nodded at me and Anatoly, and gave Erika's shoulder one last awkward pat before quickly removing himself from the room.

"I'm sorry." Erika sat up a little straighter and tucked her hair behind her ears. "I know that I was just his secretary, but he was so incredibly sweet to me. He and Leah both were, and—" she anxiously tugged on her tennis bracelet "—I just can't believe he's gone!"

Anatoly had reopened the door to the office and was taking a visual inventory. "Have the police been here yet?" he asked.

"Yes, they came earlier. They took the computer. Other than that I think they left everything intact."

Anatoly closed the door again. "So as far as you know, they didn't find anything."

Erika hesitated. "Did you really come to get my help with the funeral arrangements, or did Leah send you to gather information about…that *woman?*" By the way she said "that woman" I was unsure if she was referring to Bob's mistress or a female Al Qaeda terrorist.

Anatoly shook his head. "We didn't come to find out about Bob's mistress, but if you know who she is, I'm sure Leah would be interested."

Erika leaned forward conspiratorially lest we be overheard by the ants currently scoping out her water bottle. "Her name's Bianca Whitman. Yesterday, before…before—"

"What happened yesterday afternoon?" I asked, quickly cutting her off before she had a chance to indulge in another shower of tears.

"It was the morning, actually. Leah called me. Bob had just broken the news to her and she was so distraught." Erika looked down at her desk as if she could see the previous day's events replaying on its surface. "It was such a shock…the very idea of Bob betraying the woman he loved—" she faltered and squeezed her eyes closed against the tears "—it was just so out of character."

"And Bob was such a character." Anatoly elbowed me and I forced myself to look more bereaved. "What I meant to say was that he had so *much* character—he was just full of it."

Erika shifted in her seat uncomfortably. "Yes, well anyway, Leah asked me to look around the office for any information on this woman. So I…I went through his things while he was at lunch." She looked up at us pleadingly. "I know I shouldn't have. I just wanted to help Leah. She's become such a good friend. And Bob…you have to understand, Bob wasn't a bad person. He was just…"

"An adulterer," I finished. I was pretty sure he was a bad person, too, but I decided to let that one drop.

"Did you find anything in your search?" Anatoly asked.

Erika nodded. She unzipped her large purse and began unloading its contents onto her desk. Anatoly's forehead creased as she pulled out a miniature package of Kleenex, a bottle of prescription pills, a lipstick, a wine cork, a small package labeled *insulin,* her wallet and finally a small, light pink envelope. I had forgotten about all of Erika's health problems. She had both severe diabetes and a heart murmur. Yet it was her hearty golf-playing boss who had checked out at the ripe old age of thirty-five. It was irony like that that made a person want to take up smoking.

Erika picked up the envelope with her thumb and forefinger. "This should give Leah most of the information she wants."

"Which is?" Anatoly asked, taking the letter.

"Her name and address. There's no phone number and she's unlisted—I checked."

Anatoly scanned the letter while I helped Erika reload her purse. "What time did Bob leave work yesterday?"

"Five o'clock, as always," Erika said.

Anatoly nodded and stuffed the letter back into the envelope. "Did you tell the police about Bianca?"

"No," Erika paused a moment to blow her nose again. "I didn't want to tarnish Bob's memory. Besides, there's Leah to consider. I know she's suffering horribly right now and if she did something in the heat of passion that perhaps she shouldn't have…I just don't want to be the one to make things worse for her."

My hand clenched the Chateau d'Yquem wine cork that I had been about to drop in her bag. "You've got to be kidding me," I said. "You're not actually giving credence to baseless allegations made by some cross-burning bitch on Channel 2 today."

"I'm sorry?" Erika blinked at me. "What are you talking about? You're not saying that Bob's mistress was a Klan member, are you? Bob would never get involved with a person like that! She must have lied to him about who she was or…or brainwashed him!" Erika dropped her head to her arms again and started weeping.

Anatoly grabbed my arm and pulled me toward the exit. "Thanks for your help. Leah will contact you to discuss the memorial service," he called over his shoulder before shoving me into the elevator.

"Sophie, I doubt a lot of people saw that report," he said when the doors closed. "I know this may be hard for you to understand, but some people might think Leah's guilty just because she had means, opportunity and motive."

"Yeah, yeah, tell it to Dershowitz." I jammed my finger against the button labeled *L*. "Let me see the letter."

Anatoly handed it over to me and I quickly unfolded it.

Dear Bobby,
I know I shouldn't be writing this, but you're all I can think about these days. Every time I drive by a restau-

rant in which we dined, or pass a park bench on which we sat, or walk down a street on which you held my hand, I think of you.

Oh, yuck.

I hope that by putting the feelings that are in my heart on paper I will be better able to sort through them and maybe even figure out the right thing to do.

I know you think I shouldn't, but I keep thinking of your wife and child. I know that she's been disloyal and that she's hurt you, but two wrongs have never made a right. Thus, it is my moral obligation to end things between us.

But I can't do it, Bobby. Whenever I force myself to entertain the idea of life without you, a little part of me dies. I can still remember the way your shirt felt against my cheek as we danced at the Starlight Room. That night you told me we were soul mates. When I recall those words I know that I will never be able to walk away from you. Does that make me a horrible person? How can an immoral relationship feel so right?

So, despite the guilt, I am yours. I have no right to ask you to choose between me and your family, but I hope that you will have pity on me and make your decision. If you choose your family I will be heartbroken but I will understand; it's the right choice to make. I just don't have the strength to make it.

Love Always,
B

"Oh, this chick is a piece of work!"
Anatoly stifled a laugh as the doors opened to the ground

floor. "Maybe she's being sincere," he suggested as he escorted me to the sidewalk.

"Nah. All that 'I'll be heartbroken but I'll understand' stuff is total passive-aggressive BS. She actually had the nerve to try to guilt him into leaving his wife and child!"

"Mmm, maybe—"

We stopped in front of his bike and he handed me the spare helmet.

"We'll find out soon enough," he added.

"You think?"

"I know. We're going to pay her a visit right now."

CHAPTER 4

"But she can't be a slut," Sara said with a confused shake
of her head. "She buys her bras at Mervyn's."
—*Words To Die By*

As it turned out, Bianca lived in an eight-story building at
the top of Nob Hill. Anatoly found her name next to a buzzer
for the seventh-floor flat. "A twenty-one-year-old with a
condo kitty-corner to Grace Cathedral." Anatoly made an appreciative clucking sound with his tongue. "Pretty impressive
prize for a man you described as the world's biggest schmuck."

"She probably has buck teeth and a lazy eye."

Anatoly shrugged and pressed the buzzer. A few seconds
later a feminine voice come through the speaker. "Yes?"

Anatoly held up his hand to stop me from saying anything.
"Hello, Miss Whitman? My name is Anatoly Darinsky. I'm
a private investigator. I was hired by Bob Miller's family to
investigate his death."

There was a moment's pause and then we heard a loud
buzz as the door before us unlocked. Anatoly held it open
for me and we waited at the elevator.

"At what point do I get to rip her hair out?" I whispered.

"No hair ripping. We're going to make her feel as comfortable as possible."

"You think she's going to be comfortable talking to the sister of her lover's wife?" I let out a bitter laugh. "Give me a break."

"You're not Leah's sister," he said as we stepped onto the elevator.

"I'm not?"

"Not for this interview. You're my assistant and you will behave as such."

I tapped my finger against my lips thoughtfully. "I like that. You know, I bet that a few weeks of working with you would be enough to drive me to the edge of insanity. I might just have a breakdown and start tearing out the hair of some adulterous slut for no reason."

"Sophie…"

"Relax," I said. "I'm just kidding…sort of."

The elevator doors opened to the seventh floor, and standing in a small foyer was a pretty petite blonde wearing khakis and a white button-up blouse. A pink cardigan was draped over her shoulders.

Anatoly extended his hand to her. "Miss Whitman? Thank you for seeing me. This is—"

Bianca's hand flew to her mouth. "You're Sophie Katz, Leah's sister!"

Well, so much for that plan. Anatoly looked away to better hide the pained expression on his face.

"You know me?" My hand instinctively clenched into a fist.

"Yes, of course! I've read every one of your books! I…oh, you must hate me. I don't blame you. I didn't mean for any of this to happen." She bit her lip and looked down at her kitten-heeled sling-backs. "I keep thinking that this is some kind of nightmare—that none of this could possibly be true."

"No, it's true," I said flatly. "Someone shot the bastard."

Anatoly looked up at the ceiling and mumbled something in Russian, and Bianca's eyes welled up with tears. "God help me, this is all my fault!"

Now, that was interesting. Anatoly and I exchanged quick looks. He put a comforting hand on her arm.

"Why don't we step inside and talk."

Bianca nodded weakly and turned to lead us into her home. The place was tastefully appointed in a very Laura Ashley way. She waved a hand at a floral couch and Anatoly and I took our seats. Bianca went to her purse, pulled out a lace handkerchief and gently dabbed her eyes. First Cheryl and now Bianca—at what point did hankies come back in vogue?

"Can I get you two anything? Coffee, tea? I think I have some ice tea left over from yesterday."

"We're fine," Anatoly said. "I know you're going through a lot right now."

"Yeah, so is my sister," I muttered under my breath.

Anatoly discreetly gave my arm a painful pinch and a little whimper escaped Bianca's heart-shaped mouth as she sat down on the love seat opposite us. She lowered her head and looked up at me with misty blue eyes.

"As I said, I don't blame you for hating me. I know what I did was awful. If I could take it all back—" Her voice caught and she looked away. "If I could just go back in time and make things right…"

"What did you mean when you said all this is your fault?" Anatoly asked.

"I started the chain of events that led to Bob's death." Bianca laced her fingers together and scrunched the hankie between her hands. "I knew getting involved with him was a mistake. Even if Leah was cheating on him…"

"*Hello?*" I jumped to my feet. "My sister never cheated on anyone in her life. It was the scum she was married to who had a hard time keeping it in his pants!"

Bianca looked startled for a moment, then compassionate. "I shouldn't be surprised that she didn't tell you. It's hardly the kind of thing one brags about. But she did cheat on him. It was her indiscretion that first brought Bob and me together. Both of us discovered that we had been betrayed by the people we loved and we sought solace in each other."

I shook my head and opened my mouth to defend Leah against Bob's lies, but Anatoly grabbed my hand and yanked me back down onto the couch. He cleared his throat and looked at Bianca. "Please continue. You were explaining how you started a chain of events."

"Yes." Bianca looked at me pityingly. "It started as just a friendship. I was at the bar at Boulevard waiting for a friend and he was there waiting for his associates to show up for a business dinner. He inadvertently overheard me while I was talking to my sister on my cell. I was telling her about what happened with Kevin—Kevin was my fiancé. He…he left me for someone else. When I hung up, Bob introduced himself. He told me he knew what I was going through because he was going through something similar—that was right after he had walked in on Leah in the arms of her personal trainer…"

"Are you kidding? My sister would rather die than get involved with anyone who worked at a gym."

"Sophie, shut up," Anatoly said calmly. He smiled again at Bianca and gestured for her to continue.

Bianca looked nervously between the two of us. "Well, we became friends, and the more time we spent together the more we discovered we had in common." She fingered a delicate gold crucifix that hung around her neck. "When Bob first told me he was leaving Leah…"

Anatoly scooted forward on the couch. "When exactly was that?"

"Well, this was the first time he planned on leaving, so that was about nine months ago."

My eyes widened. "Bob had this planned for that long?"

"Perhaps *planned* isn't the right word. He had been thinking about filing for divorce long before he met me, but it wasn't until he found evidence that Leah was continuing to be unfaithful that he decided to go through with it. Once his mind was made up he immediately made his intentions clear to Leah. That's when we…became more than friends."

Anatoly's eyes darted in my direction, presumably to assure himself that I wasn't going to interrupt Bianca with another tirade. Frankly, I was too stunned to speak. I never would have thought Bob clever enough to pull off this level of deceit. I knew damn well that the only thing Bob had made clear to Leah nine months ago was his refusal to help with potty training.

"As you know, Bob and Leah worked things out," Bianca continued, "if only for the sake of their son. It was awful for Bob, and Leah's insistence that they sleep in separate bedrooms didn't help matters. Nonetheless, he was willing to stick it out so that Jack would be raised in a two-parent home. But what we had…it was so powerful, I just don't think either of us knew how to resist it." Bianca hesitated and looked at me. "I'm so sorry. I know how this must sound to you."

"I really don't think you do," I mumbled, thinking about the bedroom Leah had shared with her husband for the duration of their marriage.

"Well, we just couldn't take it anymore. We loved each other so much and we had to be together. Bob told me he was going to be leaving Leah and this time nothing was going to change his mind. And I…I know this is so awful, but I was overjoyed. I was so sure that we would have this perfect future, but I didn't think of Leah, now did I."

"I would say the answer to that is a big no," I agreed.

Bianca nodded and looked at her petal-pink nails. "Bob had told me how delicate her mental state was. He warned me she wouldn't take it well—and who would? Who could possibly be gracious in the face of losing Bob?"

She had a point. If Bob had left me I would have been too busy celebrating to be gracious.

"I just didn't anticipate that our betrayal would push her over the edge," Bianca continued. "And now look what I've done! Leah may have been the one to pull the trigger but I'm the one who set this whole thing in motion." Bianca's lower lip began to tremble. "It's all my fault that the love of my life is dead!"

The really frightening thing about this monologue was that she actually seemed to be buying into her own bullshit. I tried to see her the way Bob must have: a soft-spoken, white, Christian, polished, naive girl with a pedigree and a knack for co-dependency. In other words, she was everything Leah was not.

Anatoly studied Bianca for a moment before speaking. "There's evidence that indicates Leah is not the one responsible for Bob's death."

He told the lie so effortlessly that I almost believed it myself.

"There is?" Bianca's tears momentarily stopped. "But she's the only one that had any kind of motive. Bob was so gentle and thoughtful—no one other than Leah would ever hurt a hair on his head."

"I would," I whispered. But if Anatoly or Bianca heard, they chose to ignore me.

"What about your ex-fiancé, Kevin?" Anatoly asked. "Is there any chance he wanted to reconcile with you? Perhaps Bob was in his way."

Bianca tucked her hair behind her ears and shook her head sadly. "Kevin proposed to his new girlfriend three months ago and the two of them moved to Boston. He could care less who I'm with. The only man who really cared about me was…was…"

"My sister's husband," I finished for her.

Bianca shot me a pleading look. "I want you to know that I don't intend to contact the police. If they come to me I guess I'll have to answer their questions, but I don't want to make any more trouble for Leah. I know I'm as much to blame as she is, and I…I don't want to take both of Jack's parents away from him. I don't want that at all." She averted her eyes and her shoulders began to tremble. "All I really want is for Bob to be alive again."

Anatoly sighed and drummed his fingers against the armrest impatiently. "Bianca, do you know for sure that Bob informed Leah he was leaving her this last time?"

Bianca nodded without making eye contact. "He came over here right after he broke the news to her. It was the last time…we were together." She swallowed hard. "I can't understand how he could be gone when just yesterday he was making love to me."

I tried to swallow my disgust, but it was impossible.

"Did he say anything about the rest of his plans for that day?" Anatoly asked.

"He said he was going to work and then he was going to go home and pack. He was planning on moving in with me that night, but said he might not get here until late. I waited and waited, and when he wasn't here by eleven, I turned on the news and—" She stopped herself and stared fixedly at the hardwood floor.

Anatoly cleared his throat. "Did Bob ever talk about anyone he disliked or who he felt disliked him?"

"Other than Leah?"

"Yes," Anatoly and I said in unison.

"No, everyone loved Bob."

Those were the same words Leah had used. I had a quick flashback of a *Saturday Night Live* skit in which the audience of a Broadway play came out of the theater and one after another recited in a monotone voice, "It was better than *Cats*, I'd see it again and again." Maybe Erika was on to something with the brainwashing thing. Worse, maybe Bob had turned all the women he had contact with into San Francisco's version of a Stepford wife. But that didn't work because San Francisco's version of a Stepford wife would probably be a drag queen.

"All right, I think I have all I need for right now." Anatoly stood up, and Bianca followed suit. "May I contact you again if I have further questions?" he asked.

Bianca nodded. She looked at me and pulled nervously at the sweater draped over her shoulders. "Please tell Leah that I'm sorry."

"I can't imagine that your apology would mean anything to my sister."

Anatoly took hold of my wrist. "We're leaving now." He pulled me toward the door, but I resisted.

"One more thing," I said. "May I see the bracelet?"

Anatoly shot me a questioning look. I had forgotten to tell him about the Tiffany's receipt Leah had found.

Bianca flushed. "You know about that?"

I fixed her with a cool stare. Bianca bit her lip.

"I'll go get it," she whispered, and retreated into the next room.

"What bracelet?" Anatoly hissed.

"Yesterday Leah told me she found a receipt for a six-thousand-dollar bracelet."

"And I'm just hearing about this now?"

"It's not like it's important. The only reason I brought it up is that I want to see what it looks like."

"Really," he said dryly. "This isn't about trying to make Bianca feel guilty about the gift?"

I shrugged. "It's an added perk."

Bianca reappeared with a wide gold bracelet that was covered in small, sparkling yellow stones. She cupped her hand and held it out for my inspection. I poked it gingerly with my finger. "Wow, Liz Taylor's got nothing on you. Are these diamonds?"

"Yellow sapphires."

"Huh, those suckers must have been on special or something."

"He gave it to me to celebrate the one-year anniversary of the day we met." Bianca's voice took on a dreamy tone. "He got the date wrong by six and a half weeks but I never corrected him. It was just such a romantic gesture."

Extravagant seemed like a better word for it. Still, Bob clearly had better taste than I had given him credit for. I pulled my hand away from the bracelet. "It's amazing how profitable immorality can be, isn't it?"

Bianca's lower lip started doing its trembling thing and Anatoly grabbed my arm again. "We're really going now," he said, more to me than to her.

Bianca trailed behind us and watched glumly as we stepped onto the elevator.

"I can't believe I allowed you to come on these interviews," Anatoly muttered after the doors had closed.

"I'm sorry, but she messed up my sister's life and I don't really give a shit how sorry she is about it. She's probably the one who killed Bob. I mean, if she loved him so much, why is she extending her apologies to the woman she believes to be his murderer?"

"That was a bit strange." Anatoly stepped out of the elevator on the first floor and escorted me to the sidewalk. "Do you think there's any truth to Bianca's assertion that Bob tried to leave Leah nine months ago?"

"No way. Leah would have told me."

"Are you sure?"

"Leah doesn't suffer quietly. Ever."

Anatoly sighed and looked back at Bianca's building.

"What are you thinking?" I asked.

"I'm thinking that if the police end up talking to Bianca they're going to think that she..."

"Has an unhealthy lack of cynicism?" I offered.

Anatoly laughed softly. "She is incredibly naive, but what I was going to say was that she comes across as being credible." He looked at me and the gravity in his expression chilled me. "They're going to think she is a lot more credible than your sister."

I didn't say anything, and Anatoly was wise enough not to push the issue. We mounted his Harley and rode to my apartment in silence. When he stopped the bike in front of my doorstep I muttered a goodbye and walked swiftly to the door.

"Sophie?"

I turned to see that Anatoly had gotten off his bike and was standing with his helmet in his hands. "I know this is hard, but for a moment I want you to pretend that you don't love Leah. I want you to think about the things she's done in the past and the things she hasn't, and then I want you to tell me if you believe she could be capable of murder."

I swallowed and turned away.

"Sophie, even if the answer is yes, I'll still help you protect her."

"Why?" I shook my head in bewilderment. "It's not like you owe me anything. If anything, it's the other way around."

"Because," Anatoly said softly, "I have a brother."

This was news to me. Fifty million questions flooded my mind. Did he live nearby? Was he still in Russia? Or had they immigrated together to Israel but not to America? But it didn't seem like the right time to ask.

"So about Leah..." Anatoly prodded.

"Right—Leah." I thought about the woman who was

my sister. I replayed the conversation we had had the afternoon before Bob's death and then I thought about Brad Thompson. Brad was from Leah's pre-Bob days and he had been the "love of her life." She had assured me, our mother and everyone else who would listen that he was going to propose. And then it happened—the breakup. He told her that she was fun to mess around with but not nearly good enough to marry. I sat by her side as she cried into her pillow and listed off all the things she wanted to do to him, his car and his reputation. But when I had suggested that we get some of my male friends to start a fight with him at a bar and rough him up, Leah had been horrified.

"She didn't do it," I said slowly.

"Are you sure?"

I smiled and nodded enthusiastically. "I'll admit that I had some fleeting doubts, but I know my sister. She didn't do it."

"All right, then. I'm going to do a background check on Bianca. Maybe she's not as credible as she seems."

As I watched Anatoly put his helmet on and drive away, I was overcome with relief. Fear had clouded my judgment, but now I was thinking clearly and I knew Leah was innocent. All I had to do was prove it.

I let myself in and was just opening the apartment door when my phone started ringing. I looked down at Mr. Katz, who was watching me expectantly. "I'll feed you right after I get this," I assured him before grabbing the phone. "Y'ello?"

"It's me."

There was no mistaking the husky voice of my closest and most abrasive friend. "Hey, Dena, what's up?"

"What's up? How about the murder of your brother-in-law?"

"Oh, yeah, that." I went to the kitchen and poured Mr. Katz some kibble then took the phone back into the bedroom with me.

"Jesus, just when I thought things were getting back to normal."

"Tell me about it." I sat on the edge of my bed and pulled my boots off and threw them in the general direction of my closet. "At least Leah's okay."

"Is she? Did she ever find out if he was screwing around on her?"

When I didn't answer, Dena groaned. "Shit, do the police know about the affair?"

"Nope." Mr. Katz wandered into my room and glared at me. Undoubtedly he had seen the bottom of his food bowl.

"Thank God for small favors. Look, I'm with Mary Ann, can we stop by?"

"Sure, I'm not doing anything."

"Perfect, we're in the car and about a block from your place, so with any luck we'll be able to find a parking spot within the next fifteen minutes."

It would be so nice if Dena was being sarcastic, but fifteen minutes to find parking in my neighborhood was a pretty realistic estimate—assuming she didn't mind parking four or more city blocks away.

By the time Dena and Mary Ann arrived I had brewed a pot of coffee and was midway through my second cup.

The minute she walked in the door Mary Ann pulled me into a hug. "Sophie, I'm so sorry your family has to go through this."

"Thanks," I mumbled into her chestnut-brown curls. I pulled back slowly, careful not to spill the coffee I still held on to her white three-quarter-length sleeve wrap top. It was slightly cropped and exposed a little over an inch of perfectly flat abs.

Dena's hug was briefer and a little less emotionally charged, but then again, Dena wasn't exactly the touchy-feely type. She walked over to the covered mirror and knitted her thick Sicilian eyebrows. "What's up with the new wall hangings?"

I grinned and stepped into the kitchen to pour them both a cup of caffeine. "It's Jewish tradition to cover the mirrors after a family member dies."

"With sarongs decorated with rainbow-colored salmon?" Dena asked. "Oh, wait, I get it! Lox! The salmon are there to remind us that some things are more enjoyable dead."

"Dena, that is not funny!" Mary Ann said. But even she couldn't keep a straight face as Dena and I collapsed into giggles.

"My God, we're horrible human beings." I handed a cup of black coffee to Dena and a cup half filled with cream and a few tablespoons' worth of sugar to Mary Ann.

"Tell me something I don't know." Dena sat down on my couch and propped her feet up on my coffee table so that the thick heels of her boots stuck out like phallic symbols. "Seriously, though, how could anyone find Bob interesting enough to kill? There's no way that little bean counter could inspire that kind of passion."

"Mmm, I don't know about that." I sat down opposite her on my love seat and Mary Ann quickly took her place by my side. "When Leah told me he was leaving her and Jack for his mistress, who just happens to be twenty-one years old, I entertained some pretty violent thoughts."

"Yeah, but you're always entertaining violent thoughts. You write murder mysteries, for Christ sake."

"That's not fair," Mary Ann said. "You don't have to be a violent person to write about murder. I work at the Lancôme counter and I don't think about makeup all the time. I'm not even wearing any now."

I looked at her flawless porcelain complexion and tried to suppress my jealously.

"And I doubt Marcus thinks about hair all the time," Mary Ann continued, "and you work..." Her voice trailed off.

Dena was the sole proprietor of Guilty Pleasures, an establishment she affectionately referred to as an erotic boutique, and if there was ever a woman who brought her work home with her, it was Dena.

Dena smiled at her cousin mischievously and Mary Ann rolled her eyes. "Not everyone's you."

Dena shrugged and ran her fingers through her cropped hair. "Do the police suspect Leah?"

I nodded. "But she didn't do it."

"Of course, she didn't." Mary Ann used her hand to make little soothing circles on my back. "Anyone who's ever met Leah would know she's not capable of hurting anyone. The poor thing must be devastated by all this."

"She's not at her best," I admitted.

"Is there anything I can do?" Mary Ann asked.

"No—wait, that's not true." I shifted my position so I was facing her. "Leah wants to make sure her mourning attire is appropriate in a *W* magazine kind of way."

Mary Ann nodded encouragingly. "There are a few recently widowed women who I work on at Neiman. Of course I only do their makeup, but I always take note of what they're wearing."

"Jesus, is fashion really Leah's biggest concern?" Dena asked. "What about her kid?"

"Trust me, Jack is always a concern." I took a long sip of my drink. "In fact, she and Jack will be staying with me for the next few days."

Mary Ann gasped and Dena's tan complexion got almost as white as her cousin's.

I ran a jagged fingernail around the rim of my mug. "It's not as bad as all that. I can deal with Jack."

"Of course you can," Mary Ann said. "You do still have rental insurance, right?"

"And smoke detectors," Dena chimed in. "You're going to need lots of smoke detectors."

"He's eighteen months old. He's not going to be setting fire to the apartment." I glanced nervously at the smoke detector in the living room. When *was* the last time I checked the battery on that thing?

I heard the sound of a key jiggling in the lock and then Leah burst in with Jack in her arms. Despite my concerns I felt a little tug at my heart. Cuddled up against his mother Jack looked like a little cherub. If he didn't have the temperament of a Tasmanian devil he'd be irresistible.

"Have you listened to the radio?" she asked, skipping the formality of a greeting.

"Not today but—"

"There was this woman on the air and she was talking about me!" Jack squirmed in her arms and she placed him on the ground. "She was talking about how my new status as a suspect is a perfect example of how underprivileged women of color still have to struggle to be seen as contributing citizens rather than potential criminals. *Underprivileged,* Sophie! I have never been less than upper middle class in my life, and this woman has me sounding like some kind of black, blue-collar soccer mom!"

Dena put her cola can on the coffee table. "I don't think she was trying to make you look like a soccer mom…welfare mom, maybe."

"This is all Cheryl's fault!"

"Ah." I brought my fingers to my temples. "So you know about her comments to Channel Two."

"Yes, I know! And the sad part is I don't even think she's

a racist. She just knew this was her one and only chance at grabbing her fifteen minutes of fame. After all, it's not like she could ever make it as an actress. The senior citizen who fell and couldn't get back up was a better thespian than she is. Cheryl's only talent is making other people's lives miserable. That and her obnoxious ability to quote from *Entertainment Weekly*."

Mary Ann blinked. "I've never met Cheryl. Is she into celebrities?"

"Oh, she's way beyond that," Leah said. "They need to make up a new word for what Cheryl is."

"That's the understatement of the century. I don't think there's an E! Television show that she hasn't seen or an *Us* magazine she hasn't read five times over," Leah explained. "That's why she got a job at Hotel Gatsby. She read some article about how Gatsby hotels are always filled with young A-list celebrities, so when they opened one in San Francisco she rushed over and strong-armed some unwitting HR girl into letting her work the front desk."

Dena rolled her head toward her right shoulder in an effort to stretch her neck. "I thought Cheryl worked at the Ritz."

"She did, but that didn't stop her from accepting a few graveyard shifts at Gatsby," Leah said. "Never mind the fact that the Ritz has a policy against working at another hotel while working for them. The management at the Ritz just found out last week and terminated her employment." Leah allowed herself a brief moment of smug satisfaction before continuing her tirade. "I suppose she'll go to full-time at the Gatsby now. But it gives you an idea of what kind of woman she is. I mean really, what kind of person is that disrespectful of the Ritz-Carlton?"

Jack toddled over to Mary Ann and she bent over to kiss him on the forehead, then quickly withdrew her head as she caught a whiff of his current odor. "Oh," she said in a nasal voice that implied that she was holding her breath. "Does he have a poopy diaper?"

"Of course he has a poopy diaper. Do you think my son smells like this all the time?"

Leah strode forward and reached for Jack, but Mary Ann picked him up before she had a chance. "You seem a little stressed," Mary Ann said, blatantly understating the situation. "Why don't you sit down and relax and I'll change Jack."

"You'd do that?" Leah's expression softened.

"Of course. You've been through so much. This is the least I can do."

"Thank you." Leah's mouth relaxed into a genuine smile. "I'm sorry I snapped, but I'm just at the end of my rope."

"Any of us would be," Mary Ann said reassuringly.

Jack pointed to Mr. Katz, who was busy grooming himself. "Kitty lick."

"Yes, that's what cats do when they're dirty," Mary Ann explained as she carried him down the hall. "I guess you both need a little cleaning."

Leah waited until Mary Ann had disappeared into the bathroom before turning her attention to Dena. "I haven't seen you for a while," she said coolly. "Sophie tells me you're dating a vampire."

"He's not a vampire," Dena said with a yawn. "He just wants to become one. Anyway, I broke up with him last week."

"What?" I scooted forward. "Why didn't you tell me?"

"It's no biggie. He was getting a little too…" Dena waved her hand in the air as if trying to physically grab the word that was eluding her.

"Intense?" I volunteered.

"Insane?" Leah pitched in.

"Conventional," Dena finished. "When I first met him

he was so dark and mysterious, but then he got a job at the Gap and it was bye-bye gothic, hello 'Songs by Your Favorite Artists.'"

Leah shook her head. "Do you ever get tired of being a freak?"

"I beg your pardon." Dena raised herself to her full five feet two inches of height. "And the term is *super freak*." She turned to me. "I've got to check in with the shop."

"I left the phone on my bedside table."

Dena nodded and disappeared down the hall.

"So," I said, turning back to Leah, "you're having a bad day."

"A bad day?" Leah collapsed onto a chair by the dining table. "My husband was shot yesterday!"

"Yes, I know." And it couldn't have happened to a nicer guy.

"You know, the cruelest thing I ever did to Bob was serve him a cold dinner. And now Cheryl's accusing me of shooting him?"

"Like you said, she's just trying to grab her fifteen minutes." I could hear Jack screaming in the guest room. I eyed Leah to see if she was going to help Mary Ann out, but she stayed glued to her seat.

"I guarantee you Bob never told Cheryl about our marriage problems." Leah's eyes narrowed as she looked out into space. "The two of them were hardly on speaking terms! And now she runs out and gets herself a pink hankie and starts comparing me to OJ? Is she *joking?*"

"Let's focus on what we can control," I said. Jack was still screaming in the background and now I could hear Mary Ann's pleas for cooperation. Clearly Jack wasn't one of our controllables. "I found some stuff out today that you should know."

"Oh?"

"Yeah, for one thing I…well, I spoke to Bob's mistress."

Leah flinched but didn't say anything.

"She says that Bob almost left you nine months ago. She implied that you and Bob actually talked about it."

"She's lying."

"So he never said anything at all?"

"You would take the word of a whore over mine?"

I sighed and started massaging my temples in earnest. "You know, it would be so much simpler if she were a whore, but after meeting her I don't think that title really fits."

"Really? How would *you* describe the woman who was sleeping with my husband?"

"I'd describe her as a wide-eyed innocent who bought Bob's BS hook, line and sinker."

Leah pressed her lips together.

"I'm sorry. I wish I could tell you that she was some kind of siren whose unearthly song led Bob to the rocks. Although, I'm not a hundred-percent sure she isn't the one who killed him, if that makes you feel any better."

Leah shrugged peevishly. "A little."

I smiled, glad to be able to deliver at least some good news. A fresh-smelling Jack toddled into the living room followed by a somewhat haggard-looking Mary Ann. Leave it to my nephew to break someone's spirit with one diaper change.

Leah smiled at Mary Ann and pulled out a chair for her, which Mary Ann immediately dropped into. "Thank you so much for doing that."

"It was no problem," Mary Ann lied. Mr. Katz stretched his legs and wandered out of the room. Jack went after him, keeping a cautious distance. Leah started to get up to follow him but Mary Ann's words stopped her. "Sophie tells me you have some fashion questions."

"Yes," Leah said urgently. "I need to know what widows are supposed to wear."

Mary Ann reached out and patted her hand. "The key to the look is earth tones."

"Earth tones." By the awe in Leah's voice you would have thought Mary Ann had just spoken the true name of God.

"Hey, Sophie."

I looked up to see Dena standing just outside of the kitchen.

"Is it okay for Jack to be getting into the cabinet beneath the sink?"

"Oh, my God!" I yelled.

Leah and I ran into the kitchen, pushing Dena aside just as Jack grabbed the Clorox scrub and dumped it onto Mr. Katz. Jack looked up at Leah with pride in his eyes. "Dirty cat."

Leah scooped up Jack and I raced after Mr. Katz, who almost sent Mary Ann sprawling as he tried to pass her in the hall. I lunged for him and managed to throw him in the bathtub as he ran his claws down my arm. While I turned on the shower, Mr. Katz hissed and desperately tried to escape. I managed to rinse off the cleaning solution just as Mr. Katz punished me with a particularly painful scratch across the back of my wrist. He jumped out of the bathtub and darted out of the room. I looked up to see my three guests standing in the doorway.

"I know this might be an inopportune moment to bring this up," Leah said slowly, "but is anyone else impressed that my son made the connection between Mary Ann's statement that the cat was dirty and Clorox? It really is an amazing mental leap for an eighteen-month-old."

I pressed my hands against my wounds. The only leap I wanted Jack to make was into a playpen for the rest of the night. "You're right, Leah, the moment's definitely inopportune."

Leah handed Jack to Mary Ann, who took him with no little trepidation. "Let me see your arms." Leah peered at them and then pulled some cotton balls and rubbing alcohol out of my medicine cabinet. She sat down next to me on the edge of the bathtub and held my arms under the running faucet before patting them dry and applying the alcohol. "Spare me the dramatics," she said as I gasped in pain.

I narrowed my eyes. "This from the girl who was voted 'most likely to overreact' in high school?"

"I've changed." She tossed the used cotton balls in the wastebasket. "Besides, you don't know what pain is until you've—"

"If you finish that sentence with 'given birth,' I'm going to have to punch you," Dena said flatly.

Leah glared at her. "It's true. Not that you would know anything about childbirth or anything else that involved any kind of commitment."

"I'm plenty committed. I'm committed to my friends, my career, and I'm very committed to my quest to help the women of San Francisco find their G-spot."

Mary Ann sighed disapprovingly and took Jack out of the room before Dena could inadvertently corrupt him.

Leah stood up stiffly and put the first-aid supplies back in their place. "Do you ever miss an opportunity to advertise your scandalous behavior?"

"Come on, guys." I squeezed my arms in hopes of alleviating the stinging. "Let's not get into this now."

"I don't do anything that's immoral." Dena took a step closer to Leah, totally ignoring my last comment. "There is nothing shameful about sex between two consenting adults. Hell." Dena smiled slyly. "There's nothing shameful about sex between three consenting adults, either."

"There you go again, bragging about being a slut."

"It's not like you were a virgin bride, Leah."

"Yes, but unlike *some* people in this room, *I've* never slept with a man on a first date."

"Really?" Dena leaned casually against the wall. "I seem to remember a certain incident at Sophie's college graduation party. What was that guy's name again? Or did you even get his name?"

"Oh, *please,*" Leah spat. "That wasn't a *date!*"

Dena opened her mouth, but for once she seemed to be at a loss for words. I took the opportunity to drag Dena into my bedroom for a quick heart-to-heart.

"Listen, I know you and Leah see the world a little differently—"

"You're kidding me, right? She basically said it's acceptable to screw a stranger but it's not okay to have a sexual encounter with a man who's bought you dinner. No one sees the world the way Leah does."

"Yes, well, Leah has all these rules of behavior that she wants to adhere to." I sat down on the edge of my bed. "She's going through a really hard time right now and it would mean a lot to me if you could try to get along with her while she's here."

Dena stared up at the ceiling. "You're asking a lot."

"It's that or we're not going to be able to see much of each other in the next few weeks, and I don't want that." I shot her a pleading look. "I know she's nuts, but so are you. Can't we just try to combine our collective neuroses and hope that we balance one another out?"

"Fine," she said with an air of exasperation. "If I can put up with Mary Ann I guess I can put up with your sister for a while—"

"Thanks a lot—"

We turned to see Mary Ann standing in the doorway smiling at us.

"I love you, too, Dena," she said.

I giggled and pushed myself off the bed. Unlike Leah, Mary Ann knew better than to take Dena's rumblings seriously.

"Leah was just telling me that Jack usually goes to sleep around eight," Mary Ann said. "She also told me that she hasn't had a chance to get any of her stuff from home, so I was thinking that I could come back after Leah puts Jack to bed and stay with him while you and Leah go to her place and pack some things."

"She needs help with that?" Dena asked.

I shrugged. "She probably doesn't want to go back to her house by herself. Hey, I have an idea, why don't you come with us, Dena?"

"Because I don't want to?"

"Come on, it will be the perfect olive branch to extend to Leah. And if the two of you do start arguing while we're there, then at least she'll be distracted from all the memories."

"I don't know."

"Or maybe you could babysit with Mary Ann. I mean, Jack might wake up…."

"I'll go with you to Leah's."

"Great." I patted her shoulder. "I'll go tell her."

Mary Ann stopped me in the doorway. "You don't really think he'll wake up, do you?"

"No, of course not." I stepped past Mary Ann and swallowed my guilt over that last lie.

CHAPTER 5

"One should never go back to the scene of a perfect crime," Jonathan said. "But it's a good idea to go back if the crime was mediocre."

—*Words To Die By*

Although Mary Ann and Dena did arrive at my place at eight, Jack refused to go to bed before ten, so my friends and I watched Donald Trump fire people on national television while Leah dealt with her son. The delay was not exactly unexpected. As far as I knew Jack had only fallen asleep at eight once in his life. However, Leah continued to insist that the one incident had been "normal" and all the other nights of Jack's life had been "exceptions to the rule."

Eventually Dena, Leah and I arrived at Leah's door. The house was pitch-black and I tried the light switch in the foyer only to find that the light bulb needed to be replaced.

"Perfect," Dena muttered as she felt her way down the short hallway to the dining room.

Leah pushed past her and turned on a lamp before going into the kitchen. "Let's start by packing up some food."

I wrinkled my nose. "I have food at home."

"You don't have the *right* food," Leah explained. "I'm doing South Beach."

Dena gave her a quick once-over. "How much have you lost?"

"I've gained a pound, but I think I have a thyroid condition. So going forward, I'll have to be a little more diligent about following the rules of the diet."

"*More* diligent about following the rules?" Dena leaned against the counter. "Let me make sure I'm interpreting this correctly. You cheated on your diet, gained a pound, and you blame this on a self-diagnosed thyroid condition."

"It makes perfect sense to me," I said as I opened up the cupboard.

Dena rolled her eyes. "So you two *do* have something in common. You both have the same messed-up dieting strategies."

"Shh!" Leah motioned for us to be quiet. "Did either of you hear that?"

I shook my head. "Hear what?"

"I thought I heard something…like something upstairs fell over."

We were all quiet for a moment until Dena broke the silence. "I don't hear anything. Maybe it was just the sound of your two brain cells knocking into each other."

Leah shot her the look of death. "I refuse to stand here and be insulted by the whore of Babylon."

"Will you two cut it out and start packing stuff up? Mary Ann was nice enough to offer to babysit, so the least we can do is try to get back before Jack wakes up."

The floorboards above us creaked. Leah froze, a box of low-carb cereal bars in her hand. "You heard that, right?" she whispered.

Dena nodded.

"It could be nothing," I said softly. "Houses creak."

Dena was staring intently at the ceiling. "You're right," she said. "It could be nothing. It also could be something—or someone." She pushed herself away from the counter and walked into the dining room.

I could hear the crackle of tinfoil packaging as Leah inadvertently crushed the bars within the box she held. She put her free hand on her stomach and took a deep breath. "Something's off. I can feel it."

Dena poked her head back into the kitchen; her face betrayed her alarm. "Come here!" she demanded.

We followed her into the living room. Every pillow on the couch had been removed and was on the floor.

We heard a noise again. This time it sounded like soft footsteps, headed in the direction of the stairwell.

We all exchanged looks, and for the first time in our lives we were all on the same page. We ran toward the front door, knocking over a lamp in the process. I thought I could hear the footsteps descending the stairs but I didn't dare turn around and find out if I was right. Instead, we tumbled out into the cold night air and ran to my car. I jumped into the driver's seat and Leah got in next to me; Dena got in back. No one came out after us but I wasn't going to wait around and give the person more time. I put the car in gear, slammed my foot on the gas and screeched out of my parking spot.

"What should we do?" Leah asked. "Should we call the cops?"

I checked the rearview mirror and confirmed that we weren't being followed. "I don't think calling the cops is a good idea."

"Are you serious?" Dena yelled. "We could have been killed back there!"

"We don't know that," I said. "It could have been just some kid looking for a TV to snag."

"Under the sofa cushions?" Dena asked.

"Maybe he was looking for the remote control." I checked the rearview again. In a matter of minutes I had put several blocks between us and the house. "Whoever was upstairs didn't follow us." I slowed the car down to a more moderate speed. "Maybe he was more afraid of us than we were of him."

"Let's call the police and let them figure out how scared the intruder is," Leah suggested.

"But the intruder isn't going to sit around and wait for the police to show up." I pulled the car over to the side of the road. "He's probably long gone by now, and if we call the police it's going to look like we're trying to deflect their attention away from you, Leah, and that will make you look more guilty than ever."

"So what are you suggesting?" Leah asked. "That we just sit here and allow some stranger to go through my things?"

"Like I said, the intruder probably left by now."

"No, no, no." Dena shook her head furiously. "I know what you're thinking and you can just forget it. I am not playing Nancy Drew with you again."

"I wouldn't dream of playing Nancy. I'll play my own literary heroine, thank you very much," I retorted. "Besides, there are three of us, and it's not like we don't know how to handle ourselves."

"But we're unarmed! Unless…" Leah pivoted in her seat so she could see Dena. "Do you have any S&M toys with you today?"

"Not so much as a nipple clamp."

I squeezed the steering wheel a little tighter and tried not to think about what nipple clamps would feel like. "Why don't we go back and stake the place out. If we see any signs that there's someone there, we'll call the cops. If not, we'll go in and investigate."

I pulled a U-turn and headed back in the direction from which we had come. Leah was staring at me as if she were seeing me for the first time. "I used to wonder why you've had so many life-and-death experiences," she said, "but I think I'm beginning to figure it out."

Dena groaned. "If one of us gets killed tonight, I'm going to be so fucking pissed off."

We ended up sitting outside Leah's house for an hour before reentering. Leah stepped in first and went straight for the front closet. She reached up to the top shelf, pulled down three old boxes and handed one to each of us.

Dena took hers gingerly. "What are these?"

"Unwanted wedding gifts that Bob and I never got around to giving away." She pointed to the box in Dena's hand. "That one's a poor-quality crystal bud vase, and Sophie and I have equally poorly made condiment containers."

Dena stared at her box for a beat before looking back up at Leah. "Why?"

"For self-defense, of course. If there's still someone in the house you can hit him over the head with it without worrying that you might be breaking something that's valuable to me."

"Thank God for that," Dena said dryly.

I exhaled loudly. "Come on, Leah, if someone was still here, we would have seen—"

"Excuse me, but it was my husband who was killed. I think that entitles me to insist on a few extra precautions."

Dena removed the contents of her box with an air of disgust. "Well, if the intruder offers us flowers and homemade jam, we'll be prepared."

"Just humor me, all right?" Leah pulled out her condiment container and held it above her head threateningly. "Now, let's investigate."

Dena blinked and turned to me. "Is she kidding me with this?"

I shrugged and opened my box. "It'll make her feel better."

Dena watched as Leah and I moved forward, armed with our crystal. "Oh, for Christ's sake." She raised her bud vase and followed us through the house.

We walked into the living room first. All the pillows had been replaced. I sucked in a sharp breath and Leah quickly turned on the overhead light.

"This is good," I said uncertainly. "Whoever was here obviously tried to cover up the evidence, which means he's probably not the type who likes to hang around the scene of a crime."

"Nothing about this is good," Leah snapped. "All of this is very, very bad."

Dena carefully checked behind the curtains. "I can't believe I'm saying this, but I'm with Leah on this one. The whole situation sucks."

"Things could always be worse," I said doubtfully. "Let's check the other rooms."

We thoroughly checked the kitchen and dining room before gathering at the bottom of the stairwell. "Shall we?"

Leah and Dena nodded silently and we crept upstairs. Everytime one of us pulled back a curtain or knelt to look under a bed I felt my heart rate accelerate, but no one was there. We ended our search in the master bedroom. After Leah checked her closet, she slammed the door shut with enough force to send an echo through the room.

"This is too much! How am I supposed to wear anything in here when I know some pervert might have been sorting through all of it less than two hours ago?"

Dena fell back on the bed. "You really need to reexamine your priorities."

"This had to mean something," I said, glancing around the room. "Nothing's stolen—so what did they want?"

"Perhaps the goal was to make my life a living hell." Leah

started yanking open each of the drawers in her dresser. She pulled out a plum-colored cashmere-blend sweater and held it up.

Dena propped herself on her elbows. "Cute top," she said, eyeing the plunging neckline. "I bet it looks hot on you."

Leah's mouth formed a sad little smile. "I thought it did when I bought it. The salespeople told me the color was perfect for me, and even a few of the other women in the dressing area encouraged me to buy it, but when I tried it on for Bob…" Leah's voice trailed off and she folded the sweater back up and returned it to the drawer. "He said the neckline was too low and the cut too tight. He said I looked like a tramp. Ironic, since he was sleeping with one at the time." She eyed the sweater wistfully. "I did like it, though."

Dena paused for a beat before clearing her throat and standing up. "Leah, I'm sorry about Bob. I'm sorry he was killed and I'm sorry he was such a major prick."

Leah used the back of her hand to wipe away a tear. "I tried so hard to be a good wife. But I was never able to get it right."

Dena took the sweater back out and draped it over her arm. "You need to pack this and wear it. And you should never allow a man to give you shit about your wardrobe. You shouldn't allow a man to give you shit, period."

I smiled as I watched them. It was probably the nicest exchange the two of them had ever had. I glanced at the door to the bedroom. "Now that we know we're alone, maybe we should comb this place again and make sure there really isn't anything missing."

We spent the next fifteen minutes searching Leah's and Jack's rooms. We didn't find anything amiss until we reached the office and Leah started going through the desk where the computer once sat. She stared into the top drawer for a full minute before speaking.

"All the floppy disks are gone."

I walked over and looked in the drawer. "What was on them?"

Leah gave me a sharp look. "Why is that important?"

"I don't know," I said slowly. "That's why I'm asking."

Leah pursed her lips and shut the drawer. "I don't think they knew what they were stealing."

"Oh, for Christ's sake," Dena said, "just tell her what was on the disks so we can get on with things."

Leah shifted her weight from foot to foot. "Occasionally when Bob was working late and Jack was asleep I would surf the Internet, and when I found something that interested me I would cut and paste it and, you know, save it on a disk."

Dena perked up. "Leah, were you saving Internet porn?"

"Ew! No! I was saving…short stories."

Dena nodded knowingly. "Some of the best erotica is on the Internet."

"It wasn't erotica! They did include a few sex scenes, though." She blushed and looked at the ground. "I was saving Fan Fiction from a site dedicated to *All My Children*'s Kendall and Ryan."

Dena blinked. "Is this a joke?"

"Well, it's better than porn!" Leah snapped. "And in the fan fiction Ryan dumps Greenlee and ends up with Kendall. It's the way it should have happened. And since these fan Web sites sometimes go under, I always save the stories that I may want to reread on disk."

"I agree," I said. "The intruder definitely didn't know what he was taking."

Dena laughed. "Won't he be surprised when he gets home? So assuming that we're not dealing with a crazed soap fan, what do you suppose our burglar expected to find on the disks?"

Leah planted her hands on her hips. "I bet it was Bob's little Jezebel who broke in here."

Dena lifted her eyebrows. "What makes you say that?"

"Because I talked to Erika earlier. She screened all of Bob's calls at work and she thinks the only way he could have been corresponding with that woman without her knowing would have been through his e-mail account."

"So what?" I asked. "Why would that make Bianca want to break in and steal poorly written fiction?"

"The stories were beautifully written," Leah snarled. "Bianca obviously thought that Bob cared enough about her to save their correspondence. So she came in here to steal it and spare herself the embarrassment of someone else stumbling across it."

Dena cocked her head to the side. "Are you aware that your theory makes no sense, or has ABC daytime TV warped your brain beyond repair?"

"Look, the little witch already slept with my husband, and as far as I'm concerned she's probably the one who shot him, so what's a little burglary?" She made an attempt to toss her hair, but it had long since formed itself into a frizzy, unmovable mass. "It all makes perfect sense."

My cell rang and I fished it out of my handbag. "Hello?"

"Sophie, is that you?" Mary Ann's desperate voice floated through the earpiece.

I could hear Jack screaming in the background. "I take it he woke up."

"Yes, about a half hour ago— Jack, stop it!" She sucked in a deep breath before addressing me again. "Are you coming home now?"

"Well, Leah still hasn't really packed anything...."

"But she can do that tomorrow if she really has to, right? Jack, I told you, no socks on the cat!"

"We're coming right now." I hung up the phone. "That was Mary Ann, we have to leave immediately. Both Mary Ann's and Mr. Katz's lives are at stake."

★ ★ ★

My plan was to get home, go straight to bed and try to solve the mystery of Leah's lost fan fiction (along with the lesser mystery of her husband's murder) the next morning when I was better rested. Instead I was up most of the night listening to my young nephew torment my sister at the top of his lungs. By three in the morning I had decided that Jack wasn't a normal child. I mean, if all children were as much trouble as Jack, corporal punishment would never have been curtailed.

At nine the next morning I stumbled out of bed. Leah was already up and had apparently spent the morning instructing Jack on how to destroy my kitchen. Every pot, pan and Tupperware item I owned was strewn across the floor.

Leah smiled at me and poured some freshly brewed coffee into a mug. "I made it strong, just how you like it."

My mood lifted a bit. "I can't believe you made it at all. That's so sweet of you!"

"Well, it's the least I could do considering what you're doing for me this morning."

My eyes narrowed into what I knew were puffy red slits. "*What* am I doing for you?"

The buzzer rang and I looked at the clock above the stove. None of my friends was self-destructive enough to ring my place before noon.

"That would be my moms' group," Leah explained. "They all wanted to come over this morning and offer me moral support."

I looked down at the stained oversize T-shirt I was wearing as a nightshirt. "Were you planning on telling me about this?"

"As soon as you got up." Leah crossed to the front door and buzzed her friends in. "It's not my fault you can't get yourself out of bed at a reasonable time."

"No, that would be your child's fault."

Jack banged two pot lids together to emphasize my point.

"Leah!" Miranda swept into the room wearing black capris and a red T-shirt. Her daughter Courtney was tucked under her right arm, wearing a matching outfit. She threw her free arm around Leah's neck and pulled her in for a quick air-kiss.

Behind her was a woman with long auburn hair and a body that was greatly enhanced by breast-feeding. Her bald dumpling was strapped into a carrier secured to her back.

Leah led them to the living room. "Sorry about the mess," she said, sitting down on the edge of my sofa. "Sophie's never been very domestic."

"Excuse me?" I put my hands on my hips, then quickly dropped them when I realized how short the move made my T-shirt.

"I completely understand," Miranda cooed. "Artistic types always need a bit of chaos in their lives." She turned her attention back to Leah. "Donna and Marcy should be here any minute. They're bringing bagels and croissants."

"Perfect." Leah looked up at me. "Sophie, do you mind getting Miranda and Cecily a cup of coffee?"

"Yes, I mind!"

Miranda and the other woman, whom I assumed was Cecily, looked at me in surprise. I rolled my eyes and stormed into the kitchen to start pouring coffee.

Leah followed me in. "I'm sorry," she whispered. "I should have given you more notice. I just needed to do something *normal* today."

I didn't respond. It wasn't *normal* for me to be half dressed and serving coffee to my sister's friends while they discussed the benefits of disposable diapers.

"Listen, I want you to know how much I appreciate you," Leah said.

That got my attention. "You do?" I asked carefully.

Leah nodded. "Last night I couldn't stop thinking about what I would do if the police somehow pinned this on me. Can you imagine me—in jail? How would I survive, Sophie?"

I put my hand on her shoulder. "I'm not going to let that happen."

"I hope it won't, but even you can only do so much." Leah's eyes got a little watery. "I try to take some comfort in the knowledge that you'll make a wonderful mother to Jack if I can't be here for him."

My hand involuntarily tightened around her shoulder. "Leah, you're not going anywhere. I am going to make sure that you will always be the one to take care of Jack. I mean that."

Leah flung her arms around my neck. "You're such a good sister!"

I disentangled myself and quickly handed out the coffee before running to the shower, my sense of urgency at an all-time high. Once dressed and presentable I locked myself in my bedroom with the phone and called the Gatsby. After being informed that Cheryl Miller had the day off, I retrieved Leah's address book from the guest room and flipped to the *M* page. All of Cheryl's information was there. She must have moved recently because her outer Sunset address was scratched out and a Cow Hollow address was written in its place. The prestigious address told me Cheryl hadn't expected to be laid off by the Ritz. I wondered how she planned to pay her rent now that she had only one front-desk job. Perhaps I could help her out by securing her a place at one of the state's more renowned penitentiaries.

I dialed Anatoly. He didn't answer his home phone, but when I tried his cell, he picked up on the first ring.

"Hello, Sophie."

"Hey, listen," I said, sitting down on the edge of my bed.

"I think we should talk to Bob's sister, Cheryl. She's not working today, so we might be able to catch her at home."

There was a pause. "You're not armed, are you?"

"Why would I be armed?"

"I'm just trying to figure out your motivation for wanting to see Cheryl."

"I don't want to kill her—or at least I'm not going to. But I was thinking that maybe she wanted to kill Bob and maybe, just maybe, she did."

"Why would she do that?"

"Because she's an evil bitch and that's what evil bitches do—they kill people."

"I think you're confusing reality with a James Bond film."

"It's worth checking out," I said. "Cheryl and Bob never got along. She's clearly trying to convince everyone that Leah's the guilty party, even though she has no basis for the accusation. Maybe she's trying to draw attention to Leah so that she can slip under the radar."

"It seems like a long shot."

"Look, we can't afford to leave any stone unturned here. Leah is not cut out for prison and I am not cut out for motherhood!"

Anatoly took a moment before responding. "Explain to me how talking to Cheryl is going to keep you from getting pregnant."

"Not *pregnant*. Don't be dense. Leah just told me that if she gets convicted she's going to leave Jack in my care."

Anatoly's laughter rang in my ears.

"It's not funny!"

"Think about it, Sophie, you and Mr. Katz could become the legal guardians of the Antichrist. Even you have to admit that's rather amusing."

"No, I don't. Now, get over here and take me to Cheryl's or I'll have you pummeled to death in my next book."

"Not many women can be sexy and insane at the same time, but I have to say, you blend the two traits masterfully."

"You're sick." I looked in the mirror and thanked God that Anatoly couldn't see me smiling. "Be here in a few minutes."

Fifteen minutes later I met Anatoly at the front door so he wouldn't be subjected to the scrutiny of Leah's moms' group. He greeted me with a quick once-over that made my heart do a little flip-flop.

"I take it from the short length of your skirt that we're not taking the motorcycle."

"My car's just three blocks away and street-cleaning's tomorrow, so I figured I'd drive." I started down the street and Anatoly fell into step with me. "I stopped by Leah's place last night."

"Oh?" Anatoly checked his watch, then stuffed his hand in his pocket.

"Yeah, we kind of interrupted a break-in."

Anatoly stopped in the middle of the sidewalk. "Did you call the police?"

"Um…"

"Why? Why do you always do this?"

"It wouldn't have helped," I said defensively. "I didn't realize anyone else was there until I was already inside the house, and then I just ran out. By the time we had a chance to call the cops, it was clear the intruder was long gone."

"If he left in a hurry he might have left something behind that could implicate him, or at least give us an idea about what he was looking for." He checked his watch again. "We should go over there now and check things out."

"I already did that last night."

Anatoly's jaw dropped. "You went back to the house after you knew someone had broken in? What if he had still been there?"

"I wasn't alone. Dena and Leah were with me the whole time."

"So the trespasser would have had to use three bullets instead of one."

"In case you've forgotten, I've been in more dangerous situations in the recent past."

"But why test your luck? You can't take those kinds of chances with your life." He took a step closer to me and reached out to touch my hair. "You have too much to look forward to," he said, his voice taking on a considerably softer tone.

I felt a jolt of electricity shoot through me. "What do I have to look forward to—?" My voice caught as I asked the question.

Anatoly took another step closer and leaned in so that his lips were no more than a centimeter away from my ear. "I know this is hard to believe," he said, his breath tickling my skin, "but Starbucks is coming out with another variation of the Frappuccino."

"Oh," I breathed, "I wouldn't want to miss out on that."

Anatoly laughed softly and moved back. "So, no more needless risks. If you don't want to call the police, at least call me and let me deal with it. That is what you're paying me for, right?"

I nodded and willed my breathing to come out at an even pace. "Right, no more needless risks."

"Good, now why don't you tell me what you found at Leah's when you went back."

I filled him in on everything as we walked to my car. It didn't take long, since there really wasn't much to tell. I slid behind the wheel as he turned the whole thing over in his head.

"They took *all* the disks?"

"As far as I can tell." I started the car and turned down the radio.

"What the hell could they have been expecting to find?"

"That's the sixty-four-thousand-dollar question. Leah thinks Bianca was trying to find records of her and Bob's e-mail correspondence. It doesn't seem likely, but I've yet to come up with an alternative hypothesis."

"What makes Leah think they corresponded by e-mail?"

"Erika put the idea in her head. Who knows if it's actually true or not, but—" I stopped short.

"What's wrong?"

"I thought I just heard my mother's voice—there it is again. Oh my God, it's coming from the radio!" I pulled my car to a stop in front of someone's driveway and turned up the volume.

"So you don't think your daughter bore her husband any ill will?" the interviewer asked.

"No, I don't. Let me tell you something about my Leah. She's a nice girl. She was nothing but good to her husband and that was no small feat because he was a real *schlemiel*."

"You didn't like him?"

"What's to like? I'll never understand why she married him. In a church yet! But that's the problem with girls today. They always take up with the nogoodniks. Her sister Sophie did the same thing and married some putz in Las Vegas. Now she's divorced and running around town with a Russian. This one's Jewish at least, so I don't mind so much, but he needs to find himself a real job."

I squeezed my eyes shut. "Please make it stop."

But Mama continued. "Right now people hire him to take pictures of their husbands schtooping other women! You tell me, is that any way to make a living?"

Anatoly grinned. "Taking pictures of people schtooping—I think I'll put that on my business cards."

"Um, I see…" The interviewer's voice was shaking; I was pretty sure he was trying to contain his laughter. "Do you think the police are treating your daughter Leah as a suspect because of her race?"

"Never you mind about her race," my mother said sharply. "It's not polite to talk about such things. It doesn't matter what color my daughter is. What's important is that she's a real beauty and she's single now. When all this nonsense about Bob blows over, she'll have to beat them off with a stick, you just wait and see."

"Oh, my God, why don't they cut to a commercial?" I moaned.

"Right, well, that's all the time we have…."

"Thank you!" I turned the radio off and looked at Anatoly. "I think I'm going to change my name."

"What? And break your mother's heart?"

"Go to hell." I pulled the car back onto the road and drove toward Cheryl's.

CHAPTER 6

"I like fanatics. They always make me feel well balanced."
—*Words To Die By*

Anatoly unbuckled his seat belt as I pulled into a parking spot. "Presuming she's home, what are you planning on saying?" he asked.

"I'm working on that."

"Perfect."

I ignored his sarcasm and got out of the car. I had been forced to park seven blocks away from Cheryl's building, so I had had some time to come up with a plan of action. Normally the best way to win Cheryl's confidence was to drop a few celebrity names, but after her latest comments to the media she would expect me to be on the warpath and no name I could ever drop would convince her otherwise.

Anatoly and I walked together in silence as I racked my brain, and when we arrived at Cheryl's door I had yet to have a lightbulb blink on over my head. Anatoly looked at me expectantly and I flashed him a nervous smile before pressing the appropriate buzzer.

"Hello?" said a voice from the intercom.

"Cheryl? It's Sophie."

She took her sweet time responding. "What do you want?"

"Listen…" I sucked in a breath, and then it hit me. "I was contacted by *Channel Four News.* They're doing a piece featuring different perspectives on how the SFPD are handling Bob's homicide case. They're interested in interviewing both of us—"

The door buzzed open. I held the door for Anatoly before stepping in after him. "Am I that good, or is Cheryl just an idiot?"

Anatoly smiled at me appreciatively. "A little of both, I suspect."

Cheryl met us at the top of the stairs. "Why didn't *Channel Four News* contact me themselves?" she asked.

"They didn't contact you?" I eyed her outfit. It was a replica of the one that Drew Barrymore had worn on the cover of the most recent issue of *Us* magazine. "Well, they did say they were thinking of asking you. I'm sure that if I nudge them a little, they'll follow through."

Cheryl lifted her chin half an inch. "Why would you do that?"

I shrugged innocently. "Oh, I don't know…maybe I just want to have the opportunity to rip you apart in front of a few hundred thousand viewers."

Cheryl smiled. "I don't think it would work out that way, but you're welcome to try." Her eyes traveled to Anatoly and she immediately lowered her head and peered at him through her heavily mascaraed eyelashes. "I don't believe we've met." She reached out her hand in a manner that would suggest that she wanted it kissed.

Anatoly shook it unenthusiastically. "I'm Anat—"

"Anatoly Darinsky. I saw you on TV right after Sophie had you arrested. I must say, not many guys are as forgiving as you." She put her hand on her heart. "My brother was like that, too. Of course I'm sure things will work out better for you than it did for him—just because Sophie's sister is out of control doesn't mean Sophie is—or at least not as much so…hopefully."

"Oh, what-the-fuck-ever." I yanked my purse strap up before it could slide off my shoulder. "Look, Cheryl, I don't have a lot of time. If I'm going to convince the producers to let you share the air with me then I'm going to have to tell them what they can expect from you. Do you have time for a few questions, or not?"

Cheryl tossed her hair behind her shoulder and gestured for us to follow her into her apartment.

This was the first time I had ever visited Cheryl's home. One look at her place told me she wasn't the type to leave dishes on the counter or mail strewn over the coffee table— not because she was exceptionally neat, but because there were so many trinkets that if she were to leave a lipstick on a countertop it would immediately become lost amongst the kitsch. I walked forward and examined some cute but badly displayed martini-glass-shaped votive candleholders.

"Aren't those just fabulous?" cooed Cheryl. "They're the same ones Jessica Simpson has in her living room."

I looked up at her and then studied the other knickknacks with a new eye. I was willing to bet that they were all duplicates of things Cheryl believed to be in celebrity homes. It was amazing—in a pathetic kind of way.

"Cheryl," I said, working overtime to keep the disdain out of my voice, "why have you been telling the media that Leah and Bob's marriage was in trouble?"

"Um…because it *was*." She rolled her eyes at Anatoly to underscore her feeling about my question. "Anyone with half a brain could see how unhappy they were."

"There's a big difference between not being happy with your husband and wanting to kill him," Anatoly said.

I averted my eyes. It had been my experience that the two emotions went hand in hand, but it didn't seem prudent to argue the point.

"You don't know Leah like I do." Cheryl put a hand on Anatoly's arm and scooted closer to him. "She's not stable."

"How could she be?" I asked. "She's a black Jew and you know how we can be. If we're not shooting someone in a crack-induced frenzy, we're controlling the media with our fellow conspirators."

Cheryl's eyes narrowed. "Do you have any more questions, or are you done?"

I sat down on her couch and made myself comfortable. "I'm sure that the guys at *Channel Four* will want to know exactly when you spoke to Bob last."

"The last time?" Cheryl swallowed and started toying with a framed, autographed photo of Matt Damon. "I'm not exactly sure when that was. Things have been kind of crazy lately."

"You mean with all the demands put on a front-desk clerk you've had a hard time managing anything else." I smiled sweetly. "I can see how that could happen."

"I'm sure I spoke to him less than a week before he died," she growled.

"Really?" I asked. "Was that on the phone or did you meet him somewhere?"

"Why does any of this make a difference? My brother's dead and your sister killed him. That's what matters."

Anatoly raised an eyebrow.

"Come on, Cheryl." I leaned forward and leveled my gaze on her. "The police must have asked you about this. What did you tell them?"

"They did ask." She flipped her hair again and walked over to the bench she had placed by the bay window. "I told them what I told you."

"And what did you tell me again?"

She whirled around and glared at me. "That I didn't remember. It may have been longer than a week before his death, okay? It may have been more like a month. I've been busy. I just moved, and it took a lot of time and energy to really infuse this place with my own personal flare."

My eyes scanned the apartment again. "Is that what you were going for? I thought you wanted to infuse it with the flare of JLo."

"You have no intention of recommending that *Channel Four News* interview me, do you." She put her hands on the armrest of the sofa and leaned forward so that she was invading my space. "You just came here to harass me."

Anatoly came up behind Cheryl and, taking her shoulder, gently drew her back into an upright position. "Don't let her get to you." He turned her around so she was facing him. "The idea to get you on *Channel Four* was mine. I thought it would be better if you and Sophie could be on the air together. Otherwise the interview would come off as one-sided and meaningless. But if you're there—" he smiled and let his hand slowly slide down her arm as he withdrew it "—people will hear your impassioned plea and your intelligent arguments and they'll be forced to think about the facts. And that's all we want—for people's assumptions to be educated ones."

Cheryl smiled. "I should have known it was your idea to come here. You're obviously the kind of person who likes to play fair—unlike other people we know." She lowered herself onto a brown leather armchair without breaking eye contact with Anatoly. It was amazing that anyone as calculating as Cheryl could be this gullible. Or maybe she knew Anatoly was playing her and hoped that if she went along with it he'd manipulate her right into the bedroom. That was so not going to happen. "You know, it's not like I'm in cahoots with the police in order to put Leah away. The cops aren't even being very nice to me. Can you believe they actually asked me to retract my last statement to the media?"

"Nooo." I pulled out the word, and made a face to emphasize how shocking I found that.

Cheryl ignored me. "I didn't say anything bad, you know. Leah's desperate, and if by some miracle she hasn't played the race card yet, it's just a matter of time before she does. And as for those people who say my statements reeked of anti-Semitism—I don't get that at all. All I said was that her family was Jewish—and yeah, okay, I implied that Jews are traditionally wealthy, but why is that a bad thing? Everybody wants to be rich and famous, right? And most Jews are rich and everyone knows they hold all the top media positions, so it seems to me that they should be proud of their accomplishments. It's the American dream."

"I understand exactly what you're saying," Anatoly said, before sneaking me a look that told me he did understand Cheryl and was properly disgusted. "Cheryl—" he swiveled back in her direction "—it must have been horrible when Leah called and told you the news."

"Yes." She blinked and looked away. "It was."

"What were you doing at the time?"

"You know, the usual. Hanging around the apartment watching *E* and doing some decorating."

Anatoly shook his head sympathetically. "Isn't it strange to think that while you were carrying on with what must have seemed like a normal day at home, something as sinister as a murder was taking place a few miles away?"

Cheryl reached out and grabbed Anatoly's hand. "It's so good to finally talk to someone who understands."

"I'm trying to envision it." Anatoly creased his forehead and shook his head. "What were you doing earlier that day? Were you working? Out with friends?"

"No, I was home all day."

She had no alibi. The image of Cheryl being carted away in handcuffs flashed before my eyes and I had to bite my lip to keep from grinning.

"You must have loved your brother very much," Anatoly said.

"I did." Cheryl nodded and dabbed her eyes, although I couldn't see any tears.

"Did the two of you spend much time together?"

She shifted in her seat. "Bob and I are very busy people."

"So, you mean to tell me that a brother and sister who lived in the same city were never able to make time for each other?" Anatoly dropped her hand. "I don't understand. I have a brother in Israel and not a day goes by that I don't wish I could see him more often."

"Well, we did see each other occasionally," Cheryl said quickly. "Sometimes he would stop by the hotel if he had a spare moment to say hi."

"Ah." Anatoly's tone softened. "So you did make some time for each other. I was being harsh. I didn't know Bob, but Sophie said that he wasn't always the easiest person to get along with and obviously you don't share that opinion. Maybe the two of you just didn't have much in common."

"He did share my good taste." She nodded toward her disastrous stab at decorating. "But we had our differences, too. His priorities were a little confused. It's like, I would tell him about how Steven Spielberg was staying with us, you know, at the Ritz, and how he took the time to compliment me personally on my exemplary service, and Bob would act like he didn't even care." She shrugged, apparently mystified by the memory of her brother's indifference. "Maybe he was just jealous. It must have been hard for him to have a sister who was always getting to rub elbows with the celebs."

"Uh-huh." Anatoly looked like he was beginning to get

a headache. "So would you say that was your main source of contention—his lack of appreciation for Hollywood celebrities?"

Cheryl put her fingernail in her mouth and pondered that for a moment before nodding. "Pretty much."

My cell phone rang, interrupting what had become a less-than-stimulating question-and-answer session. My caller ID read "Private Number." I pressed it to my ear. "Y'ello."

"Miss Katz? It's Detective Lorenzo. I was hoping you could come in to the station. We have some more questions for you."

My heart dropped to my stomach. "Has something happened?"

"We'll talk about it when you get here."

"Okay, I'll be right over." I hung up and looked at Anatoly. "Who was that?"

I was going to answer him truthfully, but then I saw the inquisitive look on Cheryl's face and decided that the honesty could wait. "It was *Channel Four*. They said that they might not want the interview after all."

"What!" Cheryl jumped out of her seat. "But you have to change their mind!"

"Yeah, I know." I stood up and crossed to the door. "I'll go over there right now and see if I can make things right."

"I'll go with you," Cheryl offered.

"No," Anatoly said as he opened the door for me. "We don't want to bombard them. They called Sophie, so she's the one who should talk to them." He smiled at her. "I promise to call you when we have it all worked out."

"Okay," Cheryl said uncertainly. "If they want to interview just me…"

"I'll be sure to give them your number." I grabbed Anatoly's sleeve. "We really need to go now."

Anatoly nodded. "Talk to you soon, Cheryl."

We walked down the stairs together, but it wasn't until we were on the street that he addressed me. "Who was that really?"

"Detective Lorenzo—he said he had some more questions."

Anatoly hesitated. "It's to be expected that he would have some follow-up questions. It doesn't mean he has discovered anything new."

"You mean that he might not have found out about the affair," I said quietly.

"It's possible." But he didn't sound all that convinced. We walked the rest of the way to the car in silence.

It wasn't until we were on the road and halfway to the station that I dared speak my thoughts. "What if he asks me something I don't want to answer?"

Anatoly sighed and rubbed his eyes. "When in doubt, tell the truth."

"I'm sort of a poetic license kind of girl."

"I've noticed. Unfortunately so have the police. They're going to try to trip you up, and I'm sure you've heard the expression—if you tell the truth you don't have to remember what you've said."

I stopped at a crosswalk and waited while an elderly Chinese woman and her rottweiler crossed the street. "I don't really want to let on that Leah told me about the affair."

"Sophie…"

"I just think you were right when you said that the revelation should come from Leah." I shifted gears and turned the corner.

Anatoly let out a heavy sigh. "Fine, don't tell them that you knew about the affair."

"And I don't want to tell Lorenzo that I have a letter from Bianca to Bob. I mean, no one but Erika, you and me know we have that letter, and Erika's not going to say anything, so there's no real reason to volunteer this information."

"Sophie, is there anything you *do* plan on telling them?"

We weren't that far from our destination so I decided to pull into a parking garage.

"I think I'll tell them that Leah's innocent and that if they really want to be of service to the public they'll just arrest Cheryl and be done with it. The woman is whacked and she has no alibi."

"Yes, it's been my experience that the police love it when civilians tell them how to do their job."

"It's not like I'm trying to order them around—it'll be more like a friendly suggestion."

"And I'm sure there were a lot of whacked people alone on the night that Bob died." Anatoly drummed his fingers against his thigh. "That doesn't make them killers."

"But—"

"She has no motive, Sophie."

I found a spot and killed the engine. "If Cheryl did have a motive, do you really think she'd tell us about it? Even she's not that stupid."

Anatoly shook his head. "You can't mold this case to turn out the way you want it to. Let's look at the facts we have and follow them where they lead us, instead of following clues that aren't there."

"But the facts we have all lead us to Leah!"

Anatoly turned to me, his eyes caring but serious. "I know."

I swallowed hard. "Come on, let's go to the police station and get this over with."

He looked like he wanted to say something more, but instead he just nodded and got out of the car.

We walked down the street, rounded the corner and then stopped short. In front of the station was a mass of people, some of them chanting *"SF Justice is skin deep,"* others waving signs that read Leave Sistah Leah Alone or The Jewish Defense League Supports Leah.

"Oh, my God," I gasped. "It's the Rainbow Coalition, and they're seriously *pissed*."

Anatoly shook his head, clearly riveted by the scene in front of him. "This is such an interesting country."

He took my arm and we pushed through the crowd.

"Yo, check out the beautiful multicultural couple," someone screamed.

Cheers rose up into the air as people slapped us on the back and congratulated us on our exceptional PC-ness.

I bit my lip to hold back my laughter. "I'm dying," I whispered.

"Don't die," Anatoly said. "If Bob's death can cause this kind of madness, just think what yours would do. They'd probably call out Reverend Sharpton."

We bent our heads and pushed our way through the throng into the police station. Guards were posted at the door; no doubt they were there to help with crowd control, but it looked like a pretty peaceful bunch. Totally insane, but peaceful.

I announced my presence to the officer sitting at what passed for a check-in desk, and then Anatoly and I took a seat in the rather expansive waiting room. The place was filled with several other civilians who were undoubtedly awaiting their own special interrogation sessions. You'd think that the atmosphere would have been one wrought with anxiety but instead the overall mood seemed to be one of bewilderment and mild amusement thanks to the spectacle outside.

In a matter of minutes Lorenzo appeared in the doorway wearing a dark brown suit that was cut a little too wide for his slim physique. He motioned for me to follow him down the sterile hallway to his equally bland office. I glanced at the linoleum floors and his desk that was completely devoid of personal touches. Would it have killed the man to do a little decorating? If he didn't have family photos to put up, the least he could do was buy a fern to love.

"Have a seat, Miss Katz."

I nodded and for a few seconds Lorenzo and I sat on opposite sides of his desk and simply stared at each other. He had gotten a haircut since I had last seen him but the barber he had gone to obviously had no idea how to handle curls. The result was a style that made Lorenzo's head appear oddly misshapen.

"So," he said, "it seems your sister's plight has inspired a lot of people."

"I think it was Cheryl's blatant ignorance and racism that was inspiring."

Lorenzo's chair creaked as he leaned back. "Well, what do you know? We do agree on something."

"I'm sure it's just a fluke," I said.

Lorenzo laughed. "All right, I just brought you in because I wanted to go over some of the information you gave me on the night of your brother-in-law's death."

"Shoot."

"Let's start with your impression of your sister's marriage."

I lowered my gaze to the floor.

"I believe you said it was going well."

"Yes, I believe I said that."

"Tell me again why you thought so."

I shrugged noncommittally. "Leah seemed happy. On the very afternoon before his death she was telling me how much she loved being Mrs. Bob Miller."

"Did she have any reason to think she wasn't going to be able to keep that title?"

"None that I know of."

"I see. So you didn't know Bob was having an affair?"

I flinched. "I was unaware of that."

"That's funny because I just finished questioning his mistress, Bianca Whitman, and she says she talked to you about the affair just yesterday."

"Oh—" I smiled and slapped my knee "—you mean, did I know yesterday! Yeah, I knew by then, I just didn't know before Bob was shot."

The detective pushed his chair back and crossed his ankle over his knee. "You know, I could charge you with obstructing justice."

"Oh, give it up. I just recently found out about the affair and I confronted the woman Bob was sleeping with. I didn't threaten her. I didn't stalk her. I just talked to her. I don't need to report my every move to the police."

"I'm not interested in your every move, just the moves that are pertinent to this case. A man was killed in his home. That would be the same home in which your sister and nephew live. If we're going to catch the killer, I'm going to need a little cooperation from you."

"I'm nothing if not cooperative."

"Right." Lorenzo didn't even bother to hide the fact that he found that amusing. "Tell me again about the conversation you and Leah had on the afternoon before Bob was shot."

"Oh, you want to know what we talked about?"

"That would be nice."

"I can't tell you that," I said matter-of-factly.

Lorenzo's head dropped forward. "Why not?"

"I don't remember much of it. I was drunk."

"In the middle of the afternoon?"

"Yes. I'm an alcoholic."

"Really."

"Mmm-hmm, a big one."

Lorenzo cracked his knuckles and tried not to flinch at the sound. "You didn't seem to have a problem recalling the conversation on the night of Bob's death," he pointed out.

"But I was still somewhat intoxicated at that point.

That's why Anatoly insisted he be the one to drive to Leah's. Ask him."

Detective Lorenzo looked up at me without lifting his head. "Do I have to?"

I couldn't help but smile. Of course, that was a mistake because it signaled that my guard was down and Lorenzo went in for the kill. "Where were you on the night Bob was shot?"

I felt the hairs on the back of my neck stand up. "I was at home," I clipped each word at the end.

"Alone?"

"No, Anatoly told you he was with me."

"All evening?"

I pressed my lips together. I knew Anatoly would maintain his own lie that he was with me when I got the call from Leah, but I wasn't sure if he'd back up any of my elaborations on that. "He came over a few minutes before Leah called," I said. "Prior to that I was alone."

"Alone—drinking in your apartment."

"Yes," I exhaled, thankful to finally be telling the truth.

"Detective Lorenzo?" said a female voice through his phone intercom.

Lorenzo quickly took her off speaker. "Yes? Good. Stay with her and I'll be right there."

He hung up the phone and stood up. "Well, Miss Katz, it was interesting as always."

I smiled sweetly and pushed myself to my feet. "I wish I could say the same."

Lorenzo's grin widened. "I do have one more question. Do you think your sister would be willing to make a statement that she has not been the victim of racial profiling?"

"Is my sister a suspect?"

"At this point I can't rule her out."

"Yeah, well, until you do, I doubt she's going to be in the mood to help build the department's PR," I replied.

"That's what I thought you'd say."

He escorted me out to the waiting room, where Anatoly was still seated—but now he was in the company of Jack, who was busy untying Anatoly's shoelaces while Leah stared into space. A uniformed policewoman stood by her side.

"Oh, there you are!" Leah eyed both me and Detective Lorenzo. "What was so important that I had to come down here now?"

"We'll talk about it in my office, Mrs. Miller." Detective Lorenzo motioned to the female officer that he would take it from here.

"I was in the middle of planning my husband's memorial service when you called. Then I had to drop that, come down here, only to be confronted with *that!*" She pointed to the crowd on the other side of the door. I wondered what the denim- and tie-dye-clad protesters had thought of their heroine's peach polo shirt and navy chinos.

"I am sorry about the protesters," Lorenzo said. "Why don't we sit down in my office with a nice cup of coffee and we can get this over with quickly. I'm sure your sister here wouldn't mind watching Jack while we talk."

I gaped at him. This man really hated me.

Leah, on the other hand, looked somewhat appeased. She bent down and patted Jack's head as he nibbled on Anatoly's laces. "Jack honey, Mommy will be right back. You be good for Auntie Sophie."

Jack happily ignored her and Lorenzo escorted Leah to his office. I sat down next to Anatoly and leaned my head back against the wall.

"They know about Bianca."

Anatoly sighed. "I figured as much. Do you think Leah will volunteer that information?"

"I doubt it."

"Great."

We waited there together for fifteen minutes, periodically offering Jack new clothing items to munch on. Finally Leah and Lorenzo came out of his office. Leah looked slightly unsteady on her feet. Her eyes darted around the station in a way that suggested she expected something sinister to come slithering out from under a desk or a darkened corner.

"Thank you for your time, Mrs. Miller," Lorenzo said mildly. "I'll be in touch."

Leah didn't say anything. She bent down and gathered Jack up into her arms as the detective retreated into his office. I stood up and got close enough to her ear so that no one would overhear me.

"What did you tell them?"

"I told them that I knew about Bob's affair but that we were going to stay together and work out our problems."

That was good—she had lied without lying. Maybe Leah *had* learned a few things from me.

"What did you say about what I knew?" I asked.

"I said that I had mentioned the affair to you but that due to your drinking problem you might not remember the conversation."

I slapped her on the back. "That's amazing! That's the same lie I told them!"

"What are you talking about?" She balanced Jack on her hip and gave me a withering stare. "Everything I said was true."

Anatoly smirked. "This isn't a good place to talk." He gestured toward the door leading outside. Leah bit her lip and eyed the door warily.

"Come on—" I gave her an encouraging smile "—as fanatics go, the people in this crowd seem pretty harmless."

Leah nodded and walked outside with Anatoly and me on either side of her. The waiting crowd began screaming Leah's name as soon as she came into sight. A few people reached out to touch her like she was the next messiah. I quickly scanned the outskirts of the group and noted that a few TV crews had arrived to capitalize on the commotion.

Anatoly made a grunt of disgust, fell back and put one hand on my back and one on Leah's as he rushed us past the demonstrators. Unfortunately there was no ignoring the reporters. A female in a navy suit stuck a microphone in Leah's face. "Mrs. Miller, do you feel you're the victim of racial profiling?"

"No comment." Leah's voice trembled only slightly as she tried to move forward.

Another mike was thrust in front of her. "How do you feel about the attention your husband's death has brought to interracial couples?"

"No comment."

"Do you have any opinion about the pressure many activists have been putting on Hotel Gatsby to fire Ms. Cheryl Miller?"

Leah stopped in her tracks. Her head pivoted in the direction of the reporter who had asked the question. He wasn't the only black journalist there, but he had the darkest skin by far and, unlike many of his colleagues, he was not accompanied by a camera, just a notepad and pen. The other thing that set him apart was the fact that he was drop-dead gorgeous. Leah took a cautious step toward him.

"I'm sorry," she said, "but do you mind repeating that?"

He nodded and raised his voice. "Jerome from *Flavah Magazine*," he said, needlessly introducing himself. "Many of your supporters, along with several African-American and Jewish political organizations, have been putting pressure on the Hotel Gatsby to fire Cheryl Miller due to the racist statements she made about you two days ago. How do you feel about that?"

Leah locked eyes with him. Her chin went up half an inch and a hush fell over the reporters as they readied their microphones for what they hoped would be Leah's first statement to the media.

For a minute I didn't think she was going to say anything at all. Then a slow smile spread across her face. "Excuse me a moment." She handed Jack to me and whipped around so that she was facing the protesters. She threw her head back, launched her fist in the air and shouted, "Black Power!"

A roar rose up from the crowd and Jerome broke out in a full, rich laugh. In seconds people were chanting Leah's name. The other reporters started shouting out other questions, too many to respond to. Anatoly grabbed Leah's arm and yanked her through the horde.

"I'll be calling you for an interview," Jerome called after us. Leah looked over her shoulder and gave him a friendly wave.

"You are not helping matters," Anatoly said as he dragged her in the direction of my car.

"Trust me," she said, still grinning, "if this gets Cheryl fired it will be well worth it."

I trotted behind them as Jack pulled out several strands of my hair. "Where did you park, Leah?"

"Miranda dropped us off. She was going to find parking and meet me at the station, but when I saw Anatoly, I called her cell and told her we'd ride with the two of you."

"But I don't have a car seat."

"I put one in your trunk yesterday. I figured you would need it if I…if you end up being Jack's primary caregiver."

Jack pulled out a new handful of hair. I shot Anatoly a pained look. "God help me," I mumbled.

On the way home Anatoly tried to coax Leah to give him more details about her interview with Lorenzo, but she waved off his questions in favor of bringing the conversation back to Cheryl and her impending misfortune. When we finally got home Leah and Jack went in ahead of me while I stayed outside to chat with Anatoly.

He stuffed his hands into the pockets of his jacket and his eyes idly followed a young child with pigtails walking past with a man who was most likely her grandfather. "Your sister needs to keep her focus. Cheryl's career is not the issue that we should be concerning ourselves with."

"I'll talk to her." I tried to sound casual but I was worried. Not about her lack of focus; that would be an easy problem to correct. It was her overall demeanor since she finished talking to Lorenzo that bothered me. She'd been contrite. It was as if her over-the-top excitement about Cheryl's problems was a way of masking another emotion, namely fear. I looked up at the window of my apartment. "I think I'm going to stick by Leah's side for the rest of the day. If she says anything more about her interview with Lorenzo, I'll let you know."

Anatoly nodded and started to walk away, but something stopped him. He turned back and fixed me with his stare. "You're not thinking about going back to her house, are you?"

"I wasn't planning on it. Why? Do you think that someone will break in again?"

"If they didn't find what they were looking for—possibly. At this point we have no idea who or what we're dealing with."

I shrugged. "Okay, we won't go to her place tonight."

"No, you won't go to her place today, tonight, tomorrow, or any other time in the near future. Not without me."

"Let me get this straight," I said. "It's not okay for me to go there with Dena and Leah, but it's safe for me to go there with you? How chauvinistic can you be?"

Anatoly took a step forward. "Promise me, Sophie."

I put my hands on my hips and was about to come back with a snappy retort, but something in his expression stopped me. I swallowed my annoyance and dropped my arms. "I promise." I glanced back at my apartment. "So where are you off to now?"

"I'm going to the Gatsby," Anatoly said. "If we're lucky, one of Cheryl's coworkers will have some insight into why she might have wanted to see her brother dead."

I sighed. "Good luck and let me know if you find out anything." I went back inside and found Leah sitting on the floor next to Jack while he worked on what looked to be a fairly new coloring book. I would never expect a toddler to be able to stay inside the lines but it would have been nice if he had been able to keep the Crayola markings on the page and off of my wood floors.

"Leah, can we talk?"

"I'm incredibly tired, can it wait? Unless of course you want to talk about Cheryl's career problems," she looked up at me with a mischievous twinkle in her eyes, "I definitely have the energy to talk about that."

"I just wanted to tell you that if you're scared you can talk to me."

The twinkle disappeared and she looked back at Jack. "Just promise me you'll send Jack to Adda Clevenger Junior Preparatory school when he's of age. It's the best."

"Okay, first off you're going to be around to enroll him yourself. Secondly—" I paused and sat down next to Leah on the floor "—can we talk about this whole custody thing? I mean you can't honestly think that I'm the best person to name as the guardian of your son."

"Who would you have me leave him to? Mama? The woman will be seventy this year. She's in good health, despite her claims to the contrary, but she wouldn't be able to care for Jack full-time."

I had to concede that point. After all I couldn't handle Jack and I was only thirty. "What about Miranda? She seems to do well with Jack."

"Sophie, you're going to be a great mom," Leah said, while snatching a crayon away from Jack before he could stick it in his nose. "And it's not like you have to worry about child-care. All you do is hang around the house writing novels, it's the perfect job for a parent!"

"I think I might have difficulty being creative with a child screaming in the background dumping cleaning products on my cat." Although my murder scenes might improve.

"You're resourceful, you'll figure it out. And eventually you'll settle down and get married, maybe even to Anatoly..."

"Okay, hold up. Who said anything about marrying Anatoly? I don't even want to date him!"

Leah laughed and took another crayon away from Jack, but not before he managed to draw a large circle on the leg of my coffee table. "Really, Sophie, you're usually such a *good* liar."

"All right, maybe I wouldn't mind dating him, or at least sleeping with him. But there's no way that I would allow him to put a ring on my finger, now or ever."

"Never say never. I know he can be a bit abrasive and egotistical but that's just the way men are. You can't be too picky, Sophie."

"So what are you saying? That I should settle the way you did?"

The words had popped out before I had a chance to stop them. For a moment the only sound was the snap of crayons as Jack gleefully broke them in half. Mr. Katz walked in the room, took in the scene and then, with an imperious swish of his tail that let me know I was on my own, turned around and walked back out again.

"Leah," I started.

"I'm tired, Sophie. I don't want to talk anymore," she got up and disappeared down the hall.

"Leah, come back!" I hurried back to the guest room where she was sitting on the bed with her back to the door. "I'm sorry," I said. "I didn't mean that."

"Yes you did and I told you, I don't want to talk about it."

I put my hand on her shoulder and gave it a gentle squeeze. "Please don't be mad. I'm just nervous about being named as Jack's guardian even though I know you're always going to be the one taking care of him."

Leah tilted her head back so she could see me. "You *are* going to be a good mother, Sophie," she said softly. "To Jack, if necessary, and definitely to your own kids. And I'm sure you'll make a good wife to whoever you decide to marry."

I smiled but didn't say anything. Leah wasn't getting it. I had been married before, albeit only for two years, but those two years had been informative. The most important thing I had learned about myself was that I liked being on my own. Of course I would happily welcome a lover into my life, and in a few years I'd probably go hunting for one of those rare breeds of men who weren't allergic to monogamy and emotional intimacy. But if such a man existed he was going to have to settle for the title of "long-term boyfriend" because Mr. Katz was the only guy I ever planned to share my address with. As for kids…well, I just didn't feel the yearning for motherhood that apparently other women did. I planned to model my life after that of Katharine Hepburn, except I would write rather than act and I wouldn't be having any public affairs with married men. I know there are those who would say that my lack of maternal instincts made me less of a woman, but that's just who I was and I doubted that my feelings would change.

"Mama, can't bweeth!"

We both turned around to see Jack in the doorway with two crayons sticking out of his nose. Leah jumped up and pulled them out before scooping him up in his arms. "Honey, I've told you a hundred times not to do that!"

I took a deep breath. Two things were clear to me. One

was that I was not cut out for motherhood. The other was that it would take a small miracle to get this kid into Adda's preparatory school.

CHAPTER 7

"I never understood Whitman's analogy about there being two roads in life to choose from. Everyone I know is stuck at a four-way intersection and, given the choice, I think they would all be taking U-turns."

—*Words To Die By*

At eight-thirty Leah woke me up to show me what was on *Mornings on Two*. Someone in the police department had leaked the news about Bob's infidelity. I listened as the commentators rattled on about how Leah was now on top of the suspect list, but my eyes never went to the screen. Leah's face stayed blank until the news report was over and then she looked at me and her lips lifted into a brave smile.

"Well, I guess the whole world now knows that my marriage was a joke."

"Leah, I'm so sorry."

"Nothing like a little public humiliation to start off the day." She looked over at Jack, who was trying to get Mr. Katz to emerge from his hiding place under the coffee table. "Come on, sweetie," she said, pulling him into her arms. "We need to get dressed so we can face the music."

I waited for her to retreat into the guest room before going down to the lobby to collect the newspaper. There it was on the front page, a picture of Leah, her fist thrown in the air. The headline read: "Leah Katz: Victim of Racism or Perpetrator of Murder?" I rolled the paper up and stuck it under my arm. It was an awkwardly worded headline but the message was clear. My sister was in trouble.

I went upstairs and, after hiding the paper, called Anatoly and asked if he could come meet me in a few hours. He agreed without hesitation. He was way too nice over the phone, so I knew he had read or seen what I had. Now that Leah had Jack in the other room, Mr. Katz dared to come out for his breakfast. I kneeled down and scratched him behind the ears as he inhaled his food.

"Don't worry," I told him. "Soon Jack and Leah will return to their house and everything will be back to normal." I needed that to be true. Not just because I didn't want to take care of Jack, but because Jack needed Leah and so did Mama. I needed her, too.

I got dressed and spent the next few hours at my computer working on my manuscript. I heard the buzzer for the door go off a half hour before I had been expecting Anatoly, but his early arrival didn't bother me. Nothing on my screen was worthy of publication and I doubted I would be able to improve upon it until I spoke to him about our next move. I clicked off my monitor and met Leah in the foyer.

"It's Marcus and Dena," Leah said. "I already buzzed them in."

I took a moment to absorb the unexpected information. "Marcus *and* Dena?" Marcus was my hairstylist, friend and shopping partner. He and Dena had always been friendly but I had never known them to hang out without me. I stepped out into the hallway just as they came to the top of the stairs.

"Hey, guys. Did you just happen to show up at the same time or did you come together?"

"Together." Marcus paused to give me a quick kiss on the cheek. "Dena says your sister's having a fashion emergency, so I rushed over here as soon as I could." His mocha skin was the perfect complement to his pearly white smile.

I looked over Marcus's shoulder and threw Dena a questioning glance.

"She needs help establishing a new look, right?" Dena said. "That's what she told Mary Ann."

"Well, yeah," I answered uncertainly. "She wanted help looking like a fashionable widow—"

"Nothing says 'I'm in mourning' like a good haircut," Marcus interjected.

I shook my head. "You're thinking of divorce. Everyone gets their hair cut when they get divorced."

"Divorce, homicide—it all falls under the same umbrella," he said, and swept past me into my apartment, Dena close behind.

"Hello, darling." Marcus crossed over to Leah and held up a few locks of her hair. "My God, look at these split ends. No wonder you're depressed!"

Leah smacked his hand down. "I'm depressed because my husband was killed."

"No, darling, one does not get depressed over a violent murder. Such incidences call for dramatic displays of anguish. Depression is inspired by hair that hasn't been properly cared for."

Leah looked at me for some kind of explanation for Marcus's brand of lunacy. I shrugged helplessly. There was really no explanation other than Marcus was just kind of nuts, but in a good way. Whenever I was feeling sorry for myself I could count on Marcus to trivialize my problems and distract me with eccentric behavior. Why he was focusing his energy on Leah was beyond me, although I suspect it was out of devotion to me. That's the thing about Marcus—those who don't know him think he's flippant and shallow but the truth was that he was the most loyal friend a girl could have and could at times be amazingly self-sacrificing.

I sneaked a peak at Dena who was perched on the edge of my dining table. She was definitely loyal but she had to be seriously moved by a cause before she was willing to sacrifice anything, which made her new interest in helping Leah all the more puzzling.

Leah turned back to Marcus. "I'll have you know I get my hair done at the most expensive salon in San Francisco. It's located right on Maiden Lane…"

"Well, that explains it." Marcus was now circling her, examining her tresses from all angles. "If you're Paris Hilton you get your hair done on Maiden Lane. If you've got Macy Gray curls going on, you take your nappy head to a brotha from da 'hood."

"First of all," Leah said sharply, "my hair is straight."

"Your hair is relaxed. I'm talking roots, honey."

"Secondly, what do you mean da 'hood?' Your salon's on Fillmore. Just two months ago I bought a twelve-hundred-dollar dining table from the shop next door to you."

"I said I was *from* da 'hood, not that I was there now. The first nine years of my life my family was constantly relocating from one all-white southern town to another. Anywhere we moved instantly became da 'hood. We would just kick back and watch the real estate values plummet."

Dena laughed. "Mary Ann's coming over in a few minutes. She and I are going to watch Jack while Marcus does his thing."

I tried to make eye contact with Dena but she wouldn't look up. I was dying to know Dena's motivations for helping Leah but I'm also a firm believer in the "gift horse" cliché. "So are you going to be doing her hair here?" I asked.

"I had originally considered that, but no," Marcus said as he continued to toy with Leah's hair. "She needs more than a living room fix so I'll take her back to Ooh La La. I prefer to work in the salon anyway. It's a more appropriate setting. After all, you wouldn't ask a cardiologist to perform open-heart surgery in a psychiatric ward."

"Are you comparing my apartment to a psychiatric ward?"

"There are certain similarities," Marcus said and motioned toward Mr. Katz who had slipped under the coffee table and was watching my guests with a mixture of alarm and suspicion. "I've always pegged your cat as a paranoid schizophrenic."

"Hey, my cat is as well adjusted as I am!" I quickly held up my hand to stop Marcus's predictable retort. "Don't comment on that." I turned my focus on Leah. "Maybe this isn't such a bad idea," I said. "You could use a little pampering about now."

Leah opened her mouth to protest but then closed it and gave a defeated shrug. "Why not? It's not like anyone could make my life any worse than it already is."

The buzzer went off again. "Mary Ann?" I asked into the speaker.

"Anatoly."

"I'll be right down."

"No, I'd rather come up and talk to Leah."

I glanced over at Leah, who was now passively allowing Marcus to maul her hair. "She's kind of busy right now. Can it wait?"

"No."

I sighed and buzzed him in. I could pretty much guarantee that Anatoly was not going to help Leah achieve the peace of mind Marcus and Dena seemed determined to give her.

He appeared in the door and nodded briefly to both Dena and Marcus.

"Oh, I'm sorry." I gestured toward Anatoly. "Dena, this is Anatoly. Anatoly, Dena. And of course you've met Marcus." Both Dena and Anatoly mumbled a greeting while looking at the floor. This may have been their first face-to-face meeting, but Anatoly had taken the liberty of spying on Dena when she was with me and Dena had (at my request) broken into his apartment. After all that, an introduction seemed uncomfortably formal.

"Leah," Anatoly said, "I want to talk to you about Cheryl."

Leah brightened. "Did she lose her job?"

"Not that I know of. Sophie thinks she could have been involved in Bob's death."

Her eyes widened. "Why didn't I think of that? She's just the type of person who would murder her own brother."

Marcus did a quick double take. "That's a type? Honey, who have you been hanging with?"

"There's a problem with the theory," Anatoly said. "Cheryl has no motive."

"Of course she has a motive." Leah bent down to prevent Jack from swallowing a dust bunny. "They didn't get along. Actually, that's putting it mildly. Bob flat-out hated her."

Anatoly pulled out his notebook. "Any particular reason for that?"

"Yes, she's a hateful person," Leah said.

Anatoly smiled. "All right, I'll give you that. But how did *she* feel about *Bob?*"

"She could never spare him the time of day. Cheryl has two goals in life—to meet multitudes of celebrities, and to name-drop as much as possible. I think it's just a matter of time before she moves to L.A.—unless of course she's arrested first." Leah straightened up and looked at me. "Cheryl could be arrested instead of me!" She broke into a huge grin and clapped her hands together like a child. "Oh my God, that would be wonderful!"

"So was Bob somehow standing between her and her... goals?" Anatoly asked.

"Not really. He just didn't do anything to help her achieve them." She broke away from Marcus and started pacing the apartment with a new energy. "He didn't know any celebrities, and he didn't care to hear about them, so as a result they never spoke."

"They never got together for coffee or anything... Thanksgiving?" Anatoly asked.

"Not unless you count the coffee I served them after Thanksgiving and Christmas dinners. But those are obligatory. I swear, if people weren't expected to be nice to unpleasant relatives on the holidays everyone would enjoy the season a lot more."

"I'm with you, sweetie," Marcus said. "I hate the Christmas spirit. And I'm thoroughly opposed to all that love your neighbor stuff, too. My neighbor is like a flatulent Attila the Hun. You'd *have* to be Jesus to love him."

"Did he ever stop by the Gatsby just to say hi?"

Leah rolled her eyes. "I thought detectives were supposed to be good listeners. Bob never went out of his way to see Cheryl, period. He had better things to do with his time."

"Yeah," Dena piped in, "like fuck his mistress."

Leah glared at Dena, but Dena continued without apology. "I know you're not supposed to speak ill of the dead," she said, "but let's face it, the guy was an asshole and you can do better."

Leah cocked her head. "Why is it that you can never say anything nice without simultaneously being unbelievably disrespectful?"

Dena exhaled loudly. "Here's a bit of advice—when offered an olive branch it's best not to knock the tree from which it was plucked."

"That's your 'olive branch'?" Leah put her hands on her hips. "You tell me that I can do better than my unfaithful dead husband and then you have the nerve to chastise me for not embracing your remarks as some kind of peace offering?"

The phone rang and I quickly answered it. "Hello?"

"Hi, this is Jerome Bader from *Flavah Magazine.* I was hoping to talk to Leah."

"Jerome," I repeated. "You're the reporter who asked Leah about—"

"It's Jerome?" Leah leaped forward and grabbed the phone out of my hand before I had a chance to finish my sentence. "This is Leah."

Marcus sidled up next to me while Leah directed a series of *uh-huhs* and *okays* into the telephone. "Who's Jerome?"

"He's a journalist from *Flavah*—you know, that fanatically left-wing local magazine that's always slamming da man."

"Oh yeah, I like that mag. I don't mind a little fanaticism when it's cushioned by at least one picture of a shirtless hottie. But why is Leah champing at the bit to talk to him… wait…nooo!" Marcus's eyes took on the shape of saucers. "Is Leah gettin' jiggy with it?"

"No one here is going to get jiggy," I said, ignoring Dena's laughter. "Leah is in mourning."

"Okay," Leah said for what must have been the hundredth time, "I'll meet you here at eleven on Sunday." She hung up the phone, and I couldn't help notice the little smile playing at the corners of her mouth.

"He just wanted an interview, right?" I asked hopefully.

"Of course. Yes. That's what he wanted—an interview."

"You see?" I said to Marcus. "It was just a business call. Leah is nowhere near ready to start dating again—isn't that right, Leah?"

"Absolutely not," Leah confirmed. "I'm not ready at all. Now let's get down to the matter at hand—my hair." She looked at Marcus. "If I let you style my hair, you have to promise not to give me one of those cuts that looks great when you walk out of the salon but horrible the next day. I need to look cute for at least…well at least until the end of the weekend."

"Honey—" Marcus perched himself next to Dena "—when I'm done with you, all the homies will be wanting private interviews."

"Nothing too outrageous, guys," I warned. "She has a public image she needs to maintain these days."

Dena looked at Marcus, who in turn looked at me with big innocent eyes. "Of course, Sophie," he said. "I would never mess with a woman's public image."

"Will you and Mary Ann be watching Jack at the salon or here?"

"As soon as Mary Ann arrives we'll head to the salon," Dena said. "I want to see this transformation."

I took a little comfort in that. Mary Ann had a tendency to err on the side of caution and I knew I could count on her to speak up if Marcus tried to do anything too drastic with my sister's hair.

Anatoly glanced at his watch. "We should head out."

I nodded, although I had no idea where we were heading out to. I glanced at Leah. "Please don't let your kid kill my cat while you wait for Mary Ann to get here."

"What are you talking about? Jack's wonderful with animals. If you think about it, his attempt to clean Mr. Katz was a very sweet gesture."

Dena laughed. "Talk about killing someone with kindness."

"Go already." Marcus stood up and made a shooing motion with his hands. "Your nervous energy is impairing my creative genius."

I was beginning to have some major misgivings about Dena and Marcus's plans for my sister, but Anatoly was clearly impatient so I followed him out of the apartment.

When we reached the street, he turned to me. "I was just at the Gatsby talking to some of Cheryl's coworkers. Bob did go there to see her from time to time. Do you think he just failed to mention the visits to Leah, or was he deliberately concealing them?"

"I honestly don't have a clue." I wrapped my arms around myself to form a barrier against the wind. "It doesn't seem like something that he would need to hide unless…" I looked up and met Anatoly's eyes.

"Unless he was going there with Bianca," Anatoly finished for me. "According to the people I talked to, Bob did come in there with a woman a few times. As far as I can tell, he never took a room, but a reservation could have been made in the name of his girlfriend."

I pressed my palms together in mock-prayer position. "Just tell me how this new info could translate into Cheryl being a murderess."

"It doesn't," Anatoly said. "It points to Bianca."

"Bianca? How?"

"Based on the descriptions of the woman who accompanied Bob, I'd say Leah wasn't the only woman he was screwing around on."

"No. Way." I searched Anatoly's countenance for some sign of jest. "You're serious," I gasped. "But how could a man like Bob get three different women to agree to sleep with him?"

"Having never met the man, I'm not the person to ask. But I think I know who is." Anatoly gestured in the direction of Nob Hill.

"Oh." I let out a low laugh. "This is going to be good."

Bianca lived only a little over eight city blocks away from me, so Anatoly and I opted to hike up to her building. Unfortunately, I was wearing a mid-thigh-length skirt that was a tad too tight and rode up with every five steps. But the constant tugging at my hemline did serve the purpose of getting Anatoly to look at my legs, and damn if he didn't seem appreciative.

When we finally reached her building Anatoly pushed the button for her apartment.

I gazed at the little park across the street where the hired dog walkers were attending to the pocket-size poodles of their socialite clients.

"Yes?" The woman's voice that came through the speaker was not Bianca's. It was less girly and had a bit of an edge to it.

"Hello, my name is Anatoly Darinsky. I'm here to see—" The buzzer that released the door activated before Anatoly could finish his sentence.

When we got up to the correct floor we found a woman with cropped golden-blond hair blocking the entrance to Bianca's condo. She was about Bianca's size, but her features were more chiseled and her overall look more severe. She wore a pair of tailored pants and a red button-down shirt that nipped at her nearly microscopic waistline.

"Hello, Mr. Darinsky—and you must be Ms. Katz."

Anatoly nodded, his eyes doing a quick appraisal of the woman, much to my annoyance.

"I'm Porsha Whitman, Bianca's sister. I'll be staying with her for the next few weeks."

"Ah." Anatoly smiled and extended his hand. "I'm glad Bianca has family she can—"

"I'm also an attorney," she said, cutting him off without accepting his hand. "I'm here to look out for Bianca and to ensure that our family name isn't marred by this mess."

"Whitman isn't exactly a rare name," I pointed out. "I'm

sure it's dragged through the mud with a certain amount of regularity."

"I've instructed my sister not to talk to you. If there's something she wants to say, she'll say it to the police." She turned on her heel and started for the door.

Anatoly took a step forward. "Miss Whitman, it must be obvious to you that the Katz/Miller families desire the same level of discretion you do."

"Lots of things are obvious to me, Mr. Darinsky." Porsha turned and stared directly into his eyes. "It's obvious that Bob Miller took advantage of my sister's innocence. It's obvious that his wife is unstable. And it's extremely obvious that this little surprise visit of yours is completely inappropriate—"

"Porsha, please—"

I glanced behind the gatekeeper to see Bianca looking as sweet and innocent as ever.

"I don't mind talking to them," she whispered.

"Bianca, don't be an idiot."

"Just for a few minutes, Porsha." Bianca looked at the ground. "I owe them that much."

Porsha shook her head in disgust as Anatoly and I followed Bianca inside. If Porsha was staying with Bianca she was an extremely neat houseguest. Bianca's apartment was as immaculate as it had been the last time Anatoly and I had been there. As far as I could tell the only thing that had changed was the flower arrangement on the end table—this time the lilies were yellow instead of pink.

Bianca flinched at the sound of Porsha slamming the door. "Can I get you two anything?"

"For God's sake, we don't need to entertain them, B," Porsha spat. "What exactly *are* you doing here?"

I swallowed my irritation and attempted a smile. "I hope you can forgive our barging in, but we're just trying to figure out who really killed Bob so that my family can have some peace again."

"I can help you with that," Porsha said with a sneer. "It was your sister."

"See, I don't think so," I said, maintaining my friendly tone. "I think it was yours."

"What?" Bianca gasped. "I would never hurt Bob! I loved him!"

Porsha waved off my accusation with a flick of her hand. "I understand that you want to pin this on someone else, but you've made a bad choice in scapegoats. My sister has no motive."

"Sophie misspoke," Anatoly said quickly, and shot me a look of warning. "We don't suspect you of anything, Bianca. But it is becoming increasingly obvious that Leah isn't guilty, either. Think how horrible it would be for Jack if he not only lost his father, but also lost his mother to prison, particularly if she is innocent."

"Oh!" Bianca put a hand to her mouth and spoke through her fingers. "I couldn't bear that!"

"Maybe it doesn't have to happen," Anatoly said reassuringly. "If the real murderer is brought to justice, Jack will have his mother, and everyone who loved Bob will have a sense of closure."

I did a double take. Hearing Anatoly use a word like *closure* was kind of like listening to President Bush talk about his "posse." It was just utterly out of character. But one look at Bianca's quivering lower lip told me he was getting the desired response. Maybe he *was* worth twelve thousand dollars.

"How can I help?" Bianca's voice came out in a squeak.

Porsha smacked her left fist into her open palm. "Bianca, he's playing you!"

Bianca shook off Porsha's warning. "I want to help," she repeated with more determination.

"All I need right now are the answers to a few quick questions." He sat down on the couch and gestured for her to sit beside him.

Bianca avoided looking at Porsha and took her assigned place.

"During the time that you were with Bob, did you ever go with him to the Gatsby?"

"Hotel Gatsby?" Bianca wrinkled her forehead. "You mean to dine?"

"No, I mean as a romantic getaway."

"No, Bob and I never got a hotel room together. It would have made what we shared seem cheap."

I suppressed a smile. I was pretty sure that nothing at the Gatsby was cheap.

Anatoly nodded. "I understand. So you've never been there?"

"Only by myself. They have a wonderful day spa."

"But you didn't go with Bob," Anatoly clarified.

"No, never."

"I know this may be difficult for you—" Anatoly reached over and gave Bianca's hand a reassuring squeeze "—but in recent months Bob visited the Gatsby on several occasions with an auburn-haired woman who has been described by those who saw her as being tall, powerfully built and extremely striking. Do you have any idea who that might be?"

"I don't understand." She blinked a few times as if absorbing the new information was a challenge. "Are you saying…?"

"Okay, that's it." Porsha brushed by me and pulled Bianca to her feet. "We don't need this. I'll see you both to the door."

Anatoly stood up. "If Bianca wants to answer the questions, then it's not really your place to stop her."

"I disagree. Bianca's my little sister, and I protect the people I love from being needlessly harassed. Now are you both going to leave or do I need to call the police."

"You can't have us arrested for entering an apartment after we were invited in. But if you insist, we'll leave." He smiled at Bianca. "So you don't know who the other woman might be?"

"No…I…I didn't get to meet many of Bob's friends. But I can't believe…Bob would never…"

I leaned forward and tried to look sympathetic. "I understand why you would be skeptical," I said, directing my comments to Bianca. "I mean, Bob certainly gave the appearance of being fairly devoted to you—what with the six-thousand-dollar bracelets and all."

Bianca's eyebrows drew together in puzzlement. "Six-thousand-dollar bracelets?"

"The Tiffany's yellow-sapphire bracelet you showed me." Was it possible that anyone could forget that particular token of Bob's affection?

Bianca let out a short laugh. "I had that bracelet insured—it's not worth six thousand dollars."

"How much was the bracelet worth?" Anatoly asked. "Five thousand?"

Bianca shook her head, clearly bemused. "I had it insured for *fifty-one* thousand dollars."

My jaw dropped, and even Porsha looked a little taken aback. My mind flashed back to the necklace he had bought Leah for a similar price. Over a hundred thousand dollars wasted on two pieces of jewelry, yet the man couldn't manage to invest forty dollars a month in a life insurance policy?

Bianca was looking at me as if she expected me to comment. "Wow," I said, my voice coming out in little more than a whisper. "His other mistresses would be so jealous."

Porsha walked over to the door and yanked it open. "Bianca, say goodbye to your guests."

Anatoly nodded and we stepped out into the hallway. Porsha came out with us, closing the door behind her. She looked Anatoly over with new interest.

"You're good," she said. "You played on her guilt and feelings of loss in order to gain her trust, and then you just led her into the lion's den. You should have been a lawyer."

Anatoly laughed—a little too merrily in my opinion. "I think I'll stick to what I'm doing now. I lack the necessary level of corruption to pull off a career in law."

Porsha smiled. "Touché. All right, what's all this about there being another woman? Were you just fishing or do you actually have witnesses to this third liaison?"

"We have witnesses," I said. I'd be damned if I was just going to stand there quietly while she needled *my* antagonist.

Porsha turned her head in my direction. "And did these witnesses actually see Bob being intimate with this woman in any way? Were they holding hands, did they get a room, anything incriminating at all? And what's the story with the bracelets?"

"We're going to share the information we have with the police," Anatoly said, regaining Porsha's attention. "I might be convinced to share it with you if you would be willing to give me some more time with your sister."

Porsha smiled and pressed the button to the elevator. "Have fun with the police." She turned around and retreated into the apartment.

Once we were in the elevator, I said peevishly, "You're attracted to Porsha."

Anatoly smirked. "What gave me away? Was it the way I flagrantly ignored her demands that I leave until after I was done preying on her sister, or was it the cute way I sidestepped her questions?"

"It was the way you were checking out her body."

Anatoly's smirk faded into a wistful smile. "She does have a nice figure."

"You may *not* get into bed with the enemy. That's totally against the rules."

"This from the woman who promised me sexual favors when she was really trying to set me up for murder."

"Okay, so these are new rules. It doesn't make them less valid."

"Of course not," he said, as we walked out of the elevator and lobby and into the cool spring air. "I'm going to the police station to update them on what we found out. It will be helpful if they have at least a few leads that point to someone other than Leah."

"I'll go with you."

"That's not a good plan."

"Why not?"

"Because so far the only thing you've done on these interviews is piss people off."

"That's not true! Besides I don't think it's possible for me to piss off the police any more than I already have, so there's no problem."

"When you get home, I want you to pull out your dictionary and look up the word *logic*."

"Anatoly…"

"Do you want to end up as Jack's legal guardian?"

I paused. "So you'll call me when you're done at the station?"

Anatoly smiled. "You have my word. Come on, I'll walk you home."

"Um, my place is right on the way to yours, so you don't exactly have a choice."

"Still, the offer was chivalrous."

I giggled and we started walking down the hill. "Has Leah come up with any other ideas about why someone would break into her home to steal floppy disks?"

"She has yet to come up with a plausible theory, and I can't even come up with an implausible one."

"I know that burglary is significant in some way," Anatoly

mumbled. "Did she tell you anything more about her conversation with Lorenzo?"

"No, nothing she didn't tell us already." Actually, every time I mentioned Lorenzo's name, since our last visit to the police station Leah became extremely busy. All of a sudden Jack's diaper would need changing, or she'd have to call Miranda to set up a play date, or she'd pull out a pencil and a sketch pad and start to design her own line of children's wear— anything that made talking about Lorenzo an impossibility. But I knew that Leah would voluntarily spill everything in the very near future. Long-term emotional repression wasn't her forte.

We eventually arrived at my door and Anatoly waited as I got my keys out.

"Sophie, the possibility of a third woman is a good sign, but right now it's still just a possibility. Leah is far from being out of the woods."

"Are you trying to depress me?"

"I'm trying to prepare you," he explained. "I don't want you to be caught off guard if things don't go the way you want them to."

I hesitated with my hand on the door. "Thank you for being concerned, but it's all going to be fine." I looked up at him. "I won't allow it to be anything else." I pushed the door open and left Anatoly on the street. When I got up to my apartment, Mr. Katz was waiting by the door. I obediently made a beeline for the cupboard that held the kibble, but I barely had a chance to pour it before the phone rang.

"Hello?"

"Sophie? It's Erika. I hope I'm not catching you at a bad time."

"Not at all. What's up?"

"The police say they're done with Bob's office, and I thought that Leah might want to pick up some of the personal things he kept here. You know, photos and the like."

I leaned against the bookcase and pulled at a stray thread sticking out of my sleeve. "I'm sure she would, but she's not home right now. I'll have her give you a call when—"

"Maybe *you* could stop by and get the stuff? It might be easier for Leah if she doesn't have to face all the employees here right away. Particularly with all the things they've been saying on the news."

"Good point. Can I stop by tomorrow around lunchtime?"

"Um…okay…or maybe you'd like to come now?"

"I can come now," I said cautiously. "Shall I just go straight to your desk?"

Erika audibly exhaled. "That would be great. I'll be waiting for you."

"Okay, I'll see you in a bit." I pressed the hang up button and stared at the receiver. Since when had picking up a bunch of old photographs become a matter of great urgency? I flashed back to my last visit with Erika and her public displays of grief over her boss's death. No question, the woman had a flair for the dramatic. Maybe that was all there was to it. Or maybe she knew something that could help Leah.

I grabbed my coat and booked it to my Audi.

CHAPTER 8

"When people say a woman is brooding what they really mean is that she's found a way to make depression look sexy.

—*Words To Die By*

I caught sight of Erika at her desk the minute I stepped off the elevator. She was in the company of a tall woman whose back was to me. I couldn't hear their conversation, but whatever was being said was not going over well with Erika. I had never seen her look angry before, and yet at that moment the hate in her eyes was visible from thirty feet away. As I approached, the woman pivoted in my direction. I froze. Her auburn hair was pulled up in a French twist, which showcased her handsome features. She wasn't overweight but her large bone structure made her anything but petite. She fit the description perfectly. This had to be the woman Bob had been seen with at the Gatsby.

I forced a casual smile. "Hi, Erika." I thrust my hand in front of the other woman. "I'm sorry, I don't believe we've met. I'm Sophie Katz, Bob Miller's sister-in-law."

The woman grasped my hand and gave it a solid shake.

"Taylor Blake." She sounded like she had studied at one of those schools that still coached their students to speak with an upper-crust, tight-jawed accent. "I'm familiar with your books."

My smile broadened. "Oh, are you a fan?"

"My housekeeper is," she clarified.

Erika stood silently beside her desk and stared at Taylor with what looked to be a mixture of contempt and awe.

"Sophie Katz, what a pleasant surprise!"

I turned to see James Sawyer smiling down at me. He put a friendly hand on Taylor's shoulder. "Have you met Taylor? She was our last CFO. She had the nerve to leave us for another company a few weeks ago. I'm still trying to muster up enough altruism to forgive her."

"Nobody's irreplaceable, James."

Her smile accentuated her chiseled cheekbones. Everything about her exuded strength and self-assurance. There was no doubt in my mind that most men would find her intimidating.

She turned her attention to me, and her countenance took on a more serious expression. "When I left I thought my position would go to Bob." She shook her head slowly. "It hardly seems possible that he's gone."

I thought I heard Erika suck in a sharp breath, but even I recognized that my imagination was on the active side.

James removed his hand from Taylor's shoulder and used his other hand to pat Erika on the back. "Erika tells me she's helping to plan Bob's memorial service."

"Yes, I can't thank her enough."

"Wonderful, wonderful." James checked his watch. "Taylor was good enough to agree to walk me through some of the paperwork she and Bob had previously been handling, so we'll go do that and leave you two to your business."

He gestured for Taylor to join him and she gracefully excused herself without bothering to glance in Erika's direction.

Erika waited for them to disappear into the elevator before sitting back down. She ran her palms along her skirt as if trying to wipe the sweat off of them. "You don't like her, Erika?" I asked as I pulled up a chair.

"Taylor's not very nice to her employees." Erika stared at the now-closed doors of the elevator. "Can you believe Mr. Sawyer wants to reassign Bob's office to someone else already?"

Well, of course he did. Did she think Chalet was going to turn the office into some kind of shrine?

"I've been instructed to have it cleared out ASAP. That's why I wanted you to come in today."

"I figured it was something like that." It had never occurred to me that the rush could be attributed to anything so mundane. I tried to squelch my disappointment by reminding myself that Taylor Blake might have made the trip worthwhile. "What did Bob think of Taylor?"

I thought I saw Erika flinch. "They were close."

"How close?"

"They worked in the same department, so they sort of formed a relationship." Erika toyed with her tennis bracelet. "Bob had a great deal of admiration for her."

I got the feeling that Erika thought his admiration was misplaced. I bit my lip and tried to figure out the best way to pry. "Did you ever work with her directly?"

"She and Bob worked together a lot, and since I worked for Bob, there was some crossover." Erika shrugged. "She was so nice to Bob, I don't think he really saw her for what she is."

"And what is that?"

"Just another cutthroat opportunist with a pretty face," Erika said as she tidied her cubicle. "She expected all of us to bow down to her just because she was the only female upper manager in the company. Then she'd bat her eyes a few times at Bob and he'd instantly become putty in her hands."

"Taylor doesn't seem like the batting-eyes type."

"I'm just saying that she can be manipulative. And Bob's so susceptible to female manipulations. Just look what that woman from the KKK did to him."

I considered correcting Erika about the KKK thing, but exposing her as a gullible twit when it was clear that she was already suffering from feelings of professional inferiority regarding Taylor didn't seem like a kind thing to do. I crossed my legs and leaned back in the chair. "So where's Bob's stuff?"

Erika bent down and retrieved a shoe box from under her desk. I peered inside to see a collection of fountain pens, dry cleaning receipts and other miscellaneous trash. I shifted the contents around, hoping that there might be a floppy disk hiding under one of Bob's outdated parking passes. Nothin' doin'. I withdrew my hand with a heavy sigh.

"This is it?"

"The police took a lot," Erika explained. "There's also this." She opened the top drawer to her desk and pulled out a framed picture of Bob, Leah and Jack. "I kept it separate from the other things because I know how special that photo was to both Bob and Leah."

"My God, who picked out this frame?" I asked as I reached for the bright gold frame that was adorned with gaudy silver stars.

"I'm not sure but I suspect the frame was a gift from *her*."

I wrinkled my nose. "Bianca gave him a framed photo featuring him with his wife and son?"

"I think Bob's the one who put the picture in." She tilted her head to the side so she could see the photo in my hand. "It is a good picture. Bob was so incredibly photogenic."

I examined the photo, and saw none of the "good" Erika pictured. Jack was clearly seconds away from a screaming fit, Bob looked bored out of his mind, and Leah looked like she was suffering from gastric intestinal distress.

"Bob used to keep that photo right on the corner of his desk so he could gaze at it all day long. Maybe Leah could put it in a different frame."

I wrinkled my nose. "Bob *gazed* at this?"

Erika blinked a few times as if trying to stave off tears. "I've really grown to care for Leah, although I haven't been a very good friend to her. She always treated me like family—like a sister really."

I put the frame in the box without comment. If Leah really had treated her like a sister, Erika wouldn't love her so much.

"The night…that horrible night, Leah called me—she left a message saying that she was coming over to see me."

"I remember. She was at my apartment when she placed the call. She said you weren't home when she got there."

"I was house-sitting for Dora, my neighbor—actually I was cat-sitting, since that's really why she wanted me there. I was just curled up on Dora's couch drinking her port, trying to lose myself in a Nora Roberts novel, and all the while Leah was waiting in front of my house a few doors down. If I had looked out the front window and seen her car I could have talked to her. Everything could have worked out differently."

I gritted my teeth. "Leah didn't kill Bob."

"I know she didn't," Erika said quietly. "The more I think about it the more I know she would never do anything like that. She loved Bob as much as—" Erika flushed and looked away "—Cleopatra loved Anthony."

"Right," I said slowly. I made a mental note to keep Leah away from snakes for a while.

"But if I had been there, Leah might not have been the one to…to find him. And I could have vouched for her whereabouts."

I nodded. "That would have been nice."

"And Bob." Erika looked down at her desk. "I miss him horribly. I know he made some mistakes, but he really was—"

"A good person, yeah, you told me." I tucked the shoe box under one arm and stood up. "If there isn't anything else, I should get going."

"No, nothing else." Erika didn't leave her seat. She was probably reliving some memory in which Bob lovingly asked her to take dictation. I sighed and left her to her thoughts. What was it that these people had seen in Bob that I hadn't? It was like me and *The Bachelor,* I suppose. Everyone I knew loved that show, and for the life of me I couldn't figure out what the big deal was. Maybe I was the weird one. I mean, if even a woman like Taylor Blake could be pulled in by Bob's charms, then obviously he must have had a few attributes. While in the elevator I once again examined Bob's expression in the family photo. He looked about as engaged as a swinger at a Tupperware party. If this is what passed for a good catch these days I'd happily stick to my cat.

It wasn't until I found a parking spot—a mere five blocks away from my apartment—that it occurred to me that Anatoly hadn't called to tell me about his chat with the police. I tried calling him while strolling home but I was only able to reach his voice mail. I hung up without bothering to leave a message. The SOB was obviously screening his calls. That was it. Going forward I was no longer going to be attracted to him.

When I got home I expected to find Leah and Jack but when I walked in, the first person I saw was Mama. She was sitting on my couch, her nose pressed against Jack's, who had his tiny hands tangled in her halo of white frizzy hair. I was immediately filled with a familiar mixture of affection and trepidation. "Mama, what are you doing here?"

"This is how you greet the woman who gave birth to you?"

"I'm sorry, it's been a long couple of days." I leaned over and gave her a kiss on the cheek. Mama sat back and admired me. "It's been so long since I've seen you I've forgotten what you look like," she said.

I had seen my mother less than two weeks ago but I let the comment pass. "I heard you on the radio the other day," I said while moving to pet Mr. Katz who was huddled up in the corner. "You gave quite an interview."

"This man from the station called me up and said he wanted me to be a guest on his show," Mama said as she gently stopped Jack from ripping her thick gold necklace off of her. Mr. Katz glared at them. He had always liked Mama but I think he was beginning to understand that he was not the favorite grandchild.

"He said I could tell people what a nice girl my Leah is so of course I said I would do it," Mama continued. "So now I'm a bigshot radio star." She gave me an exaggerated wink. "You didn't expect that, did you, *mumala?*"

"Can't say that I did." I sat down next to her thus using her as a physical buffer against my nephew. "Where is everybody?"

As if in response to my question there was the distant sound of a toilet flushing. In a moment Mary Ann came out, looking beautiful and fresh as ever. "Hi, Sophie! Isn't it great that your mom stopped by? We've been hanging out for the last hour!" She went into the kitchen and opened the freezer. "I picked up a pint of Häagen-Dazs earlier, want some?"

"What flavor?" I asked.

"Strawberry cheesecake."

"I'll pass," I said, secretly grateful that Mary Ann had chosen the only flavor I could easily resist.

"How 'bout you, Mrs. K.?" Mary Ann was the only one

of my friends who called Mama that. Most of my friends subscribed to the Californian philosophy that the only people who should be referred to by their last names were those who had the power to flunk you or incarcerate you. Marcus was one of the few people I knew who took issue with that rule and insisted on calling Mama Mrs. Katz despite being invited to call her Esther; but that was probably because he was from the South. Mama had given up on correcting Marcus but as far as I knew she had never bothered to correct Mary Ann. I think she liked the novelty of the Mrs. K. thing.

"No ice cream for me but I would like some tea if you don't mind and maybe something to nosh on?" Mama gave me a quick once-over. "You should eat something, you're too skinny."

Of all the backward compliments Mama consistently doled out the "too skinny" one was my favorite. I got up to help Mary Ann with the snacks. "So is Leah hiding in the bathroom, too?"

"No," Mary Ann said. "She called about a half hour ago to say she had some shopping to do and that she'd be back by six-thirty."

I checked the clock above the oven. It was already five-forty-five. "How's her hair?"

"I don't know." Mary Ann dug into her Häagen-Dazs with a soup spoon before tearing open a tea bag for Mama. "When I left her, Marcus was just getting started."

I felt the subtle flutter of nerves. "I thought you were going to stay with her at the salon."

"I was, but Jack got bored and he tried to dip his hand in a bowl full of bleach so I got him out of there. He's actually been pretty good ever since."

I brought out a plate full of Egg and Onion Matzo and a prepackaged container of hummus to Mama and glanced down at Jack who was now ripping up my latest issue of *Elle*. "Mama, you're letting Jack rip up my magazine."

Jack grinned up at me. "Jack 'ike to wip."

I narrowed my eyes. It was tempting to show him what the word "wip" really meant.

"Let him have his fun," Mama said, clearly amused. "I looked through that magazine and there's nothing but pictures of skinny girls dressed up in fancy schmancy clothes. There was a bathing suit in there and you know what they wanted for it? Four hundred dollars! Who pays that kind of money for a piece of fabric that could fit in a wallet?" Mama shook her head. "Trust me, it's better that you use it to keep Jack busy than waste your time reading such nonsense."

I gritted my teeth and went back for the tea.

"Just put my drink in one of those little cups," Mama called after me. "I'll wait for Leah for a few more minutes and then get out of your hair. It's not like you need three women to take care of one little baby."

"Yes we do!" I dropped the tea kettle back onto the stove and bolted to Mama's side. "Jack needs you and Leah's under a lot of stress right now." I put my hand on my mother's shoulder just in case she planned on bolting right away. "I really think it would help if you took Jack for the night. It's been a while since you've done that, right? And I know you have extra clothes for him and that porta-crib thing, so it would be easy!"

Mama looked uncertain.

"Did I tell you he said a new word yesterday?" I asked, struggling to keep the desperation out of my voice.

"Really?" Mama brightened. "So tell me the word already."

"Baba."

"Baba! He wanted his grandmother!"

I nodded enthusiastically. "That's what he said. 'I want my Baba.' It was his first grammatically correct sentence. And whenever he sees a lady with white curly hair on the street he cries. So I think we should ease his suffering and let him spend some time at your place, don't you?"

Mama laughed. "All right, I'll take him but don't think I don't see what you're up to. Jack doesn't really cry when he sees little old ladies, does he? You're just making up stories because you want some time away from little Jack, no?"

I smiled sheepishly. "You got me."

"You and your elaborate stories and excuses," she said again. "You're lucky you don't have a nose like Pinocchio. What would have happened if you had just asked me to take Jack home so you and Leah could get some rest. Would the world end if you told the truth once in a while?"

"I *do* tell the truth...once in a while. I guess I just like to make up stories and excuses, too. I am an author after all."

"But when you start using those stories for your real life, that's what gets you into trouble. Remember that time you offered to watch Brandon's pet snake?"

"Oh, come on, Mama, I was thirteen years old."

Mary Ann came out of the kitchen, still holding on to the pint of ice cream that she apparently planned to finish off herself. "Who's Brandon?" she asked eagerly. "Did he go to high school with us?"

"Brandon was my first real crush. His family moved to Oregon right after junior high graduation. You know, Mama, we don't really need to tell this story."

"Even at thirteen my Sophie was a real beauty," Mama continued, dismissing my objections. "And those brains of hers. Any boy would have been lucky to have her on his arm. But she had to get Brandon's attention by making up stories. As soon as she found out he had a boa constrictor she went on and on about how much she loved snakes. She even told him that she planned on breeding them and raising little snake babies when she grew up!"

Mary Ann's eyes widened with horror. "You like snakes?"

"I don't *hate* them," I said. Jack was now toddling over to my music collection. I quickly snatched him up before he could use my U2 CD as a Frisbee. "You want to mess with my stuff, Jack?" I asked sweetly. "Why don't we find you something over here?" I went over to where I kept my old VHS tapes and checked to see if I had anything that I didn't watch anymore.

"No, Sophie isn't so afraid of snakes, but I am and so is her sister," Mama said, shaking her finger in my direction. "So you can imagine my reaction when she comes home with the boy's snake and tells me that she's going to be taking care of it while this Brandon and his family are off caravanning around Disneyland for the weekend. I let her know right away that there would not be any snakes in *my* house. What was I running, a zoo?"

"The boa wasn't even fully grown yet and he had his own enclosure!" I protested. I pulled out a yoga exercise video that I had bought with the best of intentions six years earlier but had never actually gotten around to putting in the VCR. "Here, why don't you take this apart," I said to Jack. I sat him on the ground and he quickly started unraveling the tape. Mr. Katz looked at him with alarm. Clearly he thought Jack was a lot scarier than a snake.

My mama on the other hand didn't seem bothered by Jack's need to destroy and continued with her story. "It's true what she says. The snake had a little Plexiglas home all his own. That's why I said it would be okay for her to let him stay in the garage. But the snake wasn't so happy about this and he made a run for it."

"But snakes can't run," Mary Ann said.

"She means he got out," I explained. "I fed the snake but I didn't want to actually hang around and watch it eat."

"What did it eat?" Mary Ann asked, although by her tone I wasn't at all sure she really wanted to know.

"He ate mice," I said. "Very cute, very alive mice."

"Oh!" Mary Ann put her hand over her mouth and looked away.

"I know," I said, "so I just dropped the mouse in, dropped the lid back on the enclosure and hightailed it into the house. But here's the thing…I didn't take the time to make sure that the lid was really closed."

"It was a real to-do," Mama said, clearly amused by the memory. "All weekend I walked around wearing three pairs of socks so that I wouldn't get snake bites on my ankles."

"Boas don't bite, Mama," I said. "But it *was* a 'to-do.' Mama wasn't the only one who was upset, Leah was beside herself. She sat up awake all night that Friday and Saturday with all her lights on clutching a pair of Dad's old shoes that she planned to throw at the boa if he should make an appearance. And of course I was freaked out about how I was going to explain everything to Brandon when he got back." I shook my head. "To make matters worse our neighbor had this little shih tzu and I was sure that it was only a matter of time before he became snake-lunch."

"Finally this Brandon character shows up with his mother, all ready to take their pet home," Mama said with a giggle. "I told Sophie she was going to have to tell them. I watched her greet them at the door and I thought she was going to cry, and as you know it takes a lot to make my Sophie cry."

Mary Ann looked at me sympathetically. "You must have felt terrible. How did they take it?"

"There was nothing to take!" I plopped down next to Mama and leaned back into the cushions. "I was all ready to confess when I hear Leah clearing her throat behind me and there she was, holding the enclosure with the boa safely inside. You could tell she didn't want to be holding it because she looked like she was going to throw up any second, but she held it nonetheless. She had spotted the boa in the garage next to her bike just moments before, and rather than force me to admit my failure to my current heartthrob she mustered up all her courage and put the animal back in it's enclosure so we could give it back to Brandon without his ever being the wiser."

"But…she was afraid of snakes!" Mary Ann cried.

"Yes," Mama said, "but she loved her sister more."

A warm feeling filled my stomach as I recalled that moment. "She saved me," I said softly.

Mama patted my knee. "And now it's our turn to save her."

I heard a key jiggle in the lock of the front door and a moment later it sprung open and Leah bounded in followed by Dena and Marcus. Leah was wearing a new knee-length leather skirt, spike heels and a very burgundy cotton top. The streaks in her hair matched the shirt.

The warm fuzzy feeling I had been experiencing evaporated. "Oh. My. God."

Leah spun around, with what seemed like a kind of manic exuberance. "You like? It's the new me!"

I turned to Marcus. "She's supposed to be in mourning! How could you give her burgundy highlights?"

"What can I say?" Marcus lifted Jack into his arms and directed his comments to him. "I took one look at your mommy's coloring and all of a sudden I just knew we had to go burgundy."

"Really, Sophie," Dena said, walking to Leah's side. "I don't know what your problem is, it's all earth tones."

"You look very pretty," Mary Ann said hesitantly. "I don't think I've ever seen you wear an outfit so…um…fitted." She turned her attention to me and it was clear she was picking up on my frustration. She'd have to be deaf, dumb and blind not to. "I think I'll be going," Mary Ann said quickly. She gave Mama's hand a goodbye squeeze and then rushed out before anyone could thank her for watching Jack and well before I had a chance to explode.

Mama shook her head. "Since when did you start wearing leather skirts?" she asked Leah. "If you're not careful people will think you're as sex-obsessed as your sister."

"I like the skirt," Leah said defensively. "Dena picked it out for me."

I pressed my fingers into my temples.

Marcus put Jack down and leaned over to give Mama two air-kisses. "Mrs. Katz, it has been so long since I've seen you. I'm loving this little floral print top of yours. It's just so retro."

"Thank you, deary." Mama turned to Jack and smiled. "Did you hear that? Your Baba's a hip cat!"

"Leah, you've got to show Sophie what else we did."

The twinkle in Dena's eyes left me with a sense of foreboding.

Leah obediently lifted up her shirt and displayed a sparkling gem strategically placed inside her belly button.

With a high-pitched squawk I lunged forward and pulled Leah's shirt back down.

"I don't understand," Mama said, staring at the part of Leah's stomach that she had just flashed us. "How does it stay in there?"

"It's a body piercing," Marcus explained. "Dena wanted to take her to this place called Body Manipulations, but there was a wait, so we went to my friend on Polk."

"Your friend on Polk?" I whispered weakly.

"He goes by the name Warlord and, girl, if you could see this man…" Marcus pretended to fan himself off with his hand. "That boy can ransack my village any day of the week."

"You let some guy named Warlord stick a needle into my sister's stomach?"

"Mmm-hmm." Marcus tapped his finger on his chin. "I think his last name is Goldberg."

Mama perked up. "A nice Jewish boy! Is this Warlord single?"

"That's it." I made a silencing motion with my hands. "Maybe you've all forgotten, but Leah's a prime suspect in her husband's murder. She needs to maintain the image of an innocent, grieving widow. That image is going to be hard to pull off with a cubic zirconium in her navel!"

"Oh, give me a break." Dena crossed her arms over her chest defensively. "It's not like she's going to be wearing midriff shirts into court. Besides, no one in their right mind is going to believe that Leah is a murderess."

"Really? I'm not sure the police or the D.A.'s office will agree with you."

"Well, they'll just have to talk to me." Mama stood up and put a hand on each of my sister's cheeks. "Such a face. Like an angel you are. I'll show them the pictures of when you were a little girl and they'll see."

I gritted my teeth. "Mama, I think you should take Jack now, okay? Dena and Marcus, you need to go, too. I need to talk to Leah alone."

"*Oy gevalt,* I'm being dismissed by my own daughter." Mama picked up Jack and gave Leah a loud kiss on the cheek.

"So, you're really going to take Jack?" Leah asked hopefully. "For how long?"

"Your sister here thinks I should take him overnight, if that's all right with you."

Leah didn't even pretend to think about it as she eagerly handed over Jack's diaper bag.

Mama turned to Marcus and Dena. "So who's going to take me home? I don't want to ride with one of those crazy cabdrivers while I'm with my only grandchild."

From the kitchen I tossed Marcus one of my spare keys. "You can get the car seat out of the Audi. It's parked on Lexington and Pacific."

"Will do," Marcus sang. "You know, Mrs. Katz, we should really do your hair next. Why be gray when you can go platinum?"

Marcus and Mama walked out first and Dena turned to follow, but I stopped her right outside the door. "I know this was your idea," I hissed. "I know you don't like Leah, but you're messing with her life here, not to mention mine."

Dena's jaw set. "I'm not messing with her life—I'm trying to help her get one. She was so fucking depressed yesterday that she even had *me* feeling sorry for her."

"And so you naturally assumed that you would fix things for her by dressing her up like a femme fatale."

"Hey, she's in a better mood now than she was this morning."

I shook my head. "Listen, Dena, it's all well and good that you want to give Leah an emotional lift, but next time just buy her a dildo and call it a night, okay?"

Dena grinned. "I just got a new one in stock yesterday. It's called the Diamond Daddy and it—"

"I'd go for a basic model to start her off." I shoved her gently toward the stairs. "I'll call you later."

I returned to the apartment to see Leah lifting up the corner of a sarong to check out her new do in the mirror.

"Leah, you know we're going to have to dye your hair back to brown, right?"

Leah turned to me with a vexed expression. "Everywhere we went today I got compliments. Compliments on my hair, Sophie. I don't think that's happened to me since I spent three hours getting it pressed for the senior prom."

"Leah—"

"This image works for me, and I have always been a believer in sticking to what works."

"If the D.A. gets a picture of you looking like this just

three days after your husband's death you'll be handed a life sentence before you can say Versace."

"So what do you suggest I do, hmm? Should I behave the way everyone expects me to?"

I took a small step back. "Is this a rhetorical question?"

"Yes, it is, because the answer is blatantly obvious. We may not have a lot in common, but we're both educated intelligent women and we both know that the definition of insanity is to do the same thing over and over again while expecting to get different results each time. I was the perfect wife to Bob. I did what was expected of me—and you know what I got for my troubles? To quote your friend Dena, I got 'fucked royally,' and not in a good way, Sophie."

"Okay, I think you need to take a deep breath—"

"Do not patronize me! I am not a five-year-old having a temper tantrum, I am a twenty-eight-year-old having a nervous breakdown!"

"I'm not trying to be patronizing, Leah, I just think we need to back up and approach this conversation in a calm, rational manner. Can I get you something? A glass of water, some Zoloft maybe?"

For a second Leah didn't move, then her shoulders slumped and I watched as all her anger was visibly washed away by a sudden wave of exhaustion. She sank down onto the couch.

"My whole world is falling apart."

I sat down next to her and leaned my forearms onto my knees as I studied the floor. "So, we'll just have to put it back together again."

For a few minutes the only sound to be heard was Mr. Katz's snoring and Leah's jagged breathing. She leaned over and got herself a Kleenex from the end table. "What is she like, Sophie?"

I didn't look up. "What is who like?"

"You know who I'm talking about. Is she…pretty?"

I squeezed my eyes shut. Of course she was talking about Bianca, since she still didn't know about Taylor. "I guess she's kind of pretty," I hedged, "in a very conventional kind of way."

Leah nodded. "The girl next door. Bob always liked that look."

"Leah, you're every bit as attractive as she is."

"*Please*. I'm ten pounds overweight, Marcus had to slave over my hair in order to make it look like this, and I don't remember there ever being a time in my life when I didn't have a blemish on my face somewhere." She bit her fingernail. "No wonder Bob was unhappy with me."

"I don't think Bob strayed because you got a pimple, however—" I took a deep breath "—maybe the reason Bob wasn't happy at home had something to do with the fact that you weren't happy, either. I mean, I used to think you were at least happy with your life overall, if not with your husband specifically. Now I'm beginning to think that was denial on my part. I just couldn't stand the idea that you would settle for a life that would make you miserable. But that's exactly what you did, isn't it?"

"I think *miserable* is a little harsh. I was *almost* happy. I honestly tried to be." Leah leaned back into the couch. "The funny thing is that I thought things were getting better. You didn't spend much time with Bob these past two years. Neither did I, for that matter, but the time I did spend with him was…different. He was different."

"How so?"

She rotated her wedding band on her finger. "I could never quite put my finger on it. He was more confident, more generous, more…well, just more everything."

"What brought that on?" I asked, although my thoughts immediately turned to the other women in his life.

"I don't know." Leah got a faraway look in her eyes. "For a while I was stupid enough to think that it had something to do with me. I had enrolled in this cooking class and had taken to throwing these wonderful dinner parties for him and his colleagues, and I thought that maybe I had finally become the wife that we both wanted me to be. I wanted that so badly. That's why I didn't argue when he asked me not to wear the plum sweater with the V-neck or cut my hair short—I was trying to mold myself to fit a certain image. I wanted to be the kind of polished and genteel homemaker that you see featured in *Better Homes and Gardens.* But no matter what I did or didn't do I could never quite pull it off."

I pulled my hair back from my face. "You shouldn't have to *mold* yourself at all. You need to figure out who you already are and stick with that."

"And who would that be? Because according to you, vamp is unacceptable." She held up her leg so that her stiletto heel was proudly displayed in the air.

"Trust me, the vamp thing isn't a good look to play with right now," I said.

She sighed and lowered her leg. "Maybe I should be a political activist. I could champion the minority cause. There seem to be a lot of people out there who want me to do that."

"You're a registered Republican who listens to Neil Diamond CDs. You're not going to make it as a Black Activist."

"How about a convict, then?" She turned to me and I noted how pale she had become. "Detective Lorenzo thinks I'm guilty, Sophie. I can tell by the way he looks at me. And the tone of his voice..." Her voice trailed off and she averted her eyes. "It's just a matter of time before he issues a warrant for my arrest."

I swallowed, hard. "All we have to do is show reasonable doubt. You're not going to prison for this. I won't let that happen."

"I see. And who died and made you God?" But her tone lacked the venom necessary to make her words biting. "I was so quick to hand Jack over to Mama, but now that I think about it I might have been too hasty. My time with my son might be limited."

"Leah…"

"So why shouldn't I wear a leather skirt and a belly-button ring? It's not like anything I wear will change the in-evitable. At least this way I can be known as the woman who was fashionable in the face of adversity."

I sucked in a sharp breath. "Is that what this is?" I stood up and made a sweeping gesture that encompassed her whole outfit. "The early signs of defeat? You couldn't just start wearing sweatpants like everyone else?"

"I'm not being a defeatist, I'm being a realist. Are you even listening to what I'm saying?"

"No, I'm not, because you're not saying anything useful." I bent forward so I was in her face. "You say you love your son, but look at you!"

"What are you talking about? I love Jack more than life itself!"

"Then fight for him! Don't just put on a pair of fuck-me pumps and roll over! Lorenzo thinks you're guilty. So what? We're the ones with the truth on our side. That and a bot-tle of Miss Clairol will get you a hung jury to call your own. Now drop the martyr bullshit and find some goddamn flats!"

Leah gawked at me, seemingly unable to move. Finally, she cleared her throat and shifted slightly in her seat. "You don't seriously expect me to dye my hair with some drugstore product, do you?"

CHAPTER 9

"She's always been a micromanager," Daniel said as he watched the police read Melina her rights. "It just goes to show, the devil really is in the details."

—*Words To Die By*

I think Leah finally heard me. After a few minutes more of discussion we reached a compromise. Since the sex-kitten stuff seemed to boost her self-esteem, she would wear it at home while sitting shivah. However, if she actually had to leave the apartment she would make a point of looking conservative and downtrodden.

After we had all that settled, I took off. I went to Starbucks for a Frappuccino and then drove around the city for a good hour. I finally ended up in Forest Hills, and despite my promise to Anatoly, I parked across the street from Leah's house. Of course I told myself that I was just staking the place out and that I wouldn't actually go inside, but deep down I knew that wasn't my plan. The house was completely dark, and after fifteen minutes of no activity I got out of my car and went in. I entered the living room first, half expecting that the cushions would be off the sofa again, but everything seemed to be in its place.

I considered searching the room but quickly scratched the idea. When Dena, Leah and I had arrived, the intruder had already worked his way upstairs, so if there was any room in the house that he had not had a chance to search it would probably be up there. I dropped my purse on the coffee table and climbed the stairs, making a point to turn on every light I came across. I wanted to make it clear to any potential burglars who might be scoping the place out that now was not a good time to break in. Of course, my plan had a few holes in it. First, unlike the burglar, I didn't know what I was looking for. Second, whatever the mystery item was, there was a good chance that the police already had it tucked away in some evidence room. But I was feeling extremely antsy and more than a little desperate, so I had to do something, and looking for a floppy was as productive an activity as anything else I could do.

I started with the guest room. Someone obviously thought that the desired disk was worthy of being hidden in the couch, so why not under a mattress? But after twenty minutes of meticulous searching, I had come up with nothing. My next stop was Jack's room. I turned on the light and scanned the pastel-painted walls.

And that's when I heard the front door to the house open and shut.

I now know what it means to have your blood turn to ice. For a moment I couldn't move. The floorboards creaked under heavy footfalls.

Okay, breathe, Sophie. Breathe and think. Maybe whoever was downstairs would stay there. My cell was in my purse downstairs so I was going to have to sneak into Leah's bedroom and call the police from there. They would come save me and arrest the real murderer all in one fell swoop.

The footsteps started up the stairs.

Okay, time for plan B. I quickly tiptoed across Jack's bedroom and closed his door. My fingers lingered on the doorknob in hopes of finding some kind of lock, but there was none. Okay, not a problem, I would just block the door with a piece of furniture. I went over to the dresser and tried to push it. It was attached to the wall with some kind of metal thingy. I stepped back and eyed the small bookcase filled with Jack's clothes and books. It took all of two seconds to determine that the bookcase had been attached to the wall as well. If there was an earthquake, this is the room you'd want to be in. However, it wasn't the best place for those who wanted to hide from murderers.

The footsteps reached the top of the stairs, then stopped. I needed something to defend myself with. I scanned the room for something heavy or sharp. Nothing. If it wasn't plush, plastic or nailed to the wall, it wasn't in the room. Even the electric outlets were covered by plastic gizmos.

I heard the door to Leah's room squeak as it was pushed open.

Okay, plan C—escape. I went to the window and tried to open it—it wouldn't budge. Something was keeping the window from moving. I stepped back and examined it. There was a large plastic thing attached to the window. The words Baby Safe were written across it in big pink bubble-letters. I tried not to hyperventilate. I was going to be the first person to die as a result of an overly baby-proofed room.

The footsteps were now moving down the hall. There was no more time. My eyes focused on the only launchable non-pillow-like item within reach—a Diaper Genie—and I picked it up and waited for the intruder.

The second the door swung open I used all my strength to hurl the object at my would-be attacker. The Diaper Genie smashed against the threshold and a string of foul-smelling but very neatly wrapped diapers came spiraling out of the plastic contraption and onto the floor.

My terror slowly morphed into embarrassment as I met the eyes of Anatoly.

"Well," he said slowly, "this is another first for me."

I strode over to him and whacked him on the chest. "Do you have any idea how much you scared me? I thought the murderer was coming up here to kill me!"

"Not an unrealistic fear, which is why I told you not to come here."

"Yeah, well…" I tried to think of a good argument but quickly gave up. "Fine, I shouldn't have come by myself, but look—" I pointed to the evidence of Jack's regularity "—I think I did prove that I can be resourceful under pressure. If you were a bad guy and someone started throwing dirty diapers at you, wouldn't you run?"

"I'm thinking about running right now."

A smile threatened the corners of my mouth and I turned my back on him to conceal it. "What are you doing here, anyway? And why didn't you call me after you spoke with the police?"

"I called your place and Leah told me you were out, and since you love to take unnecessary chances with your life, I thought I'd try here first." I turned to see him take a step backward into the hallway as he covered his nose with one hand. "Can we continue this conversation downstairs?"

"You're such a wimp," I said, despite the fact that I, too, was dying to escape the pungent odor. I gingerly stepped over the diapers and followed him downstairs. I would have to clean up before going home but that was a job worth procrastinating.

"Did you come here in hopes of finding something more incriminating than fan fiction?" he asked as we entered the kitchen.

"That was the plan, but I haven't found anything yet. How did things go at the police station?"

Anatoly pulled some glasses out of one of the cabinets. "Why don't we start by pouring ourselves a drink?"

I slumped against the counter. "That bad, huh?"

"It wasn't good."

"Give me a second to raid Bob's wine collection." I went to the walk-in pantry that Bob had converted into a make-shift wine storage facility and scanned the various cases before settling on a bottle of Chateau d'Yquem. By the time I got back to the kitchen Anatoly had already located the corkscrew.

I handed him the wine and he studied the label. "I don't think I'm familiar with this vineyard."

"It's not very well known," I explained. "In fact Bob was the only person I've ever known to keep it in stock, but for some reason the name has been floating around in my head lately."

Anatoly smirked. "The names of alcoholic beverages float around in your head, and yet you still don't think you have a drinking problem."

"Anatoly, open the damn bottle and tell me something useful."

He nodded and uncorked the wine. "I met with Lorenzo and relayed the information given to me by Cheryl's co-workers," he said as he poured the wine into two glasses, "but I'm not sure he believed me. I'm too closely connected to you."

I pounded my hand against the counter. "He can't just dismiss all the evidence that you dig up because you're my friend. That's got to be criminal negligence or something!"

Anatoly chuckled. "Not even close. The police have to consider the source of any information that comes their way, otherwise they'd spend all their time chasing false leads. I think they'll check it out, but I doubt it will sway their investigation away from your sister."

"Well, something has to!" I took a sip of the sweet wine. "She's innocent, Anatoly, which means that the real murderer is sitting back and enjoying a life free of the threat of conviction."

Anatoly studied the contents of his glass. "You're a good sister, Sophie. I admire that."

My mouth dropped open. In the past, Anatoly had expressed his anger with me, his fear of me, his amusement at my expense, and on a good day, his physical attraction to me, but this was the first time he had ever told me he admired me for anything. My eyes traveled down to his beautifully masculine hands. Why did I keep forgetting that I wasn't attracted to him anymore?

I forced myself to redirect my gaze to the half-empty bottle of wine. "Do you think the police would take our claims more seriously if I told them that I may have met Bob's Hotel Gatsby mistress?"

Anatoly's eyebrows shot up.

"I stopped by Chalet today to pick up some of Bob's things, and I got to meet the former CFO, a woman named Taylor Blake. She's tall with auburn hair, very striking, and, according to Erika, she had Bob wrapped around her little finger."

"Really." Anatoly's voice was heavy with appreciation for my expert sleuthing skills.

"Really. I gotta say, I wouldn't have pegged her as Bob's type. She comes across as being very forceful and strong. Not at all the little feminine flower that Bianca is, and I seriously doubt that she's the slave to Martha Stewart protocol that Leah is."

"Maybe his taste varied."

"I guess. I just always felt that Bob was the kind of guy who liked his women to be kind of girly and on the subservient side. I could totally see him with someone like Erika…."

Both Anatoly and I froze, the same thought crossing our minds.

I looked at the wine bottle again. "Oh my God, I know why this winery has been in my thoughts lately."

"Why?"

"Because there was a cork from this same winery in Erika's purse."

Anatoly straightened. "How long did Erika work for Bob?"

"A few years," I whispered. "And you know, when I met Taylor today she was with Erika, and it was clear that the two did not like each other. Taylor wouldn't even look at Erika— it's like she didn't want to deal with her."

"And Erika?"

"Erika seemed jealous."

"Erika was wearing a tennis bracelet," Anatoly said quietly. "It must be worth at least six thousand dollars."

"Oh, my God. We all just assumed that the receipt for a six-thousand-dollar bracelet that Leah found was for something Bob gave Bianca but that wasn't the case at all."

Anatoly lowered his wineglass to the counter. "It was clear right from the beginning that her attachment to Bob was extreme. How could we miss something so obvious?"

"How?" My heart was pounding against my chest as I put the pieces together. "Maybe I was too riled up after hearing Cheryl's comments to the media. Maybe you were too distracted by your overwhelming feelings of lust for me. Who the hell cares *how* we missed this? The point is we figured it out, and now we have to tell the police."

Anatoly put his hand up to slow me down. "I am perfectly capable of doing my job while coping with unrequited lust."

For a split second I forgot that Anatoly wasn't the reason for my current state of excitement. My eyes fell to his perfectly sculpted shoulders. Good thing I wasn't attracted to him anymore, otherwise I'd be in trouble.

"And," Anatoly continued, "we don't know anything. We just suspect."

Oh, right, right, right. We were talking about Erika's affair with Bob. I had to make a prioritized to-do list for myself: Find brother-in-law's killer, then have sex. I managed to suppress my raging hormones and turned Anatoly's last statement over in my head.

"What do you mean, we don't know?" I asked slowly. "She gets misty every time his name is mentioned, her jewelry has a market value that is well beyond her own purchasing power, and she carries around a cork to a wine that only Bob and, like, five other people in San Francisco drink."

"None of that is proof," Anatoly said, "and, considering the lack of faith the police have in us, we really need to back up any leads we feed them with a hefty amount of hard evidence."

"We don't have time to collect evidence," I shouted. "Erika had an affair with my sister's husband. She may even have killed him! She's probably at home as we speak packing her bags in preparation for her one-way trip to Barbados!"

"Sophie, think this through. If Erika *is* the killer, the smartest thing she could do is stay put and play it cool while the cops go after Leah."

"Yeah? Well, what if she isn't smart?"

"That's the problem." Anatoly drummed his fingers against the counter. "I'm not at all convinced that she has the cunning necessary to pull off this kind of crime."

"Why would she need cunning?" I started pacing the room as a hypothetical scene unfolded in my mind. "Leah went to see Erika the night of Bob's murder, but she wasn't home. So, what if she was here? She could have come over to confront Bob about Bianca. They start arguing, Erika throws a few wedding pictures around, Bob gets pissed and storms out of the room. Then Erika, who has been to this house umpteen times before and undoubtedly knows where

Leah and Bob keep the safe and their one and only security code, which they use for *everything,* goes to get the gun. Bob comes downstairs again, pours himself a glass of much-needed scotch and then *bang*—" I made a pistol out of my fingers "—Erika shoots him in the head. She then leaves, locks up the place with her spare set of keys that Bob gave her to use during the times Leah's off getting her semi-annual Calistoga mud bath, and *voilà!*—Erika has committed the perfect crime. No cunning required."

"Unless, of course, it was one of Bob's many other mistresses," Anatoly said.

"I don't understand." I wrinkled my nose. "Who are you thinking of? Bianca or Taylor?"

"Perhaps neither. My guess is that there were lots of women in Bob's life. We just have the names of a select few."

I stuck a thumbnail in my mouth and thought about that. "I don't know…I mean, there's only so many hours in a day and the man *did* have a job."

"So did Wilt Chamberlain, and apparently he slept with twenty thousand women in his lifetime."

"First of all, being a basketball star isn't so much a job as it is a lifestyle and secondly, Bob's no Wilt Chamberlain. On a good day he was about as interesting as a statistics professor."

"Apparently he was interesting enough to attract the attention of a debutante, a female CFO, a pretty admin and your sister." Anatoly stepped forward and picked up the wine bottle and studied it absently. "There may be hundreds of women in this city who had motive and opportunity to kill Bob. That's bad news for anyone trying to pinpoint an individual murderess, but very good news for someone trying to prove reasonable doubt."

I tapped the toe of my shoe on the tile floor and tried to digest this new development. Bob was a lout, but he hadn't deserved his fate. That, in addition to the fact that the real murderer was apparently content to allow my sister to be prosecuted for a crime she didn't commit, was enough to make me want to see the guilty party locked up for life. But I had to keep my eye on the real prize, and that was ensuring that Leah wasn't charged with anything.

"All right," I said quietly. "What do we need to do to convince the police of all this?"

"We start by talking to your sister. If you point out the possibility of these affairs to her, she might begin to remember things she once thought to be irrelevant. Phone calls from Erika or Taylor…maybe she walked in on a late-night business meeting that seemed a little too intimate…who knows? But we need to pick her brain."

"You mean *I* need to pick her brain." This was not going to be a fun conversation.

"Just try to keep her calm and remind her that the silver lining to all this is that Bob's infidelities may be her ticket to freedom," he said.

"Yeah, I'm sure she'll be very rational about the whole thing."

Anatoly laughed quietly. "Just one more thing." He stepped closer and looked directly into my eyes. "No matter how angry Leah gets, neither of you are to contact either Taylor or Erika. We cannot afford to tip our hand."

I took a deep breath. "Got it. No tipping." I looked at the bottle in Anatoly's hand. "I think we'll go for tipsy instead."

When I got home I found Leah in front of the television in her new outfit watching an old *Sex and the City* episode on TBS with Mr. Katz curled around her feet. The shoe box I had picked up earlier was in front of her on the coffee table. She looked up as I entered the room and eyed the overnight bag I had brought back with me.

"That's mine, isn't it?"

"I stopped by your house and picked up some more clothes for you and Jack since we were a little rushed last time we were there." I dropped the bag on the floor and sat down next to her. "I've never seen this episode."

"I've never seen any of the episodes," Leah said. "I read that this show was nothing but a portrayal of gauche, desperate single women complaining about their love lives."

"Well, I don't know if it's gauche, but the rest sounds pretty accurate."

Leah sighed. "If I had just stayed single I wouldn't be in this mess. Of course, then I wouldn't have Jack."

I nodded and kept my eyes glued to the set. I did love my nephew, despite all his eccentricities. I just wished that I could love him from afar.

Leah pointed her finger at the shoe box. "Where did that come from?"

"Bob's office. Erika called and asked me to pick it up." I could hear the contempt in my voice as I pronounced Erika's name, but if Leah noticed it she didn't say anything.

"What about that awful picture in that hideous frame?" Leah asked. "That didn't come from his office, did it?"

"Erika said it was one of his most cherished possessions. She said, and I quote, 'He could gaze at it all day long.'"

"Ew." Leah made a face. "We don't have that many photos of the three of us, but that one is by far the worst. What person in his right mind would even want to *look* at it, let alone *gaze* at it?"

"Yeah, well, that's just what Erika told me. But I don't think that she's a slave to honesty."

Leah leaned forward and poked at the frame. "I bet Cheryl gave him this frame. It's certainly tacky enough. It must have been for a birthday or something before Bob and I were together because if I had been there when she gave it to him I would have thrown it out."

My shoulders slumped. I had been hoping that my disparaging remarks about Erika would serve as a natural segue into the conversation about her betrayal, but Leah wasn't taking my lead. My eyes traveled back to the television. "Why don't I make us some popcorn and martinis?"

"No thanks." Leah sighed and turned the TV off with a light tap of the remote. "I don't think I'm in the mood for this anymore."

"In that case let's skip the popcorn and just go straight for the cocktails."

Leah eyed me warily. "What is it?"

I leaned over and freed my swollen feet from my heeled boots. "What is what?"

"There's something you want to talk to me about but you're afraid to bring it up. I can always tell, you know. It's like that time when we were kids and you had to tell me that you'd accidentally blown up my Barbie Dream House while working out the kinks in your science fair project."

"Oh, Leah," I sighed. "That wasn't an accident."

"That was on purpose?" She gasped. "I had to save my allowance for over a year to buy that thing!"

"I have some good news and some bad news," I said quickly. "Which do you want first?"

"Does Mama know you meant to blow it up?" Leah demanded. "I swear—"

"Okay, we'll start with the good." I smiled a little too broadly. "I figured something out tonight that might help you. If my deductions are correct, your days as a prime suspect may soon be over."

Leah's anger dissipated, and I could see the spark of cautious hope in her eyes.

"You've found a way to clear me? How?"

"Well, that's the bad news. I didn't exactly find a way to clear you. I just identified a few other people who had equal motives, and at least two of them might have had equal opportunity. That means the police will have to broaden the scope of their investigation, and with a lot of luck they'll catch the bad guy, or at least be unable to arrest you."

"I don't understand."

"Leah…" I paused for a deep breath. The information I was about to give her was a lot more volatile than the tidbit about the Barbie Dream House. "I think Bob was having more than one affair."

Leah stared at me for a full minute before vehemently shaking her head. "No. That simply isn't possible."

"Oh, sweetie—" I put a comforting hand on her knee "—not only is it possible, it's probable. He was seen at Hotel Gatsby with a woman who was neither you nor Bianca."

"No." Leah stood up with a jerk and stepped away from me. "Don't you think I would have known if Bob was having multiple affairs? Do you think I'm completely clueless?"

"When it comes to your husband? Absolutely."

Leah glared at me and crossed her arms over her chest. "All right then, Miss Know-It-All, who was this woman that Bob was supposedly sleeping with?"

I looked down at my hands. It seemed that I should start with the least offensive betrayal and work my way up. "Anatoly's going to the Gatsby with a photograph tomorrow to confirm our suspicions, but we think the woman described by the people at the front desk is Taylor Blake."

Leah laughed. Not a bitter laugh, but a full out "I'm watching *A Fish Called Wanda*" kind of laugh. "Taylor Blake? Are you joking? Have you even met the woman?"

I nodded. "I met her today. She's very handsome."

"Yes." Leah nodded, still smiling. "Handsome is a good word for her. She lacks the natural femininity of oh, I don't know…*Dennis Rodman,* but she is very *handsome.*"

"Come on, Leah, she's a good-looking woman. I'm sure she's had her fair share of boyfriends."

"She probably has, but not Bob. Bob would rather be strung up by his toes than partner up with a woman like that."

"We'll see," I said. I studied Mr. Katz who was now sharpening his claws on my bookcase. "There's another woman, too."

"Oh, really? And who would that be, Dianne Feinstein?"

"Erika Wong."

Leah's smile disappeared. Her right hand made a clutching motion over her heart. "No," she whispered, "she wouldn't…Bob wouldn't…"

"It's obvious that she was very close to Bob," I pointed out. "God knows she's distraught over his death."

"That doesn't mean anything. She worked for him, and they were close, but that doesn't mean…"

"She's pretty bitter about his affair with Bianca, and it's clear that she has some beef with Taylor—"

"But her problems with Bianca have to do with her loyalty to me. Erika and I have become friends, for God's sake!"

I forced myself to meet her eyes. "When Anatoly and I were talking to her the other day, Erika dropped a wine cork that she's been carrying around in her purse."

"Yes, she's been carrying that around for a while," Leah explained. "She said that it was from a magical evening with a special someone." She squeezed her hands together. "She was talking about someone else, though, I'm sure of it."

"The vineyard was Chateau d'Yquem."

Leah blinked and looked away. "It's a big coincidence, but that doesn't mean—"

"Have you checked out Erika's jewelry lately?"

She didn't say anything.

"She's got a tennis bracelet, and I'm pretty sure it's from Tiffany."

Leah's mouth set in a thin straight line. "That back-stabbing bitch."

I nodded. "You got that right. And here's the kicker—she doesn't have an alibi for the night Bob died."

Leah's entire being looked like it was ready to explode into an impressive display of fireworks. She walked past me, grabbed her purse and headed straight out the door.

"Wait!" I shouted after her. "You can't go see her!" I struggled to get my boots on again, but when I wasn't able to do so fast enough I simply held them with my left hand and raced down the stairs after her.

"Leah!" I screamed as I stepped out onto the sidewalk. She was almost a block away. How the hell was she able to make that kind of time in those heels?

She stopped next to her car and pulled her keys out of her bag.

"Oh, shit," I moaned. I sprinted forward and caught up with her as she was turning over the engine. I threw open the passenger side door and tumbled in just before the car screeched onto the empty street.

"Leah, you need to rethink this."

"You should have heard Erika when I told her about Bianca!" Leah took a sharp turn in the direction of California Street.

"Uh-huh, tell you what, why don't we find a Starbucks and you can tell me all about it over a couple of Frappuccinos."

"At first she started making excuses for Bob, talking about how the heart works in mysterious ways and I should try to be more understanding—" Leah made another sharp turn. She was definitely heading toward the freeway.

"Okay, forget the Frappuccinos. How 'bout we go somewhere and get those cocktails we were talking about? You want a cocktail, Leah?"

"Then when I told her that the woman he was leaving me

for was twenty-one, she just freaked out. Erika asked me over and over again if I was sure I had heard him correctly."

"Hey, I know! We can buy drugs! A little weed and this whole thing will be funny."

"Are you hearing me?" Leah demanded. "Before I recited Bob's description of Bianca, Erika thought he was leaving me for her! After everything I've done for her, that little witch tried to break up my family!"

I seriously doubted that Leah had done a lot for Erika, but that was hardly the issue at the moment. What was important was that we were clearly headed straight for Erika's Daly City home.

"Leah," I said carefully, as she merged the car into the lane that would take us to 280, "Anatoly specifically told me that we shouldn't make our theories known to Erika or Taylor. Right now, we have the upper hand because they don't know that we know about the affairs…but if you confront them—"

"I have no intention of confronting Taylor Blake. I hardly know the woman. In fact, the only thing I *do* know about her is that she wasn't sleeping with my husband. But Erika, ooh, she's going to be sorry she messed with me."

"Is she, Leah? What exactly are you going to do? Kill her? The threat of a life in prison isn't enough for you? You want to try for the death penalty now?"

"I'm not going to kill her." Leah pulled the car onto the freeway. "But I am going to give that little hooker what-for."

"Give her what-for? You're going to risk everything just so you can give her what-for?"

"I've made up my mind, Sophie."

"And what if she's the killer?" I flinched as Leah cut in front of a Lexus SUV, barely missing its bumper. "As far as we know Erika could still have Bob's gun. She could shoot us, Leah!"

"Don't be silly—Erika's not the type."

"Are you serious? Ten minutes ago you didn't think she was the type to sleep with your husband!"

Leah narrowed her eyes. "If she did kill him—if she actually had the nerve to both sleep with Bob and then shoot him in *my* house…I swear to God I—I don't know what I'll do."

"Well, you could always give her what-for. I hear that makes a real impact on the cold-blooded killer."

Leah fell into an icy silence and put a little more pressure on the gas pedal. Maybe she'd attract the attention of the California Highway Patrol. Then she'd have to stop. On the other hand, that might not be so great, either. The last thing Leah needed was for the police to see her at her most insane.

We continued our journey until we finally reached the Daly City Freeway exit, which I assumed was nearest Erika's home. Leah pulled onto a residential street with cookie-cutter houses in pastel shades. The neighborhood was completely quiet, the glow coming from behind a few curtained windows being the only sign of conscious life.

I took a deep breath and tried one more time to stop my sister. "Leah, if you could just take a moment to calm down and think about this, you'd see that we would be in a much better position to make Erika pay for what she's done if we bide our time a little. I mean, how much fun would it be to see her taken away in handcuffs? It would probably make the news, and you could tape it and re-watch it whenever you needed a lift." I gave her a half smile.

Leah stopped in front of a pale pink house. "Sophie, I am a woman scorned. You don't ask a woman scorned to bide her time."

"Are you kidding? Have those years of watching *All My Children* taught you nothing? The women scorned *always* bide their time."

Leah got out of the car and stormed up to the front door of the house. I ran up to her side and grabbed her arm.

"Listen, you've done some stupid things in your life but this could easily take the cake. I mean, this actually tops the time you agreed to go out with Seymour Dickman…."

Leah yanked her arm away and started to knock on the door. But when her fist made impact with the wood, the door creaked open. For a second I forgot that I should be talking Leah out of destroying her life. Why wasn't Erika's door closed and locked? It looked like a decent neighborhood, but still…

Leah was much less fazed. She pushed the door open and stepped into the entryway. "Erika," she called, as I quickly closed the door behind us. "Erika, I know you're here. There are a few things that I'd like to discuss with you."

There was no answer. I glanced around. The only light was coming from the street lamp outside. "I think it might be a good idea if we left now," I whispered. "You can give her what-for tomorrow."

"You know this can't wait." Leah marched ahead of me. "Erika? Where are you?"

She stepped into the living room with me right on her heels. There was a strange smell that I couldn't immediately identify, but that for some odd reason reminded me of the days I hung out with Leah during the early part of her pregnancy.

"Oh, for God's sake," Leah muttered. "Aren't there any lights around here?" She reached over and switched on a large lamp resting on one of the end tables.

The place was in shambles. There was a roll-top desk in the corner with every drawer open and papers littered all around. Pictures had been taken off the wall and the cushions of the love seat and couch had been removed. There was an empty bottle of Baileys lying horizontally on the coffee table, along with two glasses that looked recently used.

Someone had thrown up on the couch (which explained the memories of Leah's first trimester) and on the floor between the couch and coffee table lay Erika. She was on her stomach, and her face was hidden by her hair, which also had traces of vomit clinging to it. But there was something about the awkward way she was positioned that set her apart from the average passed-out drunk. She was so still. I couldn't see her back rise and fall with breathing. I stepped in front of Leah and bent over Erika to examine her more carefully.

"Erika?" I whispered.

Behind me I could hear Leah clucking her tongue.

"My God, she's really fallen apart, hasn't she," she said flatly. "Do you think this little breakdown is due to the fact that she's lost the love of her life, otherwise referred to as *my husband?*"

From the corner of my eye I could see Leah wandering around the room. "Look at this place. She must have thrown quite the party here and now she's passed out like a common drunk. I guarantee you Bob never saw this side of her."

I was tempted to turn around and slap some sense into Leah. I don't know what kind of parties Leah had been going to, but in my circles people didn't usually get trashed and then ransack their host's file cabinet.

"Oh, damn it, I just broke a nail."

I didn't acknowledge Leah's manicure problem. Instead, I reached my hand out and pushed aside a few of Erika's raven locks so I could see her better. Her eyes were open.

I shot up and stumbled back, crashing into Leah.

"Ow! You just stepped on my foot!"

"Leah, she's dead."

Leah looked at me like I was insane. "Of course she's not dead. She just drank herself into unconsciousness." She stepped around me and glared at the body. "Erika, wake up! I'm not leaving until I speak my mind!"

The silence that followed her words was unbearable. Leah hesitated and walked around to the other side of the body. "Oh, my God." Leah's mouth dropped open and she looked up at me with a new, terrifying comprehension. "But she… but…I don't…"

The horror that had paralyzed me disappeared and was replaced by a powerful survival instinct. I spotted a box of Kleenex next to the lamp and gingerly pulled out several sheets. I handed half of them to Leah. "I'm going to get your fingerprints off the lamp—you go work on the door."

"But—"

"Now, Leah!"

Leah numbly took the Kleenex, but didn't move. I resisted the urge to shake her, and carefully wiped off the part of the lamp she had touched. I then turned it off and pushed her toward the front door. I wiped the doorknob and the entire area around where she had first tried to knock. Then I peered outside. No one was around to see us.

Unless, of course, the murderer was watching.

The thought spurred me to hurry. I half pulled, half pushed Leah to the car and shoved her into the passenger seat before jumping behind the wheel. It took all of my self-control to obey the speed limit as we drove away from the scene of yet another crime.

# CHAPTER 10

"The problem with telling someone to drop dead is that there's always the chance they might comply."
—*Words To Die By*

Leah was silent as we rode along on the freeway. Then again, I didn't exactly try to engage her in conversation. The image of Erika was still vivid enough to make my heart beat an unnatural rhythm. Someone had been there moments before we had arrived, and killed her. Or worse yet, they had still been in the house when we found her.

But fear was only one of the emotions I was experiencing. I was also seriously pissed off at my sister. All we had had to do was stay home and wait for Anatoly to give us instructions. Had that been so much to ask? Was it really necessary to confront her late husband's mistress facing an impending murder charge?

I glanced over at Leah, who was now staring blankly out the car window. "Leah," I said a little too sharply.

Her only response was a slight shake of the head.

"Leah, can you abandon your catatonic state for a few minutes so we can go over our story?"

"All I wanted to do was tell her off."

"Yeah, that didn't work out so well, so let's come up with a different strategy."

"Sophie, do you think I'm a witch?"

I let out an exasperated sigh. "No, Leah, you're not a bitch. Although you do have a tendency to fly off the handle, and you didn't think things through—"

"Not a bitch—a *witch*. You know, the kind that flies around on a broom."

I glanced over at her quickly before looking back at the road. "Please don't lose it on me right now. In a few weeks you can go crazy, but not now, okay?"

"I'm not crazy," Leah said. "It's just that when Bob told me he was leaving me I had some horrible thoughts. I wanted him to suffer. And then I came home and he was dead. And now, no sooner do I find out about Erika and want to give her what-for, then she turns up dead."

"So you think you're an ethnic version of Carrie?"

"This isn't funny, Sophie!" Leah pulled her newly highlighted hair back with a jerk of her hands. "Two people I was angry with are dead. Mama always told us that people thought our grandmother was a witch. Maybe we shouldn't have been so quick to laugh those stories off."

I took the Sixth Street exit and drove through downtown. "If every person you disliked automatically died from violent causes, Cheryl would be decapitated, our elementary school music teacher would be stabbed to death, and every hardcore Raiders fan would be lying at the bottom of some river."

"You have a point." She looked over at me, a slight smile playing on her lips. "And you're still alive, so my powers must not be *that* strong."

"Yeah, but I'm invincible. After the nuclear holocaust, it's gonna be me, Cher and the cockroaches."

Leah laughed, but the tone was a tad on the hysterical side. I gave her a sidelong glance and some of my anger melted away. Reaching over, I put my hand over hers and gave it a gentle squeeze. "I know what you're feeling but I need you to suppress it for a few hours. If you can pull it together, I would like to take you to Redwood. They should be busy tonight."

Leah stopped laughing and shot me a look of disbelief. "We just found the dead body of my late husband's mistress, and you want to go clubbing?"

"It's a bar, not a club. I think I can get some of the employees and patrons to remember us without being able to recall exactly what time they saw us or be able to swear to how long we were there. It's a weak alibi, but it's better than none."

"I can't go to some trendy bar right after losing my husband!" Leah said, suddenly concerned about her image. "I didn't even go to bars when he was alive! No one will believe it!"

"Is there anyone who would have believed that you would go and buy yourself a skintight leather skirt?"

Leah took a moment before answering. "Do you think we'll find street parking?"

We did end up going to Redwood. Leah managed to pull off the role of the depressed widow being dragged to bars by her well-meaning sister. That didn't exactly make her Meryl Streep, but it did help us to establish an alibi without making it appear that she was celebrating her hubby's sudden demise.

When we got home around midnight we found Anatoly sitting on my doorstep.

"Where have you two been? I've been trying to reach you for over three hours."

"Really?" I said, checking my watch. "I must not have heard my cell ring—we were at Redwood."

"Redwood—as in the forest?"

"As in the *bar*." I pulled out my keys, opened the door and ushered in Leah, who was studiously keeping her eyes on the ground.

"You took her to a bar?" Anatoly scooted in after us before I had a chance to close the door. "Are you trying to find a way to make the defense attorney's job a little more challenging, or are you both just insane?"

"I prefer the term *eccentric*." I looked over at Leah, who was now ringing her hands again. She was clearly having a flashback to our discovery earlier in the evening. I put a hand on her back and pushed her up the stairs. "I figured she might as well get some mileage out of her new look."

I opened the door to my apartment and let Leah in ahead of me, then stood in the door frame blocking Anatoly's admittance. "It was a bad idea," I confessed. "She had a miserable time and so did I. What we both really need is some shut-eye. Do you mind if we talk tomorrow?"

Anatoly didn't look very sympathetic to my fatigue. "Did you ask Leah about Erika?"

"No!" I said a little too adamantly. "I think we may have been wrong about that. Let's just keep our suspicions to ourselves…no need to smear Erika's reputation for no reason."

Anatoly's brow creased. "What's going on?"

"Nothing. Why would you ask?"

"You're keeping something from me."

I rolled my eyes. "Okay, you got me. I didn't have a horrible time at Redwood. It was actually fun. Are you happy now?"

Anatoly was beginning to look alarmed. "That was one of the worst lies you have ever told me."

I hesitated for a moment. "Was it the lie itself that was bad, or was the problem in the delivery?"

"Both, and it has been my experience that when pathological liars falter in their area of expertise, they are hiding something big."

I glanced back at Leah, who was sitting at the dining table with her head in her hands. "I did take her to Redwood," I said slowly. "We did have a horrible time and I do think that it's important that we keep our mouths shut about Erika. Now please, it's been a long night, so can't we just leave it at that?"

Anatoly opened his mouth to answer, but I put a finger to his lips. "Sometimes it's better not to know."

Anatoly looked conflicted as he studied me in the doorway. "You don't want me to go to the police with our suspicions about Erika."

"No."

"You don't want me to talk about it at all or even look into it."

"You're catching on fast."

"I don't like being kept in the dark, Sophie."

"Then you shouldn't come over to people's homes in the middle of the night." I glanced at the clock behind me. "Good night, Anatoly." I shut the door without waiting for him to walk away. I had dealt with enough for one evening. Anatoly was going to have to go on tomorrow's to-do list.

I had nightmares all night long about finding Erika. Every time I woke up in a cold sweat I would force myself to visualize something pleasant, like George Clooney. But when I closed my eyes again, it was Erika's prone body that I saw. At four o'clock I gave up on trying to focus on positive imagery and had a couple of shots of vodka to help me relax. The one thing about being a writer is that you don't have to wake up early in the morning to go to work. Of course, judging by my level of productivity lately, I didn't need to wake up at all. I went back to my bedroom and let my head sink back onto the pillow. I would first figure out everything for Leah, then I would be able to focus on the manuscript I was supposed to be working on. I felt the effects of the alcohol on my already tired mind. Everything would fall into place. But for the moment the only thing I needed to concentrate on was sleep.

Two hours later, Leah woke up. I know this because the clock read 6:05 a.m. when I awoke to find her shaking me. "Sophie, Sophie are you awake?"

"No."

"Sophie, the police aren't here."

I opened one eye. "Did you just say the police *aren't* here?"

"That's right."

"And you felt the need to wake me up and tell me this?" I propped myself up on one elbow. "You know who else isn't here? Johnny Depp. So now that we've finished stating the obvious, can I go back to sleep?"

"No."

"I hate you."

"*Why* haven't the police come to question us about Erika?" Leah asked. "Don't you think that I'll be a suspect?"

"Probably." I yawned. "But my guess is that we're the only ones who know she's dead."

Leah gasped. "You think she's just rotting away on her living room floor?"

"Well, I wouldn't have phrased it quite like that but…yes."

"How long will it take before someone else finds her?"

"What do I look like, Nostradamus? She won't come into work, she won't return her calls, and eventually someone will go check on her."

Leah shook her head. "I don't like this."

"Oh, really? Because I'm having the time of my life."

"There's no need to be sarcastic." Leah stood up and threw my robe on top of me. "Get up. I need to figure this all out before I have to pick up Jack."

I swung my legs over the side of the bed and pulled on the robe. "When do you plan on picking him up? Next year?"

"I'm serious, Sophie." Leah led me out of the room and into the kitchen, where I immediately made a grab for the coffee beans. "I'm tired of this cloak-and-dagger nonsense. I have things to do. I have a memorial service to plan, for God's sake. Do you think that's easy? It's like planning another wedding! And, well, Erika's not exactly around to help anymore—not that I would have let her, considering what I learned about her…."

"Mmm, so have you been interviewing photographers?" I ground the beans and threw them in the coffeemaker.

"What? No, but I am putting together an album documenting Bob's life. And I do need to start talking to caterers—"

"And coffee—if Bob's friends are going to be making speeches, you're going to need lots of coffee for the rest of us."

"And I know exactly where I want the service to be held," Leah continued, ignoring my thinly veiled insult. "And while I don't need to send out actual invitations, I do need to make sure that the word gets out to the right people."

I froze with my Brita pitcher poised over the coffeemaker. "Oh, my God, I just realized who the right people are."

"Well, it's not too difficult to figure out. There's the Cavlins and the VanSambes…."

"And the Whitmans, Leah. You can't forget Bianca Whitman."

Leah blanched. "You're not serious."

"Of course I'm serious." I absently poured the water into the coffeemaker as I planned our next move. "Bianca won't expect to be welcome there, so we'll have to tell her to come. Why don't I call her up right now and invite her to come on over for brunch?"

"Why don't you?" Leah mocked. "Other than the little

issue that she has completely dismantled my life, I don't have any real problem with her."

"Leah, don't you see? We'll invite her over to make it clear that while her actions were hurtful, we don't bear her any ill will. To further illustrate that, we'll ask her to come to the memorial service."

"Over my dead body."

"No, over Bob's. It's his memorial." I pulled a couple of mugs out of the cupboard and handed one to Leah. "Then, while she's here, we'll subtly inquire about her whereabouts last night."

Leah gasped. "You think she's the one who killed Erika! She must have found out that she wasn't his only mistress and lost it, why didn't I see it before?"

"At this point I'm not sure I care all that much who killed Erika, as long as *we're* not blamed." I leaned my back against the cream-colored tiles of the counter. "It's possible Bianca didn't know about Erika, but it's just as possible that she did, and if she doesn't have an alibi, then the police will have to look at her."

"That's assuming the police find out about Erika's affair with Bob."

"And if they don't, all the better." I shrugged and watched as the coffee drizzled into the coffeepot. "Then they won't be able to come up with a motive for you at all. The point is that if we make nicey-nice with Bianca, then we could get some useful information out of her, her bulldog of a sister might lighten up a bit, *and* you won't look like a jealous, vindictive wife who is capable of murder."

Leah pressed her lips together and looked down at her empty cup. "Fine, I'll invite her to the service. But she can't sit in the front row and she can't stand up to speak." She peered up at me. "I already shared my husband with her, and I'll be damned if I'm going to share the spotlight."

★ ★ ★

I waited until 9:00 a.m. to call Bianca, and as it turned out, my timing was impeccable. Porsha had stepped out for a morning jog, so no one was there to tell Bianca that having a private breakfast with the woman believed to have killed her lover wasn't the most prudent thing a girl could do. Bianca had accepted my invitation to brunch without so much as a hesitation. Once again Bianca's naiveté didn't sit well with me. She just didn't seem to have the savvy or even the intelligence to pull off a murder without leaving mountains of evidence behind.

Leah was busy in the kitchen, muttering to herself like the schizophrenic housewife she had become. I sighed and leaned against the counter and watched as she chopped up some fresh fruit to place in what was quickly becoming an elaborate salad. "I don't get you. If you hate this woman so much, why are you going to all this trouble?"

"You want this to look good, right?" Leah turned away from the salad and started arranging the croissants, which she had picked up a half hour earlier, on what was apparently my "only presentable serving dish." "If she's as polished as you say she is, she'd suspect something the minute we put an onion bagel and smoked salmon on the table. Honestly, who wouldn't?"

"Me?" I looked behind me to examine the perfectly set dining table. "So are you saying that if we serve her croissants on good china, she won't suspect that we're trying to poison her?"

"Yes, that's exactly what I'm saying— Wait! No, I'm not trying to poison her!" Leah suddenly shot back. "Which is why… Besides, I'm serving Perrier as a beverage. Nobody poisons Perrier."

The buzzer went off, masking the groan that escaped my lips. Leah put the finishing touches on the meal and gave me a nod to indicate that I should press the intercom.

"Bianca?" I spoke her name with the most positive inflection I could muster.

"Porsha."

I pressed my forehead against the wall. "Porsha, will you be having breakfast with us, too?"

"Bianca's not coming."

Of course she wasn't. That would have made everything too easy. I jabbed my finger against the button to allow Porsha admittance into the building, while Leah wrinkled her brow in confusion. She was undoubtedly weighing her disappointment over not being able to show Bianca up with her gentile domesticity against the thrill of playing socialite with someone named Porsha.

Porsha managed not to make any noise as she climbed the stairs, despite the three-inch Manolo Blahniks she was wearing. She walked to my door but didn't step inside.

"I want you to know that I have informed the police of my whereabouts."

I couldn't help but grin. "And why is that? Are you on probation?"

"They know I'm here, so if I disappear, they'll know where to look."

"I'm not going to kill you, Porsha. I don't even want to see you. I only invited Bianca."

"*We* invited Bianca." Leah stepped forward and peeked over my shoulder. "I want her to know that I don't hold any resentment toward her. What's done is done and now we should all be focusing on our loss and our mutual love for *my* husband."

Now it was really hard not to laugh. Porsha, on the other hand, just looked sick. Albeit sick in a kind of powerhouse, sexy way. She was wearing a white dart-seamed top, paired with a navy knee-length skirt that was a little too tight to be considered conservative. She narrowed her eyes as she focused on Leah.

"So, you're the wife."

I looked back to see Leah nod uncertainly. "I'm sorry, but you are…"

"I'm Porsha Whitman, Bianca's sister and lawyer."

Leah's expression hardened and she took a step back. "Well, I suppose if I was going to extend my hospitality to your sister, I can certainly extend it to you." I could tell she was trying to sound polite, but her words sounded stilted and cold. "Would you like to come in for some croissants and Perrier?"

"Did you poison it?"

I shook my head. "Nobody poisons Perrier. Only the less expensive brands like Calistoga."

Porsha's chin jutted out but despite her obvious misgivings she stepped into my apartment. "What do you really want with my sister?"

"We wanted to feed her," I said, pulling out a chair at the dining table. "She's too thin."

"Apparently Bob didn't think so," Porsha remarked venomously.

Leah took in a sharp breath, and I bit into my lip. I really hated this woman.

"My husband," Leah said slowly, "clearly found your sister to be…amusing. I'm so disappointed that she won't be joining us. I do hope she didn't stay away because she felt ashamed or…cheap."

It was comebacks like that that made me proud to claim Leah as my sister.

"Bianca stayed away because I told her to," Porsha said. "If you have a message for her, you can give it to me."

"We wanted to invite her to Bob's memorial service," I said.

Porsha cocked her head to the side. "And why would you want to do that?"

"Because it's the polite thing to do." I smiled sweetly. "Didn't they teach you anything in finishing school?"

"Are you trying to prove to the police that you're not bitter?"

Damn it. Not only was she a bitch, but she was a smart bitch. Those were the worst kind. "We're not trying to prove anything to anyone," I lied. "We're honestly trying to do the right thing."

"I don't believe you."

I sighed and looked to Leah for help. She had more experience dealing with the Porshas of the world than I did.

Leah pulled out a chair. "I'm sorry you doubt us. Why don't we all talk about it over breakfast? I made a lovely fruit salad, so if you're worried about the calories in the croissants, there's an alternative." She looked pointedly at Porsha's skintight skirt.

Porsha sat down and crossed her arms in front of her. "I'll just have the Perrier."

Of all the things she could have done, refusing food that my sister had prepared specifically for her was the one thing most likely to set Leah off. I saw Leah's nostrils flare and quickly stood up and gave her a gentle shove toward the kitchen. "I'll have some fruit and a croissant," I called after Leah, as she rigidly walked into the kitchen to retrieve our food. I sat down again and smiled. "You know, I think I saw Bianca at Redwood last night."

"What's Redwood?" Porsha asked, her eyes following Leah's movements.

"A bar downtown. I'm sure it was her. She was wearing this cute little pink number—"

"Bianca was home all night."

"Are you sure? I could have sworn it was her."

"It wasn't."

"Oh." I leaned back in my chair and smiled as Leah returned to the table with our food and drinks. "In that case, did the two of you catch *Saturday Night Live?* I meant to tape it but—"

"I doubt Bianca watches anything that inane."

"You doubt it? Didn't you notice if she was watching television?"

"I was at the movies. However, I know my sister and she's not the type to watch late-night TV."

It took a huge effort to keep myself from breaking out into a grin. "So Bianca spent the night by herself, not watching *Saturday Night Live.*" I made eye contact with Leah, who looked incredibly relieved. "How lonely. Maybe if she would allow us to get to know her, we could provide comfort to one another."

"She has friends for that," Porsha said.

I poured myself some of the cyanide-free sparkling water. "So what movie did you see?"

"Why are you so interested in where Bianca and I were last night?"

I shrugged dismissively. "I'm not. I was just trying to make conversation."

"I have no interest in conversing with either of you." Porsha stood up. "I came over to find out what you were up to and to tell you to stay the hell away from my family. If you don't, I'll make sure you'll regret it."

I smiled. "Are you threatening us? My, my, how...*violent* of you."

"I'm not the murderer here."

"If you say so." I tore off the end of my croissant and popped it into my mouth.

"Porsha," Leah said sweetly, "why does Bianca need a lawyer? I hope she's not in any kind of trouble."

"She needs someone to give her legal advice so she's better equipped to keep psychotics like you at bay."

"Are you a criminal defense attorney?" Leah asked, her voice dripping honey.

Porsha shifted her weight from one foot to the other and

looked toward the door. "No, that's not my area of expertise." She walked briskly toward the front door. "Don't call my sister again or I'll get a restraining order."

"Oh, give me a break," I called after her. "You can't get a restraining order just because we invited her to breakfast. I would think a lawyer would know that. What kind of law do you practice again?"

"That's none of your business," she said as she exited my apartment.

I jumped up and ran after her. "Oh, come on, give me a hint." I leaned over the banister as Porsha started down the stairwell. "Civil? Personal injury?"

"Go to hell," she shouted back, and then stopped as she realized that her path was being blocked by Anatoly.

"Anatoly!" I said warmly. "You're just in time. Porsha was just about to tell us that she's an ambulance chaser."

"The hell I was!" Porsha craned her neck up to look at me. "I'll have you know I practice family law!"

"You're a divorce lawyer?" I laughed. "Well, that's perfect. If Bob hadn't died, you could have represented Leah."

"What are you doing here, Porsha?" Anatoly asked in a voice that I found to be entirely too warm. "Has something happened?"

"These harpies tried to lure my sister here under the pretense of wanting to treat her to tea and crumpets!"

Anatoly's eyes traveled up to me. "Tea and crumpets?"

"They were croissants!" Leah screamed from inside the apartment.

"I'm done here." Porsha pushed past Anatoly and swiftly walked the rest of the way down the stairs.

Anatoly turned to watch her go before coming up. "It's really amazing," he said as he walked back inside with me. "I have never seen two women conduct themselves so poorly during a murder investigation."

"There is nothing sinister about croissants," Leah said, glaring at the food in front of her. "I can't believe she had the nerve to leave without eating one."

"Yes," Anatoly said, "clearly that's the important issue here." He sat down in Porsha's vacated chair and dumped some fruit salad on her empty plate. "I showed Taylor's picture to a few employees at the Gatsby. She was definitely the woman who was seen there with Bob."

"Bob would never have slept with Taylor," Leah said.

"Maybe not, but he took her to the hotel, and that can only help us redirect the police's attention away from you." He pierced a strawberry with his fork. "It would be even more helpful if we could show that he was having additional affairs."

"Anatoly," I said in a warning voice.

"Did Sophie talk to you about that possibility?" Anatoly continued, ignoring me.

Leah looked up to meet my eyes. "She told me about your suspicions regarding Taylor, but that's it."

"She didn't tell—"

Leah stood up abruptly. "I don't want to talk about this anymore." She threw her napkin down on the table and hurried down the hall to the guest room.

Anatoly turned to me. "What the hell is going on?"

"Well, it sounds to me like Taylor was shtooping my brother-in-law."

"That's not what I meant."

"Let's pretend it is." I sat down next to him. "So what's our next move?"

Anatoly shook his head in confusion. "Why are we avoiding the topic of Erika?"

I looked away and took a long drink.

Anatoly made a noise of frustration. "In that case, I think we should visit Taylor Blake and talk to her about the true nature of her relationship with Bob."

Spectacular. With my luck she'd be hanging from her showerhead. "Why don't we call first?"

Anatoly examined me carefully. "Are you trying to avoid a face-to-face confrontation?"

"It seems prudent."

"Now I know something's wrong."

"You know, maybe we *should* talk to Erika," I said slowly. "Why don't we pop in on her at work?"

"I thought that was precisely what you didn't want to do."

"I just don't want to spread rumors about something that may never have happened." I tore off another piece of croissant. "But if we just ask her directly while she's at work, then I suppose it won't do any harm."

Anatoly was watching me carefully. "It's not the kind of information most women would want to discuss at their place of business. Erika might be more forthcoming if we catch her at home."

The croissant caught in my throat and I had to make a grab for my drink to keep from choking. "You know, I'm not even sure where she lives. Besides, we might be able to find someone at Chalet who has information about Taylor. We could knock out two birds with one stone."

"Kill," he said. "You *kill* two birds with the stone."

"I'd really rather wound them."

Anatoly stared at me for what felt like an hour. "Fine," he said. "We'll go to Chalet."

We both stood up, but Anatoly grabbed my arm before I could go to tell Leah that we were leaving. "Sophie, I know we haven't always been honest with each other, but if you're in some kind of trouble you need to tell me. If I can, I'll help you."

"And if you can't?"

"I'll help you anyway."

I broke into my first real smile of the day. "Has anyone ever told you that you're a lamb in wolf's clothing?"

Anatoly grunted and released me. "I give up. Get your coat—we have an interview to get to."

CHAPTER 11

"You know how some people say that with every step forward they're forced to take five steps back?" he asked. "Well every time I try to move forward I inevitably step right off a cliff."

—*Words To Die By*

It took us a while to find out that Erika had been reassigned to James Sawyer's office and a lot less time to find out she hadn't shown up or called in. I made an effort to put on my best surprised face as James relayed the news.

"Has she done this before?" Anatoly asked, leaning against the desk that Erika had just begun to make her own.

"No, the reason I offered her the job as my assistant was that I knew I could count on her," James said. "I'm actually very worried."

"Has anyone called her?" I asked innocently.

"I've called several times but there's no answer. I'm at a loss as to what to do next."

Anatoly absently jotted something down on a Post-it on Erika's desk before stuffing it into the pocket of his jeans. "If you give us her address, we'd be happy to stop by her house and check on her."

"Unfortunately, I don't think we have the time." I kept my eyes glued on James so that I could better avoid Anatoly's questioning stare. "We have a pretty full day ahead of us. But as long as we're here, perhaps we could ask you about Bob's relationship with Taylor Blake."

"What exactly would you like to know?" James asked cautiously.

Anatoly shrugged, his eyes shifting from me back to the items decorating Erika's desk. "Were they just coworkers, or did they share a friendship?"

"We're all friends here at Chalet. We strive to maintain a warm, family atmosphere."

I resisted the temptation to puke and instead studied James's stance. He had shifted his weight back onto his heels and his arms were now crossed over his chest. He wasn't making eye contact with me or Anatoly.

"James," I said, in a purposely familiar tone, "Taylor and Bob were seen at Hotel Gatsby together on a few occasions. Why were they there?"

James's shoulders sagged. "Why don't you step into my office."

We followed him inside the double doors, which he quickly closed behind us. He gestured for Anatoly and me to use the two available leather upholstered chairs and sat down behind his desk. "I didn't want this to become public knowledge. It seems disrespectful of Bob's memory and it could only harm Taylor's flawless reputation as a businesswoman."

Anatoly's lips formed into a wry smile. "It's not going to look too good for Chalet, either."

"You must understand, as soon as I found out about them I pressured Taylor to resign her position," James said. "I gave her a stellar recommendation, of course—she deserves it. She was offered an executive position at JVW and will be starting there within the next few days. There's not a doubt in my mind that she'll be a major asset for them. But she broke company policy. We don't allow upper management to get romantically involved with those who report to us."

Anatoly crossed his ankle over his knee. "What exactly is the wording of your company policy?"

"It's very clear-cut," James explained. "Any romantic involvement with a coworker can result in immediate termination. Employees have to sign a document saying they understand that, among other things. So, as you can see, Taylor knew the risks."

"Your corporation seems to have some sexist leanings," Anatoly pointed out. "Why else would Taylor be asked to leave while Bob was offered a promotion?"

James's eyes narrowed. "If Bob had offered his resignation I would have been content to have Taylor stay. That didn't happen, and since Taylor was officially Bob's supervisor, it was her actions that left the company open for a possible sexual harassment suit. I assure you, sexism had nothing to do with it."

"No need to get defensive." Anatoly threw up his hands, as if to surrender the argument. "But hypothetically speaking, you could have fired both Taylor and Bob without the fear of legal repercussions. Bob *did* sign the same document."

James hesitated before nodding his agreement. "I could have gotten rid of both of them, but then I would have been left with a royal mess. Taylor and Bob were the two top executives in the financial department. To lose both of them at once would have been devastating for Chalet." A pained look crossed his features. "Unfortunately, that's exactly what ended up happening. Thank God our sales are strong, otherwise the stockholders would be fleeing in droves."

"How did Taylor react to your decision?" Anatoly asked.

"Taylor accepted her fate fairly graciously. Granted, she did contact me a few times after all was said and done in hopes that I might have changed my mind, but when she determined that I hadn't, she certainly didn't make a fuss. And as soon as she found out about Bob, she offered to come in a few times to help me figure out which of Bob's projects could be delegated to the rest of the accounting staff and which needed to be taken care of by me personally."

I wrinkled my nose. "That was excessively generous of her."

"I suspect Taylor is grateful to me for my discretion." James glanced at his watch. "She's due here any minute to go over a few things with me and the new comptroller one last time."

"If she did ask for her job back, would you give it to her?"

"Perhaps. Unfortunately, I think my chance at wooing her back has come and gone." James released a troubled sigh. "Normally, I don't like to rehire former employees, but as I said, it doesn't look good for a company that just went public to lose both its CFO and comptroller in the space of a month...." James's voice trailed off and, with a tired smile, he sat farther back in his chair. "I'm getting ahead of myself. Now that Taylor has another job she may not want to come back. She could simply be helping me today out of the goodness of her heart."

Anatoly nodded, although he didn't look all that convinced of Taylor's altruism. "Do you have any reason to believe Bob was carrying on with anyone else here? Perhaps someone who worked for him?"

I shot Anatoly a warning glance, but he ignored me.

"Of course not," James said. "Why do you ask?"

"Bob was a married man having an affair with his boss." Anatoly flicked a piece of lint off his jeans. "That had to speak to a certain moral flexibility that would lend itself to future misconduct."

"Now you sound like one of those right-wing puritans who made such an issue over Clinton's affair." James laughed as if he had just made a hilarious joke. "Bob had a weakness for women, but he learned from his mistake with Taylor. He was determined to keep his personal and professional life separate, and that's all that mattered to me. It was not my job to punish Bob for the questionable decisions he made with regard to his personal life. My job was to reward him for the good decisions he made at Chalet. If he had lived to fill the CFO position, it would have been his second promotion in as many years. You don't get that kind of advancement without being damn good at what you do. Taylor was a great worker but, truth be told, Bob was better."

"James? I—" Taylor stopped short as her eyes fell on Anatoly and me. "I didn't realize that you had company. You haven't forgotten our meeting, have you?"

Anatoly's mouth stretched into a satisfied smile and he stood up to face her. "Actually, Ms. Blake, we were just talking about you."

Taylor's posture stiffened. "Do I know you?"

"Taylor, this is Anatoly," James said. "He's a family friend of Bob's. He's also a private detective."

"I see." Her voice had a new edge to it. "Are you investigating something?"

James sighed and steepled his fingers. "Close the door, Taylor."

Taylor did so but didn't bother to enter the room.

"They're looking into Bob's murder," James said. "I know that every one of us wants to do whatever we can to bring his killer to justice. Unfortunately, that means a lot of things that we've been keeping under wraps are going to become exposed. Specifically your involvement with Bob."

If we had been in a 1950s sci-fi flick, laser beams would

have been shooting out of Taylor's pupils right now, vaporizing James in a flash of cheap special effects.

"I had to tell them, Taylor." James's voice rose to an almost whiny pitch. "A man is dead. Surely the search for his killer is more important than the secrecy surrounding your short-lived office romance."

"I trusted you—"

By the look on Taylor's face I'd say she was one step away from qualifying for a restraining order.

"You tossed me aside in order to accommodate that middle-class half-wit and yet I still agreed to come in here and clean up the mess he left behind."

"Taylor, I had to let you go. You *know* that." James's voice had gotten stronger but he had also slumped lower in his chair. "You knew the risk you were taking when you took up with Bob. You made the choice, and even after you left I kept my mouth shut—"

"Only because no one asked you the right questions," Taylor snapped.

I muffled a cough with my hand and Taylor started as if she had forgotten that I was there. She recovered quickly and rolled her shoulders back.

"I suppose you think you've found another suspect."

I shrugged. "If the silencer fits…"

"What?" James's Adam's apple did its bobbing thing a few more times. "You can't think that Taylor killed Bob!"

"Of course they do!" Taylor took three advancing steps toward his desk. "You just told them I had an affair with him and lost my job because of it!"

"But you would never do that." James quickly looked at Anatoly and me. "She would never do that," he repeated.

"And what makes you say that?" Anatoly asked.

"Because she's not a murderer. And…and…wait. She couldn't have done it." A relieved smile lit up James's face. "I

ran into her at the Grand Café the night Bob was killed. I
bought her dinner."

Anatoly turned his eyes to Taylor. "Is this true?"

"Yes, it's true." Taylor never looked away from James.

"And what time did this dinner take place?"

"I got there at around a quarter to seven and she was already there. She was about to dine alone at the bar, but I invited her to join me instead. So you see—Taylor couldn't
have killed Bob."

"When exactly did your affair with Bob end?" Anatoly
asked, apparently unfazed by Taylor's sudden alibi.

Taylor's eyes stayed locked on James, and she lifted her chin
a quarter of an inch. "The affair ended several months ago."

I tried to ignore the throbbing in my head. There
wasn't enough Valium in the world to prepare Leah for
this confession.

"When *exactly* did it end?" Anatoly asked smoothly.

"When," Taylor repeated. "I suppose it ended mid-
November. It was never serious."

"But you were still working together at that point."

"I just found out about it last month," James piped in. Taylor glared at him but didn't say anything.

"How did you find out?" I asked.

"I went to her office to go over some paperwork. She
wasn't there, but next to her wastebasket was a card."

"And you read it." Taylor's voice was cold and steady. "It
was a complete violation of my privacy."

"What did the card say?" Anatoly asked.

James sighed. "He wanted her back."

Anatoly was clearly listening to James, but he was watching Taylor, who remained by the door, radiating anger. "Is
that when James asked for your resignation?" he asked.

I saw Taylor wince. "It was for the best," she said testily. "I
don't like working for spineless chauvinistic pigs."

"Yeah." I nodded empathetically. "That's got to suck."

James cleared his throat awkwardly. "Well then, now that all this unsavory business has been discussed, I suppose it goes without saying that it would behoove all of us if this conversation stays within these walls."

I clasped my hands together and brought them under my chin. "I don't think that behooves me." I looked up at Anatoly. "Does it behoove you?"

Anatoly shook his head. "I'm not behooved."

"But what's the point of telling people about this?" James sat up, clearly alarmed. "You know that Taylor didn't kill Bob and this news will obviously upset Leah, not to mention our stockholders—"

"I understand you're angry," Taylor said, cutting James off and directing her words to me. The funny part was that she was the one who sounded pissed. "Try to understand—what Bob and I shared was meaningless. I was newly divorced and Bob was a comfort. But we were never in love. It was just an ill-conceived fling."

"Yes." I stood up to face her, although I was still forced to crane my neck to make eye contact. "It seems my brother-in-law's life consisted of one ill-conceived fling after another. What I don't understand is why *you* chose Bob. Did it ever occur to you that the man you were making love to was a simpering idiot? Or were you unable to reach that conclusion until the affair was over?"

Taylor's mouth twitched at the corners. "Like I said, I was just coming out of a relationship with another simpering idiot. I was simply sticking to what I knew."

James let out a forced laugh. "Very well, now that we have that straightened out, I would like to get back to the matter of discretion. Taylor made a mistake, but I fail to see that any real harm was done. No need to make things worse than they need to be."

Anatoly pulled his keys out of the pocket of his leather jacket and smiled at James. "You're right, there's no need to cause any more embarrassment to the family or Chalet." He put his hand on my back and began to guide me toward the door, but stopped before we got there. "As I said before, we would be happy to check on Erika if you don't mind giving us her address."

I felt the muscles in my neck tighten as I struggled to come up with a reason that we wouldn't be able to go on that particular errand.

James's brow creased and he rubbed the nonexistent stubble on his chin. "I'm really not supposed to give out the personal information of our employees, but I suppose in this case…"

"No, no," I said quickly. "We don't want you to break any rules on our behalf." I grabbed Anatoly's arm. "Come on, we have other stuff to do."

Anatoly frowned but allowed me to lead him out of the office. "Why don't you want to go to Erika's?" he asked when we got onto the elevator.

"She lives too far away." I jammed my finger against the button for the lobby a few times, although the elevator was already on its way down.

"Fine, don't tell me," Anatoly grumbled as the elevator doors opened to the bottom floor. "Let's try another question. If a man had done to you what it seems Bob did to Taylor, how would you feel?"

I smiled as we stepped out onto the windy streets and walked over to where he had parked his bike. "If it were me? I'd want to kill him."

He nodded and handed me a helmet. "My thoughts exactly."

"But James says she was with him."

"Yes, but he clearly likes Taylor, or maybe he just felt

guilty for exposing her. Either way, he has reason to cover for her."

I turned my face away from the wind. "Do you think Taylor and James are involved romantically?"

Anatoly sighed. "I didn't get that feeling from them. I know where you're going with this—you're thinking James could have killed Bob in a jealous rage, but the fact that he fired Taylor without firing Bob tells me that James isn't a man who would risk everything for the love of a woman."

"You're probably right," I admitted. "Taylor, on the other hand, may very well be guilty." I zipped up my leather jacket in preparation for the motorcycle ride ahead. "The problem is that if we go to the police with this and they question either James or Taylor, both are likely to deny it."

"Of course they will." Anatoly's lips curled into a sexy half smile. "That's where my spy stuff comes in." He reached into his pocket and pulled out a mini tape recorder.

"Anatoly," I breathed, "I do love it when you're devious."

We called the police station to ask for an immediate appointment with Lorenzo, but he was out of the office. The woman who I spoke with on the phone wouldn't say if he was out having lunch or on a case, which made it impossible for Anatoly or me to guess how long he'd be out of reach. So Anatoly and I decided to hold on to the tape until we could give it to him personally. I couldn't wait to see his expression when I destroyed his hopes for an open-and-shut case.

I had Anatoly drop me off at home and I bounded up the stairs to talk to Leah. I found her humming to herself while making chocolate chip cookies.

"You're in a good mood," I noted, hanging my purse in the hall before coming into the kitchen.

"I'm in a great mood!" Leah sang. "I got the most wonderful news today."

"Really? Do tell." I tried to stick my finger in the mixing bowl, but Leah slapped it away.

"That reporter Jerome called me this morning." She stopped stirring and grinned at me. "He wanted me to be the first to know that the Gatsby caved to public opinion and fired Cheryl. I called the hotel and confirmed it!" Leah clapped her hands together happily. "Tell me how great that is!"

"It's spectacular," I agreed. "Does this news somehow tie in to your urge to bake cookies?"

"I'm making them for the management at the Gatsby as a little thank-you, and I think I'll make a few extra for the staff there since they're the ones who had to put up with her all these years."

"They're probably planning a party." I peered into the silver bowl. "Well, I have news, too, but if you want to hear it it'll cost you a dough ball."

"You're not supposed to eat food that has raw eggs in it— it could give you salmonella or something."

I shrugged dismissively and held my index finger above the bowl in preparation. "I like to live dangerously."

Leah sighed and motioned for me to help myself, which I eagerly did. I let the mixture of flour, butter and sugar melt in my mouth while I figured out how to present everything to her in the most positive light. "You might want to sit, because this is pretty big." I waited, but Leah remained standing. I took a little more dough and continued. "Taylor Blake has admitted to sleeping with your husband, and I have it on tape!" I threw my arms out in a *ta-da*-like motion.

Leah stood completely still and stared at me. "But…but there's no way. He couldn't have."

"Oh, but he did," I said. "Anatoly has the tape, and as soon as Lorenzo gets back to his office, I'm going to hand him another suspect that he can't ignore. This could be your reasonable doubt, Leah!"

Leah blinked, and then slumped against the counter.

I dropped my arms. "You're not happy."

"I liked my news better." She absently ran her dough-caked fingers through her hair. "I just don't understand it. Taylor isn't Bob's type at all!"

"Leah, maybe you didn't know Bob's type." I looked down at the floor. "Maybe you didn't know Bob."

I peeked up at her and noted the beginning of tears in the corners of her eyes. I reached out to her, but my gesture was interrupted by the sound of a buzzer.

"It's probably Anatoly." I went over to the intercom. *"Hola, como se llama?"*

"Me llamo Detective Lorenzo."

I stepped back from the intercom. Had the people at the station told him I called? But even if they had, why would he come here? I pushed the intercom button again. "Just a minute." I went into the kitchen. "Okay, Leah, step away from the mixing bowl and get out that photo album you've been working on—you know, the one featuring Bob in all the stages of his miserable life. That way you'll come across as bereaved."

"But what about the cookies?"

"We'll just say that I was making them." The buzzer went off again. I threw a dishtowel at Leah. "Come on now, wipe off your hands and get the pictures. Hurry."

I went back to the intercom. "Do you want me to come down or do you want to come up?"

"I want to come up—now."

I looked over my shoulder. Leah had pulled out her album, along with a Tupperware container full of pictures, and was tossing them around her to look as if she had recently been sorting through them.

"Okay, I'll buzz you in," I sang.

Seconds after pressing the button, Lorenzo was up the stairs and standing in front of me. "Hello, Ms. Katz. Am I mistaken or were you stalling before letting me in?"

"Oh, I'm sorry about that. I have a horrible habit of stalling whenever an obnoxious person asks to see me. I've got to work on that."

Lorenzo smiled and stepped inside my apartment. He nodded at Leah, and then at the sarongs still hanging on the wall. "I don't think you had those up last time I was here."

I had forgotten that Lorenzo had been here before, way back before Bob had died and I was mixed up in an entirely different murder investigation. Actually I hadn't so much forgotten as I had purposely suppressed the memory. I followed Lorenzo's gaze to my carefully covered mirrors. "It's part of sitting shiva," I said. "This is how Jews mourn the loss of loved ones."

"Is that so?"

"Yep, we hang sarongs over the mirrors."

Lorenzo nodded as if he had heard this before.

"Leah's been putting together a photo album with all her favorite pictures of Bob." I pointed to the pictures scattered about.

"Great. Mind if I sit?" he asked after making himself comfortable in a dining room chair.

I took a seat opposite him. "Did the guys at the station tell you Anatoly called?"

"I got the message," Lorenzo said. His eyes never left mine. I was being studied but I couldn't put my finger on why.

"Anatoly and I had a little talk with Taylor Blake today— that would be the former CFO at Chalet.com."

"Really?" Lorenzo's voice didn't hint at any interest.

"Yep," I said, forcing myself to keep my rising nervousness under control. "It seems that Taylor had a thing for her subordinates. One subordinate in particular. I don't suppose you'd like to guess who that was, would you?"

"If I answer correctly do I get a cigar?"

"No, but you might get a new suspect. She was sleeping with Bob."

Lorenzo lifted his chin. "And she admitted this?"

"Yep."

"And how does this give me a new suspect?"

"What do you mean, how?" I fell back in my chair, confused. "She had an affair with Bob, her boss found out and asked for her resignation—and guess who was offered her job as soon as she relented and quit?"

"I feel certain that you're going to tell me."

"Damn right! The job was offered to Bob! He screwed her, both literally and figuratively. Now tell me that doesn't give you the perfect motive for murder."

"Do you have any evidence of this?"

"Ah." I shook my finger at him teasingly. I was feeling less nervous now that I was about to play my trump card. "You think that this is all hearsay. You think that if you ask Taylor about any of this, she'll deny it and you'll be back to square one."

"I wouldn't say I'm exactly at square one." Lorenzo's eyes traveled to Leah, who was hunched over a photograph of Bob standing in front of a Dairy Queen.

"Whatever. It just so happens I have the best evidence of all. I have Taylor's confession on tape. Anatoly recorded the whole thing."

Lorenzo shook his head. "I hate it when PIs take it upon themselves to do things like that."

"You just hate being wrong."

"No, my main goal is to find the person responsible for killing Bob Miller. Whomever that person may be." His eyes went back to Leah. "I would be very interested in hearing that tape."

I stood up. "I'll call Anatoly right now and ask him to bring it over."

Lorenzo held up his hand to stop me. "Before we do that, let me ask you a question—when's the last time you talked to Erika Wong?"

The nervousness came back with a whole new force. "Erika?" I repeated. "I don't know. Leah, how long has it been since we've seen Erika?"

Leah and I had practiced for this. She looked up from her pictures and chewed on her lower lip while I fixed Lorenzo with an inquisitive stare.

"I haven't talked to her in days," Leah said truthfully. Of course we had *seen* her last night but she hadn't been talking. "Why? Is there something wrong?"

"How many days precisely?" Lorenzo pulled out his handy notebook without bothering to answer Leah's question.

I couldn't help but note that he hadn't pulled it out when I was giving him the information about Taylor.

"Um, I don't know…." Leah pressed her hands together as she struggled to answer Lorenzo's question. "Before Bob's—before I found him." She looked down at the pictures and swallowed hard. "I had spoken to her that morning. I wanted her to help me figure out a way to win him back. She was so kind and…" Her voice trailed off and she looked away as if to hide her tears.

"I've spoken to Erika since then—a few times," I volunteered. "I went by her work to ask her to help with the memorial service, and she called me two days ago and asked if I could pick up Bob's personal effects."

"Did you?" Lorenzo asked without looking up from his notebook.

"Mmm-hmm, it was just a bunch of photos and stuff." I pointed at the large black album that Leah had begun. "I think Leah's put some of them in there."

"How did she seem?"

"Who? Erika? I don't know, tired, maybe a little stressed.

She asked after Leah. The two of them are friends—isn't that right, Leah?"

Leah nodded but didn't look up.

"Did she talk about anything else?"

"Not much," I said. "James Sawyer and Taylor were there. She made some comments after they left that implied that she had a problem with Taylor. Detective Lorenzo, do you mind telling me what this is all about?"

"What was her problem with Taylor?"

I desperately wanted to look to Leah to see her reaction, but I didn't dare. It would be great if Lorenzo thought Taylor was jealous of Erika. That would give her a motive in both murders. On the other hand, if I let on that I suspected Erika was romantically involved with Bob, Lorenzo would assume that I had shared those observations with Leah, which would give her a motive, as well. I looked up at the ceiling as if trying to recall the conversation that was so fresh in my mind.

"I think she said something about—"

The buzzer rang again, giving new meaning to the expression "saved by the bell." I flashed Lorenzo a grin that I hoped looked more apologetic than relieved. "Excuse me for a moment." I walked over to the intercom. "Who's there?"

"It's me." I felt myself brighten at the sound of Anatoly's voice, although there wasn't a lot he could do for me at the moment. I just wanted him there to lean on. I quickly pressed the buzzer, then I heard his footsteps as he climbed the stairs.

When he arrived he paused inside the foyer the moment he spotted Lorenzo in the living room.

Lorenzo stood up in greeting. "I got a message that you wanted to see me."

"Right," Anatoly said, as if Lorenzo's statement somehow explained his presence in my apartment. "There was some information that I wanted to share with you. Sophie and I spoke with Taylor Blake and James Sawyer." He stepped inside and leaned his shoulder against the wall.

Lorenzo nodded. "Yes, Sophie's told me all about it. She also told me you have a tape."

Anatoly shifted his weight. "Uh, yes…or at least that was my intention."

My head snapped in his direction. "Your *intention?* What do you mean 'your intention'?"

Anatoly stuffed his hands in his pocket and looked out the windows. "It didn't work. There's something wrong with my tape recorder."

I shook my head, unwilling to accept what I was hearing. "Maybe it recorded the conversation but it just won't play it back. Did you try another tape player?"

The expression on Anatoly's face told me he had. Lorenzo let out a heavy sigh.

"But I don't get it! Tape recorders don't just break for no reason. What the hell's wrong with it?"

Anatoly's chin was jutting out a bit now, but I was pretty sure that the anger he was feeling was directed at himself rather than me for once. "I think it needs batteries."

Lorenzo started laughing so hard I thought he was going to fall out of his chair. Leah kept her eyes on her pictures, but she seemed to be inadvertently crushing the one in her hand.

I sidled up to Anatoly. "You don't get to make cracks about my 'amateur' detective skills ever again," I said in a hushed voice.

Anatoly nodded solemnly.

"Well," Lorenzo said while wiping a few tears away, "thanks for the laugh. But when you came in, Sophie was just about to tell me why Erika Wong had a problem with Taylor."

Anatoly raised his eyebrows at me.

"I don't remember exactly what was said." I spoke

quickly, so Anatoly wouldn't have time to give away the fact that he knew about the true nature of Erika's relationship with her boss. "Just that Erika didn't think Taylor was very nice to her employees and she kind of implied that Taylor used to have Bob wrapped around her finger."

"Is that where you got the idea that Taylor was involved with Bob romantically?" Lorenzo asked.

"Yes," I said firmly, "that and the fact that she's been seen with him at the Gatsby. Erika said Taylor used her influence on Bob to manipulate him. She didn't offer any details and I didn't ask."

"You didn't ask." Lorenzo looked up from his notebook. "That seems odd to me, since you've been so intent on launching your own personal investigation into this case."

"At the time it didn't seem relevant," I said, immediately defensive. "It wasn't until I sat down with a cup of coffee and thought about it that I began to put the pieces together."

"Right." Lorenzo made another note.

"Detective Lorenzo." Leah gently put aside the photos that were covering her lap and pushed herself to a standing position. "You're beginning to scare me. Erika and I are close. Please tell me she's not in any kind of trouble."

I suppressed my surprise. That had been so perfectly executed! Leah had sounded concerned and poised—not manic at all. Even Anatoly looked convinced.

Lorenzo straightened in his chair and studied her face. "Mrs. Miller, have you ever known Erika to use drugs?"

"Drugs?" Leah blinked and looked at me. It wasn't the question we were expecting. "She gave herself insulin shots to control her diabetes, if that's what you mean. And she had a heart murmur, I know she takes something for that."

"Actually I was thinking of illegal narcotics."

"No!" Leah took a step back as if the question had been a physical blow. "Well, I've always been a perfect friend to her but I suppose it's possible she was keeping secrets from me."

"Leah's a strong advocate for the 'just say no' movement," I explained, and shot Leah a warning look.

"So you think it's possible that she was doing drugs and not telling anyone about it." Lorenzo made another note in his book. "Has her behavior changed at all lately?"

I looked at the floor to avoid revealing my rising level of panic. Everything depended on how Leah responded to Lorenzo's questions.

There was a long silence before she finally answered. "I'm searching my brain for any signs, but for the life of me I can't think of one."

I bit my lip to suppress a sigh of relief.

"No weight gain or loss?"

Leah shook her head.

"Did she seem paranoid at all?" Lorenzo pressed. "Maybe she seemed a bit anxious or jittery?"

Anatoly pushed himself off the wall so that he was standing in a more erect position. "Do you suspect she's doing cocaine?"

"You've got to be kidding me!" I tried to visualize Erika wearing one of her homemade crocheted sweaters and snorting coke in the bathroom of Chalet. The image wouldn't come.

"I can't take this anymore." Leah stomped her foot against the hardwood. "Why are you here questioning us about Erika's possible drug use? What does this have to do with us or the death of my husband?"

Lorenzo fixed her with a steady gaze. "I hate to have to be the one to tell you this, but Erika is dead."

Here was the moment of truth. If Leah's reaction wasn't perfect, we were both in deep shit.

Her eyes widened and her color actually seemed to fade. "Dead," she repeated.

"One of her neighbors discovered her late this morning. It appears that she overdosed on cocaine."

"What?" I said again. Leah and I looked at each other in complete amazement. "You mean to tell me that Erika's been successfully hiding a cocaine addiction, only to up and overdose out of the blue?"

"Yes," Lorenzo said as he sat back in his chair, "it does seem peculiar. But there was no sign of forced entry or any other indication that her death was anything other than an overdose."

My mouth dropped open. Was he kidding? The door had been left open, the place had been ransacked…how many more signs did he need? Unless, of course, he was baiting me. I abruptly closed my mouth and lowered myself onto the armrest of the love seat. "I never would have thought Erika was the type," I said finally.

Leah was frozen in place, and for a second I thought she was returning to a catatonic state. She looked down at her hands that still clutched the picture of Bob at the DQ, rumpled as it now was. "I just…I just can't believe this." Her eyes met mine. "None of this makes sense."

Lorenzo was staring at her, his expression unreadable. "So you had no idea."

Leah shook her head furiously. "None. I would think that with all her health problems she would have had the common sense to stay away from drugs." She looked out the window as if she expected the incoming sunlight to illuminate things for her. "She always drank a little bit too much…but cocaine? That's just incredible."

"And when was the last time you saw her again?"

"Um…" Leah squeezed her eyes closed.

Only I knew the image she was trying to block out.

"It's been weeks—three weeks, I believe," she said.

"And where was that?"

"We had lunch at The Flower Market Cafe. Jack was spending the afternoon with my mother."

"When was the last time you were in her house?"

"Her house?" Leah was barely keeping it together. "I don't know…it's been a good year or so."

"I see." Lorenzo stood up. "Well again, I'm sorry for your loss." He slipped his notebook back in his pocket. "By the way, I like the new highlights."

Leah put her hand up to her hair self-consciously. "Sophie's friend Marcus gave them to me. He was trying to make me feel better."

"Did it work?"

"No."

"I see. This may seem like an odd request, but would it be all right if I took a strand of your hair?"

Anatoly stepped forward. "She doesn't have to give you a strand of her hair."

"Of course she doesn't need to," Lorenzo said smoothly. "I'm simply asking."

Leah looked to me and I shook my head.

"Let's not play games." Anatoly walked over to Leah and put his hand on her shoulder. "It's no secret Leah's a suspect in her husband's murder. She'd have to be stupid to hand over a piece of hair without consulting a lawyer."

Lorenzo smiled at Leah. "If you have nothing to hide there shouldn't be any problem with handing over a strand of your hair. If you're worried that it would somehow be used against you in your husband's murder case, you can rest assured it won't be. We know the two of you lived in the same house and we know you discovered the body. Your hair found at that crime scene proves nothing but that. So unless there's something else…something you don't want us to know, then there should be no reason not to give us a strand of hair."

Leah looked at me again, and then at Anatoly. Finally she cleared her throat. "I'm sorry, Detective, but I don't go around ripping my hair out for people for no reason." Stepping away from Anatoly, she beelined to the door and flung it open. "I believe we've answered all your questions, and after everything you've just told me, I would really like some time alone with my sister. So if you don't mind…"

Lorenzo nodded and walked toward the door, but hesitated when he was less than a foot away from Leah. "I must say, Mrs. Miller, I find your refusal…interesting." With that he walked out of my apartment, and Leah slammed the door after him.

I forced myself to peek over in Anatoly's direction. He was standing very still. His expression was completely emotionless, but for some reason I felt sure that he wanted to strangle me.

CHAPTER 12

"Lies have a habit of catching up with you, but the truth always gets you right away, so you tell me which is better."

—*Words To Die By*

Anatoly walked to the bay windows and looked out onto the street. "I'm guessing that you went to confront Erika, despite the fact that I warned you not to, and in doing so stumbled across her dead body."

Leah let out a little squeak of affirmation.

"So neither of you killed her?"

"No!" Leah and I said in unison.

Anatoly sighed. "I didn't think so, but I thought I should ask."

"But here's the thing," I said while I allowed myself to slide from the armrest of the love seat to the cushions. "Lorenzo was either baiting us or something really weird is going on. When Leah and I discovered Erika, there were signs of forced entry all over the place. Someone had been through her desk, torn apart her furniture, the works. There's no way that was a simple overdose."

Anatoly tapped his fingers against the glass. "Lorenzo agrees with you. If he didn't think Erika's death was a homicide, he wouldn't be questioning us. But my gut tells me he wasn't lying about there being no signs of forced entry."

"So, what are you saying?" I asked. "That he's either stupid or blind?"

"I'm saying that someone cleaned up the crime scene before the police got there."

My mind flashed to that feeling I had back at Erika's house—the feeling that Leah and I were not alone. "Okay," I said quietly, "I'm officially freaking out now."

"*You're* freaking out?" Leah let out something that vaguely resembled a laugh. "My husband and one of his many mistresses are dead, and the police were just here asking for a strand of my hair!"

Anatoly turned and glared at us. "This wouldn't be a problem if you two had just been up-front with me earlier. We could have come up with a story about you guys paying Erika a visit a week or so ago. Then any DNA evidence the police came across could easily have been dismissed as coincidental."

I pulled nervously on the edge of my sleeve. "I hadn't thought of that."

"I was under the impression that you were paying me to be on your side," Anatoly continued. "How can I help you if you both refuse to be honest with me?"

"Well, I'm sorry if we didn't handle things the way you would have liked us to, but I don't know how I'm supposed to act on a day-to-day basis!" Leah put her hands on her hips. "Do I talk to the press or do I avoid them? Do I go to Bob's church and light a candle for him or do I cover my mirrors with sarongs like some kind of Hebrew Hawaiian freak? And now you want me to know automatically how to behave after finding some dead Jezebel lying in a pool of her own vomit? They didn't exactly cover that one in last month's issue of *Good Housekeeping!*"

"Okay." I held up my hands in a request for peace. "It's obvious that everyone's feeling a little overwrought and over-tired. I think we all know what this situation calls for."

Anatoly looked away and Leah stared up at the ceiling. "Please don't say it," she moaned.

"I'm sorry but I think I have to. This moment requires Starbucks." I put my hand over my heart and assumed an overly dramatic tone. "Yes, there are people who would call me a sell-out for my refusal to boycott every national chain that has the audacity to be profitable but those people don't appreciate the pleasures of corporate decadence. Particularly when the corporate decadence is blended up in a cup and topped with a generous amount of whipped cream."

Leah scoffed. "If they ever create a twelve-step program for Starbuck addicts, I'm signing you up."

Twenty minutes later we were all seated around a small round table with our beverages in hand and I was feeling better with each sip of whipped cream. However, it was clear that my companions were having a harder time getting into the caffeinated spirit.

"You two still look depressed," I noted.

Anatoly swished his cappuccino around in his mouth before answering. "I think it's safe to say that our somber mood is related to all the killing that has been taking place recently."

I looked down at my drink. "Well, I'm going to go with the cup's-half-full view of things."

Leah narrowed her eyes. "How can you say our cup is anything but drained?"

"Well." I racked my brain for a silver lining. "At least the murderer is only killing people we dislike. It doesn't make the crimes less repugnant, but you must admit it's an improvement over the last murderer I had to deal with."

Leah's mouth dropped open. "My God, you've become a sociopath. I have a sociopathic sister. Can my life get any worse?"

The image of Erika lying dead on the floor flashed before my eyes and I was suddenly overcome with a fresh sense of angst and fear. I shook my head fiercely and forced myself to think happy thoughts—like running my hand up and down Anatoly's thigh while sipping an Irish coffee. I closed my eyes and tried to make the image clearer in my mind.

"It's not that I'm without empathy—I'm just very good at avoidance and denial."

"Disliking a murder victim is only a good thing if you are beyond suspicion," Anatoly pointed out, "and neither of you has that advantage."

"I liked Erika," Leah said softly. "She was always sweet to me. I think I liked her even more than I liked Bob."

I did my best to look surprised.

"You know, with everything that's happened I can't muster up any anger for either of them," Leah said, toying with the top button on her silk blouse. "Erika and I were friends. I actually thought she looked up to me. She always made a point to remind Bob of my birthday or our anniversary. I'm sure she picked out most of the gifts Bob gave me, too. Now I know those gifts were given out of guilt. Not even Bob's guilt, but hers!" Leah pounded her fist against the table. "He couldn't even take the time to relieve his own damn conscience—he had to have his mistress do it for him!"

Anatoly smiled wryly. "Well, at least you're not angry about it."

"You know," I said, "the police would have another suspect if a certain detective had remembered to *put batteries in his tape recorder.*"

I heard the hiss of the air Anatoly sucked in through his clenched teeth. "I made a mistake. There will be other opportunities."

"Oh, really?" I cocked my head in his direction. "You don't think Taylor will get suspicious if we ask her to repeat everything she said to us during our last conversation? While we're at it, we should ask her to confess to both Erika's and Bob's murder. I'm sure she'll be obliging—"

"Hello, darlings."

I looked up to see Marcus. On his arm was a sweet young thing with a head of jet-black curls. He looked a lot closer to his teens than his thirties.

"Hey, sweetie," I said, forcing myself to let go of my frustration long enough to offer Marcus a smile. "What are you doing in this neck of the woods?"

"Looking for you, of course." Marcus pulled up a couple of extra chairs and squeezed them between me and Leah. "I tried your house, and when you weren't there I figured I'd try your place of worship."

I giggled and looked over at Marcus's companion, who had chosen the seat nearest Leah. In fact, he couldn't seem to take his eyes off of her. "Marcus, are you going to introduce us?"

"Of course. Leah and everyone, this is Charlie. Charlie, this is everyone and Leah." He smiled at my sister and said, "Charlie's your biggest fan."

"My…fan?" Leah said warily.

"Yes, ohmygawd, I love you!" Charlie put a hand on his chest for emphasis. "I've been totally following your whole case. I saw you do that little black pride thing in front of the police station—that was perfect. You are such a diva."

Anatoly shook his head and stared into his drink, and Leah shifted in her seat uncomfortably. "Thank you, I never really thought of myself as a diva…" A little spark flashed in her eyes. "I *could* be a diva, though." She reached across the table and grabbed my hand. "Maybe that's what I should do! Everyone in San Francisco loves divas."

"Totally," Charlie agreed enthusiastically.

Marcus smiled and leaned back in his seat. "Charlie and I met last night at Café Fleur."

Charlie nodded. "Marcus is a Leo and I'm a Pisces." He clasped his hands together and gave Marcus a dreamy smile. "Fire and water, a perfect balance. How could we not hook up?"

Marcus sighed dramatically. "Yes, I believe it was fate that brought us to the men's room at the same time." He pulled a couple of fives out of his wallet. "Charlie, why don't you get us a few grande machiatos?" He put his hand on his flat stomach. "Make mine nonfat—I wouldn't want to overindulge right before fleet week."

Charlie nodded obediently and gave Marcus a kiss on the cheek before he went off to fetch their treats.

"He's cute," I noted. "Kind of subservient, though."

"Yes, and I'm so the alpha male." Marcus laughed. "He's probably nothing more than short-term fling material but he does have some intriguing qualities."

I eyed Marcus curiously. "Such as?"

"His job at the Gatsby for one. He works in Room Service." Marcus waved a finger at Leah. "You said that Cheryl and Bob never spoke, but my boy Charlie spotted them at the Tonga Room having a little after-work powwow."

Now even Anatoly looked interested. "What were they talking about?"

"I'm not entirely sure. What grabbed me was that Charlie said the two of them seemed very nervous and conspiratorial. But I think Charlie had been popping pills shortly before we hooked up, because, out of the blue he went all 'Age of Aquarius' on me and I couldn't make heads or tails out of what he was saying. I figured you and Sophie might get more out of him with your little Sherlock-and-Watson thing."

"You dragged him over here just because you thought he might know something that could help me?" Leah beamed. "That is so thoughtful of you! Isn't that thoughtful, Sophie?"

I smiled genuinely at Marcus. "You're a regular Mother Theresa."

"Mmm, never been a big fan of hers." Marcus twisted one of his short dreadlocks. "Sure she helped a lot of kids and stuff, but so did Princess Di and *she* did it in Valentino." He held his palms up to depict a scale. "Like Charlie said, it's all about balance."

Anatoly smiled as Charlie came back to our table. "So, Charlie, Marcus was just telling us that you know Cheryl from the Gatsby."

"Mmm-hmm." Charlie gave Marcus one of the two drinks he had purchased and put a scone down in front of his own seat. "Did he tell you the whole Bob story?"

"He started to," Leah said. "He mentioned you saw them at the Tonga Room."

Charlie nodded. "They were sitting at the bar together and I wasn't about to pass up the opportunity to give Scary Cherie a hard time."

"Scary Cherie?" Leah asked.

"It's a little nickname that some of us Gatsby folks gave to your sister-in-law."

Leah regarded him fondly. Clearly Charlie's distaste for Cheryl raised her opinion of him considerably.

"Anyhoo, I walked up to them and they were sitting there passing a note—"

"Excuse me?" I leaned forward. "They were doing what?"

"I know, it's weird. At first I thought Cheryl was the one giving the note, but as soon as I walked up, she pocketed it, so maybe she was on the receiving end."

"Did you see what it said?" Anatoly asked.

"She was too fast for me to see much, but I did get a glimpse of a name that was written on it—Maria E. Souza."

Leah wrinkled her brow. "That name means nothing to me."

"Well, it meant something to me," Charlie said. "The Souzas are this cute little Brazilian couple with matching parrot tattoos. At the time they were honeymooning at the Gatsby. I should know since I was the one constantly bringing the oysters up to their room."

"Did you talk to them about the note?" Anatoly asked.

"Yes, Bob said the Souzas were acquaintances of his, and Cheryl was going to deliver a message to them. Of course, I didn't know what Bob's relationship was to Cheryl at the time—I just figured he was a poor bloke who suffered from a mental disability."

"You thought my husband was mentally disabled?"

Charlie shrugged sheepishly. "Why would a mentally sound person have drinks with Cheryl?"

Leah paused. "Good point. Continue."

"Well, the whole thing was just strange," Charlie continued. "Why not just call the hotel and talk to the Souzas? But Scary Cherie got all huffy about my intruding on her private time, and she and Bob picked up and left."

"This doesn't make sense," Leah said, pushing her hair behind her ears. "Bob doesn't know any cute Brazilians. Are you sure they weren't cute Germans? He knows lots of Germans."

"Oh, yeah." Marcus nodded solemnly. "People are always getting those Germans and Brazilians confused."

"I'm just saying that it doesn't make sense for Bob to be sending a note to a couple of Brazilians! And ones with parrot tattoos?" Leah rolled her eyes. "There's just no way he would have befriended people like that."

Anatoly sat back in his chair. "Other than the parrot tattoo, what did the woman look like?"

"Like I said, she was cute," Charlie looked at the ceiling as he conjured up the memory. "A little shorter than me—she was really feminine in a hip kind of way."

Anatoly nodded as if that meant something to him. "Did she spend all her time with the man she came with?"

"Not all of it… I remember seeing her in the restaurant eating alone. But that could have been a one-time deal. I just remember them because I like the sound of Portuguese. Even the name of the language has a certain style to it. Porchegēz." He rolled the *r* so that he sounded like an exaggerated Ricky Ricardo.

Leah turned to Anatoly. "I know where you're heading with this and you can stop right now. Bob was not romancing some neglected Portuguese tattooed lady."

"I never thought of that!" Charlie put his hand on his cheek. "What a little shit."

"Major understatement," I muttered.

"But the Souzas seemed like such nice people," Charlie continued. "They were at the hotel for at least a week, and every time I brought something up to them they took some time to chitchat with me. One night they tipped me fifty bucks—that's the other reason I remember them."

"Maybe her wealth was part of the attraction," I suggested. "That could be the common denominator that we're overlooking while comparing the women in Bob's harem."

"My husband did not have a harem! And he certainly wasn't some kind of male gold digger. After all, I didn't come from a lot of wealth, despite the nonsense Cheryl has been spewing."

I put my elbows on the table and leaned forward. "Maybe his taste for rich chicks is a recent phenomenon."

"And how would you explain his interest in his secretary?" Leah spat.

"I don't know…maybe Bob jumped into bed with Erika

in order to distract himself from his more important rela-
tionships with you and Bianca…maybe he was having a hard
time deciding if he should honor his marriage vows or pick
Bianca as his new life partner and he was just using Erika
as a…a…"

"A filibuster!" Marcus snapped his fingers in the air.
"Something to do in order to put off a vote!"

I gave Marcus an appreciative slap on the arm. "That's
good. Do you mind if I use that in one of my books?"

"Hello?" Leah brushed off the comforting hand that
Charlie had put on her shoulder and glared at Marcus and
me. "Are you two listening to yourselves?"

"What do you mean?" I asked.

"What she means," Anatoly said, "is that your theory
doesn't make any sense. People don't have affairs in order to
distract themselves from their other affairs. And Erika isn't
the only hole in your gold-digger theory."

"Oh, really," I said defensively. "And what's the other
problem?"

"If Bob was dating women for their money, why did he
spend all *his* money on those same women?"

"You got me there." I looked over at Leah. "Did you
guys take out a second mortgage on your house or something? I mean, how the hell was Bob able to buy Bianca a
fifty-thousand-dollar bracelet?"

Leah gasped. "*Fifty thousand dollars?* Are you sure?"

"I'm sorry, Leah—I forgot to tell you. Bianca let us know."

Leah put her head in her hands. "I can't believe this. No
wonder he balked when I said I wanted enhancements for
my birthday. He had already spent all his money on Bianca."

"Enhancements?" Charlie shook his head in confusion,
and Marcus just clucked his tongue.

Anatoly finished off the rest of his drink and focused on
Charlie. "Do you remember Maria's husband's name?"

"Yes, it was Mario, or maybe it was Pablo—I remember it sounded very Latin."

"Great," Anatoly muttered. "Do you think you could get me some more information about this Brazilian couple? Like a home address or a phone number?"

Charlie shook his head so hard I thought it might come off. "The Gatsby has very strict rules about protecting the privacy of its guests."

"Just a hometown, then," Anatoly coaxed. "No one will ever know."

"No, no way."

Charlie started to stand up, but Marcus gently pulled him back down. "You wouldn't need to break into the computer system," he said as he brushed a lock of hair away from Charlie's face. "You could just ask around. You said these Brazilians liked to schmooze with the staff, so they might have mentioned a hometown to someone, and if they were handing out Ulysses S. Grants like they were George Washingtons, people will remember them."

Charlie looked at Marcus uncertainly. "I guess I could ask around." He smiled at Leah. "It's the least I can do for my favorite diva."

"I can't tell you how much I would appreciate it." Leah beamed at him over her drink. "You're just—" Her voice trailed off as she searched for the vocabulary that would flesh out her diva image. "Fabulous," she said shyly. "You're absolutely fabulous!"

Anatoly and I dropped Leah off at my place a half hour before Mama was scheduled to bring Jack back. I suggested that the two of them spend some private mommy–child time together. I pretended that I was only thinking of the best interests of her and her son, but I'm pretty sure everyone saw through that facade. The truth was, I was desperate for some time *away* from my family. Anatoly and I walked down toward North Beach to hash things out.

"Do you think they have DNA evidence that could link Leah to Erika's death?" A light breeze caused goose bumps to materialize up my arms. "Is that why Lorenzo asked for one of her hairs?"

"If they had that kind of evidence, Lorenzo would have shown up with a warrant."

"Then why request a hair sample?"

"Either he's hoping to get that kind of evidence soon or he just wanted to see how she would react to the request." Anatoly stuffed his hands into his leather jacket.

"So maybe it was just a test." We paused for a bicycle to go by before crossing the street. "If that's the case, how do you think she scored?"

"Somewhere in the sixty-percent range."

"That means she got a *D*."

Anatoly shrugged. "Possibly a *D+*."

I stopped walking and looked up at the wispy white clouds that covered the sky. "What do we do now?"

"I still think our best bet is to try to offer the police as many suspects as possible. We need proof that Taylor was sleeping with Bob, and that she had reason to hate him."

"That's the nice thing about Bob and his sister," I said. "They're both so easy to hate."

Anatoly laughed. "I can see that."

"Well, as far as the suspect thing goes, I do have some good news." I started walking again and Anatoly quickly fell in step. "I tricked Porsha into admitting that Bianca didn't have an alibi for the night we found Erika. That's got to be helpful for us."

Anatoly creased his forehead. "You tricked Porsha? That couldn't have been easy."

"What is that supposed to mean?" I glared at him. "You

think Porsha's some kind of sexy female Einstein and I'm the frizzy-haired village idiot?"

Anatoly smiled. "No, I don't think Porsha's Einstein."

"Very cute. I'll have you know that not only did I trick Porsha into giving me the information about Bianca, but she's still none the wiser for it." I glanced at the Muni bus that was letting some of its passengers out in front of us. "But if Bianca or Taylor killed Erika, why did they search her place? Were they looking for the disk?"

"That would be my guess, but I'll be damned if I can figure out what they think is on it," Anatoly said. "We can't make that our focus, though. Let's just get the information that we need to prevent Leah from being arrested and leave the rest be." He glanced at his watch. "Speaking of which, we should talk to Cheryl again."

"You think the little tête-à-tête that Charlie walked in on is significant in some way?"

"Only one way to find out. Care to take a ride to Cow Hollow with me?"

"What the hell, I might as well put all my pent-up hostility to good use." I smiled at Anatoly. "Let's go nail her ass to the wall."

 **CHAPTER 13**

"I think I would like children better if they weren't so incredibly immature."

—*Words To Die By*

Unemployment didn't seem to be agreeing with Cheryl. Her hair was stringy and greasy, and there were dark circles under her eyes. She didn't even bother flirting with Anatoly as she wordlessly allowed us entrance into her apartment. Her place was suffering, too. It had gone from cluttered to downright messy. There were dirty dishes on the coffee table and nylons hanging from her chairs. Either Cheryl was severely depressed, or heroin chic had come back in a big way.

Anatoly and I waited for her to offer us a seat, and when she didn't, he pushed aside some clothes and made himself comfortable. I remained standing, not wanting to inadvertently sit on a leftover piece of pizza.

"We heard about what happened with your job," Anatoly said in a voice that oozed sympathy. "You must be incredibly upset."

Cheryl sank into the armchair behind her. "I didn't do anything wrong." Her eyes sparkled with tears.

Anatoly shook his head. "They didn't actually fire you over those innocent remarks you made about Leah, did they?"

By the blank look on Cheryl's face one would have thought she was having difficulty understanding the question.

"You think…" She faltered. Then she straightened her posture and used her sleeve to wipe away a tear. "That's not the reason the Gatsby gave, but yeah. They said I was late three times or something like that, but really it was about Leah. My brother gets killed and then I get fired for insulting his murderer." Her voice got stronger with each word. "It's so not fair. She's the one who killed him, not me. She did it."

Anatoly and I locked eyes. Something was off.

"Cheryl," Anatoly pressed gently. "Why didn't Bob listen to you when you told him how wrong Leah was for him? You're his sister. Surely he must have respected your opinion."

"Bob was never a good listener. Leah and Bob together were like—well, it was like that show *The Nanny*—you know, the one where Fran Drescher gets together with her boss?" Cheryl scornfully blew out a puff of air. "It never should have happened."

I wrinkled my nose. "They never should have gotten together?"

"No, I mean the whole show shouldn't have happened! It was a stupid premise and that's exactly what was wrong with Leah and Bob's marriage—the whole premise of their relationship was stupid."

"And what would that premise be?" Anatoly asked.

"Simple. Bob wanted someone who would play the role of a good corporate wife, and of all the women who auditioned for the part—and there weren't many—Leah did the best." Cheryl leaned farther back into the cushions. "What Bob never understood is that you don't marry a woman just so she can play second fiddle to your career. When you pick a spouse, you should think about who they know and where they come from. Anyone can be a housewife, but only a select few can get you into the right VIP rooms."

I stared at Cheryl, nearly speechless. "You are one of the most bizarre and twisted individuals I have ever met, and when you consider my list of acquaintances that's saying a lot."

"Don't talk to me about being twisted," she snapped. "I know you lied to me about that interview on *Channel Four.*"

"Oh, you figured that out, did you?"

Anatoly shot me another warning look. "Cheryl, did Bob ever introduce you to Taylor Blake?"

Some of the color drained from Cheryl's face. "I may have met her once or twice."

Anatoly leaned forward. "What about Maria E. Souza? Does that name ring a bell?"

"Maria E. Souza." Now Cheryl looked like she was going to run screaming from the room. "That does sound familiar—she was a friend of Bob's too, wasn't she?"

"You know the answer to that." Anatoly's tone, while still gentle, had become firm and confident. "We spoke to Taylor. She confessed to everything."

There was a scratching noise as Cheryl's nails scraped against the upholstery of her chair. "I didn't know Taylor had anything to confess to."

"You don't have to lie anymore, Cheryl," Anatoly said soothingly. "Everyone knows about the affair. Taylor even admitted to her rendezvous with Bob at the Gatsby."

Cheryl's mouth dropped open, giving her the look of an overwrought guppy. "Taylor admitted to having an affair with Bob? I can't believe that."

"It was going to come out sooner or later," Anatoly said, and crossed his ankle over his knee. "I understand why you would want to help Bob—he was your brother. But helping him required some bending of the rules, didn't it? For the women like Maria, there were husbands to consider. Did you let Bob know when Mr. Souza wasn't around? Did you act as a lookout person so that Bob and his mistresses didn't suffer any surprise interruptions?"

Cheryl's eyebrows drew together. "Wait a minute—"

"And then his relationship with Taylor presented its own unique problems. They wouldn't want to reserve a room under either of their names. Perhaps they wouldn't have wanted to reserve a room at all considering that neither of them planned to spend the night. Is that the real reason they fired you, Cheryl? Were you granting your brother unpaid access to the rooms?"

Cheryl stared at Anatoly, disbelief coloring her features. "Is that what you think?" She shot to her feet, her voice taking on a strangled quality. "That I was trying to turn Hotel Gatsby into my brother's personal whorehouse? Is that really what you both think?"

She turned her back on Anatoly and faced me. I looked at Anatoly, who was nodding his head furiously.

"Yes," I said slowly. "That is what I think." Actually the thought had never occurred to me. Why would Cheryl do something so stupid for a brother she didn't even care about?

"No one's judging you." Anatoly stood up and held his hands up for peace. "He was your brother and he was trapped in an unhappy marriage. Of course you would want to help him in any way you could."

Cheryl whirled back around to confront him. "I would never have allowed him to take advantage of me or the Gatsby in that way! Maybe I would have done it for someone like, I don't know…Matt Damon, but I would never bend the rules like that for someone as unimportant as my brother! What kind of person do you think I am?"

"How many times do I have to say it?" I said. "You're bizarre and twisted."

"Get out of my apartment."

"Cheryl, I don't want to accuse you unjustly," Anatoly said, "but that's what Taylor told us. Why would she lie?"

"I said *out!*"

"Okay, we'll leave." I stood up and smiled sweetly at Cheryl. "But you realize that the next person who's going to be kicked out of here is you. It's not like you're going to be able to afford the rent on a place like this anymore."

Cheryl took a step back. "What are you implying?"

"Isn't it obvious? Judging from the location and size of this apartment, I think it's safe to presume that an unemployment check isn't going to cover a lot more than your utilities."

Cheryl squeezed her eyes closed. "I want you out of here," she said quietly.

Anatoly nodded and gestured for me to follow him. The minute we stepped out into the hall, Cheryl slammed the door behind us. We listened to the clicks of the dead bolt and the chain lock being secured.

"Okay, so what the hell was that about?" I asked Anatoly as we walked down the stairs.

"I knew she would take offense at my accusation." On the main floor he pushed the heavy glass door of the lobby open and we stepped outside. "I was hoping that she might let something slip while defending her innocence."

"So you don't really think she was renting out the rooms at the Gatsby by the hour."

Anatoly chuckled. "I think it's improbable. It's more likely that she was allowing Taylor or Bob to check in under a pseudonym in exchange for a bribe of some kind."

"Well, she definitely knows more than she's letting on. Did you see her face when you mentioned Maria's and Taylor's names? Can you say *blanched*? She didn't want to go there at all." I shook my head. "I'm going back to my first theory. Cheryl's the guilty one."

"I'm beginning to think you might be right," Anatoly said. "But I still can't figure out what her motive would be." He scratched the light stubble on his chin. "Even if she was breaking the company rules for her brother, that, in and of itself, isn't a good reason to kill him."

I made a little dismissive sound as I zipped up my jacket. "Maybe she purchased one of Charlton Heston's old guns on eBay and she wanted to try it out," I said sarcastically.

"Somehow I doubt it," Anatoly said. "Besides, it's Bob's weapon that's gone missing." We paused in front of Anatoly's Harley and he handed me one of the helmets. "Do you think Bob would have told her where he kept his gun?"

"It's always possible." I put the helmet on and waited until Anatoly started up the bike before climbing on behind him. "Hey, maybe she has a thing for the host of *America's Most Wanted* and she thought killing her brother would get his attention."

Anatoly revved the engine and started down the street without answering.

"Anatoly?" I yelled. "Can you hear me?"

"I'm trying not to," he yelled back.

I rolled my eyes and wrapped my arms around him partly to help secure my position but mostly because I liked the way his abdominal muscles felt when I pressed my hands against them. I had no idea why Cheryl would want to see her brother dead, but if Little Miss Hollywood was responsible for setting my sister up for his murder, I'd make sure that the only stars she saw were the kind that appear after you've been knocked unconscious.

I was pretty good at keeping the image of Erika's lifeless body out of my conscious mind during the day, but lying in my bed that night I found that the visual came to me every time I closed my eyes. If that wasn't enough, I couldn't stop thinking about all the bizarre information regarding her cause of death. It wasn't until sometime after two o'clock in the morning that I fell asleep. As it turns out I didn't have to worry about dreaming, because beginning at 2:25 a.m. Jack started waking up every ten minutes. And just when I started to get used to the sounds of *his* screams, Leah would get frustrated with him and start screaming, too. At three I finally gave up and started working on my next manuscript. I had an idea for a storyline in which a mother forced her mentally unstable sister-in-law to babysit her son, thus driving her to take her own life.

It was approaching 6:00 a.m. when I finally got back in bed. I was able to sleep for another three and a half hours before Mr. Katz started kneading my pillowcase. I opened one eye and looked at him. "I suppose you want food," I muttered.

I interpreted my pet's angry expression as a yes. I crawled out of bed and stumbled down the hall. Leah was in the living room staring at five different outfits she had laid out on the couch.

"Hot date?" I asked as I went into the kitchen and retrieved the kibble.

"It's not exactly a date, just a first meeting."

"Wait a minute!" I rushed back into the living room, kibble in hand. "I was joking. You're not seriously thinking about going out on a date with everything that's going on in your life, are you?"

"No, of course not." Leah selected a navy blue sleeveless sweater and held it up against her torso. "I misspoke. What I meant was that I agreed to give an interview today. I thought it would be a good idea to tell my side of the story to the press."

"Oh...okaaay." I pivoted and went back to my chore of feeding the cat. "Who's the interview with?"

"The man from *Flavah* Magazine. Jerome."

I bit my lip as I felt the beginning of a headache come on. "I forgot that you had agreed to meet with him."

"I did, too. But he called this morning to confirm. He has such a nice deep voice. Do you think I should wear that plum sweater that Bob didn't like?"

"So you *do* like him!" I slammed my hand against the tile counter. "Damn it, Leah, this is not good!"

"I told you, it's just an interview." She opted for the sleeveless number instead, and picked a pair of brown cigarette pants to go with it. "You know, I've never been with a black guy before."

"Leah," I said in my best warning tone.

"I've dated Latinos before, and I went out with that Japanese guy in high school, but I never dated anyone of my own race. Why do you think that is?"

"I don't know. Can we examine this issue at a different time—say, after Bob's case has been closed?"

Leah smiled and came into the kitchen. "I swear on our father's memory that I will not so much as bat an eyelash at Jerome."

I let out a sigh. "Thank you."

"On one condition."

"One condition? Maybe you're not getting this, but you're the one facing prison time. You should be suppressing your urge to flirt with Jerome for your own sake!"

"It's just a small favor, Sophie."

I threw my hands up in defeat. "Fine, what is it?"

"I need you to babysit Jack today."

"In what universe is that a small favor?"

"Just while I'm talking to Jerome. He wants me to show him around my house so he can get a better sense of the kind of life I shared with Bob. It shouldn't take too long."

"You know the saying 'time flies when you're having fun'?" I asked. "Well, the reverse is true, too."

"Don't be selfish," Leah reprimanded. "Besides, you owe me."

"How do you figure?"

Leah took a step forward and looked me in the eye. "Three little words. *Barbie. Dream. House.*"

I closed my eyes. "Damn it, I knew that would come back to bite me."

Less than two hours later, I had drunk an entire pot of coffee and it still hadn't given me the lift necessary to deal with my now awake and inexplicably unhappy nephew. I bounced him up and down while pacing the living room singing every kids' song I could think of from "Rock-a-Bye Baby" to the theme song from *The Incredibles*. Jack was having none of it.

When the phone rang I shifted Jack to my right hip and tucked the receiver between my ear and shoulder. "Yes," I screamed, in hopes of making myself heard over Jack's howls.

"Hi, um, is Leah there?"

"Does it sound like the mother of this child is here?" I put Jack down on the floor, which just made him scream louder.

"Okay, I'm thinking this is a bad time."

"Wait, who is this?" I sat on the edge of the couch and desperately started sorting through Leah's diaper bag to find a magic toy to pacify Jack.

"It's Charlie…"

"Marcus's Charlie?"

"C'est moi."

"Oh, I'm so glad you called!" I found a small stuffed clown hiding under a supply of baby wipes and tossed it in Jack's direction. "Did you find anything out?"

"Sort of."

"Define 'sort of.'"

"Well, nobody remembers the name of the husband or what part of Brazil they were from. But Maria went to our day spa while she was staying here. Wendy, the masseuse who worked on her, remembers her."

"Sounds like you've got a knack for this detective stuff, Charlie." I started unzipping pockets in Leah's bag, looking for something more effective than the clown. There was a small outside pocket in which I found a supply of Leah's makeup. I put my hand over the mouthpiece of the receiver. "Here, Jack, try some Estée Lauder."

"Sophie? Are you still there?"

"I'm here." I glanced at Jack, who was showing a surprising interest in his mother's cosmetics, notably a shiny cylinder of lipstick. "Okay, so what did Wendy say about Maria?"

"Basically that Maria was one of those clients who liked to talk when she was supposed to be relaxing. She spent the whole time quizzing Wendy about San Francisco's hidden treasures—you know, the cool hangouts that the tourists don't know about. But here's the kicker. She said that it was her first visit to San Francisco and she didn't know a soul here."

"Really?" I tapped my finger against my lips. "She could have been covering," I ventured. "You know, making a point of saying that she didn't know people here so no one would suspect she was having an affair with a local."

"I could see it if the conversation was with her husband or his family, but why make a point of lying to your masseuse?" Charlie reasoned.

"You're right, that doesn't make sense." I sighed. Why was it that the more information I got, the more confused I became? "Okay, here's another question for you. Is there any chance that Bob was checking into the hotel under a pseudonym?"

"Unlikely. We need a credit card to make a reservation. Celebs sometimes ask us to refer to them by a fake name, but our records in the computer have their real info."

I sighed again and then looked down at Jack. "Charlie, I've got to go."

"Okay, I'll call you if I get more dirt."

"Yeah, okay, gotta go." I hung up the phone and bent down to Jack's level. "You ate all the lipstick, didn't you."

Jack looked up at me with big innocent eyes and flashed me a giant smile, his baby teeth now covered with Crystal Rose.

I picked up the canister of lipstick and looked to see if there were any instructions concerning accidental ingestion.

"I'm so not cut out to be your guardian."

CHAPTER 14

"Of course I don't own you!" Samantha spat. "I don't own the road either, but that doesn't mean I want to share it."

—*Words To Die By*

Anatoly showed up at my house an hour later. By that time Jack was screaming again. I hadn't bothered calling Poison Control since, judging from the raw waste that he had pushed into his diaper, it seemed reasonable to assume that there was nothing left in his stomach to pump. I had gone through Leah's things, and if something didn't have a warning label on it, I offered it up. Nonetheless, apart from a brief interlude he had with a super-absorbent tampon, Jack was not to be appeased.

Rather than help me, Anatoly seemed content to stand in the corner of the room and passively observe the execution of my nephew's diabolical plot to drive me to the brink of insanity.

"So, tell me what Charlie said again?" he asked, leaning his weight against the wall.

"Anatoly, look at me. It's everything I can do to get a sentence out without this child yanking out another lock of my hair, and you actually have the nerve to ask me to re-peat myself?"

"I just want to make sure I have everything straight." He crossed his arms in front of his chest. "Unless, of course, you want to be taking care of this child on a full-time basis."

I shot him a lethal glare, then turned my attention to the phone that had begun to ring again. It occurred to me that Jack's screams might have spurred one of my neighbors to call Child Protective Services. I snatched up the receiver. "Is this CPS?"

"What?" Leah screeched. "Why would CPS be calling? What have you done to my child?"

"Nothing bad, which speaks to my unbelievable level of self-restraint." I mouthed the name *Leah* for Anatoly's benefit.

Anatoly pushed himself off the wall. "Ask her if she has any of Bob's old credit card statements."

"Leah, do you have any of Bob's credit card statements?"

"No, Bob always shredded the bills after he paid them. Why is Jack screaming?"

"I don't know, maybe because he's Jack." I shook my head at Anatoly to indicate that Leah didn't have what he wanted.

"Have you tried feeding him?" Leah asked.

"Of course I have!" I didn't bother mentioning that her lipstick had been one of the items on the menu.

"Has he been sticking his hand in his mouth? He was doing that a lot last night."

Anatoly waved his hand in the air to get my attention. "Ask her if Bob's job ever required him to meet with out-of-town business associates."

I nodded at Anatoly and spoke into the receiver. "I haven't noticed Jack putting his hand in his mouth, but he did try to bite my pinky off a few minutes ago. Leah, is there any chance that anyone Bob worked with would have stayed at the Gatsby?"

"If that was the case, don't you think I would have mentioned it when Charlie was telling us about the Brazilians? My husband didn't have to entertain clients, he was a comptroller. The only business people he ever interacted with socially were his superiors who actually worked for Chalet. You know, maybe he's teething."

"Who, Anatoly?"

"No, Sophie—Jack. The pediatrician said that if Jack was teething I could give him some children's Advil. I have a bottle in your bathroom but I don't like to give it to him unless I'm sure."

"What are the side effects of the Advil?" I asked as I rescued a section of my hair from Jack's clutches.

"He tends to get rather drowsy and sedentary."

I covered the mouthpiece and turned to Anatoly. "Go to the bathroom and find the children's Advil." I gave him a shove down the hall.

"Don't give it to him now," Leah continued. "I'll be home in a little bit, and if he's still cranky, then I'll check his gums."

"Right." Anatoly came back from the bathroom with the Advil and I immediately started pouring the purple fluid into the plastic measuring cup. "Whatever you say, Leah. When are you coming home, anyway?"

"Well, Jerome and I are at my house."

I swallowed hard. "Please, please, please, tell me you're not getting to know each other better."

"Don't be silly. I'm just walking him through the events of…that night."

"Great idea," I said absently, as I pried Jack's mouth open and coaxed him to take the Advil.

"And after that, I'm going to show him some of the places Bob used to take me during our courtship. I'm going to walk him through our entire relationship so he can accurately relay the love Bob and I shared to his readers."

My heart dropped into my stomach. "I thought you were just going to be gone for the morning."

"Change of plans."

"Leah, you can't do this to me."

"What? I'm sorry, but I think there's something wrong with my phone—you're cutting out."

"Leah…"

"Nope, can't hear you anymore. I'll check in again in an hour or so. Ta!"

"Leah!"

At the sound of the dial tone I tore the phone from my ear and threw it across the room. "I can't believe this! Leah doesn't need to worry about going to prison—because I'm going to kill her!"

Anatoly nodded distractedly. "So what did she say about Bob's clients and colleagues?"

"She has no reason to think that Bob would have been visiting anyone at the Gatsby, colleague or otherwise." I used both hands to lift Jack so that he was eye to eye with me. His screams had been reduced to a peevish whine.

"Sophie, I have to go," Anatoly said.

"What?" I put Jack down. "But you can't leave me alone with this child! That would be…be…"

"The way the cookie crumbles," Anatoly finished. "I know this is difficult to believe, but I have a life outside this case."

"Excuse me, but twelve thousand dollars of my money says you don't!"

"I have errands to do and a few bills to pay. I'll call you later in the day and we'll do some more brainstorming." He leaned down and gave Jack a playful punch on the arm that started him screaming again. "See you later, Jack. Have fun torturing your aunt."

I stood there with smoke coming out of my ears and watched as he walked out. Jack's screams went up a notch in volume and I looked down at him sympathetically. "For once, I don't blame you. I feel like screaming, too."

I picked the remote off the top of the television set and started flipping through the channels. Leah didn't like Jack to watch TV, but I was past caring about her parental preferences. Besides, watching television had to be healthier than digesting cosmetics.

Unfortunately, Jack wasn't a big fan of *Mr. Rogers* or *America's Funniest Animals,* and after a few other poorly received programming choices I was about ready to give up. And then I found it—the secret to domestic harmony right there on the Disney Channel. Five hyperactive Australians who called themselves The Wiggles were jumping around singing about fruit salad with a giant dog, and Jack was immediately transfixed. I sat down on the edge of a chair and waited for the spell to be broken—but Jack became more engrossed by the second.

Mr. Katz peeked into the room to investigate. "I don't know why, but he loves this show!" I explained to my clearly skeptical cat. I looked back at the screen and watched the brightly dressed men strike up a conversation with their door. "I wonder if you have to be a kid to really get this."

Mr. Katz didn't seem to have an answer, so I let the question drop and grabbed a Corona from the refrigerator. I decided this was the perfect opportunity to sort through the shoe box of Bob's life. Sitting down on the couch, with Jack in full view, I examined each dry cleaning receipt and parking stub in hopes of finding something useful. Perhaps he had parked somewhere unusual, like Brazil, for instance. But no such luck. I was about ready to give up when I found a torn-up scrap of paper. The words "Jan Le" and the numbers "517-8" were written on it. By the way the paper was torn it looked like "Le" was the first part of a last name. I rummaged through the box again to find the other torn pieces, but they weren't there. Jan could be anyone—a mistress, a prospective employee, an exorcist, the possibilities were endless. There was no reason to think that this name had anything to do with the case.

I got up and ripped out a blank piece of binder paper from a notebook I had resting by the phone. By the time the credits were rolling on *The Wiggles Show,* I had listed all the facts I had collected on the case so far. Despite my deep-seated desire to see Cheryl get her just desserts, my most likely suspects were still Taylor or Bianca. This Maria person was a possibility, but that piece of the puzzle didn't fit as nicely as the others. And I couldn't figure out how the floppy disk fit in at all. Mr. Katz was now sitting at my feet, eyeing Jack warily.

"Bianca doesn't have the temperament of a killer," I said aloud. Jack ignored me, but Mr. Katz was all ears. "Maybe I just haven't been pushing the right buttons. Maybe if I piss her off, the bad Bianca will rear her ugly head."

Jack grinned at me. "Piss off!" he said proudly, then turned back to the show.

"Shh! You shouldn't say that," I chastised while ducking my head down to hide my barely contained laughter.

Jack giggled but kept his eyes trained to the television set. I put my virtually untouched beer down on the table with a solid *thump* and punched Bianca's number into the phone.

She answered on the fourth ring.

"Hey, Bianca, it's Sophie. Do you have a minute?"

"More questions?" Her voice sounded weary.

"Just a few. I talked to Taylor Blake yesterday and she admitted to having an affair with Bob."

"So I've been told."

I sat up a little straighter. "You knew? For how long? Who told you?"

"I've known for approximately fifteen minutes and it was Anatoly who told me."

"Anatoly called?"

"He stopped by—you just missed him. I'll tell you what I told him. I've only met Taylor once and I've never even heard of anyone named Maria Pizo—"

"Souza."

"Whatever. All I know is that Bob would never cheat on me. He wasn't capable of that kind of betrayal."

"Are you serious? He cheated on the mother of his son!"

"But he didn't love Leah. He did love me."

I scoffed. What she didn't know about men could fill a concert hall. "Is your sister there to hear you spout this drivel?"

"No, she left with Anatoly."

I froze. "Say that again."

"She left with Anatoly." Bianca's voice started to shake. "I know she—all of you think I'm being naive, but you didn't see Bob and me together. We—"

"Why the hell did she leave with Anatoly?" I asked.

"What? Oh, she had some errands to run for work. Make some copies, send some documents by FedEx, that kind of thing, and Anatoly offered to give her a ride."

How fucking thoughtful of him. "How could someone named Porsha not have a car?"

"The name Porsha is much older than the actual car. You see…"

I pressed the base of my palm against my forehead as Bianca droned on about the history of names and the German automobile industry. It hadn't been my intention to imply that someone named Porsha had to drive a Porsche. In fact, I would assume that good taste would necessitate the opposite. What I meant was that by naming a child Porsha, parents were essentially putting a sign over their daughter's head saying, "My blood's bluer than a Polo University sport jacket and I have more money than God." And such a person shouldn't be riding around on the back of a Harley.

"Plus, she doesn't know how long she'll be in the city." Bianca had come back to the matter at hand. "And she prefers taking cabs to dealing with a car rental agency."

"Okay, I get it. So do you think these will be quick errands?"

"She told Anatoly they would be."

I sighed in relief.

"But after she's done, the two of them are going out to lunch."

"What?" Now I was on my feet. "Where? Where are they having lunch?"

"I think they said The Ramp. Is there a problem?"

"Yes, but I'm going to fix it." I hung up the phone and called Marcus.

"What's happening, hot stuff?" Marcus cooed into the receiver, apparently having gotten my name off his caller ID.

"I need to take you to lunch at The Ramp."

"You *need* to take me?"

"Anatoly's having lunch there with another woman."

"Are you having one of your jealous fits? Do you want me to set her up with an appointment at Vladimir's Salon? She's guaranteed to come out with hair worse than The Donald's."

"I don't have time for that. I need to spy on them."

"Ooh, I love spying! But wait, I still don't understand why you need me."

"Because I have Jack. I need you to keep him quiet so that he doesn't blow my cover."

There was a moment of silence before Marcus finally responded. "Honey, I've spent time with Jack. The only thing that's going to keep that child quiet is duct tape."

I stamped my foot so hard that Jack turned away from the

television. I held my breath until he turned back. "Are you going to help me or not?"

"Of course I'm going to help you. When do we rendezvous?"

"Immediately." I hung up and glared at Jack. "If you blow this for me, there'll be no more lipstick for a month!"

Jack blinked at me, smiled and shouted, "Piss off!"

Marcus, Jack and I got to The Ramp before Anatoly and Porsha. We settled down at an inside table near the bar that had a perfect view of the outdoor dining area where I assumed they would eventually be seated. Marcus was bouncing Jack up and down on his lap. My eyes were glued to the outside entrance when I heard something sweet and gurgling. My head snapped in Marcus's direction.

"What?" Marcus asked, noting my expression of shock and disbelief.

"Did Jack just…laugh?"

"Yes, he did—didn't you, cutie?"

"Sooo, he likes you?"

"Mmm-hmm. Jack and I are shopping girlfriends. He helped Dena and me pick out his mommy's new leather skirt." He turned his attention back to Jack, "Didn't you, sweet cakes…didn't you help Mommy look like a hottie?"

I watched the two of them in awe. "Would you like to keep him? Leah will probably want him back eventually, but I'd say you'd have a good month before that happens."

"Sorry, but if I had to change a diaper I would never be able to look at a butt in the same way again. And you can imagine how devastating that would be to a gay man's social life. Speaking of social lives—" Marcus scooted a little closer to me "—I didn't want to drill you with Leah there, but what was all that talk yesterday about Bob making boom-boom with his gal Friday?"

"Ugh, you don't know the half of it." I spent the next few minutes filling Marcus in on everything I had learned about Taylor. "And then today I found a piece of paper with a woman's name and partial phone number on it."

"Partial?"

"The paper was ripped up."

"My, my, give him a pipe and some satin pj's and Bob could be the next Hefner."

Jack pointed to a Bloody Mary being held by a woman at a neighboring table. "Jack want."

"Good eye." I waved the waitress over. "Can I get a Bloody Mary?"

"Um, Sophie?" Marcus leaned in closer to me. "He's *eighteen months old.*"

"I know that. It's for me." I smiled at the waitress. "My nephew will have a virgin."

Marcus shook his head at the waitress. "Change the Virgin Mary to a Bloody one and give it to me. The child will have straight apple juice." He gave me a pointed look. "I don't do virgins."

The waitress giggled and jotted down our order. "Anything else?"

"Chips and guacamole would be great," I said.

"So," Marcus said, picking up where we had left off. "Do you think Bianca found out about all this and decided that she'd rather kill Bob than live with him?"

"Stranger things have happened. And of course Taylor had motive… Oh! Oh! They're here!"

I scooted down in my chair and held the appetizer menu in front of my face so that only my eyes were visible. Marcus was considerably less discreet and craned his neck so he could have a better view when the hostess seated them at one of the outside tables.

"So that's the other woman." Marcus clucked his tongue.

"I can see why you're worried. Girlfriend's got great hair. Are you sure you don't want me to set her up with Vladimir?"

"*Please,* I'm not that petty." I sat up a little straighter now that they were seated and less likely to spot us. "Do you see those long drop earrings? Those are so last year."

"Yeah, you're not petty at all." Marcus smiled at Jack. "Jack, can you say 'catty'? Come on boy, you can do it—cat-tee."

Jack smiled and tried to duplicate the sound. "Khaki."

Marcus gasped. "Did you hear that? He named the color of my shirt, and he didn't even call it tan, he called it khaki. He's like a budding Mizrahi!"

"Yeah, that's great, Marcus. What do you think they're talking about?"

"I don't know, piña coladas? Walks in the rain? Making love at midnight?"

"Are you trying to tick me off?"

"Of course not. Trying and succeeding are two very different things." Marcus gently placed Jack in his high chair. "They're probably talking about Bob and his murderer."

"You think this is a business lunch?"

"Well, it's not like they're making out at the table."

I shook my head dismissively. "The fact that they didn't start making out the minute they were seated doesn't mean it's not a date. It just means that neither of them is you." I leaned back in my seat as our waitress brought our order.

Marcus took a sip of his cocktail. "For the sake of argument, if Anatoly *was* talking about the case, why would he need to talk to Blondie?"

"I don't know—I guess he could be confirming what I told him about Bianca not having an alibi for the night Erika was killed."

Marcus froze. "Come again?"

"Oh, I forgot to tell you—" I took a long sip of my drink "—somebody went and offed gal Friday."

"What?" Marcus screeched, then covered his mouth and scooted down so that Anatoly and Porsha wouldn't join some of the other patrons in staring at him.

I smacked his leg under the table. "They're too far away to hear, but be more careful next time." I popped a chip in my mouth and swallowed it before continuing. "It wasn't in the papers. Officially she died of an overdose, but I don't buy it—and I don't think the police do, either."

"What do they say she OD'd on?" Marcus asked.

"Cocaine. Not a good drug for someone who is already shooting up insulin for her diabetes and has a severe heart murmur."

"Huh." Marcus toyed with one of his locks. "Any chance it was suicide?"

"You could make a good case for that. She was grieving over Bob, and the revelation that he had planned on leaving Leah for a woman who wasn't her didn't exactly improve her mood." I watched Jack stick his fingers into the bowl of guacamole and then proceed to paint his face green. "Erika was very much the ingenue. I can see her trying to stage a Romeo and Juliet–like ending, but I don't think her weapon of choice would be cocaine."

"I see," said Marcus thoughtfully. "And what are ingenues killing themselves with these days? Daggers with pearl handles?"

"I'm just saying that Erika wasn't the type to go to Hunter's Point to buy a vial of coke. Besides, if she were trying to kill herself, snorting cocaine seems like a very imprecise way of going about it. What if she hadn't died? She could have just ended up in some hospital bed with a state-appointed twelve-step sponsor."

"But you just said that she wasn't the cokehead type," Marcus replied. "Maybe she didn't know the odds. Maybe she *did* want to do the Romeo and Juliet ending but the local drug dealer was fresh out of hemlock."

I was suddenly distracted. Anatoly must have said something clever, because Porsha had just burst out laughing. Bitch.

"One thing I don't get," Marcus said. "If Erika's death wasn't in the papers, how do you know about it?"

"She ordered calamari instead of a salad."

"I'm not following."

"The waiter just put a plate of calamari in front of Porsha. You know what this means, don't you?"

"That she's not allergic to shellfish?"

"It means she's trying to impress him. Look at her. She's totally the green-salad type, but she didn't order the green salad because if the lettuce isn't cut into perfect little pieces, it can be a disastrous first-date faux pas. Stuff falls off your fork, it gets stuck in your teeth—it's just a mess. So she ordered the more caloric but neater calamari."

"My God, you're right. Now if she orders scallops for her entrée, we're cooked!"

"It's not funny."

"Sophie, it's insane. Now how do you know about Erika?"

"The police came over and questioned Leah and me about it."

"What? Why? Do they think you forced Erika to 'just say yes'?"

"I have no idea what they think. I don't even know if they suspect that Erika was sleeping with Bob. All I know is that either Detective Lorenzo is lying to me or he walked into a very different scene than Leah and I did."

"Come again?"

"Oh, did I forget to mention that Leah and I are the ones who originally found the body?"

"What!"

"Yeah, but that's kind of a secret so *shh*." I held a finger up to my lips.

"Oh. My. God. Do you and Leah ever get tired of discovering dead bodies?"

"Absolutely not. Nothing makes my day like a good corpse sighting." I sucked the alcohol off the celery stick in my drink before handing it over to Jack.

Marcus jabbed his finger into my arm. "Porsha's getting up. Oh my God, Sophie, I think she's going to the ladies room."

I turned and cast a desperate glance at the restrooms, which were less than fifteen feet away from our table. "We need bigger menus to hide behind!" I squealed.

Porsha turned and started walking in our direction. Without another thought, I ducked under the table. Jack started giggling uncontrollably as I tried to curl my body into an invisible little ball. I watched Porsha's Stuart Weitzmans walk past and disappear behind the door with the little figure of a woman on it, then sighed with relief.

"God, that was close." I climbed back up into my seat and came face-to-face with Anatoly.

"Did you really think I wouldn't notice you?"

"I don't know what you're talking about. Marcus and I just came here for lunch. I didn't even know you were here."

"Then why were you under the table?"

"I…wanted to see Marcus's shoes."

"His shoes."

Marcus kicked a foot out for Anatoly's examination. "They're Prada. I bought them for less than half price on Fashionbliss.com."

Anatoly barely glanced at the shoes. "Can I see you for a minute, Sophie?"

I grimaced and followed Anatoly out to the patio.

"How did you know I was going to be here?" he asked.

"I told you, I didn't—"

"Sophie."

"I called Bianca."

"Why?"

"I wanted to see if I could make her violently angry."

Anatoly released a heavy sigh. "Why?"

"Well, you have to be violent in order to commit murder…"

"So you figured if she murdered you it would move her farther up the suspect list." Anatoly shook his head. "What's more frightening—that you thought that was a good idea, or that I'm not surprised?"

"Look, this conversation isn't really relevant because I barely had a chance to say hello before Bianca told me you had just taken off with her sister. So you're the one who needs to explain himself."

"Remind me—why do I owe you an explanation?"

"Because Porsha is related to one of the major players in this case. It's a conflict of interest."

"First of all, I'm not a police officer. If I want to dine with the sister of a suspect I can. Second, I would think you would be happy about this. You were the one who first decided to pump Porsha for information."

"*Me,* not you! Under no circumstance should you be pumping Porsha—!"

"What the hell are you doing here?"

We turned to see Porsha glaring at me.

"I was hungry?" I looked at Anatoly and wondered if he would challenge me in front of Porsha, but he just shrugged and looked out at the bay.

"Really?" Porsha asked. "I find it rather curious that of all the restaurants in San Francisco we both chose the same one at the same time."

"It's just a coincidence," Anatoly said firmly. "Sophie comes here all the time. I just didn't predict that she would come here today."

He covered for me! I felt my deviant heart flutter. But my cell phone started ringing in my purse before I had the chance to throw myself at him.

"Hello?"

"You've kidnapped my child," Leah said.

"Are you kidding me? I'm trying to give him away!"

"Very funny. Can you two come home now? I need…" Leah's voice trailed off, and when she spoke again her voice was much softer. "I need Jack. I just need to hold him."

"Leah, what's going on?"

"Lorenzo just left. He had a warrant, Sophie."

There was a tightening in my chest. I pivoted and walked away from Anatoly and Porsha. "A warrant for what? Are you under arrest?" I jumped as a hand closed around my shoulder. I turned to see Anatoly's concerned eyes looking down at me. One glance told me that Porsha was back at their table, pouting.

"No, not yet…but Sophie—" Leah's voice broke off and I listened to her attempts to control her ragged breathing. "He took…he took a strand of my hair. I think they may have found something to link me to Erika's death."

CHAPTER 15

"Jerry brought home some of that edible chocolate body paint in hopes of spicing up our sex life," Carol said with a sigh. "Unfortunately I was PMSing that night so I ended up eating everything in the container before we had a chance to get our clothes off."

—*Words To Die By*

Anatoly made up some excuse for Porsha and offered up Marcus as a means for her to get home, so that he could follow Jack and me to my place. Normally I would have been thrilled that he was so willing to ditch my rival, but at that moment I had bigger things to think about. Since the Harley made parking a two-minute dilemma versus the twenty-minute headache that I was faced with, Anatoly beat me to my apartment. When Jack and I entered, Anatoly was seated at the dining table looking over notes that he had presumably just taken, and Leah was curled into an upright version of the fetal position. When she saw me she leaped off the couch and took Jack from my arms.

"Hi, sweetie. Mommy missed you! Did you miss Mommy?"

"Khaki."

Leah looked at me quizzically. I shrugged, grateful that of all the new words he had learned that day he had chosen *khaki* to share with his mom.

Anatoly closed his hand around my arm. "Let's give them some time alone."

I did a quick double take. "I can't leave Leah when she's in the middle of a crisis. She'll have me strung up by my thumbs!"

"No, Anatoly's right." Leah smoothed Jack's sparse head of hair with a shaky hand. "This may be the last time I'll be able to be alone with my child for a long time."

Now I was really scared. I looked to Anatoly for answers. "I'll fill you in on what she told me," he whispered, then pulled me toward the door. "Leah, we'll be back in a few hours. Call Sophie on her cell if you need us."

Leah didn't respond. Instead she just pressed her forehead against Jack's and whispered his name.

I swallowed and followed Anatoly out onto the street before speaking again. "Please tell me what's going on. What do the police have on my sister?"

"I'm not exactly sure." Anatoly tilted his head upward and squinted at the dark clouds that had begun to gather in the sky. "Lorenzo gave her some information, and when I walked in she was on the phone with that reporter from *Flavah*—I think his name's Jerry…"

"Jerome," I said impatiently. "What does he have to do with anything?"

"He was with Leah when Lorenzo showed up, so he offered to call a few contacts over at the police station to help figure out what's going on."

"And?" I prodded.

Anatoly gently guided me in the direction of his place. "It seems that the cocaine Erika OD'd on was injected."

"So?"

"So Erika used insulin injections to control her diabetes."

"Again, so wha—wait a minute!" I almost tripped on the curb as we started to cross the street. "Erika didn't know she was shooting up cocaine. She thought she was taking insulin!"

"Maybe." Anatoly took hold of my elbow to prevent me from inadvertently walking in front of a bike messenger. "The syringe that was used came from the package of needles that she got with her supply of insulin, but there are other things to consider. Cocaine needs to be melted down immediately prior to being injected. It would have been impossible for someone to sneak a vial into her medicine cabinet hours before the injection without its changing consistency."

"So someone would have had to make the switch just minutes before Erika put the needle in," I said slowly.

"Yes, assuming Erika gave herself the injection." We turned onto Anatoly's street and started up the hill. "There's some question about that, since there were no fingerprints on the syringe, or even on the box in which it had been stored."

"Could the person who gave Erika the shot have been wearing gloves?"

Anatoly shrugged. "That or they wiped the needle down after it was used. Either way it doesn't look good."

My mind flashed back to the night Leah and I discovered Erika, and I did a quick mental inventory of all the things I had wiped down. The lamp, the doorknob…no, I was sure that if I had stumbled across a syringe or even a box of insulin during my little cleaning session I would have taken special notice. "Where did they find the needle?"

"That's the other thing…they apparently found it at the bottom of Erika's toilet. It appears that somebody tried to flush away the evidence."

"Okay, hold up." I raised my hand to stop him. "Some murderer was clever enough to kill Erika with an overdose of crack but they weren't smart enough to figure out how to flush a toilet?"

"Apparently Erika has one of those toilets where you have to hold the handle down in order for it to work properly."

I wrinkled my nose. "I hate those."

"Yeah, I think our killer is with you on that point." We had reached his building, but he hesitated before putting the key in the lock. "Sophie, you need to understand something. They wouldn't be asking for Leah's hair if they didn't have some kind of DNA evidence to compare it to. If her hair matches what the police want it to match, she's going to be locked away until this whole thing goes to trial."

"No—" I shook my head and looked past him "—I don't accept that."

"It doesn't matter what you accept, those are the facts."

"Facts are overrated," I argued. "Just ask any young earth creationist."

Anatoly sighed. "So what are you going to do? Hold a public prayer session and protest the teaching of criminal justice within our school system?"

"All I'm saying is that I have faith. I have faith in God, I have faith in my sister, I have faith in myself and I have faith in you. And between the four of us we should be able to make everything turn out all right."

Anatoly smiled. "So you still think the glass is half full."

"I think it might be down to a quarter full, but it's still not empty." I looked down at the scuff marks on the tips of my boots. "You're not throwing in the towel or anything, right? Please tell me you're not."

Anatoly reached forward and lifted my chin. "I can't guarantee that things will work out the way that you want them to, but I can promise you that I will never throw in the towel. Not when it comes to you and your family."

Our eyes met, and for a moment I was actually speech-less. It's not something that happens to me very often. Ana-toly's mouth formed into one of those half smiles that I love so much and he stepped forward.

"What are you thinking?"

I took a deep breath and then forced myself to pull back. "I'm thinking that we have a lot of work to do."

Anatoly shook his head. "At this point there's nothing to do but wait. The DNA results should be back within the next twenty-four hours, and at that point we'll plan our next move."

"Yeah, well I'm all for spontaneity, but not when it comes to my sister's life. I say we come up with two alternative plans of action so that when the results come in we're ready."

Anatoly sighed. "How does the saying go? 'There'll be no rest for the wicked'?"

"Something like that." I glanced at my watch. "Why don't we go upstairs and do a little brainstorming. Do you have any coffee?"

"Of course," Anatoly said, and opened the lobby door.

When we got upstairs I did a quick inventory of his apart-ment. I had never actually been inside before. It was consid-erably smaller than mine and the decor was definitely on the stark side. There was a sofa, a leather La-Z-Boy, a pool table that had seen better days and a television set that was prob-ably a few years younger than me.

"So I take it you didn't spend the advance I gave you on an interior designer."

"I spend my money on things that are important to me," he said as he took my coat and walked out of the room.

"Like what?" I called after him.

"Like this."

I followed his voice to the kitchen, and gasped. The room was as big as the living room, but unlike the latter, was filled with state-of-the-art accessories. A food processor with at least eight settings sat proudly on the counter next to a bread machine nice enough to make any Sur La Table connoisseur jealous. There was a Viking stove and a very impressive set of cooking knives, but by far the most stunning item in the kitchen was a gourmet, top-of-the-line Starbucks Barista Digital Italia Espresso 2000. I was vaguely aware of Anatoly getting something out of the refrigerator as I walked over to the machine and let my hand hover over its top.

"May I touch it?" I asked in an awed whisper.

Anatoly smiled and walked to my side. "Usually when a woman asks me that she's not talking about my coffeemaker."

I shot him a disgusted look. "How dare you refer to this miracle of technology as a coffeemaker!"

"Forgive me." Anatoly moved his hand over mine and then pressed down until it was sandwiched between the glistening steel of the Espresso 2000 and the slightly rough texture of his palm.

Images of making love in a field of Arabica coffee beans filled my head. "Will you…" My voice faltered as I looked up into his eyes. "Will you work it for me?"

Anatoly broke into a grin. "Sophie, I thought you'd never ask."

Without removing his hand, he maneuvered himself behind me. Now my back was pressed against his stomach. He reached his right hand up to open a cabinet door above my head and he pulled out a coffee grinder.

I swallowed. "You use whole beans?"

Anatoly nodded and moved his mouth closer to my ear. "It's better when it's strong."

Okay—orgasm time. I closed my eyes and tried to resist the temptation of the moment. What was it that guys did when they wanted to last longer? Think about sports, right? But you would have to know something about sports to think about them, and my knowledge in that area was limited to the game of Frisbee. There was no way that a flying disk was going to distract me from the organ that was beginning to press into the small of my back.

"So…um…should we grind the beans?"

"Shh." Anatoly's lips had moved from my ear to my neck. "We don't want to rush the process." His breath tickled my skin. "It was you who pointed out that we weren't just talking about coffee."

"No." I breathed, and turned to face him. My breasts pressed against his pectoral muscles. "We're talking about espresso."

Anatoly's hand went up to the back of my head and he pulled me into a heated kiss. I spread my hands out to either side of me and grasped the edge of the counter. My arm brushed against the item Anatoly had retrieved from the fridge. I opened one eye and saw the brown-and-gold bag. The label read Special Reserve Estate 2003—Sumatra Lintong Lake Tawar—only the best espresso beans money could buy. I groaned and moved my hands to his shirt. What difference did it make if he was an egocentric chauvinistic womanizer? Clearly he was my soul mate. His hand moved to my butt and I felt myself being lifted up onto the counter next to his machine. I spread my legs to pull him into an erotic embrace. Anatoly's right hand had moved to the top button of my jeans and I gasped as his left cupped the prize that he coveted. In the past when Anatoly and I had come this close to having sex, something had always stopped me. Usually it was the nagging fear that he was actually trying to kill me. But now I had put all those fears to rest. How could anyone who owned an Espresso 2000 be capable of something as sordid as murder?

Murder? Wait a minute…another gasp escaped me, but this one didn't stem from passion. "Anatoly, what are we doing? We should be thinking about ways to help Leah."

"We will—later." Anatoly had undone the last button of my Levi's and was busy trying to maneuver them off me.

The temptation to agree was overwhelming, but… "I don't think Leah's problems are something we can afford to put off."

Anatoly pulled back just enough to make eye contact. "You really want to stop now?"

"Umm…"

"What if I told you that in the drawer directly beneath you there was a box of chocolate-covered espresso beans?"

"Dark chocolate?"

"What else?"

"Let's get it on."

Anatoly grabbed me, his mouth closed over mine once more and all thoughts of Leah, and Bob's murder, flew out of my head. All I could think about was how good it felt to be pressed against Anatoly and how awesome it was going to be to eat those espresso beans. As if reading my mind, he reached behind my legs and pulled the small box out of the drawer. He took a half step back and slowly rolled a bean along my lower lip. My tongue flicked out in a desperate attempt to taste the chocolate, but Anatoly was working at a more leisurely pace. After what seemed like an eternity he slipped the bean into my mouth, along with his index finger. Now I could taste espresso, chocolate and Anatoly's skin all at the same time. I moaned in pleasure and sucked gently on his finger as he slowly withdrew it.

"More?" he asked teasingly.

I swallowed the delicacy and nodded. "Lots more."

Anatoly put another bean in my mouth, but this time his other hand was at work untying my wrap top. It fell open and he gazed at me appreciatively. His hand traveled in a straight line from my throat, to my navel, to the elastic waistband of my bikini briefs. His other hand stroked the inside of my thigh. "We need to get rid of these jeans."

He didn't have to ask me twice. I wiggled my hips to help

Anatoly remove my clothing, then promptly ripped his shirt right off him. My God, the man had a beautiful body. His hands wrapped around my waist. He leaned forward and gently sucked on the sensitive area at the base of my throat. I moaned and threw my head back, banging it against the cabinet behind me.

"Are you all right?"

"Fantastic. Can I have another espresso bean?"

Anatoly laughed. "I feel like I'm using your addiction to obtain illicit sexual favors."

"Well, of course you are. You don't have a moral problem with that, do you?"

"I think my conscience can take it."

He fed me another bean and slipped his other hand inside my panties. When I felt his finger push inside me, I almost exploded. I would have called out his name if I wasn't so busy chewing. He leaned forward so that he was closer to my ear.

"I have wanted you since the moment I saw you."

"Even when you thought I was a murderess?"

"Even then," he confessed. "I know it's twisted, but I couldn't help myself."

"Nothing wrong with being a little twisted—" I gasped. Anatoly had now employed a second finger to his task. It was only fair that I reciprocate. I moved my hand to the bulge in his jeans. "Well, it's not a gun...so you must be glad to see me."

Anatoly chuckled. "You have no idea."

I closed my eyes as he trailed kisses along my right shoulder. "You know you're going to have to use a filter," I whispered.

Anatoly laughed again. "I think I have some in stock." He picked me up and threw me over his shoulder.

"Okay, this is so not sexy," I said as he lugged me potato-sack style toward the bedroom.

"Maybe not, but it's a lot easier on my back than cradling you in front of me as if you were some kind of fairy-tale princess."

"Hey!" I snapped. "It just so happens that I'm Jewish *and* I'm American, which makes me a princess by default—so carry me the right way!"

Anatoly put me down inside the doorway of his bedroom. "You don't like being carried over my shoulder?"

"Nothing slips by you, does it?"

"Fine." He picked me up and threw me onto his bed, then quickly fell on top of me and pinned my arms down against the mattress. "Was that better?"

I smiled. "Actually it was rather fun. Kind of like a roller-coaster ride."

"How appropriate." He kissed me again and I wiggled my arms free so that I could pull him against me in earnest. Anatoly moved off me long enough to remove his own jeans, and then reached for the bedside table.

"You don't keep them in the bathroom?"

"My feeling is that the best place to store condoms is by a bed."

"But then it looks like you were expecting to get lucky….oh!" I sat up with a bolt. "You weren't planning on bringing Porsha back here, were you?"

Anatoly shot me a withering look. "I hadn't expected to bring anyone back here today—" He tore a condom free from the others in the pack and pushed me down on the bed again "—but I'm damn glad that I did."

I felt a jolt of electricity shoot through me as he slid his hand inside my bra and fondled my nipple. "Yeah, this afternoon is definitely looking up."

He unhooked my bra and then lowered his mouth to my left breast, his right hand lifting me so that I was arching toward him. I moaned as the last of my undergarments were removed. He caressed me slowly and methodically until it was all I could do to breathe.

Finally, he sat up and removed his own briefs. My eyes widened in disbelief. "Oh my God, you're not circumcised!"

Anatoly looked down at his erection. "Nice of you to notice."

"I've never seen an uncircumcised penis before."

"Well, you're welcome to become more acquainted with mine."

I reached out my hand and stroked him slowly. Anatoly's breath quickened. I glanced up at him. "It looks different."

"Sophie, when men say they want women to talk during sex, this is *not* the kind of conversation they're thinking of."

"It's like it has a little hat."

Anatoly muttered a Russian curse and gently removed my hand. "You're lucky you're so damn sexy, you know that?" He hid the object of my fascination beneath a layer of latex.

"Hey, if you don't like what I have to say, then give me something else to talk about."

"Happily." He pulled me up so that we were both sitting on the bed, my legs wrapped around him once more. He parted my lips with his tongue. I felt him pressing against my inner thigh, and then with a slow, deliberate movement he entered me and I forgot about Mr. Happy's little hat. At first our movements were slow and sensual, but they quickly picked up speed. We fell back on the bed and I clenched the sheets in my fists as a wave of heat and pleasure spread from my groin to every other inch of my body. I breathed in, and the smell of our sweat mingled with his cologne filled my nostrils. With each thrust he seemed to fill me more completely, and finally I couldn't hold out anymore. My body convulsed and my moans were lost in our kiss. Less than a minute later I felt him shudder, then I felt the full weight of his body on top of mine.

"That was incredible," he whispered.

"Yes, it was."

We lay there for a few minutes savoring the moment, but eventually I knew that I was going to have to break the silence. There were things that needed to be attended to—things that couldn't be taken care of in the bedroom. I ran my fingers through his hair.

"Anatoly, I don't want to ruin the mood, but do you think you could make me that espresso now?"

Less than a half hour later Anatoly and I were dressed and in his living room sipping a latte that rivaled any of the ones I had ever ordered at Starbucks. I thought about asking if he had whipped cream, but the inevitable innuendos that remark would elicit made me hold my tongue.

"So, by the look of your kitchen I would say that you know how to make a lot more than espresso," I remarked.

Anatoly lifted an eyebrow. "I thought I just demonstrated that point in the bedroom."

"Let me rephrase that," I said quickly. "What dishes do you like to cook?"

"I can cook almost anything." Anatoly put his cup down on a coffee table that was ugly enough to win him a reality show makeover. He smiled at me and sat down on the equally hideous sofa. "Italian, French, Mediterranean, even Japanese—you name the culture and I can probably cook you the corresponding cuisine. I enjoy being a bachelor and I enjoy good food, so learning to cook was the only logical choice."

I love him. "So why is a nice Jewish boy like yourself lugging around a foreskin?"

"In a country where extreme anti-Semitism is the rule rather than the exception, it is unwise to do something to your child that would make it easy for people to identify him as Jewish."

"So what are you saying? That people in Russia hang out in public restrooms checking to see whose penis qualifies them for harassment?"

Anatoly looked at me and something in his eyes sent a chill up my spine.

"Trust me when I tell you that Jews born in the States don't know how lucky they are."

I swallowed hard. Anatoly had always come across as strong and in control, but at that moment I realized that his bravado might be something he had cultivated for the sake of survival. I reached my hand out and let my fingers brush against the stubble that had begun to form on his cheek. There was so much I didn't know about this man.

My cell rang and I jumped up, spilling half my drink on Anatoly's already stained carpet. I flashed him an apologetic smile before retrieving the phone from my purse. "Leah?"

"Sophie, you're never going to believe this. Jerome just called me. One of his sources told him that the police did find a hair at Erika's place."

I squeezed my eyes shut and crossed my fingers. "The DNA didn't match up, did it?"

"No, the hair they found wasn't mine."

"Yay! Oh, Leah, that's spectacular!" I turned around and gave Anatoly a thumbs-up.

"It gets better."

"How can it get better than that?"

"The hair was blond."

"Bianca?" I wrinkled my nose. "But this isn't making sense. If the hair was blond they should have known right away that it wasn't yours."

"It was dyed blond."

I felt my heart flutter. "Dyed?"

"Mmm-hmm, and based on the lab results they know that whoever it belongs to was closely related to Bob."

My mouth dropped open. There was a God and he was magnificently vengeful. "That little bitch," I said joyfully.

"Come home. We need to break open the champagne."

We entered my apartment to find Leah putting several champagne flutes on my dining table. She looked up at Anatoly and me and flashed us a huge grin.

I scanned the apartment and noted that while Mr. Katz was sitting on the couch in plain view, there was no child harassing him. "Where's Jack?"

"He was tired, so I put him down for a nap. He didn't sleep well last night."

"Yeah, I know. He was very vocal about his insomnia."

"A little early for that, isn't it?" Anatoly nodded at the glasses. "All we know is that Cheryl *might* have been in Erika's house. That doesn't change a lot."

"It gives me hope," Leah said quietly, "and that changes everything." She looked at Anatoly and her eyes narrowed. "You know, I think it would be appropriate for you to refund my sister's money. She's the one who figured out who killed my husband. She knew it was Cheryl right from the beginning."

"I suspected," I said. "I didn't know anything."

"We *still* don't know anything," Anatoly pointed out again. "Even if Cheryl is implicated in Erika's alleged murder, that still doesn't mean that she'll be charged with killing Bob."

"Now you're just being a pessimist." Leah dropped down into a chair by the table and causally crossed her legs. "Seriously, what are the odds that someone who wasn't involved in Bob's murder would up and kill his secretary days after his death?"

"About the same as the odds that someone would kill my brother-in-law weeks after someone else tried to kill me. And yet, here we are." I took my place next to my cat and was starting to scratch him behind the ears when a horrible thought came to me. "Leah, you didn't tell Jerome that we were the ones to find Erika, did you?"

Anatoly's shoulders became more rigid and he stared at Leah, no doubt praying for the same answer I was.

"Of course I didn't," Leah said. "But I don't think he would tell anyone if he knew."

"But he doesn't know," Anatoly said again for confirmation.

"No, no. He had heard about Erika's death earlier and he knew the police thought it might be connected to Bob's murder, so he's asked his sources to keep him updated on any new developments. I certainly didn't volunteer anything about what I knew, and Jerome didn't ask me to. In fact, during the interview almost all his questions were about Bob and our marriage. Although he did seem interested in what kind of things I liked to do in my spare time and my views on parenting and private schools." Her voice trailed off and she smiled. "He's a fascinating man."

"How would you know?" Anatoly asked as he sat down next to me. "You just said that all the two of you talked about was you."

I giggled. "Why do you think she found him so fascinating?"

"Very funny," Leah said, but she didn't look offended. "We talked a little about him, too. He's different than any of my other male friends, or Bob's friends for that matter."

I blinked in surprise. "Bob had friends?"

"Okay—business associates. Anyway, Jerome is more...urban. When I first met with him today he was very professional, but as we spent time together he became more comfortable and he started using a lot of slang." She looked off into the distance as if trying to recall something. "Is that kind of talk still called 'jive'?"

"I think the popular term now is 'talking black,'" I said.

"Right, right, I think he told me that." She ran her fingers through her hair. "I showed him a few home movies I had made of Jack. He said he was 'a city of a child.' I'm not sure I know what that means but I kind of like it."

For some reason the image of a Godzilla-sized Jack frightening a whole bunch of Japanese people popped into my mind.

"He should be here any minute. I called and invited him over since he was the bearer of the good news," Leah continued. "This way I'll have the opportunity to kiss the messenger."

"What did you just say?" I scooted forward on the couch.

"Kiss the messenger? Really, Sophie, it's just an expression."

"Kill," I corrected. "You're supposed to *kill* the messenger, not *kiss* him."

"Really?" Leah cocked her head to the side. "That does sound right. Well, I'm certainly not going to kill him after he told me that Cheryl's one step closer to wearing an orange jumpsuit." She laughed. "Cheryl hates orange. It makes her look like a demented jack-o'-lantern."

"Here's an expression for you," Anatoly offered. "Don't count your chickens before they're hatched."

Leah made a face. "And people call *me* a killjoy." The buzzer went off and she got up to press the intercom. "Jerome?"

"Hey, girl."

Leah smiled and buzzed him in. She waited impatiently for him to climb the stairs and then waved him into the apartment. "I'm so glad you could come."

She gave him a kiss on the cheek, which, to my eye, he received with a little too much enthusiasm. Then he exchanged greetings with Anatoly and me and quickly turned his eyes back to Leah.

"Now that we're all here, I'll get the champagne." She

helped him remove his coat before retrieving a bottle of Cristal from the kitchen.

"What exactly did your source at the police station say?" Anatoly asked as Leah popped the cork and started pouring our drinks.

"Just that the police found a hair somewhere around Erika's body that wasn't hers," Leah said, and handed Anatoly a glass. "For some reason they compared it to Bob's DNA. Didn't match but it was damn close. My man says that it definitely belongs to someone related to him."

"Well, well, that *is* incriminating." I shifted slightly in my seat. "It was nice of you to call Leah and tell her, Jerome."

He nodded. "Leah and I are cool. I know she isn't guilty of any of this shit."

Jerome leaned against the wall, and I was struck again by his impeccable physique. Under normal circumstances I would have advised Leah to go for him in a big way, but until she was completely cleared of all charges, I was determined to keep her chaste and mournful. I cleared my throat.

"So now that you have all the information you need for your article, I guess we won't be seeing you for a while."

"My article isn't due for another week and I'll need to come back to check my facts. If you're worried that I'm going to be dogging Leah in print, you can relax," he said, completely misreading my concern. "I wouldn't do that, and even if I wanted to, *Flavah* wouldn't publish it."

"Why not?" Anatoly asked as he draped his arm over the back of the couch.

I wasn't sure if he was trying to get closer to me, but I inched toward the crook of his arm just in case.

"*Flavah's* a black magazine," Jerome explained. "And when this Cheryl chick started talking smack, a lot of the sistahs and brothas sat up and took notice. *Flavah* wants to make sure the people see this for what it is—just another battle in the war the police have waged against us."

"Enough politics." Leah lifted her glass. "We have things to celebrate. Let's toast to Cheryl. May she rot in jail for the rest of her miserable life."

"Works for me." I stood and lifted my glass.

The buzzer rang again, and I looked at Leah questioningly. "Did you invite anyone else over?"

"No, but it's not exactly unlike your friends to drop by un-announced. Honestly, Sophie, I don't know how you put up with it."

I was tempted to point out that it was a lot easier to put up with surprise visits from friends than the extended stay of family members, but I bit my tongue and waited while Leah inquired over the intercom who was there.

"Detective Lorenzo."

An uneasy silence fell over the room, Leah turned to me and Anatoly. "Do you think he's come to tell me that I'm no longer a suspect?"

Anatoly stood up, his expression serious. "There's only one way to find out."

Leah pressed the button to release the door, and in the blink of an eye Lorenzo was standing in my doorway, a uni-formed officer at his side.

"Ms. Leah Miller—" his tone was cool with disdain "—you're under arrest for the murder of Bob Miller."

"W-what?" Leah stammered. "But I don't understand…"

The other officer took a pair of handcuffs out and started reading her her rights.

"Wait a minute." I stepped forward and looked desperately from Leah to Lorenzo. "You can't arrest her, she didn't do anything!"

"She killed her husband," Lorenzo said blandly.

I glanced at Leah. She had lost so much color, she could

have passed as white. "Listen, don't worry about this," I said lamely. "There's obviously been some kind of mistake. I'll call a lawyer and we'll work this whole thing out."

Jerome stepped up behind me as Leah lowered her head so that her hair hid her face. "This ain't gonna hold, Leah," Jerome said. "These cops are desperate for an arrest and they probably dug up some circumstantial shit to get one. It'll be thrown out of court in no time."

"But the hair," Leah whispered to Jerome in a voice I barely recognized as hers. "You said it was Cheryl's hair."

Anatoly stepped forward. "Don't say anything, Leah. We'll go over everything when we have an attorney present."

Leah looked up, and Jerome smiled at her. "Girl, you're gonna be fine. You just keep a stiff upper lip and these cops will be unlocking those cuffs in no time."

Leah tried to smile back but she clearly couldn't manage it.

Lorenzo nodded at the other officer, who had finished with the rights. "Time to go."

I stood there, immobilized, as I watched them take my sister away. The sound of the front door to my building opening and then slamming shut jarred me out of my shock.

"I have to follow them," I said, reaching for my purse. "She can't be alone."

I was halfway out the door when Anatoly grabbed me by the arm and stopped me. "You're forgetting something."

"I'll call a lawyer from my cell on the drive over." I tried to pull my arm free but Anatoly's grip was iron.

"I'm not talking about the lawyer."

The sound of a cry came from down the hallway. My eyes widened and I looked at Anatoly in horror.

Anatoly nodded without breaking eye contact. "That's right, you have a child to think about now."

CHAPTER 16

If God only gives us what we can handle, why are there
so many suicides?
                                          —*Words To Die By*

To say that the next hour was chaotic would be an understatement. I called the police station and found out where I
would need to go to see Leah. Then I did the most difficult
thing of all. I called Mama. Calming her down was a major
challenge because I was far from calm myself. But she did
have the presence of mind to recommend a lawyer that she
knew from her synagogue. Anatoly held my hand and reminded me to breathe as I relayed the whole saga to the attorney over the phone.

Surprisingly, the person who kept Jack under control
through it all was Jerome. He simply took him into the guest
room with some wooden spoons, pots and pans and taught
him how to be his own one-man band. Normally I wouldn't
have been thrilled with this noisy child-care technique but
at that moment I was just thankful not to have my nephew
underfoot.

By the time I was off the phone, Mama was at my door.

It took a little effort but I convinced her to stay at my place with Jack rather than accompany Anatoly and me to the jail. Her arguments that Leah might be feeling the need for a little maternal love were not completely unfounded, but it was also unrealistic to assume Leah would be able to deal with Mama's hysterics while she was barely keeping it together herself, and a jail was certainly no place for Jack.

In the end I decided to let Jerome stay with Mama and help her with Jack, and Anatoly and I left to try to see Leah. Without argument, I let Anatoly drive my car.

Thankfully he wasn't overly conservative about the speed issue. "We're going to figure this out," he assured me as he weaved in and out of traffic.

"But this doesn't make sense!" I said as I searched my purse for Advil. "They didn't arrest her before because they wanted time to build their case, so why arrest her now? Why would they risk losing in court just so they could rush the arrest of a woman for what is being described as a crime of passion? She's not a flight risk and she's obviously not a danger to others."

"It's possible they found something new or…"

"Or what?" I gave up on the Advil and threw my purse on the floor of the Audi. "Are Lorenzo and his fellow officers just trying to make all our lives miserable? Does he get off on seeing newly widowed mothers in handcuffs? What?"

"Maybe they think she *is* a danger to others."

"Who would she be a threat to? It's not like she has other husbands around town cheating on her, and she's kept her distance from Bianca."

"Sophie, just because the hair didn't match Leah's doesn't mean that they didn't find something else in Erika's house that linked Leah to the crime scene. A fingerprint, maybe a broken nail—there are lots of things a forensics team could have turned up."

A fresh wave of panic washed over me. "She broke a nail while we were there. She said so and I totally forgot about it."

I turned to Anatoly, hoping that he would tell me my oversight wasn't as earth-shatteringly awful as I suspected. His expression offered no such assurances.

I brought my fingers to my temples and tried to stave off the migraine that was forming. Right now Leah was being treated like a violent criminal. They would put her in a cell with the other violent criminals. I fought back a sob as I thought about the body search that she would have to endure. How could any of this be happening? And then there was Jack to think about! I couldn't deal with him on a good day—how was I supposed to manage him full-time while sorting through all this?

Anatoly glanced over at me. "Don't overthink the situation. We need to take this one step at a time."

"You know when the guys in AA came up with that slogan they were thinking of beating alcohol and drug addictions, not murder raps."

"Did that lawyer say whether or not he was coming down to the station?"

"Posthaste." I sighed.

"Can I ask why you didn't bring an attorney on board before this?"

I looked out at the cars in the lane next to us. "I don't know—I guess I wanted to take my time researching people to make sure I retained the best guy for the job." That was another lie. I had postponed hiring a lawyer because I didn't want to acknowledge the possibility that Leah would need one. Here I had been yelling at Leah for not facing the realities of her situation, while I hadn't been willing to face them myself.

Anatoly pulled into a garage and parked his car on the second floor. Next to us a tan Mercedes pulled in. The driver was a man with a pudgy face, a high forehead and wire-rimmed glasses. "That's Timothy Weis, Leah's lawyer." I offered him a halfhearted smile and wave.

Anatoly blinked. "That was fast."

"His wife is the woman who performed Jack's bris and she loves my mom. She'd expect Timothy to go out of his way to help her daughter."

"So you think his wife's expectations are enough to motivate him to get here less than forty minutes from the time you called to retain him?"

I gave Anatoly a withering look. "If your wife was trained in the art of slicing up penises and she asked you to do something, would you do it?"

Anatoly paused, then nodded. "Yes. Yes, I believe I would do it very quickly."

We got out of the car and greeted Timothy. I had met him on three or four occasions and he had never struck me as a force to be reckoned with, but his track record was phenomenal. Mama had even told me that he was considered to be one of the top twenty criminal attorneys in the country.

The three of us slowly walked together to the Civic Center jailhouse and went over the important facts about the case once again.

"The evidence is circumstantial but there's a lot of it," Timothy said as we approached the front steps. "The one thing she has going for her is Cheryl."

"You mean the hair they found," I said, looking around to make sure no one could overhear us.

"We don't even know that the hair exists." Timothy stopped and pulled from his pocket a small black cloth, which he used to clean his glasses. "We can't base a case on the unnamed source of a severely biased reporter."

I wrinkled my nose. "Then how is Cheryl a help?"

"The comments she made on television. In two minutes

of airtime Cheryl changed Leah's status from villainess to victim. Leah couldn't have gotten better results if she had retained a private publicist."

"But you're talking about public opinion," I said. "That won't help Leah in a courtroom."

"Public opinion can always help, or hurt, as the case may be. If this Jerome fellow really wants to put out pro-Leah propaganda, then I say we give him as much ammunition as possible." He adjusted his glasses again. "I'm going to talk to the police and see what they've got."

Timothy left us with instructions to wait for him in the lobby, so Anatoly and I found a few chairs and took seats. For a long time we sat silently side by side. Anatoly seemed deep in thought. Hopefully he was thinking of a solution to this mess. Personally all my focus was on repressing a panic attack. And if *I* was fighting off a breakdown I could only imagine what Leah's state of mind must be. I turned to Anatoly.

"What if Leah says or does something to turn the other inmates against her?"

"She'll be fine. Remember, she's going to a holding cell, not prison—not yet, anyway."

I smacked his arm. "Not *ever.*"

Anatoly sighed and pinched the bridge of his nose. "We need to provide the police with other likely suspects immediately. We need proof that Taylor was sleeping with Bob."

"What about Erika—do you think they know about her relationship with him?"

"I have no idea. Considering what happened to her it might be better if they don't. It will just complicate things."

"Complicate things? Are you kidding?" I let out a hysterical laugh. "How much more complicated can all this get? Bob's dead, his gun is missing. We've been interviewing everyone who's had any kind of relationship with him, and the only thing we've learned is that while alive Bob had the libido of a rabbit in heat. In the meantime there are minority activist groups that are on the brink of rioting, and Jack is on the brink of losing both his parents."

"Are you familiar with the expression 'things can only get better'?"

"Of course, I'm familiar with it. Are you saying that things are going to start looking up?"

"No, I was about to say that the expression is a blatant lie. Things can always get worse, and they can always get more complicated."

"That's your way of cheering me up?" I shook my head, mystified. "Tell me, Anatoly, have you ever considered writing one of those *Chicken Soup* books?"

"I'm just saying that the police's case against Leah isn't as strong as it could be, and if we just dig a little deeper we might be able to dismantle it altogether."

"God, I hope you're right," I whispered.

Anatoly studied me for a beat, then put his arm around my shoulders and pulled me to him. I rested my head on his shoulder and closed my eyes.

"You know, Sophie, if you need to…"

"No, I don't want to cry."

"All right, then let's use the time productively." He gently stroked my hair. "I've been thinking about Cheryl's apartment."

"What about it?"

"You made a comment about how she wouldn't be able to afford it now that she's unemployed. My question is, how was she able to afford it in the first place?"

"Well, she was working two jobs for a while there—front desk at the Ritz and Gatsby and of course the hotel union wage rates are high." I tapped my toe against the ground. "On the other hand she was obviously spending a lot of money on knickknacks and her place was pretty nice—it can't be much smaller than mine."

"And the neighborhood is just as nice as ours," Anatoly added. "My apartment is a lot smaller and I pay twenty-five hundred a month."

"I pay the same, but I've been there for almost ten years so I have rent control on my side. But Cheryl just moved into her place, so she must be paying top dollar."

"So let's say the rent is around three thousand, and she was only working part-time at the Gatsby, so even when she was working two jobs she couldn't have been making more than forty-five thousand a year gross."

I lifted my head from his shoulder. "Anatoly, maybe Bob was giving Cheryl hush money. Maybe he was paying her not to tell people about Taylor. Or maybe *Taylor* was paying her. That would explain why she was so shocked when she learned Taylor had confessed to the affair."

"Maybe," Anatoly said slowly. "But Cheryl wasn't the only one living beyond her means."

"You're thinking about Bob. Yeah, he was definitely living large."

Anatoly nodded. "Fifty thousand dollars is a lot to blow on one bracelet."

"My ex-husband might have splurged on something like that, but then again, my ex-husband uses the lottery as an alternative to a 401K plan."

"But then there's the bracelet he bought for Erika, that was six thousand, and then the necklace he got Leah—how much was that worth?"

"It was in the fifty thousand range."

"So he spent just under a hundred and ten thousand dollars on jewelry in the course of—what, a month? Two? Was Bob making that kind of money?"

"After he was promoted last year, Leah told me that they

were making four hundred thousand a year. But they have a huge mortgage, and then there's the car payments...."

I looked up to see Timothy approaching, and I jumped to my feet. "What took you so long? It's been like—" I looked at my watch "—thirty-five years!"

Timothy released a heavy sigh. "Allow me to take you through this slowly."

"Why in God's name would I allow you to do that?" I asked.

Anatoly pushed himself up to his feet. "Sophie, let the man speak."

"Yes, thank you." Timothy's smile was a bit on the tremulous side. "There is *some* good news. As of this moment the only crime she's being accused of is the murder of her husband."

My mouth dropped open as I gauged the complete lack of humor in his expression. "Oh," I managed to say, "well, that *is* a relief. I was worried her last jaywalking offense had finally caught up with her."

"I was thinking of the mysterious death of Erika Wong." Timothy looked back over his shoulder nervously. "They found DNA evidence at Erika's house that shows Leah was recently there, and apparently when she was last interviewed, Leah claimed she hadn't been to the residence in over a year."

"The fingernail," I whispered.

"Exactly," Tim said. "I'm sure the police would have preferred to wait to arrest Leah until they had more than circumstantial evidence linking her to Bob's death, but now they think she might have had a hand in Erika's death, all of which would make her a possible danger to society. And they questioned Bob's boss, a Mr....wait, it's in my notes, something with an *S*."

"Sawyer," I supplied.

"Yes, that's it. Sawyer. Mr. Sawyer told the police that

Erika and Bob were unusually close and that she was, and I quote, 'devastated by Bob's death.'"

"So now they suspect the affair and Leah has a motive," Anatoly surmised.

He put his arm around me again, but even that didn't make me feel better. If I had just had the presence of mind to look for that stupid fingernail, Leah would be home with her son right now. How could I be so stupid?

I met Timothy's eyes. "But if they think Bob was sleeping with Erika, they must realize that Bianca has a motive, too."

"I pointed that out to them. But right now they're doubtful that Bianca was in the know. There were no phone calls between Bianca and Erika, or even any records of Bianca calling Bob's office. She always contacted him by means of his cell phone or e-mail. She barely knows any of Bob's friends or colleagues, so who would have told her about Bob's other affair? Leah, on the other hand, had ample opportunity to make the discovery. The phone records show that Leah called Erika several times just hours before Bob's death. And unlike Bianca, Leah knew about Erika's health condition."

I took in a shuddering breath. "But if Bianca did know…"

"Even if Bianca knew, the police believe it's unlikely she would have chosen to kill Bob on the same night he was leaving Leah for her." Timothy pushed his glasses up on his nose. "Of course, we'll argue differently."

I clasped my hands together in an effort to keep them from shaking. "What does this mean in terms of bail?"

"It will make it harder, but as I indicated before, the police have yet to charge Leah with killing Erika. If they don't do so by the time of the bail hearing, it will help. And even if they do, a fingernail is not exactly a smoking gun. We can try to spin it."

"What about the hair?" Anatoly asked. "Is it Cheryl's?"

"Most likely. And the good news is that the hair was actually *on* the body. They got a warrant and compared the hair found at Erika's to some hairs they took from a hairbrush found in Cheryl's apartment, and there was a match. But they can't guarantee that the hair in the brush actually belonged to Cheryl."

"So then they should yank some hair out of her head and test that," I pointed out. "Seems simple enough."

"It would be simple," Timothy agreed. "But unfortunately, Cheryl's disappeared."

"Disappeared?" I repeated.

"Yes, her car's gone and there's no sign of her purse, so it looks like she left voluntarily."

Anatoly gave my shoulder a little squeeze. "That's a good thing. It makes her look guilty."

"Yes, it does," Timothy agreed. "But now the police are toying with the theory that Cheryl and Leah were actually working together."

For a minute my distress was replaced by complete bewilderment. "Come again?"

"They think that they might have had a falling-out or something after Bob's murder, which would explain Cheryl's disparaging remarks about her. They also are considering the idea that Cheryl's comments to the press were a smoke screen so people wouldn't suspect that she and Leah were capable of working together." He smiled at my blatant confusion. "I know it sounds highly implausible, but right now they're just looking at all the possibilities."

"Have you run any of this by Leah?" Anatoly asked.

"I tried to." Timothy shifted his briefcase from one hand to the other. "Your sister's not well."

"She's sick?" My heart pounded against my chest. How much worse could this get?

"Not in the typical sense." Timothy cleared his throat.

"She's just a tad on the hysterical side. I tried to talk to her, I really did, but she just kept going on about how the jump-suit she would be forced to wear doesn't come in earth tones."

It wasn't the first time that I had sat on the opposite side of a Plexiglas window to talk to a prisoner, but it *was* the first time that I had done so with a prisoner I cared for. Looking at Leah's messed-up hair and eyes that were brimming with tears filled me with the urge to take a sledgehammer to the transparent material that separated us. Instead I put my hand against the glass and tried to keep my voice calm as I talked to her over the phone.

"Leah, Timothy thinks that he'll be able to get you out on bail. It would be different if they had enough evidence to charge you with two homicides, but right now the events that led to Erika's death are still unclear. So getting a judge to set a bail shouldn't be too much of an ordeal." At least, I hoped it wouldn't be.

"All I wanted was to be a wife and mother," Leah said, her voice listless and meek. Apparently her hysterics had passed. "I did everything right. I had a fairy-tale wedding. I helped Bob find the perfect house for us to live in, and I decorated it with all the latest styles from Pottery Barn. I dressed Jack in Baby Ralph Lauren. I read every issue of *O Magazine* and *Martha Stewart Living*. How could all of that have led me to this?" She eyed the room around her and shook her head in disgust.

"It's just one night, Leah. Tomorrow we'll get you out of here."

"They took me away from my child."

I felt a lump materialize in my throat. "Leah…"

"They took me away from my child and they put me in a cell with a bunch of dealers and prostitutes. And, Sophie—" Leah's voice began to tremble "—one of the prostitutes has burgundy highlights, too!"

"Oh, honey, it's going to be okay, really. And I'm sure that your highlights are much better than the hooker's."

Leah was crying so hard now that I had to strain to understand her. "She said...she said she got them done at Vidal Sassoon!"

I paused for a moment. "She gets them done at Vidal? God, she must be doing well.... You know what, never mind all that. Just be gracious and try not to draw attention to yourself. Remember, if Martha can survive incarceration, so can you. Hey, maybe I'll call my agent and see if I can get you a book deal. Would you like that?"

"I don't want a stupid book deal," she sobbed. "I want to get out of here!"

I sucked in a sharp breath, tried to keep my own emotions in check. "Okay, let's think this through. Now I told you that in addition to Cheryl's hair they found your broken fingernail at Erika's. What I haven't told you is that the police are toying with the possibility that you and Cheryl have been working together."

Leah instantly stopped crying. Her mouth dropped open and she leaned forward so that her forehead was just inches away from the Plexiglas. "What did you just say?"

"They think the two of you might have killed Bob together and then afterward had some kind of falling-out because, well, you know, sometimes murderers get mad at each other."

"Wait a minute—they think that I had possession of a gun while I was in the presence of Cheryl and then I turned around and shot *Bob?*" Leah's voice was getting louder by the second. "Why would I do that? Why would any self-respecting murderess pass up the chance to kill that pretentious little groupie?"

"Oh, come on, Leah, it's not like *everyone* wants to kill Cheryl."

"I'm not talking about the people who haven't met her!" Leah pounded her fist on the table in front of her. "You know what, I've had it. It would be one thing if the police really had a strong case against me, but the fact that they would even entertain the idea that I would be in cahoots with Cheryl just proves they're grasping at straws. Tell my lawyer I expect him to clear me of all charges by the end of the week, and when he's done with that, I want to file a suit against the city."

"For false arrest?"

"For slander! For stupidity—for insulting my sensibilities! My God, there should be a law against even having that woman's name mentioned in the same sentence as mine!"

I smiled and leaned back in my chair. "You know what, Leah? I think you're going to be just fine."

CHAPTER 17

"I respect a woman who's able to intimidate her ene-
mies, but when the mere sight of her causes people to
run from the room screaming—that's a problem."
—*Words To Die By*

Anatoly and I parted ways when we got back to our neighborhood. Anatoly had called Jerome while I was visiting with
Leah, and Jerome had given him the contact information for
one of his police sources, so Anatoly was going to try to talk
to him. I, on the other hand, needed to deal with my family.

When I walked into my apartment I found Mama in the
kitchen and Jerome in the living room reading to Jack. He
must have left and come back, because next to him was a pile
of kids' books I had never seen before. The one he was reading at the moment was a board book titled *Soul Food*. Jack
was curled up in Jerome's lap, completely engrossed. Rich,
wonderful scents came out of the kitchen, completing the
scene. The sight gave me an unexpected feeling of peace.
Bob had spent so little time with Jack, and he had been so
disdainful of Leah's ethnicity, and here was Jerome cuddled

up with him reading a book that clearly was meant to cele-brate his black heritage.

Jerome looked up as I walked in, and Mama turned away from her cooking and eyed me anxiously.

I took a deep breath and smiled at Jack. "Where'd all the books come from?"

"I brought 'em from home," Jerome explained. "I have lots of little nieces and nephews who like their Uncle Jerome to read to them."

"So, enough with the suspense already." Mama banged a spatula on the partition. "When are they letting my Leah out?"

"The bail hearing's set for tomorrow," I said, then walked into the kitchen and peeked at what was on the stove. "Fried chicken. And Jerome's reading *Soul Food*. I'm sensing a theme here."

Mama nodded at an open cookbook on the counter. "I got the recipe from that cookbook I gave you that you never use."

I checked the title on the cover. "*The Complete American Jewish Cookbook?* So this is…"

"Jewish fried chicken."

"Huh, I didn't know there was such a thing." I looked at the pan again. "If you're using the chicken that I had in the freezer, I should warn you I didn't buy it at a kosher deli."

"I'm not using dairy, so as far as I'm concerned it's kosher." She flipped the chicken over before covering the pan.

"Well, it smells incredible."

"How is your sister? Are they feeding her in that place?"

"It's not a POW camp—they do feed them."

"My poor *mumala*." A tear trickled into the folds of skin around her eyes. "How could such a thing happen?"

"I'm going to fix all this, Mama." I pulled her into a hug. "I won't let Leah go to prison."

★ ★ ★

The four of us sat down that night to a dinner of Jewish Soul Food, and afterward I sent both Mama and Jerome home. Jack was as challenging as always, but I found that my sympathy for his situation gave me more patience. I even took him into my bed that night rather than put him in the crib in the guest room where he'd been staying with his mom. He slept a little better than he had the night before, and surprisingly his presence gave me some comfort. When he slept, his little hands went up to his face and I put my hand on his back so I could feel it rise and fall with each breath. Maybe I *did* have a few maternal instincts. But there was no doubt in my mind that this child didn't belong with me. He belonged with Leah, and if I had to beg, borrow or steal in order to make that happen, I would.

At five-thirty in the morning my phone rang. At first I was so disoriented by the sound that I thought it was the fire alarm and I pulled the covers over my head. It was better to sleep in and let some sexy fireman come to my rescue. On the second ring Jack kicked me in his sleep. The feeling of his foot against my stomach was enough to bring home the realization that it was the phone, and that if I didn't get it immediately, Jack would wake up and make me pay for my slow response. I slipped out of bed and lunged for the phone.

"Who the hell is this?" I hissed, sneaking out of the bedroom.

"It's me," Anatoly said. "I have a new theory."

I closed the bedroom door and then slid to a sitting position in the hallway. "You have a *new* theory? I wasn't even aware that you had an old one."

"I think Taylor and Bob were doing more than having sex."

I yawned and rubbed my eyes. "Are we talking something kinky?"

"I'm talking about stealing."

I sat up a little straighter. "Stealing?"

"Embezzling, to be precise. What if Taylor and Bob were having an affair and embezzling money out of Chalet?"

I tried to come to some brilliant conclusion but I was way too tired for that. "I give up. What if they were?"

"Hear me out. Taylor and Bob were both top executives in the finance department, so they were in the perfect position to take money out of the company without anyone being the wiser. But they were so focused on covering up their crime that they didn't spend enough time covering up their affair. When James found out about that, he pushed Taylor out."

"But at that point James still wouldn't have known about the stealing," I said slowly.

"Right. Now Bob is making more money than he ever has before and he has a bright future with Chalet, so perhaps he no longer wants to embezzle money. But he's afraid that the theft that's already taken place will be discovered. So he figures he'll just alter a few documents and make it look like Taylor was acting on her own."

"That's not very nice," I remarked.

"No, it's not. And if Taylor found out about it she wouldn't think it was very nice at all."

"So we're back to Taylor being our murderer."

"And that's what could have been on the floppy disk. Some evidence that tied Taylor to the embezzlement."

I was feeling more awake now. I got to my feet and started pacing the floor. "Erika could have known about it, too," I pointed out. "That's why Taylor needed her dead. And maybe that's why she kept showing up at Chalet, even though she doesn't work there anymore. She wants to either get her job back so she'll be in a better position to cover her tracks, or at the very least make sure James isn't on to her."

"It all ties together," Anatoly concluded.

"Except Cheryl," I said. "How does she fit into all of it?"

"She could have found out about what was going on. If she did, Bob might have been giving her hush money. Or maybe not. Maybe Cheryl is just one of the millions of Americans living beyond her means. But we know she's aware of the affair Bob and Taylor were having, so she might suspect that Taylor's the person who murdered her brother."

"Why wouldn't she just go to the police?"

"Maybe she was going to but someone stopped her."

I stopped pacing. "You think she's dead?" For some reason the thought hadn't occurred to me. I didn't want Cheryl to die. A little suffering and prison time would be okay, but death was a different story.

"I think we should visit Taylor this morning before she goes to work," Anatoly said, leaving my last question unanswered.

"Okay…wait—can I bring Jack?"

"Are you asking if I think it's a good idea for you to bring your eighteen-month-old nephew to the home of a possible murderess?"

"Yeah, that's got to be on Dr. Spock's no-no list."

"I think Taylor's more likely to talk to me if you're there. Can you call your mother right now and ask her to babysit?"

I walked into the living room and looked at the wall clock. "You're not seriously suggesting that I deal with Mama before six, are you? Plus, she had Jack all day yesterday."

"Fine, I'll go alone. Or maybe I'll take Porsha, since she's the one that helped me piece this all together."

"Excuse me?"

"I just got off the phone with her. She claims she was up all night thinking about the expensive gifts Bob gave Bianca, and she suggested he might have been involved in some illegal activity. After some brainstorming, we came up with the embezzlement idea."

I was so furious I couldn't even get any words out.

"Sophie, are you still there?"

"On second thought, I don't think I like this theory anymore," I replied. "It's too convenient and neat."

"You can't knock a theory because it works too well. I'm going to call Porsha and—"

"I'll get a babysitter. Be here in an hour."

I hung up the phone and racked my brain about who I could call. I knew Marcus, Dena and Mary Ann all worked today, so who did that leave me with? I looked down at a business card that had been left on the table, smiled and dialed the home number Jerome had written on the back.

"Yo, Sophie, what's up? You hear something about Leah?"

"No, but I need a huge favor. I need a babysitter for Jack right now."

"Girl, have you checked out the time?"

"Look, this does concern Leah. There's something I need to do that could help her, but I can't do it with Jack. Please, Jerome, if you want me to pay—"

"Keep the money. I was up anyhow."

I let out a sigh of relief. "So you can come right over?"

"I'll be there in thirty."

I managed to get myself showered and dressed in fifteen minutes. I move faster when I'm pissed off. Why was Porsha suddenly interested in helping Anatoly solve this case? But I knew the reason even as I applied my burgundy lipliner. She wanted him. Well, she was going to have to find herself another Russian Love God, because this one was mine. Granted, I wasn't actually in a committed relationship with him, but we *were* sleeping together. He was the first guy I had slept with in two years. Two goddamn years! I had a lot of time to make up for and there was no way I was going to stand by and let some Ivy League ice queen receive pleasure that was meant for me!

True to his word, Jerome arrived at my place at six-thirty.

I motioned for him to take a seat at the table. "Thank you so much for coming. Want some coffee?"

Jerome glanced at his watch. "You gotta ask?"

I went to the kitchen to pour both of us a freshly brewed cup. "Cream and sugar?"

"Just serve it up black. Jack still sleeping?"

"Yes, he is, the lucky bastard." I walked back into the living room with our coffee and joined him at the table.

Jerome waved a rolled-up *Chronicle* in the air. "You seen this?"

"Do I want to?"

"Probably not. This copy was in front of your door, but I read mine earlier. There's a front-page story with a picture of Leah being led into the station in cuffs."

"Shit." I took a deep breath. "God help the photographer if Leah sees that photo."

"The publicity isn't such a bad thing. We can use it to get a protest going. Some kinda grassroots deal. The black community doesn't want this to go down the way it went down for O.J. We need her to be innocent beyond any doubt, so the people will see that the police really are pulling the racial-profiling crap. You see, this isn't just about Leah."

"The hell it isn't," I snapped. "You know, I'm sorry if the black community needs a victory, but my sister is not an icon, she's not a pawn and she sure as hell isn't a martyr. She's a person—a mother who has been taken away from her child. That's what this is about. Not some damn cause."

Jerome hesitated, then put his mug down softly on the table. "I'm sorry. I didn't mean to come off all righteous and shit. But you gotta know I'm on Leah's side. If you fill me in on more of what's going on, I might be able to help."

"And I should just take your word for it that everything

I say isn't going to show up on the cover of your magazine?" I scoffed. "Sorry, but I can't do that. You're a writer and writers lie."

Jerome looked at me quizzically. "*You're* a writer."

"Exactly."

"All right, I feel ya." Jerome laughed quietly. "Well, how 'bout I tell you what we both already know."

"I'm listening."

"We know that Bob was killed, we think that Erika was killed, and we don't know what the fuck happened to Cheryl."

I put my cup down. "How do you know about Erika and Cheryl?"

"Like I said, I have my sources." He paused, then grinned sheepishly. "In this case, my source is called the *San Francisco Chronicle*. It was all in today's article. They also said Erika might have been messing around with Leah's old man, same as that Bianca chick."

"Ah." I started massaging my temples. "Well, I'll tell you this, I never fully believed that Erika's death was a simple co-caine overdose. She was a diabetic with a heart condition, so it seems to me that she would have had the sense to avoid a drug that often contributes to premature heart attacks. I think someone else injected her with the drug, hoping it would kill her. They found Cheryl's hair on the body, which means it might have been her, but this evidence is certainly not conclusive."

"Whoa, hold up. Her hair was *on* the body? Sounds pretty damn conclusive to me."

"There could be another explanation."

"Like what?"

I toyed with the wristband of my watch, thinking. "She could have stopped by Erika's after she was killed, found the body, freaked out and left."

"Doesn't sound too likely."

"It's a possibility," I snapped. "Anyway, as much as I hate Cheryl, I can't figure out why she would want to kill Erika."

"And you think the person who offed Erika also took care of Bob?"

"I'd say there's a ninety-five percent chance of it."

"Well, it wasn't Leah," Jerome said definitively.

The buzzer rang and I got to my feet. "That would be Anatoly. You still have my cell number, right?"

"Got it." Jerome reached into his pocket and waved a piece of paper in the air. "Where are you two gonna be?"

"We're going to pay a visit to our new friend, Taylor Blake."

I grabbed my jacket and went downstairs to meet Anatoly, who smiled as I came out the door, his eyes crinkling in the corners.

"I see you survived an entire night with your nephew."

"Yeah, and you'll be happy to know that he survived, too." I accepted the helmet he offered me, but hesitated before putting it on my head. "Did you tell Porsha about what we're doing?"

Anatoly's grin widened. "I haven't spoken to Porsha today. I just made all that up so you would be motivated enough to find a babysitter."

"You manipulative jerk…" I said, before quickly putting my helmet on to hide my smile.

While we were riding I closed my eyes and fantasized about how nice it would be if we could just ride into an alternative universe where Leah was free as a bird, Cheryl, Taylor and Porsha didn't exist and there were enough lubricated condoms and chocolate-covered espresso beans to keep Anatoly and me busy for days on end. But disappointingly, he took me to Telegraph Hill instead. We parked in front of a beautifully appointed building.

When we reached the door, I grabbed Anatoly's hand just as he was about to ring her apartment.

"Did you bring a tape recorder?"

Anatoly nodded. "I even put new batteries in it."

I let go of his hand and waited to see how long it would take Taylor to respond to the ring. It took her all of thirty seconds.

"Hello?"

"Taylor, it's Sophie Katz—may I talk to you for a moment?"

There was a long pause before she answered. "I was just about to leave for work."

"It will just take a minute," I assured her.

Another pause. "What is this about?"

"Look, I'm sure that you heard Leah's been arrested. They think she shot Bob, but personally I think it was his mistress, Bianca. I was hoping you could tell me a little about your impressions of Bob and what he was like when he wasn't with my sister. The information may help me clear her and bust Bianca."

"I can't help you with that."

"Well, maybe the media would have better luck nailing you down for an interview. I'm sure if I told them about your relationship with Bob—"

The door to the building released, and Anatoly and I entered without another word. We climbed the stairs and found Taylor waiting at her front door. She was perfectly put together and wearing a beautifully structured suit that I pegged as an Armani, giving credence to her claim that she was heading out to work. She narrowed her eyes as she caught sight of Anatoly.

"You didn't tell me that you weren't alone."

"Him?" I pointed my thumb in his direction. "Oh, you can just ignore him. That's what I always do."

Not so much as a smile. "I don't have much time." She

stepped away from the doorway and walked back into her living room without bothering to invite us to follow her, which we did anyway.

Taylor's condo was magnificent. Either she had hired an interior designer or she had missed her calling. The floors were a cool marble and the furniture looked like she had bought it right off the auction block at Christie's. She crossed to her bay window and stared out at the view of the Golden Gate and Bay Bridge.

"Taylor, it's obvious to me that Leah didn't see Bob for who he really was. I'm hoping that you had better insights into his character, so that I can make sense of his relationship with Bianca."

"It's not as if the man was complex." Taylor turned around, her face a mask of impatience. "He was a self-serving opportunist with a taste for womanizing. What else is there to know?"

"So what was it that attracted you to him?" I asked. "His opportunism or his womanizing?"

Taylor's eyes shot daggers in my direction and I fought the urge to beg her forgiveness and hightail it to the door. I scanned the room quickly to verify that there were no weapons within lunging distance.

"What Bob and I shared was brief and meaningless. As I said before, I had just ended a relationship—"

"Yeah, I remember the story," I said. I heard Anatoly mutter a curse under his breath. I threw him a questioning glance before I realized I had just screwed up a golden opportunity to have Taylor repeat her story for the tape recorder. "I'm sorry," I said, "I didn't mean to cut you off."

"No, you're right. I have told you everything there is to tell, so there's no real reason for you to be here."

"Perhaps you could tell us about your professional relationship with him," I urged. "Was he hardworking? Detail oriented? Ethical?"

I thought I saw her flinch, but it had been so fleeting that I couldn't be sure. "As far as I know, Bob saved his unethical behavior for his personal life. Why, do *you* have reason to believe otherwise?"

"No, but Bob did seem to spend a lot more money than he made and it's not like he had a lot of credit card debt, so it begs the question…"

"Bob told me he dabbled a lot in the stock market, but I'm certainly not the person to be asking about that."

"Did Bob spend a lot of money on you during your relationship?" Anatoly asked as he openly admired the flat-screen TV.

Taylor looked genuinely amused. "If you think I involved myself with Bob because I wanted a man to spoil me, you not only don't know Bob but you've completely misjudged me."

I chewed on my lip and took another look at the contents of Taylor's home. "Did you buy *him* stuff?"

"Are you asking if Bob was a kept man?" Taylor shook her head. "With the exception of those few nights at the Gatsby I never spent a dime on him." She placed her hands on her hips and stared directly into my eyes. "I fail to see how any of this will help you transfer the blame for Bob's death from Leah to this Bianca woman."

I nodded and let my fingers run over the top of a low mahogany bookcase. "I was just thinking that Bianca has money and you obviously do well for yourself…"

"I'm a corporate executive," Taylor said tersely. "Of course I make a good salary."

Anatoly hooked his thumbs through his belt loops. "I don't think Sophie was implying that your affluence wasn't earned."

"I'm sorry." Taylor's hand went up to pat her hair, which

was once again pulled back into a severe French twist. "I just get tired of defending my lifestyle to the abundant number of misguided socialists that populate this city."

"I'm all for capitalism." I picked up a porcelain candlestick and verified the Lenox label. "It's murder that I have a problem with, which leads me to my next question. Is there any chance you and Bob earned some of your affluence in a manner that might have been frowned upon by the rest of Chalet's executives?"

Taylor's jaw set. "What exactly are you suggesting?"

I looked over at Anatoly and he nodded, letting me know it was okay to proceed. "Is it possible that in addition to screwing Bob you were also screwing your place of business?"

Taylor took three advancing steps. "Get out of my home. Now."

"Just one more question," Anatoly said. "When you had dinner with James on the night Bob died, what did you order?"

"I don't need to answer your questions."

"Am I to take that to mean you don't remember, or that you were lying about ever being there to begin with."

"I had the pan-roasted squab." She walked to the door and yanked it open. "I've had enough of this. If you don't leave, I'll call the police."

Anatoly gently took my arm. "Thank you for talking to us, Ms. Blake. It was enlightening."

The minute we had recrossed the threshold, Taylor slammed the door behind us. "What do you think?" I asked as we made our way down the stairs.

"I did some checking. James's credit card records show that he did eat at The Grand Café that night."

I looked up at him, squinting as we stepped into the sun. "How did you get hold of his credit card records?"

"I have my contacts."

"But isn't it illegal to give out that kind of information?"

"Since when have you been concerned with following the rules?"

"I'm not—just curious." I stuck my hands in my pockets. "You know, there's a possible suspect that we haven't looked at."

"And who would that be?"

"Porsha." Anatoly rolled his eyes, but I held my hand up to stave off his protests. "Listen, what if she found out about Bianca's affair and she just lost it? We know she's fiercely protective of her sister. Maybe she went a little overboard?"

Anatoly shook his head. "I figured you'd try to pin this on her at some point, so I did a little research. She has an airtight alibi for the night Bob was killed."

"Oh yeah? What was she doing? Playing croquet?"

"She was at a fund-raiser for her alma mater."

"I was close," I muttered. "I still think it could have been her."

"The fund-raiser was in Connecticut, Sophie."

"Yeah, but you know women like Porsha and Taylor are way too smart to get their own hands dirty. One of them probably hired a hit man or something."

"That's a nice theory but it's a bit far-fetched."

"Why's that? I'm sure they both have the money to pay for one."

"Do you have any idea how one goes about hiring a professional hit man?"

I hesitated before answering. It seemed unlikely they would be listed in the Yellow Pages. "You got me—how does one go about it?"

"I couldn't tell you." He shifted his weight back on his heels. "In fact, there are very few people who could. I'm sure if a person was a member of an organized crime family, finding a hit man would be a piece of cake, but neither Porsha nor Taylor strike me as the Mafia type."

"Just because they're not Italian doesn't mean they're not Mafia," I pointed out. "There's a Jewish Mafia, a Chinese Mafia and a Latino Mafia, so why shouldn't there be a White Anglo-Saxon Protestant Mafia?"

"I suppose anything's possible." Anatoly's mouth moved into a slow sensuous smile. "I never thought that I would be intimate with a woman who was responsible for getting me shot, but that didn't stop me from ravishing you yesterday." He stepped closer to me. "It won't stop me next time, either."

I felt a slight tingling in my nether regions. "We've come a long way since I tried to send you to San Quentin."

"Yes." Anatoly grabbed both sides of my jacket and pulled me to him. "Some would say we've gone all the way."

He moved in for a kiss, and for a moment the world around us melted away. The tingling I had felt morphed into more of a vibrating sensation. Then I heard music—actual music. Beethoven's Fifth, to be precise. I groaned as I backed away in order to pull the vibrating phone out of my purse.

"What!" I snapped after verifying that the call was coming from my home.

"Yo, Sophie, Leah's lawyer just called," Jerome said. "Her bail hearing's in two hours. He wants you and your mom to be there."

CHAPTER 18

"Yes, there is a light at the end of the tunnel. Unfortunately it's attached to an oncoming train."
—*Words To Die By*

Leah looked the picture of innocence and composure as she sat next to Timothy. I held Mama's hand as Timothy argued for Leah's right to bail, and I held it tighter when the DA stated their case for her continued incarceration. Fortunately, the police had yet to rule Erika's death a homicide, so the judge made his decision based on the single charge of second-degree murder, and he ended up granting her bail. My relief was quickly quelled when she announced that it would be set at five hundred thousand dollars. Dollars to doughnuts crimes of passion were cheaper in France.

"What, are they *meshuga?*" Mama sputtered. "How am I supposed to get my hands on that kind of money?"

"We could start by selling Bianca's bracelet," I muttered.

"What?"

"Nothing." I offered her a reassuring smile. "I have the money in a retirement fund," I said, helping her to her feet. "I could use it as collateral for a bail bondman."

"I don't like those bondmen. A bunch of nogoodniks if you ask me."

"Have you ever met a bail bondman?"

"I watch TV. You mark my words, those people are nothing but trouble. You empty your retirement fund and bail out your sister yourself."

"Do you have any idea what kind of penalties I'll have to pay for taking the money out early?"

"Listen to you! Your sister's in prison and you talk to me about penalties?"

"She's not in prison. She's sharing a jail cell with a high-priced call girl who gets her hair done at Vidal Sassoon. Somehow I don't think she's at risk of becoming anyone's bitch."

Mama's eyes narrowed. "Leah called me two days ago. She told me that there was something you needed to tell me. She said it was about her Barbie Dream House."

"Oh, come on! That doll house was expensive but it wasn't five-hundred-grand expensive. Leah can wait another day while I get a bondman to verify my assets and advance me the cash."

"Fine, fine, so I spend a few more hours wondering what horrible things are happening to my Leah in that awful place. The doctor told me that my blood pressure has become dangerously high, but don't let that worry you. I'm sure if I have a heart attack I'll survive it."

I closed my eyes and took a steadying breath. "I'll place a call to Smith Barney and see what I can come up with."

"You're a good sister." Mama patted my knee. "Now if we can just clear Leah and get a ring on your finger, we'll be in business."

After a forty-five-minute conversation with my broker and a lot of financial maneuvering, I was able to come up with the money to bail Leah out by the end of the afternoon. Fortunately, Jerome was willing and able to stay with Jack while I worked everything out.

Leah was silent for the entire drive home. When we got to my apartment she barely acknowledged Jerome. She just beelined to Jack and swept him up into her arms. "Mommy's home," she whispered into his ear. "Mommy's home."

I nodded to Jerome. "Thanks for watching him."

"No sweat," he said distractedly as he watched Leah rock back and forth, her son's head pressed to her shoulder. "What was the bail set at?"

"Five hundred grand."

Jerome let out a low whistle. "You two need some downtime, so I'll split." He gathered up his coat and turned to Leah. "When folks read my article the SFPD and DA are gonna be sorry they ever messed with you."

Leah turned her head slightly in his direction. "Later," she said softly. "We can talk about that later."

Jerome hesitated, as if he wanted to try to find some other words that might be of more comfort. Finally he shrugged in defeat and headed out.

I waited a few minutes while Leah whispered more endearments into Jack's ear. He was being surprisingly agreeable at the moment. Maybe he really had missed his mom.

"Are you okay?" I asked finally, sitting down on the love seat.

"Would you be?"

"Point taken." I sighed and looked up at the ceiling.

"Do those idiots still think I'm working with Cheryl?"

"I think it's just one of fifty million theories."

"I bet Cheryl did it on her own," Leah grumbled. "Timothy said they haven't been able to locate her. He said she just took off without a word to anyone."

"Who, exactly, would she have left word with? Right now she's one of the most hated women in the city."

"How do they feel about me?" Leah asked as she carried Jack over to the window. "Do people still see me as some kind of ethnic scapegoat or do they think I'm a cold-blooded murderess?"

"I think you could find support for both opinions."

"What about you?"

My eyes widened enough that it felt like the lines in my forehead popped out. "Surely you know that I believe in your innocence."

"I know that you love me," she said, blinking back the tears. "But, Sophie, you must have your doubts."

I stood up and walked to her side. "Not even one." And it was true. All the doubts that had once plagued me were long gone. "I know you, Leah," I said firmly. "You're neurotic, high maintenance, and at times you are a major pain in the ass. You're also one of the best people I know. You didn't do this."

"Well, what do you know?" Leah smiled weakly. "Someone finally believes in me."

"Always."

"What if the jury doesn't agree and they convict me? What will Jack think?" Leah closed her eyes as the tears began to run down her cheeks. "He'll spend his life hearing others talk about how his mother killed his father."

"Anatoly and I are going to do everything in our power to clear you before you ever have to set foot in another courtroom. Right now he's with Timothy going over a tape recording he made of Taylor confessing to her affair with Bob. That tape alone might get you off."

"And if it doesn't?"

"If things start looking that bad we'll pack your Dooney & Bourke, buy a passport on eBay and hightail it to some little resort town in a third-world country that lacks extradition laws."

"You would lose five hundred thousand dollars if I were to skip bail."

"A worthwhile investment." I put my hand on her shoulder. "I'm not going to let you go to prison. No matter what."

Jack started to squirm, so Leah put him on the ground and we watched as he began destroying my blinds.

Leah shook her head. "You know, not all children do this."

"Yeah, your son is kind of…special." I stepped around him and went to the kitchen to get us both a soda. I wanted something stronger, but I needed a clear head. "I need to ask you a question."

Leah reached her hand out to accept the diet cola. "What is it?"

"Was Bob…unethical?"

Leah paused for a beat. "Is this a trick question?"

"I mean in his business practices. Is there any chance he was embezzling money from Chalet?"

"Are you serious?" Apparently my expression answered her question. "God, I guess it's possible. He certainly spent enough money over the past two years."

"Yet you're not in major debt. Didn't you ever wonder where the money was coming from?"

"No, I just thought we weren't saving anything."

"But there were a lot of expenses that you didn't know about, like the gifts he was buying for his mistresses."

"True… Wait a minute! Does this mean those repo people are going to start taking my things? Do I need to hide the Nordstrom bags?"

"Okay, I'm thinking you're not really grasping the significance of this. If he was embezzling, it adds a whole new angle to his murder case."

"How so?"

"Well, maybe he was embezzling with Taylor and he cut

her out of the loop, or worse yet, maybe he was setting her up to take the fall."

"That does make more sense than his sleeping with her."

I rolled my eyes but didn't comment. If Leah didn't want to believe Bob was sleeping with the boss, who was I to burst her bubble?

"If he was embezzling he must have done a great job of hiding the evidence," she continued. "James loved him."

"Well, yeah, I assume that's why he gave him all the promotions."

"And Chalet is doing really well." Leah popped her drink open and took a long gulp. "If he was taking money it wasn't hurting them much."

"But that just makes it all the more likely." I knelt down and tried to direct Jack's attention away from my blinds by handing him a discarded cat toy. "If Chalet was generating a huge revenue, it would be easy to drain ten thousand dollars here and twenty there. And Chalet just went public, so until recently they didn't have as many checks and balances as other companies."

"They must have had *some*. Three years ago one of Bob's subordinates was caught embezzling money. Bob told me she had taken the money to help her mother with some medical problem and had been secretly paying it back in small installments over a period of several months. James found out and just threw the book at her. It was horrible—she was arrested on Halloween. Her husband and kids were left waiting for her to come home to trick-or-treat with them."

"Which would make Taylor all the more desperate to avoid being caught." I looked down just in time to see Jack force the toy mouse between the blades of my blinds. I winced but couldn't find the emotional energy to stop him. As long as he wasn't physically torturing me or my cat, I was okay.

Leah stifled a yawn. "This whole thing just gets more and more confusing."

"Are you as tired as I am?" I asked.

She nodded ruefully. "I didn't sleep a wink last night. I was up all night talking to Tina."

"Tina?"

"That call girl I told you about."

I did a quick double take. "*You* spent the night chitchatting with a prostitute?"

"You act like you've never talked to a hooker before," Leah noted. "You used to go out with that Mitchell Brothers dancer all the time in college."

"Well, yeah, but that's me and you're...you."

"Normally I would agree with you, but as it turns out, Tina and I have a lot in common."

"And we're not just talking about highlights?"

"No, we're not just talking about highlights. Tina and I are both mothers, we're both single, we both cheated while on the South Beach Diet, and we both know what it's like to have the man you're most committed to be unfaithful. The only real difference is that the person who betrayed me was my husband and her significant other was her pimp."

"Okay, your exhaustion has obviously led to delirium. I only wish I was recording this conversation so I could play it back to you when you're back to your normal moderately-sleep-deprived self."

"Mmm, maybe you're right." She extended her arms into a stretch. "Maybe Jack will take a nap with me." She paused and then looked me in the eye. "Sophie?"

"Yeah?"

"I don't know how I'll ever be able to thank you for everything you've done."

I smiled and nodded at Jack. "If you can actually get him to sleep, that will be thanks enough."

★ ★ ★

The next day Leah left early in the morning to take Jack to the zoo. Despite her lawyer's insistence that she spend every spare moment preparing for her case, Leah had decided that she was going to use the time to do all the things she might not be able to do in the years to come.

Anatoly called me a few minutes after she left with an update. "I'm going over to the Gatsby to see if anyone there has theories about where Cheryl disappeared to, but before I go, let me fill you in on the details of a conversation I just had with James Sawyer."

"Okay, fill away."

"I told him our theory about Taylor and Bob's possible embezzlement."

"How'd he react?"

"Initially he expressed disbelief, but when I started going over Bob's recent expenditures, his disbelief morphed into what I would call outraged suspicion. He's going to have an outside auditor go over the books and get back to me."

"Any chance James was in on it?"

"I don't think so. His salary is almost a million a year and his stock options are considerable. Plus he sincerely seems to love his company. He built it from the ground up and I think it's doubtful that he would undermine it for the sake of a few illegal bonus checks."

"So if there was any corporate monkey business going on it probably all falls on Bob's and Taylor's shoulders." I sighed and rubbed my eyes. "Well, this could be a good thing. If there's any evidence that Taylor and Bob were taking money from Chalet, James will undoubtedly find it. Then the police will be forced to move Taylor to the top of their suspect list."

"Not necessarily. I had hoped that the mere possibility of

internal theft would be enough to get James to refuse to be Taylor's alibi, but he stuck to his first statement, only amending it by saying that he wished he had known all this at the time of the dinner so that he could have taken the opportunity to stick her with the check."

"So what you're saying is…"

"What I'm saying is that it doesn't matter how many crimes Taylor is found guilty of—if she has an alibi for the night in question it doesn't help us."

I drew in a deep breath. "Surely you have *some* good news for me."

"None that I can think of."

"Well then, make some up! This is one of those times where a little placating is appropriate. Now I want you to repeat after me—'Sophie, your sister will be cleared of all charges, everybody will be happy and your next book will sell better than the *Da Vinci Code.*'"

"I can't tell you that."

"Shmuck." I hung up the phone and stared at Mr. Katz, who was curled up by the windows. "*You* think Leah will come out of this okay, don't you?"

Mr. Katz blinked, which was clearly his way of saying yes.

"And I'll sell more books than Dan Brown?"

Mr. Katz got up and left the room.

I looked down at the floor. This is why I don't gamble. I'm incapable of quitting when I'm ahead.

I spent the next two hours pounding out what I hoped would be blockbuster prose before Mary Ann showed up on my doorstep bearing gifts.

"A light Java Chip Frappuccino with extra whipped cream and a box of Neiman's exclusive chocolate-covered macaroons."

"Oh my God, it's been forever since I've had a macaroon!" I took the box from her enthusiastically, then hesitated. "They're low fat right? I'm trying to lose four pounds."

Mary Ann pulled nervously on a curl. "Well…"

"Oh, for God's sake, doesn't anybody lie anymore?"

"They're diet macaroons."

I smiled and popped a cookie in my mouth.

Mary Ann slipped off her Keds and kicked them under the coffee table. Her eyes zoomed in on the shoe box that was already there. "New shoes?"

"Old junk. Those are the personal effects Bob had at his office."

"May I?" she asked, gesturing toward the box.

I nodded and she handed me my Frappuccino before taking the box to the couch.

First she pulled out the family photo encased in the hideous gold frame. Mary Ann pressed her lips together as if trying to resist the urge to gag. "Did…Bob pick this frame out himself?"

I laughed. "Erika told me it was a gift but we don't know from whom."

She examined the photo with what I took to be morbid curiosity. "Bob and Leah look so…so…"

"Disgusted with life?" I supplied. "Yeah, they weren't exactly a Norman Rockwell kind of family."

"Rockwell…is he the guy who built Rockwell Center in New York?"

I suppressed a grin. "You're thinking of Rockefeller. Bob wasn't him, either, although you would never know it from the way he spent money." I took another cookie before sitting on the love seat with my coffee. "You know what's funny? As hard as this whole ordeal has been on Leah, in some ways I think it's helped her grow as a person."

"How so?"

"Well, as long as I have known her she's always been a

wannabe something. A wannabe cheerleader, a wannabe debutante, a wannabe domestic goddess—and Bob just encouraged that."

"Really? In what ways?"

"Oh, in lots of little ways. She used to say 'oy vey' a lot, but Bob said it made her sound low-class, so she stopped. She bought this cute little plum-colored V-neck sweater, but Bob thought it made her look slutty, so she didn't wear it. Basically he had an idea of how she should be and it had nothing to do with who she was."

Mary Ann put one hand on her heart. "That's awful!"

"It is awful. But it seems like in the past few days Leah's forgotten to try to be someone else. It's like she's been forced to look at what's most important to her and she's discovered that it's not a white-picket fence and a lace tablecloth."

"I didn't know Leah even had a white-picket fence."

I stared at her from over my plastic cup and wondered how someone could manage to be that dense and still survive. "I'm speaking figuratively. What I'm trying to say is that in a strange way this horrific situation has forced Leah to come into her own."

There was the sound of a key being wiggled in the lock and a second later Leah slipped in with Jack sleeping in her arms. She mouthed the word *hi* and went down the hall into the guest room.

Mary Ann smiled at me. "I like her highlights."

"She's getting rid of those soon," I grumbled.

When she came back out into the living room and sat down next to Mary Ann, her eyes fell on the macaroons that I had put on the coffee table.

"Have one," Mary Ann urged. "I bought them for both of you."

"Are they sugar-free? I'm on a low-carb diet."

"Sugar-free? No…" Mary Ann saw the pleading look on

Leah's face and immediately understood her mistake. "Yes, they're sugar-free. No sugar at all."

"That's exactly what I wanted to hear." Leah smiled and dove in. "So I've made a decision."

"What kind of decision?" I asked.

"I've decided to have sex with Jerome."

Mary Ann turned bright red and I nearly choked on my low-fat/sugar-free cookie. Maybe Leah wasn't so stable after all. "Wasn't it you who told me you should never sleep with a man on the first date?" I asked.

Leah nodded. "I still believe that, which is why I won't be dating him. This will strictly be a wham-bam kind of deal."

"A wham-bam deal?" My voice came out in a strangled squeak. "Who are you and what have you done with my sister?"

"Really, Sophie, what's the risk?" Leah asked. "It's not like anyone will see us holding hands in public. Besides, do you know how long it's been since I've had good sex?"

"I don't know…a month, two…"

"Seven years ago. You remember Steven, don't you? He was the man I dated before Bob."

"Seven years?" Mary Ann's eyes widened. "What about Bob?"

"I said *good* sex." Leah must have heard herself because she suddenly blushed and looked down at the floor. "Bob did try but…" As her voice trailed off she held up her hand and made a small space between her thumb and index finger.

"You mean he had a small penis?" Mary Ann blurted out, then sank down into the couch, clearly embarrassed by her own contribution to the conversation. "Well, I guess that's not the *most* important quality in a husband."

"Yeah," I said dryly. "There's honesty, loyalty, moral values—all things Bob just had in spades."

"So you understand why I want to sleep with Jerome."

"Of course I understand why you *want* to, but that doesn't mean you should do it."

"And what *should* I do? If I behave like a nun do you think the DA will drop the charges? No, he won't. My life is on the brink of ruin and it's all because I married some adulterous jerk-off with a small penis!"

And with that she turned around and threw the frame against the wall. The glass shattered and the backing dislodged, thus displaying a floppy disk that had been hidden behind the photo. Mary Ann, Leah and I all exchanged quick looks before dropping to our knees to study it. I carefully pulled away the shards of glass and picked up the disk.

"Do you know what this is?" I asked Leah.

"It's what that burglar was looking for," she whispered.

My mind went back to the day Erika called me to Bob's office. She had been so adamant that I come get everything immediately. And then there was the way that she had presented the framed photo. She hadn't put it in the box with the other things. Instead she had made a point of personally handing it to me and telling me that Leah should reframe the picture.

"Erika put this here," I said quietly. "She wanted you to find this."

Leah gasped. "You think?" She reached out and touched the disk. "If that's true, it would be as if she was speaking to us from beyond the grave."

Mary Ann stood up. "I just got a chill." She looked over her shoulder as if expecting to see a ghost.

"We have to see what's on this." I rushed to my laptop, which I had left in my bedroom, Leah and Mary Ann on my heels. When I attached the external floppy drive and stuck the disk inside, only one file popped up. It was titled "Orders." I clicked on it, and in a matter of seconds the purchasing history of several of Chalet's customers appeared on the screen.

I shook my head. "I don't get it. Why would Erika want us to have this?"

"Maybe she didn't." Leah's voice was heavy with resignation. "Maybe she didn't put it in the frame after all."

"If she didn't hide it, someone else did. But why someone would want to save the purchasing history of a select number of Chalet customers on a floppy is beyond me." I scrolled down the page. "These people weren't even *good* customers." I pointed to the screen. "Look, this woman bought twenty-five thousand dollars' worth of stuff in June and then here in July she returned it all."

Leah bent over so her face was closer to the monitor. "So she did. Look, this woman did the same thing—except she only spent seven thousand."

"I know what this is!" Mary Ann clapped her hands together. "It's a classic buy-and-return scam. We see it at Neiman's all the time. People buy a dress, wear it once and then try to return it."

I shook my head and pointed to one of the orders. "A dining room table is not a dress."

"Maybe they were having a dinner party," Mary Ann offered.

Leah squinted at the screen. "Will you look at where this woman lives? Who buys an eighty-five-hundred dollar table and then has it delivered to the slums?"

"That is weird," Mary Ann said, noting the Hunter's Point address. "Maybe it was a gift?"

"For who?" I asked. "Her drug dealer? Are they accepting tables and armoires in the place of cash these days?"

Leah tapped the arrow button, scrolling down to expose more orders and returns. "Okay, so these people like to return things. How is this relevant to my life?"

I shook my head. "I have no idea, but it must mean *something*."

"That's great, Sophie," Leah said sarcastically.

"Hey, we just found this. Give me a few minutes to figure out—oh my God, Leah, look!" I pointed to the name of one of the customers.

Leah gasped. "Maria E. Souza! That's the Portuguese woman from Hotel Gatsby!"

"Wait a minute." I quickly scrolled back up. "Jan Levine." I got up and ran to the living room and then came back with the torn piece of paper. "Jan Le—this must be her!"

Leah looked at the paper. "Where did you get this?"

"I found it in the shoe box!" I jumped up and down excitedly. "Check her phone number—see if it starts with the numbers 5178."

"It says here that her number starts with 4153." Mary Ann tapped the screen. "It's not her address, either."

Leah studied the screen and then gasped. "Oh. My. God. It's her credit card number."

"Holy shit." I slapped my hand over my mouth.

Leah scrolled back down to Maria. "There's something wrong here. The delivery address for Maria is in San Francisco."

"There's another buy-and-return scam that I know about." Leah and I turned to Mary Ann.

"Remember when I used to work at Dawson's? Well, sometimes if a department was really close to making their monthly sales goal the managers would ask the salespeople to buy merchandise and return it when the month was over."

I looked at the screen again. "All these purchases were made in March, June, October and December, and all the returns were made the following month."

Leah brought her hand to her cheek. "Every three months."

I chewed on my thumbnail. "What happens every three months?"

"The seasons change?" Mary Ann offered.

"Business quarters," Leah said quietly. "Business quarters change every three months."

My mind flashed back to the conversation we had with Charlie. "That note that Charlie saw Cheryl handing Bob— she was using her position at the Gatsby to help Bob commit identity theft."

"Why would she do that?" Mary Ann asked.

Leah looked at me and I saw my own comprehension mirrored in her eyes. "They did it to keep stock prices up. Artificially inflating stock prices coupled with identity theft… that's enough to land someone in prison for quite a while."

I lunged for the phone and dialed Anatoly's cell number.

"The subscriber you are trying to reach…"

I hung up, sat back down at the computer and quickly saved the information on the disk onto my hard drive. "Mary Ann, Anatoly should be at the Gatsby. I want you to find him and give him this disk."

"Okay," Mary Ann said uncertainly. "What are you going to do?"

"I'm going to Cheryl's." I ejected the disk and gave it to Mary Ann, who took it with some hesitation.

"You're not going to do anything stupid, are you?"

This seemed like a particularly ironic question coming from Mary Ann. "I'm not going to do anything stupid. Now go!" I pushed her toward the door. She slipped the disk in her purse and took off to carry out her mission.

"So," Leah said. "You're going to break into Cheryl's place?"

"You got it. There's got to be more evidence of Cheryl's involvement in all this, and I bet you anything it's somewhere in her home. All I need is a few minutes to look around."

"Jack and I are coming with you."

"Leah, you can't bring a baby to a break-in."

"I'm not going to go *in* with you. I'll just sit in the car and make sure no one walks in while you're there—like a...a lookout person."

"I really don't think that's a good idea."

"If you go to jail, I'll have to leave Jack with Mama. Think about what it would have been like to have been raised by Mama without Dad around to keep her balanced. I refuse to sentence my son to a childhood filled with guilt and gefilte fish!"

I smiled despite myself. "Okay, you can come, but only because I know we won't be caught." I squeezed her hand. "It's the Katz sisters against the world."

Leah gave me a curt nod. "The world won't know what hit it."

CHAPTER 19

"You wanna know if she's a devil worshiper?" Al laughed bitterly. "That broad's so evil the devil worships *her!*"
　　　　　　　　　　　　　　　　　—Words To Die By

"Just when I thought it wasn't possible to hate Cheryl any more than I already did, she goes off and kills my husband." Leah glared out the front windshield and ran her fingers through her hair. "I can't believe she would do this. What would her hero Arnold Schwarzenegger say?"

"We don't know that she killed Bob." I paused at a stop sign before hitting the gas again. "It could have been James Sawyer. I *know* he's at the center of all this."

"Don't even get me started on James Sawyer. It was just a few months ago that I had his family over for dinner. I made a soufflé, for God's sake! And this is the thanks I get?"

I gave her a sidelong glance. "If it's any consolation, I'm sure everything was set in motion long before the whole soufflé event."

"Wouldn't it make more sense for us to go to Chalet? It seems like that's where the evidence would be, and the police have already searched Cheryl's place."

"We'll never get into Chalet on a Saturday, and even if we did we wouldn't get into James's office. Besides, the police didn't know what to look for when they searched Cheryl's. We do."

"I can't believe she was actually providing Bob and Taylor with the information to steal people's identity. Surely one or two of these people had a credit report done."

"Think about it. They were probably opening new accounts under these people's names and every purchase that was made was credited back within thirty days of the purchase. And I assume Bob, Taylor, or whoever, had the presence of mind to close the accounts right after crediting them. If someone did notice it on a credit report they might have seen it as a computer glitch and decided it wasn't worth the effort to pursue the problem with the credit bureaus."

"If I thought there was even the slightest possibility that someone was charging things on accounts with my name on it I would put out the effort to find out who it was and stop them."

"Okay, let's say a few people did report it. How would they know who got their credit info? Every time we hand our credit card over to a salesperson we risk being ripped off."

"How comforting." Leah turned and looked at Jack in the back seat.

"He's being really good," I noted.

"I know. I wonder if he's feeling all right."

I pulled onto the sidewalk in front of the garage in Cheryl's building. "I'm going to give you one last chance to back out of this whole lookout-person deal. Keep in mind that aiding and abetting a break-in is a felony."

"What are they going to do, throw me in jail with a bunch of other criminals?" she said scornfully. "Been there, done that."

"Fine, but I don't think you should wait in the car. Why

don't you pretend to wait at that bus stop across the street. That way if something goes wrong, you and Jack will be able to just stroll away."

"Fine with me."

We all got out of the car and Leah pulled the stroller out of the trunk and strapped Jack in.

I looked up at the building. "Cheryl's apartment is on the first floor. I think if I climb on top of the car I should be able to pull myself up to the fire escape and climb in the window."

"Really," Leah said flatly. "Am I mistaken or are you the same person who dropped out of gymnastics after three classes."

"I was six!"

"Yes, but I don't remember you signing back up at seven."

"Do you have a better idea?"

"As a matter of fact I do. I'll climb in the window and open the door for you."

Before I could say anything she was on top of the car. She reached her arm straight up in the air, but there was still about a foot between her hand and the bottom of the fire escape.

"Leah, you really shouldn't be doing this."

She bent her knees and jumped. For a split second I didn't think she was going to be able to make it, and I wondered how I was going to explain my dented roof to the insurance company. But Leah did grab hold of the bars. Now she was dangling in the air, holding on for dear life.

A young couple who was walking by, stopped to stare. I smiled nervously. "We locked ourselves out," I explained.

They looked at each other, shrugged and kept walking. That's what I love about city dwellers. More often than not they'd rather walk away from a potential crime in progress than waste their cellular minutes calling the police.

"Anything I can do to help?" I called up to Leah.

"Climb up on the car and help hoist me up."

I was impressed. Leah had only achieved her criminal status a short while ago but she had already become pretty competent in the role. I made sure the wheels on Jack's stroller were locked, climbed up on the Audi and, with a little help and a lot of struggling, got Leah up on the fire escape.

"The window's unlocked!" she called down excitedly.

"Great." I climbed back down as Leah crawled inside the apartment. My heart pounded as I waited to see if cops were going to come rushing out of their unmarked cars to haul us all in. But that didn't happen. Instead the buzzer to unlock the front door sounded and I quickly opened it and wheeled Jack inside. I waited for Leah to come down to the lobby, and when she didn't, I cursed under my breath. I had been hoping she would just leave the door to Cheryl's place open, take Jack from me and wheel him across the street. Instead I was going to have to bring Jack right to the scene of the crime, which was not only irresponsible from a parenting perspective but also incredibly inconvenient. I was now going to have to lug him and his stroller up a flight of stairs.

I rubbed my hands against my jeans before undertaking the endeavor, and when I finally got to Cheryl's door I was out of breath and seriously irritated at Leah. But oddly enough, Jack didn't seem bothered at all. He was quieter than I had ever seen him. I rearranged him in his stroller and opened Cheryl's door.

Leah was in the middle of the living room looking incredibly pale. Cheryl was standing at her side.

"Oh God." I stepped forward. "Cheryl, I know this looks bad but I can explain."

"No need." I turned just in time to see James Sawyer closing the door behind me. The polished metal of a small revolver sparkled in his hand.

"Go stand with the other ladies, please."

I opened my mouth but words failed me.

"Now."

I mutely walked to Leah's side, pushing Jack along as I did.

James's eyes traveled down to Jack and I thought I saw a flicker of regret cross his features.

"That's Bob's gun," Leah whispered. "He was about to use it on Cheryl when I walked in."

"I would have thought that would please you," James said. His laugh had a slightly hysterical ring to it. Cheryl choked back a sob.

My hand tightened around the handle of Jack's stroller. "You don't want to do this, James. You don't want to kill a mother in front of her child."

"Of course I don't want to do this!" James snapped. "I didn't want to do any of this! Bob is the one who put me in this position. If he had had the common sense of a gnat none of this would be necessary." James waved his gun at Leah accusingly. "It was your husband who set all this in motion."

"What went wrong?" I asked. Jack was whimpering in his seat. I had never heard the child whimper before—maybe he sensed the fear in the room. "Did Bob figure out that identity theft was...you know...immoral and stuff?"

"So you know about that." James let out a heavy sigh of resignation. "It was a temporary game plan and no one was going to get hurt. Not even the people whose credit information we used. Everything we charged to those accounts was promptly credited back. All Bob had to do was get the credit information on a few of the more affluent guests at the Gatsby and wait for his stock options to start paying off."

I looked over at Cheryl, but she didn't seem to care about being exposed as a criminal. She appeared much more concerned with the prospect of her imminent death. For once she had her priorities straight.

"What did Bob do?" Leah's body was shaking. "Why did you kill him?"

"He got greedy, that's what he did! He didn't bide his time like the rest of us. Instead he immediately started spending money like he was Bill Gates and he expected me to support his expensive tastes. He told me that if I didn't give him money right away he would act as a whistle-blower. He said he would cut some kind of deal and give the DA my head on a platter. He made a floppy disk that illustrated what we were doing and gave me a copy to show me that he meant business. He was too stupid to see that even with the best plea bargain he would still have to deal with felony charges, and he was too callous to care that his sister would be sent to prison along with Taylor and me. What kind of man doesn't care about his own family?"

"Good question," Leah muttered.

"You still didn't have the right to kill him!" Cheryl cried. "You could have let me talk to him or…or you could have just given him his stupid money! You didn't have to murder my brother!"

"Don't pretend that you gave a damn about Bob," James scoffed. "You have never cared about anyone but yourself. When I asked you to get close with Erika and shoot her up with cocaine, you didn't so much as flinch."

"But you didn't tell me she had a heart condition!" Cheryl protested. "You said that we just needed to make her look like a drug addict to ruin her credibility. I didn't know she was going to die! And then you lied to me again to get me to come back to the city. You told me that you had a way of fixing everything. But really you just wanted the chance to kill me, too!" She turned to Leah. "None of this is my fault!"

"Are you serious?" Leah hissed. "You have been stealing people's identities in exchange for money! You told a woman you were going to administer her insulin and you shot her up with crack instead! I can't believe the depths to which you've sunk!"

"It wasn't supposed to go this far," squeaked Cheryl. "I just wanted to make a little extra money—just enough to get into the social events with high celebrity attendance, like award ceremonies and Democratic Party fund-raisers. I never meant to kill anyone!"

"But you knew James killed Bob," I said, my anger matching my fear. "Yet you were perfectly happy to tell everyone Leah was the guilty one."

"James told me she did it! He told Taylor that, too! He said that if she wasn't arrested quickly, everything we had been doing would come out!"

"You believed what you wanted to believe," James said.

"That's also why Taylor came up with that stupid lie about having an affair with Bob," Cheryl continued, ignoring James's comments. "James told us it was the only way to explain their being together at the Gatsby, and he promised to be her alibi for the night Bob was killed so she wouldn't be a suspect!"

"I *knew* he wasn't sleeping with her!" Leah cried, then quickly shut up, apparently realizing that this wasn't the time to gloat.

"I don't get it," I said slowly. "Anatoly said your credit card record shows you *were* at the Grand Café that night."

"There are advantages to doing charity work." James's Adam's apple slid up and down. "For instance, if you befriend the troubled youth, they will help you access drugs when necessary and they don't question you when you tell them to enjoy a gourmet meal on your credit card."

"My God," I whispered. "You really are a slimy SOB."

"No one was supposed to get hurt! When I went to see Bob that night I wanted to talk some sense into him. Killing him was a last resort. But what was I supposed to do?"

"Well, you weren't supposed to kill him!" Leah screamed.

"I don't expect you to believe this, but I didn't want any-

one to die." He looked down at Jack, and to my utter amazement, a real tear rolled down his cheek.

Leah moved closer to the stroller.

"It's just that Bob's demands kept getting bigger and bigger," he said. "When Erika found out, he told me we could
buy her silence for fifty thousand dollars. When I gave him
the money, he used it to buy some jewelry for his mistress
and bought Erika's silence by romancing her. He had no
morals, no scruples—he was going to ruin all of us!" He
looked down at the gun in his trembling hand. "I have a son,
too. I've worked so hard to build a legacy for him. I couldn't
allow Bob to take it all away."

"What about *my* son?" Leah pleaded. "I'm the only parent he has now. If you kill me, what will happen to him?"

"And he needs his aunts, too—right, Sophie?" Cheryl
looked at me to back her up.

I had to bite my tongue to prevent myself from asking
James to kill her first.

James stepped closer so that he was just a foot away from
Leah. "I promise you, Jack will be provided for. I'll pay for
his education. I'll make sure he's okay." He bent down so that
he was eye level with Jack. "I'm so sorry," he whispered. "Dear
God, I am so incredibly sorry."

Jack's eyes widened, and for a moment I thought he was
going to tell James to "piss off." But instead his little body
convulsed and then lurched forward and before any of us had
a chance to react, an obscene amount of vomit came spewing from his mouth. For a split second the room went silent
as we watched James stagger backward, his face covered in
regurgitated Cheerios. His foot caught on the floor rug,
causing him to lose his balance and fall to the ground. With
one look, Leah and I knew we were on the same page. We
pounced on James. In one fluid movement Leah kicked the
gun out of his sweaty palm and I jumped on top of him,
punching him in the nose and then the chin.

"Call the cops!" I screamed at Cheryl. But she just stood in the corner jumping up and down and screaming.

Leah tried to move past me and James so she could get to the gun, but James recovered from his shock and grabbed her ankle. Leah went sprawling. I pressed my knee into his groin. James screamed and pushed me to the side with one arm, his other hand holding on to Leah's leg.

"I'm going to kill you both!" he yelled.

"The *hell* you are!"

We looked up to see Anatoly pointing the gun at James's head. James slowly opened the hand that had been clutching Leah and raised it above his head. His left hand went to cradle his injured balls.

I squeezed my eyes closed and thanked every one of my lucky stars.

"Anatoly," Cheryl cried. "Thank God you're here!"

If I hadn't been so giddy with relief I would have strangled her.

Leah rolled away from James and we both got to our feet, leaving James on the ground. I tried to will my heart to slow down but it wasn't cooperating. Leah, on the other hand, seemed much more composed. She brushed herself off and stepped up to Cheryl.

"We both could have been killed just now."

Cheryl nodded and dabbed her eyes.

"Are you all right?" Leah asked.

"I think so," Cheryl answered weakly.

Leah punched her in the jaw so hard that Cheryl was knocked against the wall and slid to the ground. "How 'bout now?" Leah asked sweetly.

I turned to Anatoly with a huge smile on my face. "Is my sister awesome or what?"

CHAPTER 20

Sex is so much better than Prozac.

—*Words To Die By*

"This has got to be the most fun I have ever had at a memorial service." Marcus popped a cheese puff in his mouth.

"Leah really did a good job, didn't she?" I surveyed the crowd gathered together in Leah's home. "Plus I think people are a little less depressed about Bob's death than they usually are when someone they know dies."

"Leah looks great. That plum-colored sweater is to die for."

I giggled. "She's been waiting to wear that for a while."

Marcus nodded and grabbed one of the mini knishes. "So give me an insider update on the evil trio."

"Ah, James, Cheryl and Taylor. Well, Taylor's faring the best of the bunch. She still claims that she didn't know anything about Bob's or Erika's murder, and I think I believe her. She just went along with the whole story about Bob and her having an affair, to cover up the identity theft and fraud stuff."

"You know, normally those seem like pretty big offenses, but considering everything that's happened..."

"They don't seem all that serious?"

"Not so much." He smiled at a young man who reached around him to get to an hors d'oeuvres.

"Nonetheless, she'll still be doing time. Of course Cheryl and James are going to be doing a *lot* of time."

"Has anyone figured out how James got his hands on Bob's gun?"

"Bob usually left his keys in the top drawer of his desk while he was working. James just waited for him to step away from his office and then stole the keys long enough to have a copy made. Then he broke in here when no one was home and found the safe. He figured out the combo because it's the same as all of Bob's other combinations. I think at the time he was just looking for the floppy disk, but he saw the gun, and when James finally did decide to get rid of Bob he knew exactly where to get the weapon for the job."

"Mmm." Marcus nodded thoughtfully. "I have another question for you. See that gorgeous homeboy over there drinking champagne like it's beer? I'm getting a straight vibe, but I'm fighting a cold so I'm hoping my gay-dar's on the fritz."

"Your gay-dar's working fine, he's very straight. Besides, Leah has dibs."

"Is she dating already? How wonderfully scandalous!"

"She's not dating—she's decided that Jerome is going to be her grief-avoidance sex guy."

"Excuse me?"

"According to Leah, many high-society widows have sex within a few months of their husband's death as a means of avoidance. Or was it transference? I don't know—the point is they get lucky with somebody they're not serious about."

"That is so great!" He stomped his foot playfully. "*I* want to be a widow!"

"Yeah, well, Jerome's not getting lucky tonight. Apparently you have to wait a week or two for the grief avoidance to really kick in. Otherwise it's uncouth."

"Has your sister ever thought of writing a book? She would just blow that Emily Post chick out of the water."

"I don't think books are her thing. Actually, she's been thinking about getting a job as an event coordinator." I elbowed Marcus. "The Gatsby's hiring—how ironic would *that* be?"

"Excuse me, may I have everyone's attention?" Leah tapped her glass with a spoon until the room fell silent and all eyes were on her.

She smiled graciously. "I want to thank you all for coming. As many of you know, it's been a hard few weeks for me for a variety of reasons and I really appreciate all the support everyone has shown me." She smoothed her hands over the bottom part of her sweater. "Many of you have commented on this top I'm wearing. Normally I would say that this neckline is a little too low to be appropriate for a memorial service, but when I wear this sweater I remember the look in Bob's eyes when he first saw me in it." She held her glass up in the air theatrically. "So here's to you, Bob. Wherever you are—" she looked pointedly at the ground "—I want you to know that I will be wearing this sweater frequently, and whenever I do I will remember that moment and I will smile."

"That is so sweet!"

I looked to my right to see that Bianca had sidled up next to me without my noticing. "Did you just get here?" I asked.

She nodded. Her hair was pulled back by a black headband that matched her black Wilkes Bashford dress. "I had to drive Porsha to the airport."

"Oh, so she's gone?" My mood matched Leah's smile.

"Yes, back to practicing law in New Hampshire. Leah was sweet to invite me to this."

I didn't say anything. Since she was no longer under police suspicion Leah had seen no need to be anything but disdainful of Bianca—until we rented *Gone with the Wind*. After seeing the scene in which Scarlett shows up at Melanie's home in a red dress, Leah decided that Bianca simply *had* to attend the service—in hopes that it would bring attention to Bianca's transgression and Leah's overwhelmingly generous spirit.

"That was some speech." Anatoly approached our little group. "May I see you alone for a minute, Sophie?"

I handed Marcus my glass and followed Anatoly into the kitchen.

"You look good in dresses." His eyes moved over me appraisingly as I leaned my back up against the counter.

"Thank you. You look…uncomfortable in a suit."

"Very perceptive of you." He put his hands on the counter—one on either side of me, and leaned in so he was only half a foot away from me. "I was just talking to your sister a few minutes ago, and do you know what she told me?"

"That earth tones are the new black?"

"She told me that many people have sex after funerals as a way of dealing with their grief."

"Ah, I see. But this is just a memorial service."

"You're a writer." Anatoly leaned in closer. "Use your imagination."

He was an inch away now. "I can do that." I took a breath deep enough to make my breasts press up against his chest. "Do you want to go back to your place and make…espresso?"

Anatoly smiled. "I love a woman with a one-track mind."